SECOND LIFE CHANCES

GOOD VS. WICKEDNESS

By

M. W. INGLEHART

DEDICATION

This book is dedicated to my loving and supportive wife, Loretta, and my children and grandchildren—who can read it when they are old enough!

INTRODUCTION

Second Life Chances by M. W. Inglehart is a captivating tale of redemption, transformation, and the pursuit of new beginnings. The story follows a protagonist at a crossroads, grappling with past regrets and the desire for change. Inglehart's writing is notable for its vivid descriptions and emotional depth, effectively engaging readers.

The story hooks the reader from the first chapter, offering a seamless blend of introspection and action. The protagonist's journey is marked by unexpected twists and pivotal moments that challenge his resilience and determination. The supporting characters are thoroughly developed, each contributing depth and intrigue to the narrative.

Inglehart creates a vivid and immersive setting, allowing readers to visualize the protagonist's world. The thematic exploration of second-life chances is handled with nuance and sensitivity, resonating deeply with anyone seeking a fresh start.

As the story unfolds, the pacing remains engaging, balancing moments of reflection with exhilarating action. The protagonist's transformation is believable and inspiring, offering a message of hope and perseverance. By the book's conclusion, readers are presented with the idea that altering one's course in life is always possible.

Second Life Chances is a beautifully crafted novel that delivers a powerful and emotional reading experience. It highlights human growth and the potential for renewal, making it a must-read for every age.

CONTENTS

CHAPTER 1

Three Days of Dark

Lincoln, Nebraska

At sunrise, Matt and Paula strolled along the beach. The sky was painted in glorious orange and pink, contrasting with the storm in Matt's mind. He tightened his grip on Paula's hand, which offered a fleeting sanctuary from the chaos that plagued his thoughts. His SEAL team's distant, raucous laughter shattered the morning silence, returning him to the reality that he wanted to escape. His chest tightened painfully, a reminder of the battles he'd fought and the scars he carried that refused to heal.

In the distance, Matt's SEAL team gathered by the old lighthouse; their voices could be heard over the beach. They were more than just comrades; they were his brothers, a team forged in fire and blood, each carrying wounds both seen and unseen. But they all stood tall, united by warfare. Suddenly, there was another pain—sharp this time, burning and agonizing. He clutched his chest as darkness closed in around him.

Matt was jolted awake, drenched in sweat, his heart racing from the familiar nightmare that haunted him. Thankfully, Lucy, his ever-faithful dog, was there, nudging his chest and showering his face with licks. Then, barking again as if to say, "Hey, it's time to wake up!" Her eyes showed concern, reminding him he wasn't alone.

Oh man, that barking scared me out of my dream! He thought she needed to go out as he tried to shake off the remnants of his nightmare.

"Hey Matt, I'll take her out now; you can get some extra sleep," Paula said in her cheerful and calming voice.

"Thanks, Paula! You're the best."

I'm so glad Paula is here; she helps me feel better. He grinned, grateful for the support and a chance to catch a few more z's—such a sweetheart.

I love cuddling up under these warm blankets in the morning… Matt drifted off to sleep for a moment. Lucy jumped on the bed and gave him kisses and hugs. She was wet from being out in the rain. He guessed it was time to get up; she wouldn't leave him alone now.

To get up, Matt had to roll over to his right side and onto his right shoulder, which had been bothering him lately after such second-rate surgery. Then he pushed up to a sitting position. Sitting with his feet on the floor, pain radiated from his war-damaged left hand and lousy back, which they finally fused after three surgeries. The most awful pain he'd felt in his entire life.

He'd thought he was going to die a second time.

Matt exited the bed and forced himself to stand. *Getting old is hell.*

Matt just stood there, trying to stay upright. He finally walked to the bedroom door and out to the hallway. He had to feel his way along the wall. With all his aches and pains, sometimes it wasn't easy to keep his balance and navigate just to the kitchen to make coffee.

When he finally entered the living room, Paula was sitting on the couch, doing her cross-stitching.

"Good morning, dear."

"Good morning, Matt. I'm sorry Lucy woke you up. You were sleeping so soundly; I was trying to let you sleep. You were having another tough night. Nightmares again?"

"Yes, I am so sorry if I kept you awake! You certainly don't deserve to live with all my problems. Lucy woke me from my bad dream, however. She seems to sense when I'm having a stormy night."

"Ah, Matt! We have been married for forty-five years. We both have dealt with good times and bad. I love you as much or more now as we were first married. Please have confidence in my assertion. I have asked you to go back to counseling, Matt."

"OK, Paula, I hear you. Let's not talk about it now!"

"Same thing you always say. Why don't you talk to me about it? I will listen."

"Paula, I don't want to burden you with my problems; you sure don't need anything more to deal with after your brother's death this year. I'll make some coffee, and we can watch the news together and learn what's happening on Planet Earth today."

"I already made coffee, bacon, eggs, and hash browns, which are keeping warm in the oven. You can make some toast if you want. And happy birthday, Matt. You do remember today is April 20, your birthday, don't you?

"Yes, I remembered. Another year older for this old fart."

"Bring me a coffee, old man, and I will turn on the news for you."

"Paula, you are so good to me. I marvel at how lucky I was to have found you."

"Remember how lucky you are! Remember when we met Matt?"

"Yes! Of course, I remember when we first met. Our friends introduced us at a dance they took you to, where I met you for the first time, chatted a little bit, and danced a couple of times. And then I called you for a date. We went to a sports bar to watch a Nebraska football game.

"If I recall correctly, you were tall and had long dark hair tied in a ponytail. You were a college track athlete, right? You started with a teaching degree and then changed to nursing. You were so beautiful; what was not to like?"

Matt went into the kitchen and poured two cups of coffee. He returned to the living room, handed Paula a cup, and placed his cup on the end table next to his recliner. He returned to the kitchen, opened the oven, pulled out his breakfast, carried it back to the living room, sat down, and started eating.

"What's the news about today, dear?"

"Much the same: The western states are burning, California is experiencing earthquakes, and the East Coast is drowning from hurricanes and tornadoes. And nobody can figure out who will be president this year."

"As if it matters. This is good stuff; thank you, dear!"

"April is going to be hot, Matt. We should take a trip to Colorado and go fishing. You always enjoy our time in the mountains."

"Paula—what just happened?"

"Matt, the TV and all the lights just went out."

"What the heck, that shouldn't happen. All our electrical lines are underground."

Paula got up and went to look out the window. "Matt, everybody's lights are out. There are no lights, no streetlights, and it's still dark."

"OK, Paula. I'll go outside and look around. I don't think it would take the power company long to get the lights back on.

"But just in case, Paula, you should find some candles, and when I get back, I'll see if I can find some flashlights."

Matt opened the front door and used his knee to open the screen door. He stepped out onto the deck and looked up and down the street. It wasn't quite sunrise yet. He could just make out his neighbors doing the same thing, looking around and trying to figure out what was happening. Matt just waved, turned around, and went back into the house.

"Paula, everybody has the same problem, trying to figure out what's happening. I'll get the flashlights." Matt walked out to the kitchen, knowing exactly where the flashlights were in the junk drawer. He picked one of the flashlights up and turned it on, but nothing happened. *Strange, I know I put new batteries in this one just the other day.*

Returning to the living room, he saw Paula trying to light a candle.

"Matt, I tried but can't get these candles to light; I don't understand."

"Well, I can't get the flashlights to work either."

"Matt, could you call the power company? Get somebody out here to see what's going on."

"Paula, someone would have called it in since we were not the only ones in the neighborhood without power!"

"Matt, will you please call?"

"I won't right now; let's wait and see what happens."

"Matt? Was that a knock at the door?"

"Let me see." As Matt opened the door, he saw Chuck, his neighbor from across the street, looking bewildered.

"What's up, buddy?"

"Matt, we don't have any power, and it looks like the whole block is out!"

"Yeah, Chuck, I know we don't have any power either."

"Also, Matt, none of our vehicles will start, and none of the neighbors can get theirs started either."

"Chuck, you mean you can't get that big-ass Ford diesel of yours started?"

"No, and my wife's car won't start either. Nothing's working, and the other vehicles on our block have the same problem. Matt, do you know, or have you heard anything?"

"No, Chuck. We were watching the news when the power went out, so I can't answer you."

"OK, look, Matt. You are the most educated man on the block—more educated than the rest of us! Make a guess!!"

"I don't know, Chuck; it could be an electromagnetic pulse or high-altitude explosion. It could be anything that produces gamma rays that ionize the air molecules to produce positive ions, a quick pulse of energy that would knock out all electrical equipment. Remember that I'm giving you quite a simple and partial explanation.

"So, Chuck, before you ask, yes, it's possible it could be nuclear, which is artificial; it could also be natural, such as lighting or a solar flare. I am sure it could be other things as well."

"Is that your answer, Matt?"

"Yes, and Paula is not happy with me either for not having any answers."

"OK, Matt, I'll talk to you later, see yah!"

Chuck walked down the steps and back across the street to his house.

Matt watched him walk away and then looked to the northwest. A big rolling black cloud, a fast-moving storm, appeared on the horizon. He wondered if it was what had knocked out the power.

Matt yelled out to Chuck, "HAY!!! There's a huge black cloud moving in from the northwest. Tell everyone to take cover!"

Matt walked back into the house, shut the door, and locked it, returning to the living room to see whether Paula's had any luck with her candles.

"Paula, have you gotten your candles to light yet?"

"No, none of them will light. Do we have more matches? I used about all I could find."

"Yeah, there are more in the corner cupboard, a jar full of them, clear at the top. I'll get them.

"And Paula, not to scare you, but a vast black cloud is rolling in from the northwest. It's possible that within 30 minutes, the house will be pitch black."

"What are you saying? What cloud?"

"Right now, Paula, just get something to light and work on your candles. I've got a camping light in the garage cupboard. I'll get it, and we'll be okay." On his way out the door, he grabbed the car key.

Matt went to the utility room, opened the garage door, and could barely see the car. He carefully walked down the steps into the garage, past the car, to the other side and the cupboard where the lantern should be.

His good old camping light runs on white gas. He gave it a couple of pumps, grabbed some matches, and struck a match; he could hear the gas hissing. He held the match to the mantle, but nothing. The match burned out, and he lit another one, but there was still nothing. Strange, it should've started quickly; it had never failed him.

Matt went around the car to the driver's side, opened the car door, and slid in. With these new cars nowadays, you have a thingamabob in your pocket.

You put your foot on the brake and push a button on the dash to start the vehicle. The thingamabob has a battery, which would be dead.

Humm, that's why it will not start; it should have been a no-brainer. I must be slipping; I'll just call it a brain fart, ha-ha.

Walking back into the living room, he could barely see Paula sitting on the couch with Lucy.

"Any luck with the camping light, Matt?"

"No, and it doesn't make any sense at all. It uses white gas that has never failed to light before. I used a couple of matches and got nowhere.

"And Paula, I tried to start the car, but it wouldn't start or even turn over, and there was no radio or lights.

"Paula, what time is it on your nurses' watch?"

"Why? Are you going someplace?

Matt, you have a watch that tells you the time, your heart rate, and how far you walk during the day, just to name a few things."

"Yes, it doesn't work either—nothing battery-operated works. Look around the house. Your favorite old-school clock, which runs on a battery, has stopped. None of the flashlights or battery candles work. Chuck told me it was happening around the neighborhood. So, what time is it?"

"You didn't tell me everything, Chuck Mazeroski said. How come?"

"Darling, I didn't want to worry you, and I don't know if I believed him!"

"OK, Matt, it's 11:50 and too dark for this time of day."

Matt walked over to look out the living room windo*w. "Paula, it's getting dark fast, and there still are no lights, sun, moon, or light of any kind, DEAD DARK*!!!!"

He turned to look at Paula. There was no light, and it would get worse when the storm arrived.

"Paula, lock all the doors and windows. I'll get some blankets, and we can hole up in the living room. And I'm grabbing my shotgun; always be prepared for the unknown."

"Matt, I still have one more thing I would like to try."

As Paula got up from the couch, he could make her out in the darkened room, and she walked by him to the China buffets.

Matt saw her light a match, and he could not believe it. One of the candles had an intense flame. She was standing holding the candle in her right hand, with the biggest grin he had ever seen on her beautiful face.

She slowly returned to the couch, shielding the candle with her left hand.

"Wow, that's amazing! Paula, please explain why only one of your candles is working.

"Matt, I remembered I brought this candle and others two years ago at a church fundraiser. The candles are guaranteed to light in the days of darkness. And this other one you should recognize. It's the one with Mary engraved on the side of it. Remember our trip to Wisconsin?"

"Yeah, we had an exciting time in Wisconsin. We went to the Field of Dreams in Iowa, Sheboygan, Wisconsin, and did some fishing. I caught a 7-pound rainbow, which the guide turned loose."

"Yes, Matt, and then we went to the Green Bay Packers game."

"Yes, Paula, it was the most impressive thing I have ever seen. What an incredible thrill to see Rogers play for the Packers."

"Well, Matt, remember the Catholic Church on the hill? The one Mary was supposed to have appeared in to heal all those people? You paid $20 for this candle to help support the poor; it's also a blessed candle."

"Okay Paula, what is all this mumbo jumbo?"

"Matt, three days of darkness, the punishment imposed by GOD!"

"Paula, are you telling me three days of darkness is some of your church's crap? What have they been filling your head with?"

"Well, Matt, what I remember from my mumbo jumbo church stuff is that when God gets pissed at humanity, he could send down a chastisement, an unmistakable sign, and everyone will know it's from God. Anybody caught outside during this time dies, and the devil gets their soul.

"So Matt, my husband, I would call this mumbo jumbo a God event: what else would you call it?"

Too-too-too-too-toooooom! Too-too-too-too-toom! Too-too-too-tooooooo-toooooo-tom!!

"What the hell is all that noise? It's getting louder, Paula; my head is pounding."

"Matt, it sounds like horns—no trumpets. It's coming from the sky above us and getting so loud that it hurts my ears.

Matt, it's NOON!"

"What about noon? Is it supposed to mean something to you and your church group? All those old ladies sewing and talking about the world's end?"

"Matt, don't you find it strange that the trumpet sounds at exactly noon? It's not the first time this has happened."

"What do you mean, Paula; this is not the first time."

"It's happened before; it's in the Bible. God told Moses in Egypt that there would be three days of darkness, and only the Israelites would have light."

"What you're telling me is this could be three days?"

"Yes, I'm afraid that's what the trumpets were at noon, the start of the three days of Darkness."

"What else is there about this dark stuff, and where did you learn all this crap?"

"Matt, while you're watching Monday night football, I went to Bible study. If you remember, I tried to get you to go with me. We discussed the Bible in detail, and there's so much in the Bible that is coming true, with all the fires, floods, pollution, killings, and wars. It's all coming to fruition, and God is unhappy with humankind.

"He has warned us, Matt. God promised chastisement for the entire world, which some people would pay with their lives, followed by two miracles. The darkness is the chastisement; after three days, there will be two miracles. Hopefully, everything will be fine."

"Paula, what do you mean people will lose their lives? It's just dark outside. After three days, it goes away, right? Isn't it the indoctrination you get when you go to church from priests and nuns and Old Testament stuff?"

"Matt, what's happened to you? You used to be a believer. You went to a Catholic school. We got married in the church, and our children were baptized there. You used to attend church. What happened? You still wear the Marvelous Mary Metal your mother gave you before you went to the military."

"Paula, I don't want to talk about it. I told you!! I don't want to talk about it; just leave it alone!! Let's talk about something else. We can't call anyone, our phones don't work, and we can't go anywhere because none of the cars will work.

"Paula, I'm concerned about our children and grandchildren. We can't reach them to ensure they're safe with the phones not working. There is no way I can think of contacting any of our family members."

"Matt, isn't there anything we can do? You're the military man; you have all the experience. Send a flare, pull out a secret radio and phone."

"All we can do, Paula, is hope they are all safe. They're probably all worried about us, too, and nobody can do anything now."

"Matt, I hear pounding at the front door. It sounds like my sister. She is calling my name. She needs help! Let her in!"

"Paula, you know it can't be your sister Mary. How would she get here? It's completely dark outside. She would not have found our house in this dark if she had walked. Besides, she lives on the other side of Lincoln. She couldn't have driven because the cars don't work.

"Paula, you must be careful. Don't open any doors or windows. Remember what you told me. The old saying goes that anybody who goes out in the dark dies, and the devil gets their soul."

"Yes, Matt, we're OK if we stay in the house and don't open the doors to anybody. The dog should stay in the house; if she has to pee, she can go into the sunroom. I will put some towels down for her, and she can pee there."

The day was thick with an eerie silence, broken only by the relentless scratching and banging at the windows. Matt's heart pounded as he whispered to Paula, "I guess the demons will do anything to fool us."

Little did they know the true horror was just beginning.

Paula's candle flickered, casting light and long shadows on the walls. "I'm not paying attention to the noises outside," she said, trembling, "but the sounds are getting louder, Matt. The scratching and banging—like they're trying to break in."

A sudden crash echoed through the house. Matt said, "The storm door glass just broke." His voice rose with concern, "But our front door is solid oak, so they can't get through it, Paula."

Paula took a deep breath and grabbed a small bottle from the living room buffet. "It's Holy water," she said, her hand shaking. She went and blessed all the windows and doors, and the scratching stopped. But then, an unearthly scream pierced the air, followed by another.

"No, it can't be," Paula whispered, her face pale with fear, "what was that?"

Matt looked out the window in horror. He saw faces, tormented, burning faces, all trying to get into their house. In all his years with the Navy, he had never encountered anything remotely close to what he witnessed now.

Paula joined him at the window, her eyes wide with terror.

"Look across the street, Paula, on top of Chuck and Mabel's house. Tell me what you see."

"A red 8-foot-tall figure with glowing red eyes, horns, and black wings," Paula's voice was barely a whisper, "Mabel is my best friend. What's happening to them?"

Before Matt could answer, the figure pointed at their house with a look of pure hatred. With one mighty flap of its wings, it soared towards them at an impossible speed.

Matt grabbed Paula and pulled her to the floor. *Is this the end?* He wondered, just as the primal scream echoed across the desolate landscape.

With a thunderous crash, the roof gave way under the demon's immense force. Shingles and splintered wood rained into the house, and the air filled with choking dust and smoke. Matt and Paula clung to each other as they were showered with debris. The walls trembled and groaned as if the house was in pain.

The demon landed in the wreckage, its fiery eyes blazing with fury. Its vast wings unfurled and cast a shadow over the trembling couple. The floor-boards creaked and splintered under its heavy steps.

As the demon's fiery form towered above them, deep choking words came out of its mouth: "Matthew, I'm here to end you."

Evil's form approached them, getting closer. The demon suddenly roared in fury, his burning eyes locking on Paula, who had just thrown the rest of her Holy water at the demon. Several spots on the demon flared up, like gas thrown on a fire.

"My mission is to kill Matthew, but it will be my pleasure to take you and rip you apart."

Returning to Matt, the flames on the creature flickered, and suddenly, the demon's wings were beating fiercely, shimmering with an unearthly light coming down from above. A ray of sunshine appeared, and with one final deafening roar, the demon was consumed by a blinding burst of light, and then it was gone.

Exhausted and shaken, Matt and Paula collapsed to the floor, clutching each other. They opened their eyes after the flash of light and saw their house was in ruins.

"Matt, what happened to our house?"

"I don't know; I only remember a white light."

"Let me help you get up; I walk you to the couch."

They both sat down, confused about what had destroyed the house.

Lucy came running into the room and jumped up into Paula's lap.

Staring out the window, Matt could see nothing but total blackness, except he could faintly see the fires around the neighborhood. He could also smell the smoke coming through the roof, which, for some reason, had caved in, making a big hole in their house.

Matthew had seen his share of death, so he wasn't afraid of dying. But he was damned if he was going to let anything happen to Paula. He reached over and grabbed his shotgun and held it close. If anything comes in, he would make sure that he was between whatever it was and Paula. To the last stand. He would die for her.

CHAPTER 2

Near Death

Present Day

"Paula, darling, are you okay?"

"Matt, it was too close; I thought we were dead."

She was sobbing, hands covering her face.

"I don't know what to do, Paula. It's all so crazy."

Matt's primary concern was to comfort her and assure her that everything would turn out fine, simultaneously thinking *something serious was going on.*

"Paula, let me help you get back on the couch. I'll get you another Diet Coke. Cover your back and shoulders with a blanket, and we will just sit here together.

"You know I love you, Paula. I will do anything for you and die for you if that's what it takes."

"Matthew, you know I love you as well. After all, who would have put up with you all these years?

"So, Matt, now we have all this time and survived death. You can tell me what happened in Afghanistan; tell me the story! You owe me the truth about what caused your nightmares."

"Okay, Paula. I'll do the best I can. It's so hard for me to think about what happened."

*****

It all started in Afghanistan and the Middle East following September 11. It was 2009, and we were getting much-needed rest at Kandahar Airfield. When I got a message, the captain wanted to see me immediately.

So, I ran up to his building across the compound, to an office door with his name on it: Captain Engel.

I knocked.

Tap, tap.

"Yes, come in."

I guessed Captain Engel was about 50 years old, with a thin face, gray hair combed to the right, about 6 feet tall, and weighing 175 pounds. And yeah! He had seen his share of combat.

As I walked through the door, I stood and saluted, "Lieutenant Dylan reporting, sir."

"Yes, Lieutenant, at ease. Shut the door and sit down."

As I sat down, I noticed the green military-issued chairs, desks, light green walls, filing cabinets, and pukey green carpet.

"Lieutenant, how is your team doing after your last mission? I know it was a tough ten days in the backcountry of Afghanistan."

"We had a lovely week of recuperating, eating hot cafeteria food, sleeping, and treating minor injuries.

"The men are bored now; we are not used to sitting around with nothing to do."

"Well, Lieutenant, I have a mission for your team. I realize you have been here for longer than two years, and I am sure you heard the rumors about SEAL Team 3 going home.

"Your team has been here longer than I have. Your team has been excellent, but they should go home after two years."

"Yes, sir. Thank you, sir."

"But as I said, I must ask you and your men to take on this last mission. One that only you and an experienced team can carry out."

"Sir, we have been lucky for the past 2 years; we should be going home!"

"Yes, you should; I agree with you.

"This mission comes from the highest level down to us; several principals must be rescued.

"The mission, Lieutenant, is a rescue operation in Pakistan."

"Sir, I thought we were not allowed in Pakistan."

"That's true, Lieutenant. However, this mission is to rescue American prisoners the Taliban took after they entered Afghan territory, raided several villages, and captured a priest and between 6 and 8 of his team, which consisted of a couple of nuns and college students from the United States. All were helping the priest inoculate the people in the Afghan mountains."

"Sir, how long ago was this information relayed to you?"

"About 2 to 3 days before we heard anything.

"Again, I cannot stress enough that this comes from the highest level down—from the President to a general, down to my boss, and now to you. It seems that the priest was once one of ours."

"One of ours, sir?"

"He was a Green Beret stationed at the forward operating base Gardez several years ago. And before you ask, he left the military, became a priest, and returned to help people in Afghanistan."

"Yes, sir, I understand the priority. Do you have a plan, sir?"

"I will send you and your team, with two Sikorsky SH-60 Sea Hawks, to forward operating base Gardez. That will put you within striking distance of the Pakistan border. You will land on this side of Afghanistan.

"The helicopters will also stay on this side of the border. The idea is to march 10 miles and reach the target before sunrise. At that point, you should be able to get an idea of the strength of the Taliban forces in the area. You will decide when you are going to initiate entry. First, take out the guards and then rescue the hostages. When the situation is under control, call the helicopters to your site, load the hostage, and bring them back to Firebase Gardez. Understand?"

"Crystal, sir. I will inform my team."

"All right, Lieutenant Dylan. It's now 07:00. Get everything together, get your team supplied, and be ready to go by 10:00. Meet on the airfield, and we will leave at the same time, headed for the Firebase Gardez."

"We, sir? Are you going along on this mission?"

"Yes, I'm taking the C-130 and a platoon of 24 Marines. We will follow you to the firebase.

"I plan on running the mission at Gardez.

"Any other questions?"

"No, sir. If you do not mind, I'll leave now. I have preparations to make. I will brief the team, give them mission parameters, and answer as many questions as possible."

"Then, Matthew, I'll meet you on the field at 10 o'clock. Here's a folder containing more information on the hostages. From what I understand, they dressed as village people to blend in. So don't shoot them!

"Dismissed!"

"Thank you, sir."

I got up from my chair and gave my commander a salute. Turned sharp to the right, opened the door, and went out. I waited till I was outside the building, and then thought *Oh crap*.

I walked across the compound to the men's quarters. Opening the door as I walked through, I looked about. Some men were playing cards, others reading, some listening to music, and some writing letters, I'm guessing, to their loved ones at home. Although expectations were for our unit to go home, I mean two years, two years of missions, all most deadly. We deserved to go home to our loved ones and families.

This was not going to go over well with my men!

I looked around, and there was Master Sergeant Ethan Jones, 28, black, 6′ 1″, built like a bull, with black hair always short—a good man to have on your side in a fight.

James Miller is Caucasian, 27, 190 pounds, with blue eyes and blonde hair. He was a charmer with the ladies. He was our radio operator and always had something to say. His nickname was Sparky.

Luke Sinclair, 26 years old, Caucasian, 5′ 11″, 195 pounds, had a shaved head and brown eyes. He was known for his precision skills and deadly sniper skills. He carried 308-caliber sniper rifles. His nickname was Punch.

Nathan Davenport, 24, Caucasian, the youngest member of the team, came in a year ago. A farm boy from Iowa with blonde hair and blue eyes. A good-looking kid standing 6′ 1″ and weighing 200 pounds. Sent to us because of his electronics knowledge and skill in setting up listening posts in various places in Iraq. Nickname: Iowa.

Stephen Fox, Caucasian 27, 6′ 2″, 234 pounds. Green eyes. Our explosives man. If you want to blow it up, he's the man—nickname: BOOM.

Adam Hart, Caucasian, 26, 6′ 1″, 200 pounds, blue eyes, also liked the ladies, trained as a military medic, and in hand-to-hand combat. Pretty efficient with small arms. Nickname: Doc.

"All right, men, listen up."

Master Sergeant Jones jumped up, "Attention! Officer on deck!"

All the men jumped up to attention and saluted me. I always appreciated loyalty. We had been together for over two years, plus the time in boot camp.

"At ease and gather around. I have something to tell you."

They all smiled at me, thinking I had some news about going home.

"When are we going home, sir?"

There was no way to sugarcoat this.

"Our captain requests that we go on another mission. Into Pakistan to rescue a priest, a couple of nuns, and 6 to 8 college students captured by the Taliban and moved to a small village in Pakistan."

As I expected, moans, groans, and disappointment from them all.

"Yeah, I know you have lots of questions, and I don't have many answers right now. We are leaving the airfield at 10:00 this morning. You will need 40-pound packs, plenty of medical equipment, any food you want to take for a day or so, water, and extra ammunition because you never know what we learn along the way. Always prepare for the unexpected! We are going on a forced march in the dark, approximately ten miles. Chopper out, land close to the border of Pakistan. We have plenty of time to cover those ten miles, so make sure you have your night vision goggles with you. Go through and check all your weapons.

"So sorry to lay this on you, but I can tell you it comes down from the president to the generals to our captain. As you know, the crap rolls downhill and stops with us. We can handle it because we are Navy SEALs.

"After you get your gear together, take your letters to the drop at the post office. Boys, just in case, we have been through this before. They always hold our letters and return them to us when we return.

"Any questions?"

"Sir, just to understand …"

"Yes, Master Sergeant?"

"Are we going to rescue a priest?

"Sir, what is so vital about the priest, nuns, and college students who should have never been there in the first place?"

"I can tell you this: the priest was once a Green Beret stationed in Afghanistan. He left the Green Berets years ago and became a priest. From what I understand, he returned here to inoculate the mountain people in Afghanistan and administer first aid. I'm guessing the nuns and college students were recruited to help with the project, all funded by the Catholic Church.

"Any other questions? I'll meet you on the airfield, right then."

Matt quickly saluted them and walked out. He had to return to his quarters across the quad in the officers' quarters.

Matt had his satellite phone that he always took on missions. *I'll give Paula a quick call.*

Phone ringing, ringing.

"Hello, who is this?"

"Paula, I'm calling from Afghanistan."

"Oh, are you calling about coming home? I can't wait and look forward to it!"

"Unfortunately, I'll be delayed for a couple of days; we have one more mission to go on.

"I wanted to let you know as soon as possible Paula.

"As soon as we finish, we will fly out and see you within a week to 10 days."

"Matthew, I can't tell you how disappointed I am, but I understand it's not the first time."

"I know, sweetheart. I love you, and I can't wait to see you as well. So, I need to go. Love you."

"I love you too, Matt. Be safe and come home to me in one piece."

"Bye, talk to you later. Paula, okay?"

Matt now had to return to business and put his pack together. He checked his M4 carbine, 8-30-round magazines, two Beretta 9 pistols, and several 15-round magazines for both.

He also needed night goggles, extra socks, clean underwear, and military chocolate bars that tasted like shit. It's all they would have, some power bars, a couple of bottles of water, plus his canteen. KA-BAR knife in a scabbard strapped to his lower leg. One attached to his bulletproof vest that he could grab with his right hand for close combat, and one in his vest,

8-30 round magazines for his M4. And of course, his lucky Packers baseball cap—he never went anywhere without it.

It looks like I'm ready to go in my camouflaged clothing and Navy-issued military boots.

Matt took a last look around. *Oh! I need to close and lock my footlocker.* It contained all his valuables. With so many years in the Navy, everything he was worth was in that footlocker.

Mat opened the door and stepped out—what an enjoyable day! He headed to the post office to drop off his letter.

Betsy was the post lady there, and she took care of them. She understood the importance of leaving their letters there until they returned.

Matt looked at his watch. It was time to head for the airport; it looked like his ride had arrived.

"Private!"

"Yes, sir, are you ready to go, sir?"

"Yes, private, take me to the airfield. There should be a chopper waiting for me."

As Matt walked around to the right side of the vehicle and climbed into the passenger side, he wondered how many times he'd ridden in these Humvees.

On his way to the airfield, Matt started to think about everything he needed to do once they reached their destination.

Matt had to decide whether or not to take the inexperienced Nathan along. Matt had been sheltering Nathan and slowly bringing him on missions.

On the other hand, Matt thought this was Nathan's last chance for mission experience, combat pay, and adding the experience to his resume.

Nathan did well on the missions when they took him along on safe missions, one without any possibility of a firefight.

Matt liked Nathan Davenport, the tall, blonde-haired, good-looking kid from Des Moines, Iowa. He was the typical freckle-faced farm boy—always smiling and very likeable.

Matt decided to wait until the last minute to make that decision.

He needed to get Master Sergeant's opinion on Nathan, which is always valuable.

"Sir, we are coming up to the Sikorsky chopper."

It was no surprise to Matt; his men were there as expected.

"All right, private, stop here by this chopper, thanks for the ride."

As Matt walked up to the chopper, Master Sergeant was standing there and paying attention.

"Morning, sir!"

"Good morning, Master Sergeant. Are we set to go?"

"Yes, sir, all equipment loaded in the chopper has been accounted for."

"Sergeant, is the second chopper ready to go as well?"

"Yes, sir!"

"Sergeant, if everything goes according to plan, the hostages should be coming home on the second one."

Matt looked around, satisfied with the arrangements, and waved his right hand.

"Okay, let's saddle up. We're headed to Firebase Gardez, a short ride. Keep your eyes open; this can be a hot zone."

As both helicopters took off in unison, whirling blades, and dust flying everywhere signaled their ascent as they started a new adventure.

It wasn't too long before they arrived at Gardez Firebase. The choppers landed, and the men disembarked onto the field and walked into the hangar where Captain Engel was waiting for them.

Matt noticed 24 Marines sitting around checking on their gear. As he walked in, all the Marines nodded to the SEALs, recognizing who they were.

Captain Engel stood in front of a map. Several chairs were arranged in a circle in front of him. Matt's team sat and waited for Captain Engel to give them their final instructions.

"SEAL Team 3, let me start by apologizing for keeping you over on one last mission before going home. You are the best we have for this mission, which is strictly a rescue mission.

"When I spoke with your lieutenant, I didn't know that one of the college students was family to our president.

"Now you understand the urgency of the president and generals to move quickly to rescue the hostages.

"One other thing, it wasn't the Taliban who took the hostages but Pakistan. It was the Pakistani military that went into Iraq intentionally to capture this young lady and take her to the capital of Pakistan because of her propaganda value as well as to force concessions from the United States.

"Our Intel is not sure exactly how many Pakistani militaries are on-site, but you are clear for weapons-free."

Engel looked into their faces, "In addition, I'm sending you two Apache helicopters to oversee and cover your asses if necessary. Along with two F-15s as needed firepower.

"Don't hesitate to call if you need help.

"I can't stress enough the importance of bringing the hostages home. The president and his brother and wife, the girl's parents, are waiting at Kandahar. As soon as you've loaded them on the helicopters, they will be flown to Kandahar.

"I'm passing around a couple of pictures of her. Her name is Linda. She is about 5′ 6″, 135 pounds, has long blonde hair, probably in a ponytail, blue eyes, and is somewhat attractive and athletic.

"Please look at the picture, commit it to memory, and ensure she's the one we bring home.

"And remember they are all dressed as villagers, so don't shoot any hostages.

"Any other questions?"

"Sir."

"Yes, Lieutenant Dylan?"

"Sir, the priest you are talking about, is he a priority?"

"Matt, he is not the primary, but he is one of us, and we should do everything we can to bring him home along with the other hostages.

"The only pictures I have of this priest are from the records here at Gardez, where he was stationed as a Green Beret. I'll pass this on to you also.

"As you will see, he is a good 6′ 1″ or so, weighs 225 pounds, and has brown eyes. He is Caucasian and has maintained his physical condition.

"All right, SEALs. We are out of time. You need to head out to the border. By the time you get there, it should be close to sundown.

"One change in the plans is that you will be dropped by chopper just inside the Pakistani border, and the Marines and Rangers will remain on this side of the border as a backup if you need it.

"Also, the Apache helicopters will be in a valley hidden from sight. Callsign Hellfire 1-2, the F-15's callsign is Dragon Fire 1-2.

"SEALs callsign remains Reaper 1.

"The callsign at the base is Delta 1.

"Remain radio silent until you're on-site, then call us at Delta 1. Message: WE ARE HOME!!

"Once you have secured the site and the hostages are secure, call on the Seahawks to pick you up. Once secure and in the air, call Delta 1. and advise that packages are mailed. You will remain with the hostages until their arrival and safe transfer to the Kandahar base.

"That is all, good luck SEAL Team 3."

Matt stood up, looked at his men, and said, "Let's go, let's hit it."

The flight from Firebase Gardez didn't take too long to get past the Pakistan border.

They landed, and the chopper was gone quickly. Matt's team kept their heads down until the choppers were gone because the wash from the blades on the helicopter picked up all kinds of dust, dirt, and grass.

Matt's men were in darkness, except for all the bright stars in the sky.

Matt was happy there was not much of a moon, so there was no light. He gave his men the signal to put on the night vision gear.

Matt looked around and signaled to move out. Luke took the lead, followed by James, Nathan, Stephen, Adam, Matt, and Sergeant Jones took the rear.

Matt had decided to take Nathan along, so he was in the middle. They were marching along some rocky terrain, but mostly it was sand, hard enough that they could make a suitable time, so that's a good deal. Moving along steadily, they covered 10 miles in good time.

Matt communicated with his team through a single-channel airborne radio system, which allowed them to talk to each other and to Matt.

Matt told Luke, "Pull up, let's take a break."

Matt told his team they were making suitable time and that they should take 5 minutes to get some water to stay hydrated. "Does anyone have any problems?"

No one responded, which meant they were good to go. "Keep your intervals between each other," Matt stressed.

Matt changed points, Stephen switched with Luke and took the lead point. Luke fell in the rear, taking over the rear guard. "Let's move out!"

Matt kept track of their progress. With about 5 miles to go, he told them, "We've maintained our pace, so keep your eyes out for any movement. We don't want to run up on a goat herder by mistake. It happened to us on another mission. It's hard to decide what to do with them. Either tie them up and gag them or dispatch them."

Some time later, Matt halted the team. "We're getting close. The village should be over this next hill. Let's take a position on the hilltop, do recon, and see what we're up against."

They all crawled to the top of the hill, and with their night vision goggles, they could see a small village below.

"Lieutenant, I see at least two bogeys on top of one building with automatic weapons; there are at least two on the ground with automatic weapons."

"Sergeant, thank you. I agree. I see 2–2. It's a small village, but we must watch out for civilians."

Matt asked through headphones whether anybody else had seen anything.

No answer. "Okay, let's move in. It looks like about one hour until sunup," Matt whispered into his headset. "The plan is simple: Sergeant Jones and Stephen will use handguns with silencers to take out the four guards. Adam and James will go with me to the front door.

"Sergeant, we will follow behind you down the hill. After you remove the guards, you will move to the rear.

"On my mark, you go through the rear, and we will take the front door and meet you in the middle." Matt waited for confirmation from his men.

Sergeant Jones replied, "Roger, Lieutenant."

Matt finished his plan, "Luke and Nathan stay on the hill and cover the team below. Luke, use your .308 with a silencer to get anybody with a weapon. I think there's got to be more than just four guards. If we are lucky, we will catch them all sleeping.

"So, everybody stays frosty, weapons hot! Kill anyone with a gun!

"All right, let's move out and take your positions."

The night was still dark enough to move unobserved, so Sergeant Jones and Stephen moved up to the building, spreading out 5 yards parallel to each other and moving quickly; the guards were dead with four quick shots before they knew what hit them.

Sergeant Jones and Stephen quickly moved to the left and around the building into the back.

Matt moved up to the front of the building with his team.

Matt was in the middle, Adam to his left and James to his right.

Matt waited for word from the sergeant's team that they were in position.

"Reaper 2 is in position."

"Roger. Go, go, go!"

Matt kicked the door open. Adam went in first, swerving to the left, James went in second to the right, and Matt entered the middle of the room.

Adam and James both opened fire, killing four hostiles, and both moved to the hostages. Matt looked in front of him as a door opened and saw a hostile ready to shoot. Then he was dead. The sergeant's team made an entrance and killed five hostiles, as well as the one standing at the door.

Matt was looking over to the left to see if all hostiles were dead when, to his right, out of the dark, came a figure right at him. Before Matt could react, he was stabbed in his stomach, and he came again at Matt with the knife from the right side, this time aiming towards Matt's throat; Matt raised his left hand to block it, and the knife he cut right through his wrist. Matt tried to reach for his knife or pistol, but the man was too close and pushing against him.

Before Matt knew it, someone came from his left, disarmed the hostile, took his knife, jammed it deep into the hostile between his throat and collarbone, and pulled down, opening his chest.

Matt collapsed. Blood was gushing from his left wrist and spurting all over the place. Matt put his right tactical glove over his wrist, trying to stop the bleeding while he also was bleeding from the gaping hole in his stomach.

All Matt could do was sit there and bleed. Quickly, the bleeding caused him to lose consciousness. His eyes blurred, telling Matt he was near the end.

Matt was now unconscious. A person came to Matt's left arm and put a tourniquet on it, stopping the bleeding. He then took Matt's hand away from his wrist, applied a bandage, and splinted it to hold his arm and wrist in place. He also gave Matt a shot of morphine before he went into shock. Next, he attended to the hole in Matt's belly. Then the morphine took over, and Matt was under.

Master Sergeant Jones came into the room, saw Matt was in bad shape, and immediately took over, taking all the hostages outside to the front of the building.

"Sparky, call Rescue 1 and 2. Also, call Dragon Fire 1-2 for backup."

"Yes, Sergeant, on it."

Matt didn't know who had taken care of him until years later. The same person laid him down and covered Matt with blankets he found inside the building.

Periodically, someone would give Matt more morphine and check his bandages while waiting for the choppers to come in for rescue.

Master Sergeant went back into the building and brought out three prisoners with slight wounds, tied up their hands and legs, and leaned them up against the building.

All the hostages were accounted for except for two; at least the President's niece was found unharmed.

The priest's face was beaten, but otherwise, he was in decent shape. He looked around at all the rescued people, "Hey, two are missing. Two nuns are not here."

After Sergeant Jones walked over and took him aside, "I'm sorry, I think around the building on the other side are two of your people. They had been hanged on two poles, stripped, and then gutted. It's not a pretty sight. I promise we will recover the bodies and take them with us; no one will be left behind."

Before Sergeant could stop him, the priest ran around the side of the building to the back where the two nuns were hanging. Then they heard a blood-curdling scream. The priest came back to the front of the building and looked at the three tied-up prisoners. The one in the middle was a heavyset-looking Pakistani.

The priest stood before the one in the middle and said, "Why did you do that?"

The Pakistani looked at him, smiled, and said, "They were so tasty, delicious, yummy!"

The other two prisoners grinned and smacked their lips, making laughing noises hurtfully.

The priest stared at them, turned, and returned to the building. He soon came out with a sword, and before anybody knew what was going on, he cut off all three of their heads, yelling at the top of his lungs," Go to hell, go to hell." And then he walked away, collapsed into a heap, and sobbed.

Sergeant and the rest of his team stood there dumbfounded, not knowing what to say. What could you say?

In the distance, Sergeant could hear helicopter rotors—the choppers coming in to pick them up.

Sergeant Jones took charge. "All right let's get everybody ready to leave. Stephen, get the stretcher from the first chopper. Nathan, you and Adam will take Lieutenant Dylan to the first chopper. Adam, stay with Lieutenant since you are the medic. Nathan can help you."

Nathan looked puzzled at Sergeant Jones.

"It will be a good learning experience for you, Nathan."

Sergeant Jones looked at James, "Help me collect the two bodies of the nuns and load them in the first chopper.

"The rest of the team, including the hostages, will go in the second chopper. So, Adam, as soon as the bodies are loaded, take off, and we'll follow.

"Get to Kandahar as soon as you can. The lieutenant needs significant surgery on his hand. Keeping him stable is your primary job, Adam."

The rotors on the first chopper started to rotate at a high pitch, lifting off the ground and making a right turn off to Kandahar.

Sergeant Jones returned to the building and made one more turn-through. He then ran back to the second chopper and climbed aboard to ensure nobody was left behind.

"Sparky, call Delta 1." The Sergeant took the microphone. "The main packages are safely mailed; the uncle and parents should be proud. Three other packages are being mailed; two are sent in bags, and one has been damaged. The damaged package is on shipment one and needs immediate care. End of message, Reaper 2."

By giving them the Reaper 2 callsign, Sergeant Jones indicated that he was now in charge and that the lieutenant was the injured one.

Chopper 2 climbed into the air, making a right turn and gaining altitude, heading to Kandahar. The Apache helicopters were approaching; one circled behind Chopper 2, and the other took the lead, both covering the front and rear of Chopper 2 containing the hostages.

Further out, Chopper 1 was reaching the Pakistani and Iraqi borders. Adam was in the back with the lieutenant, checking bandages and his IV. Nathan sat on the jump seat with his back to the pilot. Both had headphones on to communicate with the pilots. The pilots checked the situation with the lieutenant and showed genuine concern.

Nathan was sitting back. There was not much to do but hold on to the side of the seat with both hands and then suddenly …

The pilots were talking frantically back and forth with each other, then shouted, "ROCKET! Hold tight; we take evasive maneuvers, send countermeasures, turn left, and hang on!

"Delta 1! Delta 1! We are under fire; repeat, we are under fire. Unable to avoid rockets, countermeasures are exhausted."

Nathan and Adam just look at each other, confused, and then …

A rocket—BAM—went right through the pilot's cabin and took Nathan.

Adam was still holding onto the straps that held the lieutenant to the stretcher, and now they were going down hard.

The chopper was now in two pieces. The half with the Lieutenant and Adam hit the ground with a tremendous jolt, throwing out Adam and the Lieutenant. Both landed on rocky ground. Adam landed next to the Lieutenant.

Adam was still conscious after he hit the ground. His left arm was broken. He watched as the other part of the chopper hit the ground and exploded about fifty yards away. There couldn't be any survivors.

Adam got up and walked over to where Lieutenant was lying. He started to open his eyes and look around. Adam knelt beside him. "We just crashed; a rocket went through the chopper, breaking it into two pieces."

"Adam, where are the others?"

"Sorry, sir, they didn't make it; we are the only two alive."

"Nathan?"

"Yes, sorry!"

"Okay, Adam. Although my left hand is not functional, I am still capable of shooting with my right hand. We need weapons. Look in the chopper and see if you can find my pack. I have two Berettas and some extra magazines."

"Yes, sir, my left arm was broken in the crash, but I can still shoot. I'll grab a carbine and cover it to the right if you can cover in front of you to the left."

Matt was concerned that all this fire and smoke would draw the Taliban.

Adam came back with the weapons.

"Adam, make sure your shots count; we don't have much ammunition."

"Sir, you are bleeding again. Let me at least put a bandage on the pulled-out IV."

Adam grabbed his pack with his right arm and took out a large bandage. "Okay, sir, that should stop some of the bleeding."

Just then, Adam stopped talking. "I can hear something out there, sir!"

A lone Taliban came down the hill towards Matt, all dressed in black, carrying a Russian-made AK-47, firing it toward Matt, who took his Beretta and put two rounds right into the Taliban's chest, ending his life right there.

Matt heard Adam firing behind him. A couple more were coming at him, two shots each, bringing them down, six shots gone. Matt had nine more in this magazine and one other magazine lying on his chest. *Here comes a couple more.* Bam, bam. Two shots each, five shots remaining.

Matt, pausing, didn't hear any shooting from Adam, so he turned his head to see where Adam was. DAMN! He was lying there with a hole in his head.

Son of a bitch, he was a good man. At that exact moment, a Taliban appeared, stood looking at Matt, stared him in the eyes, and shot Matt in the chest.

Matt knew he was going to die. *Great, more firing and yelling, shit; the Rangers and Marines finally made it.*

As Matt faded out, he heard another shot over his head; someone had made a clean headshot and killed the son of a bitch who killed him.

As Matt passed out, his last thoughts were of his love, Paula.

"Good shot, Sergeant Stone. Damn Taliban."

"Thanks, Captain."

"Stone, check and see if the Navy guy is alive.

"The rest of you get body bags for the other people; we're taking them all home."

Stone stood up, waving, "Medic, over here; I think this one is alive."

Medic arrived, checking the Navy guy. "Yes, sir, it looks like he has taken one to the chest; wait a second; the round hit something metal in his chest, and it stopped the bullet from going all the way into his chest.

"His other wounds have been bandaged; someone took good care of him. He should make it if we can get him back to Kandahar Hospital. However, it's going to be touch and go."

Captain Engel shouted, "All right, Rangers, we are moving out!"

*****

Back in Lincoln. The Present

"Paula, you know the rest of the story. Someone told me Captain Engel got hold of you and told you they were sending me to Kandahar Hospital. With all the drugs, I don't remember anything about arriving at the Kandahar Hospital.

"I remember waking up in Germany at the hospital, and you were standing beside me, holding my hand. What a beautiful sight to see you!"

"Yes, Matt. I remember it was a long haul for you to get through rehab. You were lucky at Kandahar. The President was still on site with his doctors and surgeons, so surgeons were waiting for you when they brought you into Kandahar.

"The surgeons repaired your hand and reattached all the ligaments and nerves. Fixing the wound in your chest, they found a medallion in your chest, the one your mother gave you, which stopped the bullet from going deeper into your chest. The stab wound you had in your stomach was right where your appendix is; they went ahead and took your appendix out and stitched you up."

"Paula, I must tell you what happened at the crash site. I swear, I died, and it was impressive and terrific, and I wanted to stay there, and I didn't want to come back."

"Yes, Matt, but the medics brought you back to life and brought you back to me."

"Paula, I told you what I remember after waking up in a German hospital.

"But the rest of the story is about a Catholic priest who came around and talked to the men in our ward. He finally got to me, and I told him what happened to me when I died.

"His comment was that I was on drugs. None of it happened; it was all hallucinations, which occur when a person does too much heroin, so I had to just put it out of my mind; it never happened. And try to give up being a drug addict.

"Paula, I was so pissed he wouldn't listen to me and then told me I was a drug addict. I heard it the whole time I was there.

"Also, Master Sergeant Jones came to see me. I didn't know what happened during the rescue in Pakistan. So, he filled me in about the priest we rescued and how he killed three tied-up prisoners. He cut all their heads off.

"Now, can you see it from my point of view? I was told I was hallucinating because of drugs, and now a priest is a killer. I no longer have faith after all that has happened."

"I'm sorry, Matt. About what happened to you, but you can see outside the windows, and if everything is truly evil, there must also be goodness. Goodness must be Jesus Christ. I notice you still have the medallion of Mary that your mother gave you, even though it has a dent. It saved your life. I would call it a miracle.

"Matt, somebody was looking out for you; whether you want to believe it or not, someone was watching over you."

"I also lost some men. Their deaths, and especially that of Nathan, the kid from Iowa, trouble me deeply. I had a choice of leaving him at the base where he would have been safe. But I decided to take him along, and it haunts me. And, of course, Doc died while saving my life."

"Matt, sweetheart, I certainly understand why you have nightmares now. I'm glad you told me; I understand better. I also know there is nothing I can do to help. All I can do is be here for you and tell you I love you no matter what."

"Paula, it must be the third day. You said it would be three days before everything returned to normal, right?

"This reminds me, Paula, that you owe me an explanation of what to expect when the three days end and what is normal."

"Matthew, all I know is that after three days, according to the story, God is going to take all the chosen ones to heaven and send all the bad ones to hell. Following the first miracle, some people will be left behind. We don't know who those people are or for what reason, but they just are left behind.

"I don't know anything else and certainly don't know if everything will be normal again. What I know and am sure of is that we saw pure evil, and it scares me to death to think of anyone I knew who might have been sent to a place of evil."

"I hope that once it has returned to normal, Paula, we should be able to call all our grandkids and children and ensure everybody is safe and okay."

"I get the cell phones so we can keep them beside us."

"We'll call as soon as possible. If the car starts, we can drive to Omaha to see our children and grandchildren."

"You, Matthew, are such a great grandpa. You love your grandchildren, and I have always been impressed by how you love your children. You are such a good man; I was lucky to meet you."

"Paula, I think you have that backward. I am the one who was so grateful you are my partner, my lover, and my best friend, and for our wonderful life.

"Sweetheart, the candles are dimming. What does your Timex say the time is?"

"Matt, it is 10 minutes to noon, I am praying it is about over."

Matt looked out the window. It seemed dark yet. "If you are right, Paula, when things return to normal, I'll be one happy man."

Too-too-too-too-toooooom! Too-too-too-toom! Too-too-too-toooooo-toooooo-tom!

“Paula, the trumpets must mean it is over. Look, the sunlight is coming down through the clouds. I think we’ll make it; all will be okay, baby!”

Paula was jumping around, dancing with a smile on her face. She was so happy.

Matt looked at her, thinking, *I am so glad she’s happier and we are unharmed. Our house is somewhat in pieces, but I can fix any damage when everything returns to normal.*

“Matt, I am not feeling well. My stomach is turning over, and my head hurts badly. What is happening to me?”

Matt looked at Paula. She had collapsed on the couch, and with the sun shining in the window, he could see the agony on her face.

Matt stepped towards her, but something was wrong with his chest; it was pressing on him like a vice.

Am I having a heart attack? It felt like something was sitting on my chest, so heavy; he couldn’t stand it. *What’s wrong*? Matt dropped like a stone. A dead stone!

And so it had begun. Around the globe, people were dropping dead. Only to be reborn, to be given another chance. At redemption.

CHAPTER 3

Hot Springs Dakota

Safe Refuge Day 1

Hot Springs, South Dakota, is a wonderful little community of 3000+ citizens, 400 Native Americans. It is the home of one of the state's best VA hospitals, which sits on a hill overlooking the community. The Fall River runs through the city, where, occasionally, one can catch a trout or two. The area has many landmarks, including a house of ill repute, which is also on the hill. Patrons used to climb the hill from the railroad up the side of the mountain to get to the pleasure palace.

There are several hot springs where people come from miles around to soak.

Several churches are also in Hot Springs, one of the main ones being St. Anthony of Padua Catholic Church, where Father Mike is the pastor.

Father Mike treks up the hill daily to the VA hospital on foot. Patients keep saying, "Just drive, Father." But after morning Mass, day after day, rain or shine or snow—can't forget the snow—he continues to climb the hill to the VA Hospital.

"Yes, Father Mikie, if they only knew about your past, things would be different, but it's okay. You belong to me, and someday soon, I will come for you.

After the service, Father Mike changed his clothing, put on pants and walking shoes, and then walked up the hill to visit his acquaintances at the VA.

Today, he planned to see George. He opened the door to George's room and walked through. "Hi, George, how is it going today? It looks like I'm here in time for PT, so I brought the wheelchair. Let me help you into the wheelchair, and then we can go down to PT. You have been improving, I hear. Soon, you should be walking, George, and holding those grandchildren."

"Father Mike, I'm not up for this today; I don't feel like going anywhere. I'd rather just lay here and die."

"George, what kind of attitude is that? You've got a great future ahead of you. Besides, your wife, two children, and your grandchildren back in Nebraska await you to walk through the front door."

"Walking through the door, that's a laugh. I don't have any legs; how do you expect me to walk through any door?"

"George, Uncle Sam spent thousands of dollars to find and get you the best prosthetic legs they could.

"Let's not disappoint those grandkids. Get up; I'll help you slide off your bed and into the wheelchair. Put your arms over my shoulders. There you go, slide into the chair; that's good. All right now, we're off. Firstly, going to the elevator and then down to the fifth-floor PT room. I'll be with you the whole time, George, and when you're finished, I'll take you back to your room. So, let's give it your best and get you home soon; it's been too long for you to be away from family."

"Father, I don't understand. You have way too much enthusiasm. If you had only seen what I've seen in my lifetime, so many of my friends were lost in Afghanistan, and I'm still here, only half a man."

"George, that may be true, but you need to think the other way; they lost their lives so you could live. Now you need to live for them and do the best you can, not feeling so damn sorry for yourself; now get on with your work."

The physical therapist was a 25-year-old male who would have his hands complete with George. Good luck, young man. After George finished his PT, Father Mike returned him to his room and helped him into his bed.

"George, it looks like breakfast time. So, what are you eating this morning?

"Let's look, George. We have pancakes, eggs sunny side up, and bacon with toast. And, of course, what would we do without coffee?

"Okay, George, I'm off to see somebody else. Before I leave, let me give you a blessing.

"Oh, God, bless this man and help him heal so he can return to his family. Amen. Goodbye, George."

Father Mike walked out of George's room and down the hall, taking the elevator to the third floor. His next vet was not going to make it. Knowing this, Father knew he should not show concern; he had to be positive and expect the best.

"Master Sergeant Jones, you have so many tubes and stuff running out of your body, friend. And you still haven't gained consciousness since they brought you here two weeks ago. I know you're suffering; according to your chart, you're full of drugs. I am so sorry you ended up this way, Master Sergeant; you are one of the best.

"I know, Master Sergeant, you left the Navy with your team in one piece and returned to the States to retire.

"Why didn't you just stay retired? You went back in, and the first time you went on a mission, your team's truck hit an IED and killed everyone but you. Not too much left of your lower body, and you lost your right arm. I'll still pray you come out of this with dignity.

"Master Sergeant, I don't know if you remember me, but I remember you from Afghanistan, and yeah, it was not a happy time. I was not a good person then, but you never judged me, and for that, I'm always grateful.

"I told your family you were at the Hot Springs VA hospital in South Dakota. I understand they will try to drive up from Kansas and spend time with you. I pray God will give you a chance to talk to them and visit with your family for the last time.

"Bless you, Ethan Jones. I hope you find your way to heaven because you certainly deserve it. Bless you, in the name of the Father, Son, and Holy Spirit. Amen."

Walking outdoors and down the hill, Father Mike had the sickest feeling in his stomach; it would be the last time he saw Sergeant Jones. *God, keep him alive until his family gets here, please!*

Nearing the chapel, he saw it was time to hear confession, the most crucial part of redemption for these poor souls. He had to return to the church by 11:30 to meet with the Altar Society women, which was a pleasure and an exciting time, but there was just a little sarcasm in his voice.

After opening the church doors and walking down the center aisle, he saw all the ladies waiting for him at the front pew.

"Good morning, ladies."

"Good morning, Father, and happy birthday!"

"What? I forgot. It is April 20. Okay, thank you. Oh, what's this? It's a chocolate cake, my favorite. Thanks, ladies. Did you bring plates? I'll share this wonderful creation."

"No, Father, it's all yours. And there is ice cream downstairs in the freezer."

"Oh my! Thank you very much; how thoughtful. So, what kind of business do we have today to discuss?"

"Father, we just wanted to wish you a happy birthday. We have handled everything, so you don't have to worry. We love our job of taking care of the church, so all is well."

"Thank you, ladies. Bless you, in the name of the Father, the Son, and the Holy Spirit. Go in peace. Amen."

He sat there with his cake—what a wonderful gift! He had milk in the refrigerator. *I'm all set to have a happy birthday watching baseball. First, confessions for my parishioners—it looks like about ten or so. It shouldn't be too late.*

Father Mike finished with confessions and saw that it was almost noon. He always liked to be in the church when the sun shone through the stained-glass windows. Such a wonderful and mystifying feeling made him soulful and closer to God. *Okay, put out some of these candles and stop for the day. It's time for baseball.*

He walked up to the altar to genuflect. *Father, Son, Holy Spirit. Amen. What's so loud? It's not coming from the church's loudspeakers; it sounds like trumpets outside, coming from above the church.*

Too-too-too-too-toooooom! Too-too-too-too-toom! Too-too-too-tooooooo-toooooo-tom!

Father Mike fell to his knees. Looking around, he could tell the light was dimming, hardly coming through the windows. It was getting darker, and he thought it must be a storm. But he didn't understand the noise of the trumpets and such darkness.

People started rushing into the church scared, unsure of what to do, and looking for answers. He didn't have any.

"I'm sorry, folks. Make yourself comfortable. We will weather this storm together; we've seen worse. Stay calm."

"Father Mike?"

"Yes, John?"

"Father, the phones aren't working." Our cell phones are not working, so we can't call anybody. And the lights are out around town, and I see the lights in the church are out."

"Okay, John, we've had the lights go out before during a storm. There is nothing new about darkness caused by a storm. We will just have to wait to see. Help me light some more candles. We need some light. We are lucky we have candles still burning from mass this morning. If we need more, we have lots of downstairs."

Suddenly, the front doors flew open, and the Methodist minister and his wife entered.

"Welcome, Christopher and Joan; nice to see you both. How can I help you?" Father Mike asked.

Christopher wore his usual black coat, white collar, black shirt, pants, and black shoes. He was about 50, 5 foot 11, pudgy, balding, and had gray hair around his temples, with the usual comb-over. His wife, Joan, was 49 or so, 5 foot 5, also a little overweight, and had grey, curly hair that she always kept nice and neat. She was wearing her usual plain Walmart dress.

"Father Mike, something weird is happening; we need to talk. Alone!"

"Okay, Chris, let's go to the sacristy, and we can be alone and have a conversation without being interrupted."

Father Mike walked over to the sacristy and opened the door for Chris. After following him in, he closed the door, turned around, and said, "Okay, Chris, what's so important?"

"Father, I think it's the end of the world. All the lights are out, pitch black, and you can't see anything. None of the lights will work, none of the cars will start, and anything with a battery won't work. A couple of our candles would light, but not enough for everyone who flocked to the church. So, I've asked my congregants to come to your church for safety. All of them are waiting outside your church."

"And Chris, why would you do that? Why would you come here and not go to your church?"

"Well, I hate to admit it, but the Catholic Church has always been more practiced with all this end-of-the-world stuff. I notice all your candles are working, which supports my statement."

"Okay, Chris. If I understand what you are saying, do you think the world will end? What else?"

"Father, did you not hear the trumpets? They weren't from here; they came from the heavens, trumpets sounding the beginning of the end. It's noon. God is sending a chastisement to humankind. I think he's fed up with us."

"Chris, I know a little bit. I can find more in the Bible. I remember that Moses used darkness when he tried to free the Israelites. So yes, I guess it could be possible it's happening again. If that's true, we are safe here if we don't go outside. So, yes, bring your people in, and when all are safe inside, we can lock all the doors and windows.

"Chris, did you bring any food or water with you?"

"We did, Father, all we could carry in backpacks."

"It's lucky that we just finished our Catholic food drive. We have lots of food stored in the basement, all the necessities for three days.

"Chris, as long as people remain calm, we should be all right.

"One other thing, Christopher, that I just recalled from my seminary days: when people go outside during the three dark days, they drop dead, and the devil gets their soul. If true, you must stress that your people stay inside.

"On second thought, Chris, let's go in and talk to everyone so everybody's on the same page and nobody tries to open the doors or windows."

"Are you guessing, Father? If anyone opens doors or windows, the devil and his demons will come through and kill us; they then get our souls?"

"Chris, I'll read more about what to expect. One last thing I remember is that God said that after the chastisement of man, there would be two miracles following the three days. So, it could be a positive, hopeful way to end the conversation with our constituents."

"Thank you, Father Mike; I'll follow your lead!"

Father Mike opened the oak door, standing back to let Chris go first. As they walked to the front of the church, they saw several scared people standing around, looking for answers and wondering what to do.

"Chris, go ahead and let your people in the church. Then, put the cross-piece on the oak doors; it should keep them tightly closed. When you have finished, join me in front of the church.

"Friends, here's what Reverend Christopher and I think is happening. The prophecy known as Three Days of Darkness might be unfamiliar to you. It's written about quite a lot in the Catholic Church's history, such as when Moses tried to free the Israelites and called down three days of darkness. I'm sure all of you heard the loud trumpets from above. We're guessing noon is the start of the three days of darkness.

"Reverend Chris and I agree that the basic rule should be don't go outside! We are locking all the doors and windows, the reason being that you will drop dead, and the devil will get your soul if you go outside during the three days of dark. Sounds extreme to modern ears, I know. But this is not a prophecy we want to test. Better safe than sorry. Likewise, if you open a door, you invite the devil in, and he kills you and takes your soul. Through a window, anything connecting to the outside, darkness is death. Remember, the devil is a trickster and will trick you however he can. Don't believe anything you hear outside. If you're not sure, ask one of us. Just know he's after your soul, and God's given the devil permission to go after any souls who are foolish enough to go outside."

Father Mike looked around at all the confused and frightened people.

"Friends, we have a kitchen with plenty of food and two bathrooms downstairs, as well as two bathrooms upstairs, plenty of water, and blankets if needed. We're all stuck here together for at least three days. Yes, it will be challenging, and if any of you need to talk to us, don't hesitate to ask.

"God bless you in the name of the Father, the Son, and the Holy Spirit. Amen."

Father Mike turned to Chris; "What about the Lutherans? Did you happen to talk to them?"

"Yes, Father, I did on the way down, and they said they were good with their church. They feel their religion is as close to the Catholic religion as anybody's, so maybe they have the same beliefs about three days as you and feel they will be safe."

"Well, let's hope so; right now, there's nothing else we can do to help, so maybe God will take care of them.

"Yes, Joan?"

"If it is OK with you, Father Mike, I was thinking about circulating a sign-up sheet for anyone who could help us with health issues, cooking, or volunteering to care for those who need care. We're not going to be able to do it all ourselves."

"You are right, Joan, that's a clever idea. Right now, I could use some help lighting candles downstairs so we can start sending people down to the basement. There are tables and chairs, playing cards, dominoes, and plenty to keep them busy."

"And thank you, Father, for taking in our people."

"Joan, I am more than happy to.

"Now, shall we start to organize things downstairs? We have some great cooks among our German and Norwegian ladies."

Chris and his wife followed Father Mike downstairs to get things going.

Later, Father Mike returned upstairs to make sure all doors and windows were locked. Looking around the church, he recognized three young college students sitting in the front row on the left side of the church.

"Good afternoon."

"Hello, Father Mike!"

"I would like to assign you three to a project if you are up to it?"

"Sure, Father, we're bored sitting here with nothing to do, so okay."

"Let's see if I remember your names: Linda King, Kimberly Morgan, and Bradley Newcomb. Like most college kids, you are home for Easter and in your fourth year."

"Yes, Father, we were here only for Easter weekend. Now, we're stuck here for a few more days."

"Yes, three days anyway; let's hope that holds.

"All right, then. Some bottles with holy water are at the church's front and back. I would like you to go around every door to ensure they're locked, then bless each with holy water in the name of the Father, the Son, and the Holy Spirit. Make sure you check all the doors and windows upstairs and downstairs.

"Does it sound like something you three can manage?"

All three said in unison, "Yes, Father, we got this," and off they went. So much enthusiasm is hard on this 70-year-old man.

As they rushed to accomplish their assignments, he remembered the days each started college. Now look at them …

Linda King, 5′ 6″, 135 pounds, long blonde hair in a ponytail, wearing jeans, Nike tennis shoes, and a Chadron State gray T-shirt. Gymnastics scholarship.

Kimberly Morgan, 5′ 8″, 140 pounds, brunette, has long hair in a ponytail. She was wearing jeans and Nike sneakers. *I Love the Hot Springs* blue T-shirt. She had planned on going into nursing.

Bradley Newcomb, 6′ 1″, 185 pounds, short blonde hair, also wearing jeans and a white Chadron State Football shirt. Football scholarship, planned on being a history teacher. All three were in their professional year.

Walking around the church, Father Mike spotted his old friends, Donald and Monica Stradford, who were retired ranchers in their seventies. They were great people. Donald had a slight build of only 5′ 10″ and gray hair; he wore light pants and a blue-and-white checkered shirt.

Donald had a bad fall a couple of weeks before and broke his leg; he walked with a cane and had a cast on his leg. Monica was a little fancier, always wore lovely dresses, had her hair fixed, and went to the beauty salon at least once a week.

"Hey Donald, I'm glad you and Monica made it; how is it going for you?"

"Father, I'm glad we were close, just down the street. A vast, big, black storm cloud moved in on us, so we decided to step into the church and wait it out.

"With a cast on my leg, I used a cane to maintain my balance. I'm glad Monica was with me to help."

"I will continue wandering around and see if anybody else needs help. Let me know if you need anything. Otherwise, there's some food downstairs, and you can help yourself."

"Thank you, Father."

When Father Mike was in the middle of the aisle, he saw a couple new to him, so he walked over to introduce himself.

"Hello, I am Father Mike; how are you two doing?"

"Yes, Father, we recognized you from before. We came in with Reverend Christopher and his group. We are undoubtedly grateful you welcomed us into your church.

"My name is Doris, and this is my husband, Leonard, or Lee, as we have all been calling him for years."

"I'm glad to meet you both. I see you have blankets and pillows to make yourself comfortable. That's a clever idea, considering it might be a few days before we leave."

Father looked at Lee, about sixty-nine and five foot eleven, thin, dressed in well-worn blue jeans, wearing a red button-down shirt with an emblem on the right hand of his shirt that read TWO HORSE RANCH. He noticed a silver buckle from his rodeo days, a broncobuster at one time. He had a pair of faded Roper boots beside him and his old, sweat-stained, worn-out gray Stetson.

His wife, Dolores, was about the same age as her husband. She was a large ranch woman with gray hair swcpt back into a ponytail. Shc was also wearing faded blue jeans, a flowered button-down shirt, and an old, worn-out pair of brown shoes.

"Is there anything I can do for you two?"

"Father, Lee has a pacemaker, and it's battery-operated, so I'm trying to keep him warm and not let him get too excited."

"I'm sorry to hear that. Of course, I will do anything I can to help. Have either of you had anything to eat?"

"No, I just needed to stay sitting here and keep Lee from moving around too much. It's not good for him to be up and maybe even take a fall."

"Of course, I understand. I'll have somebody bring up a tray for you, and we have a wheelchair at the back of the church. I can get someone to bring it up for you.

"The bathrooms are at the back of the church. If you need to take Lee to the bathroom, I can get somebody to help you."

"Father, thanks; I can manage with the wheelchair; it would be perfect."

Looking around, I saw Bill, our local Ace Hardware manager. He is 68, 6 feet tall, and weighs 190 pounds. He still wore his red Ace Hardware shirt, blue jeans, and tennis shoes.

"Hey there, Bill. Can you come here and lend me a hand?"

"Yes, Father, what do you need?"

"Would you go to the back of the church and bring a wheelchair up here for these two fine people?"

"I am on it, Father."

"All right then, I will check back with you two later. I'll get some food sent up as soon as I can."

"Thank you, Father, for your help; it is appreciated."

"Don't mention it, Doris; don't hesitate to ask if you need anything else."

Walking towards the altar, Mike saw a couple of his regulars, Amel and Genevieve Conard, both in their seventies, sitting in the front pew—farmers from the south of town. Amel was dressed in his farmer jeans, suspenders over his shoulders, and a good six foot two, 185 pounds, with gray hair. Genevieve was dressed in her flowery dress. She is about five foot four, a pump lady with gray hair. All the gray hair comes from raising nine children. Amazing!

"Good morning, Amel and Genevieve. I'm glad you made it to the church. How has life been for you since you moved to the retirement home in town?"

"Father, it's been fine. Amel and I have kept busy. Since turning the farm over to John, we have been blessed with a rich life, meeting people, and enjoying playing in the church card group."

"Make sure you get food, pillows, and blankets to make yourself comfortable."

As Father Mike turned towards the altar on the right-hand side, he saw a couple of young people he knew well.

"Hau Koda, Fern Singletree!"

"And hello, Father, you still remember the phrases in Sioux? Hau Koda—hello!"

"Yes, a handful of words from you teaching me. So, how are things here with you two?

"And I see you have Dakota Johnson with you."

"Yes, we were home from college for Easter and got ready to head back to college when it looked like a storm would keep us here."

Fern and Dakota dressed like typical college kids in blue jeans, bright-colored shirts that followed the latest trends, and Adidas tennis shoes—well-worn, of course.

When these two came to Father Mike four years ago, they were troubled about their desire to attend college. Their parents, relatives, and friends criticized them for wanting to do better for themselves.

Most Native Americans lived on the reservation, and their lifestyle entailed getting government money and drinking themselves to death. Father Mike did everything possible to get them admitted to college and keep them away from their family and friends on the reservation.

Both excelled in college and they were amazing-looking young people.

Fern was 6 feet tall, 165 pounds, well-muscled, with long, black, braided hair. Dakota was 6′ 1″ and 180 pounds. He was muscular, had black hair, and kept very neat.

Both Fern and Dakota were in their senior year of college. They were very bright, intelligent young people who deserved every chance to be successful. They had never disappointed Father Mike, especially after he helped them get athletic scholarships and financial aid from the Catholic Church to attend Chadron State College in Nebraska.

Fern was a college track star who excelled in running the 100 m, 200 m, and 4 x 100 relay. She also took up archery as a hobby and competed in college competitions. Dakota was a calf-roping and steer-wrestling rider and occasional broncobuster. And they both flourished ever since. Never a disappointment, they both used their gifts to go into education and become teachers.

“Okay, you two. There is food downstairs, and we have blankets and pillows. Make yourself comfortable. It looks like we are going to be here for a while. Talk to you later!”

“Bye, Father! Thanks for all your help.”

A young girl, unfamiliar to Father Mike, was seated against the inside wall of the church. She was around 5′ 9″ and had long bleach-blonde hair tied back in a ponytail. The black roots came through as red tints in her hair. She was dressed in black, with some kind of lettering on her blouse he didn't recognize. Of course, black jeans with holes in the knees seemed like the style. Her face looked like it had caught fire, and somebody put it out with a pair of track shoes.

Sorry, God, it was not the right thing to say.

Father Mike approached her, and she pulled away, so he just left it and walked on.

He suddenly heard pounding at the front doors and ran to the back of the church.

Bradley was standing by the outside doors, about to take the crosspiece down to open the doors.

Father Mike loudly said, "NO!"

"But Father, there are people out there in trouble. They want to come in, yelling and asking for help. Shouldn't we help them?"

"No, Bradley, remember what I said? The devil is going to trick us if he can. There should not be any people out there now. How would they find the church in the dark? How did they get here? The cars are not working!

"Do not open the doors; don't open the windows. If the devil or some of his demons get into the church, we are all dead, and we all are going to hell! Keep it in mind."

"OK, Father, I had a lapse; the people didn't need help."

"Bradley, please get me a bottle of holy water. Are they still screaming outside the doors?"

"Yes, Father, still pounding on the doors, wanting to get in here, and terrible screaming and agonizing sounds."

"Okay, take holy water, splash it on the door, make the sign of the cross, and say, 'Bless you in the name of the Father, the Son, and the Holy Spirit, amen.'

"As you can hear, they are gone. If people were needing our help, holy water wouldn't stop them. But if it's the devil or his demons, it would deter them for at least now.

"So, continue your actions; consider this a learning moment. And I will expect you girls to keep Bradley in line."

"Yes, Father, we will," they said, snickering as they walked away. Life was excellent.

Walking back to the church, Mike continued checking on people, ensuring everyone was okay and seeing if they needed anything. It looked like everything was under control. *I'm glad they got more volunteers to help; that's good.*

Humm, I won't return to the rectory tonight to sleep; I should find a spot here for the night. I have some blankets stowed away in the sacristy closet.

First, I am going downstairs to get something to eat, play some pitch, and visit with some of these fine people to try to alleviate their fears.

For the next two days, the routine was banging at the doors or scratching at the windows. Father Mike and his flock did the same remedy with the holy water, keeping doors and windows locked and the people busy while waiting for the end of this darkness.

The morning of the third day was finally upon them, and about everybody had breakfast and coffee as things were looking good.

"Christopher, how about we get everybody upstairs and tell them what will happen? Should the end of three days of blackness end at noon?

"I also think one or two of us should go outside first and check to ensure everything is OK before we turn people loose and send them back to their homes. What do you think?"

"Father Mike, that sounds like a clever idea; we don't know what's happening. We're out there after what's happened, and there has been so much commotion for three days. We could smell smoke, so there must have been a fire somewhere; we don't know if our homes were burned down or if a town was left for us."

"Okay, let's start getting everybody together upstairs here, and we'll go from there."

Joan started moving people upstairs and asking them to sit in the pews so that they could discuss their next move.

Everybody moved upstairs and sat. The excitement was growing. Everyone wondered if this would end—at least, they hoped it would end.

"Good morning, people. First, I have all the faith in the world that this will end at noon.

"Chris and I have decided that only one or two of us should go outside in the afternoon to ensure everything is okay before we send you home.

"We don't know what to expect or what happened in the last three days. How did our town make it through? What happened to our homes?

"So, we have about 15 minutes before noon. Just say a prayer and thank God we made it through this trial and tribulation he sent us. We anticipate the two significant events promised to occur following the tribulation period.

"So, Chris, would you like to give your blessings?"

"Yes, thank you, Father. Heavenly Father, bless these people, for they have tolerated the worst tribulation in their lifetime. We praise your name and God and ask you to help us through the following days. Amen."

Everyone followed with "Amen, amen!"

Mike thought to himself, *Well, that was concise.*

Clocks were ticking down. It was 11:55.

Too-too-too-too-toooooom! Too-too-too-toom! Too-too-too-tooooo-tooooo-tom!

And darkness cleared, hallelujah! They could see the sun shining through the glorious stained-glass windows. Father Mike was jumping up and down for joy, and then, deep pain came to his chest and his head, and he collapsed. He was dying, and the last thing he heard was screaming, screaming.

The other people in the church all crumpled down on the floor. The people in the basement also collapsed to the floor, and nobody was left alive.

The pounding, screaming, and yelling outside stopped as the sun came through the windows, and the skies opened to blue, bright sunshine. All the candles in the church had burned out. There were no sounds—only deathly quiet.

CHAPTER 4

Free Will Good or Evil

State Prison: The Worst

The South Dakota State Penitentiary in northern Sioux Falls, South Dakota, occupies approximately thirty acres and was constructed as a territorial prison in 1881. It was given state penitentiary status when South Dakota became a state in 1889. The prison houses level IV prisoners in three separate housing units based on the degree of the offense. Building 1A houses the most violent criminals with NO possibility of parole, and building 2A houses less violent criminals with the possibility of parole. Building 3A holds criminals who have committed various deviant offenses. The facilities house the worst prisoners in South Dakota, North Dakota, and Nebraska.

The 7-foot man, all dressed in black, was sitting in his black 1980s Cadillac. He was going through the file given to him by the governor—secret files on the prison warden and other personnel in charge at the prison's administration offices.

Jason Kerr Holtz is the warden at Sioux Falls prison. He's been the warden for the past five years and was given his job as a personal favor from the governor. *Humm, fascinating; the governor failed to mention such an interesting tidbit.*

Mr. Kerr Holtz's secretary, Claire Knapp, is an older lady who has worked in the prison for almost twenty years. According to her file, she is about to retire at the end of this year.

I see from her file that she filed a sexual harassment case against Mr. Kerr Holtz after Claire's husband died a few years ago. Mr. Kerr Holtz walked up behind her when she was working on files in the filing cabinet. He rubbed his hard dick up against her from behind. She turned and punched him right in the nose, giving him a bloody nose.

It looks like he is a real charmer, but I only need information, nothing more, for now.

The tall man in black opened his car door and rolled out; he took his briefcase and walked up to the prison's administration building. Taking the stairs to the second floor, he took a right turn, ending at the warden's office door. Opening the door, he walked into the office.

Claire was sitting behind her desk, typing. She looked up and saw a big, tall man dressed in black, with black hair and dark black eyes.

"Yes, what can I do for you?"

"I would like to talk to the warden."

"I am sorry. Do you have an appointment?"

"Claire, I don't need an appointment. So, you know, I have a letter from the governor giving me access to the warden. Tell him I am here."

"I do not think it's possible. The warden is a busy man."

The man in black turned to the left and walked right around her desk through the warden's double doors, busting into the warden's office.

Claire was following. "I am so sorry, Warden. I told him you are busy, and he didn't have an appointment. Sorry, sorry."

"Who are you? Why are you in my office?"

"Warden, I have a letter from the governor introducing myself and giving me full access to all the information I want."

"What are you talking about, the governor? Why would the governor grant you any kind of privilege? This is my prison, and I am in charge. I have made all the decisions, and you must get out right now. Claire, call for security."

"Warden, I don't think you understand. You don't have a choice. You either cooperate with me, or I will call the Governor and remove you, especially if he finds out about your little thing with your secretary."

Poor Claire started bawling and turned away, walking through the doors closing behind her.

The big, tall man in black pulled up a chair and sat in front of the warden's desk. "Okay, Warden, now that we cleared the air. Let's start."

"What do you want?"

"Warden, I want the list of your worst prisoners incarcerated here in this beautiful spot in Sioux Falls, South Dakota. Please give me a complete rundown of each one's history and tell me about the operating procedure in this prison.

"Start at the beginning."

"Very well, I will start with the prison yard.

"All criminals are given freedom outside, about half the size of a football field. The yard holds basketball, weightlifting, and handball courts, where the inmates can sit and spend the day.

"Outdoor activities are divided into levels, and 1A is first for two hours. Followed by 2A, repeated for approximately two hours. Finally, 3A for two hours. The worst watch takes more guards to keep an eye on them because somebody is liable to slip in and beat them. 3A prisoners are separated from the other two levels. Other inmates in the prison hate and despise the sex crimes of level 3A prisoners.

"1A is the first scheduled exercise in the yard following breakfast. It will last from 10:00 AM until noon. During this time, guards are in the towers with heavy weapons and walk around in the yard, keeping an eye on the inmates. They carry no weapons, only a nightstick and a taser.

"Billy Stone, a.k.a. Wolf, is 68 years old, 6′ 2″ tall, his 250 pounds is solid muscle. He has black silvery hair swept back, is Caucasian, and when he opens his mouth, you can see all his teeth, which is why he is called Wolf. He has an Army background, sniper recon, and was dishonorably discharged for taking ears of Iraqi kills. He was arrested in Rapid City, where he was cutting ears off dead Iraqis in the neighborhood he lived in—no possibility of parole.

"Jeffrey Plugge, a.k.a. Bear. Age 64, light-brown skin, bald head, 6′ 2″, weighs 275 pounds.

"Joseph Kelly, a.k.a. Preacher. He is 70, 6′ 3″, 180 pounds, Caucasian, with long, combed silver hair piled high on his head—life in prison. There is no possibility of parole. He was guilty of embezzlement from a local church where he was the preacher who killed the church accountant to keep his embezzlement secret from the church members.

"Billy Stone runs the prison from the inside. I agree with this because he keeps violence to a minimum. His day starts with playing chess with Preacher."

*****

Prison Yard Day Time

Billy Stone is sitting at the table playing chess with Joseph Kelly. The conversation usually goes like this. "So, Billy, how many people did you kill? 10, 15, or 20?"

"Why the hell do you want to know? Why do you keep asking me? I won't tell you. If you don't stop asking, you might be one of the next ones!"

"And what about you, Preacher?

"You are seventy-some years old, a church preacher, and a large church that takes in how many thousands a week? And you embezzled how much, two million? And when your accountant caught you, what did you do? Oh yeah, you killed him.

"So, Preacher, how can we play chess? Since we must endure this daily, I'm getting sick and tired of it."

*****

Also in The Yard

Standing against the wall was William Haglett, a.k.a. Creepy: age 67, 5′ 11″, 169 pounds, Caucasian, fragile, wispy brown hair, some front teeth are missing.

He usually stands against the wall with a smirk on his face, always staring at people while smiling at them in such a way that it is creepy; he killed three people during an armed robbery. He has few friends but is known to do the boss's dirty work. Billy Stone.

Billy Stone controls all drugs and alcohol; if you want cigarettes or any other kind of contraband, Stone will get it for you at a price.

On the other side of the yard by themselves are a bunch of inmates known as the Ogallala Sioux convicts. Most are from the Pine Ridge, South Dakota, area and are some of the most violent criminals.

Vern Two Shoes, age 65, 5′ 8″, 180 pounds, black grayish hair always kept in braids, and distinguishing features include a four-inch-long scar on his right cheek. Very dark eyes, yellowish teeth. He was known to use a hatchet to finish off his victims. Armed robbery was his thing. The problem was that he killed too many people in doing the robberies. Life in prison, no possibility of parole.

Timothy Blackbird, age 67, is six feet tall and weighs 190 pounds. His black hair has some gray streaks and is tied back in a ponytail. He has a flat nose, and some teeth are missing in the front. He used a knife to cut up his girlfriend's new boyfriend after she dumped him and then turned on her. An O.J. Simpson scenario. Timothy did not get off, life in prison without the possibility of parole.

James Red Cloud, a.k.a. Comanche. Age 66, stands 6′ 1″, weighs 200 pounds. He has long black hair down to his waist, black eyes, a pock-marked face, and most of his teeth. He and his friends killed three people in an armed robbery for $60. So he could buy some more drugs. When they finally caught him, he was so high that he started shooting at the police officers. It was an unwise decision to shoot, but he survived and was sentenced to life in prison without the possibility of parole.

One particularly dangerous individual is the Kiowa Apache named Pacer. At 68, Pacer stands 5′ 11″ and has 145 pounds of solid muscle. He gets very agitated and hates white men. His long black hair, kept in braids, gives him a menacing look, and people leave him alone.

The south side of the yard is usually the weightlifting equipment area, where you will find several Black inmates who keep to themselves. Some have a reputation for killing inmates in the prison.

The leader is John Washington, a.k.a. Snake. Age 66, 6′ 2″, 200 pounds, black skin, a large nose, a square jaw, and short black hair. A big drug dealer in Sioux Falls, South Dakota, killed a federal agent from the DEA during a drug deal. Life in prison, no possibility of parole.

Daryl Johnson, a.k.a. Roach. Age 64, six feet tall, 190 pounds, black curly hair. Has pockmarked skin, deep brown eyes, and a scar over his right eye. Killed his wife in a drug-induced fit of rage. Life in prison, no parole possibility.

Brett Samuelson, a.k.a. Stretch. Age 65, Black, 6′ 4″, 260 pounds. Long, curly black hair in braids. Facial expression menacing, long facial scars on both cheeks and tattoos of different weapons on each arm. An arsonist who set fire to an apartment complex in Vermillion, South Dakota, in which five people died. They were all retired individuals—no possibility of parole.

Kevin Rothwell, a.k.a. Deuce. Age 67, Black, stands 6′ 2″, 200 pounds, black hair, bald spot on the back of his head. Distinguishing marks are the tattoos up and down his left and right arms of family members who have died. He killed the local sheriff in Rapid City, South Dakota, by running over him with a 2-ton truck—life in prison with no possibility of parole.

The Hispanic prison population usually spends their days in the yard over in one corner playing handball or just staring at everybody else. The small population just keeps themselves and tries to avoid trouble.

The leader is Dustin Toby, age 63. Called Bulldog. Light brown skin, short, black, curly hair, 5′ 10″, 185 lbs. Distinguishing marks are tattoos on his arms, back, and neck. He had a small goatee on his chin, brown eyes, and a narrow face. Robbed a convenience store in the small town of Marshall, South Dakota. Killed the owner and his wife and one female bystander. Life in prison, no possibility of parole.

*****

Before Noon

"Okay, Warden sounds precisely like what I need. Thank you for being so cooperative; I will be leaving now."

"For what purposes do you want all this information?"

"Warden, I am going to turn them all loose." The man in black got up, turned, went to the door, turned around, looked at the warden with those piercing eyes, and said, "Starting today, in three days, they will be free." He turned, opened the door, and walked out.

*****

Prison Yard

"Preacher, I think I have you checked; I win. You're not much of a challenge, Preacher."

"Bill, to pass the time, we could play pitch or get a couple of other guys and play cards. What do you think?"

"Preacher, I don't think there are many people here with whom I would play cards. I don't trust any of them; they all cheat. Ha, ha, ha.

"OK, Preacher, It is about time for dinner anyway. Let's head to the cafeteria and get in line first.

"Too late, Preacher, it's the noon bell; let's get in line for some chow."

As they stood in line, Stone looked at the cafeteria's high windows designed to keep prisoners in. He could see clouds and a massive storm approaching from the west.

The inmates filed into the cafeteria, standing in line for the noon meal as they sat down to eat marginal food.

*****

Exactly Noon

Too-too-too-too-toooooo om! Too-too-too-toom! Too-too-too-toooooo-toooooo-tom!

"Okay, what the hell was that, Preacher?"

"Billy, I do not know what the hell it was. It sounded like trumpets, loud trumpets up above."

"The lights are out, and we can't see anyone."

The guards yelled, "Everybody go back to your cells NOW!"

"I can hardly see, Preacher. How do I get to my cell? Okay, I see our cell."

All the inmates filed out, going to their cells, where they were locked in. It was getting darker, and all the lights were out.

*****

Inside the Prison

The guards discovered that no lights, phones, or other electronic devices worked, and anything that ran on batteries wouldn't work either, so they panicked.

Some guards ran out and got into their cars to go home, but the vehicles wouldn't start because the batteries didn't work. They returned inside and told the rest of the guards that the cars would not start; there were no radios, and all were dead.

None of the flashlights or emergency lights were working, either. They realized they would have to wait until they got some help—just hole up in the cafeteria and wait for the lights to return.

Billy was thinking, *What do you do when you sit in a cell with no lights, and can't see anything, can't read, can't even see to piss?*

Some prisoners had matches and lit paper for light, even for fleeting periods. Billy, we are not getting any help from the guards, either."

"The worst thing, Preacher, is that I didn't get to finish eating. We don't have any water, food, or light. What's next?"

"Billy, what day is it?"

"What time is it?"

"How am I supposed to know?"

"You have a watch, don't you, a wind-up one?"

"How do you suppose I will see the time without light? I ran out of matches a long time ago."

"I'm hungry, Billy. Do you have anything to eat?"

*****

Deal or No Deal

Suddenly, all the prison lights came on. In the middle of the main floor was a tall man, all dressed in black, with scary-looking features.

"Good evening, gentlemen. This is near the end of your second dark day. I'm here on behalf of my Master to offer you all a proposition or job, depending on how you want to look at it. All of you in this building are here with no possibility of parole. If you agree to work for my Master, you'll be given free rein over the land once you're out. All the riches you want, all the land you might want, and you can kill as many people as you wish.

"You don't have to answer me right now. I will return on your last day tomorrow and set those who want to join us free. Do you have any questions?"

"Yes. I'm Billy Stone; who the hell are you?

"Who is your master?" Preacher asked, "who is this person we are supposed to work for, and why isn't he here?"

"All good questions, Mr. Stone. Does it matter who he is? He's not here because he has work to do to prepare your way.

"So, tell me, there are three buildings here. This is 1A, right? And in building 2A, what kind of inmates are there?

"Anyone can talk and speak up!"

"The people in building 2A have a possibility of parole. Do-gooders..."

"Okay, so who's in the third building? 3A?"

Billy Stone was going to have his say, "That is a building you don't want anything to do with. All are perverted sex offenders, the worst kind of people in the world, except for the ones in this building. But we don't kill children or rape women and kill them sexually."

"Mr. Stone, I didn't think you would be against perverts. However, my Master has used those kinds of people before, so I will visit them next. They will have the same offer, and they will also be turned loose on the world.

"I will be back tomorrow. Until then!"

And with that, he raised his right arm into the air, snapped his fingers, and was gone. And the lights went out.

Everybody was yelling, "What the hell, who was he?"

"Why didn't he leave the lights on?"

"All right, everybody, calm down. We're dealing with someone who walked in here, turned the lights on, and then disappeared, after offering us a deal."

"What the fuck Bill? Who put you in charge?"

"Pacer, everybody must decide to take the deal or leave it.

"I want the hell out here. No matter what the cost might be later, I'll deal with it later. But I want out, and he sounds like he's given us the opportunity.

"Indeed, you have enough time to sit and think about it. So, if you want to discuss it, look at it. So, until tomorrow, I'm going to sleep now."

"Bill?"

"Yes, Preacher?"

"These guys will be up all night discussing this. It's hard to get any sleep.

Bill, didn't you think that guy was creepy?"

"I don't know, Preacher; There are a hell of a lot of creepy guys in here. What difference does it make?

"Now shut up, Preacher. I need to get some sleep. Gotta quit thinking about food."

*****

The Next Morning: Last of the Dark Days

All the inmates in the prison were awake. You could hear them talking and moving around, flushing the toilets. They were waiting to see what would happen at noon.

Everyone was on edge. There was craziness, screaming, hollering, and yelling—a bunch of frightened, angry, anxious people.

"It must be getting close to noon, Preacher. What is your decision going to be?"

"Bill, I'm unsure what I'd be getting into. Is there a way out afterward?"

"The answer for that, Preacher, is something you can discuss with him if you like when he shows up. If he shows up, and if it's not some kind of scam."

"Okay, be an asshole. I'll just sit here with my matches and light one occasionally; leave you in the dark, Bill."

"Whatever, Preacher. While you light your matches, I will eat my Nestlé's chocolate bar with peanuts."

Bill could hear a noise. "Hey, who the hell is up there?"

"Frank, what's going on down there with you Bill?"

"We don't have any food or water; what about you, Frank?"

"The same goes here; there is still nothing from the guards."

"Billy, somebody is in the building, and I can hear them walking."

"Wait a second; the lights just came on. Bill lights just came on."

Everybody rushed to the front of their cells, and the lights were on.

A man was standing in the middle of the floor, a 7-foot-tall boxlike figure dressed in black.

"Okay, gentlemen, I will open all the cell doors. Those of you who will take me up on my deal, step out and stand in front of your cell. You'll hear some trumpets—you heard them before at the start of three days of darkness. You might feel weak and fall asleep—that's good—according to plan.

"After you wake, you will see a miracle, which will be hard to believe, but it's true. So, when that happens, remember you must move towards the west and the Black Hills, kill everybody in between, and take what you want.

"Oh, watch for women prisoners from Pierre, South Dakota. They will join us soon. Word of caution if you try to play footsie with any of these women, they will cut your dick and balls off.

"So, shall we begin?"

Too-too-too-too-tooooooom! Too-too-too-toom! Too-too-too-tooooooo-toooooo-tom!

Everyone in the prison collapsed and was knocked out. Many died, including all the guards and the warden, but not the secretary—she merely passed out.

CHAPTER 5

The Chosen

Death Comes Knocking

Matt was on his back, floating in the air; he felt everything in his life was peeling away, lost forever. All his problems, pain, injuries, lost friends, his wife and children, and grandchildren. Everything he had known or did in his lifetime was gone. A grand feeling of freedom, such a wonderful feeling, ecstasy, and entirely at peace.

A light in the distance, he was so happy. *Have I been here before? It's sort of a funny feeling of familiarity.*

Matt didn't care about the past or future, and he had no words for how he felt beyond ecstasy and the realm of celestial beauty.

Matt felt he was not moving up anymore. As he looked up, he saw two figures approaching from a distant light. What was happening to him?

As the bodies approached, one looked like an Angel with beautiful white wings and fantastic armor. The other he seemed to recognize. *Can't it be, Nathan?*

Finally, the two were right in front of him. Matt blinked, and now he was standing in a gorgeous green field surrounded by amazing flowers.

Nathan was speaking.

Matt raised both his arms, "I can't hear you."

Then Nathan waved his right hand, and now Matt could hear him.

"Lieutenant Matthew Dylan, you must return to Earth to represent good and overcome evil. Some people on Earth remain, and if they choose Good, they will need your help and protection from evil."

Nathan continued that all people remaining on Earth had an opportunity for redemption.

"However, we know some of the humans have already chosen evil, and their agenda is to destroy all humankind and send who they kill to hell.

"When you find these people, dispatch them."

"Nathan, your words are in my head, but I can't answer you; I have no speech."

Matt just stared at Nathan with a perplexed look on his face.

Finally, Nathan understood, waved his hand again, and said, "Speak."

Matt choked out, "Nathan, is it you?"

"Yes, Matthew, it is me."

"I'm so sorry, Nathan. I took you along on our last mission and should have left you at the base."

"Matthew, it was not your fault; I wanted to go. I was grateful you trusted me enough to take me along.

"Now, I am thrilled, joyful, filled with ecstasy and love. Surrounded by family and friends, don't feel sorry for me."

"Nathan, what happened to my wife Paula? She was on the couch in pain. I couldn't get to her and help her."

"Matthew, your wife, all your children, grandchildren, and all the people you know are here with us. They are all safe and happy, except for a few, and you know who they are. Some have been in purgatory for some time; they have retribution to finish.

“Now, Matthew, back to the mission.

“You have a choice: will you take the mission or not?

“Which is it going to be?”

“It doesn’t seem to be a choice, so to begin ....

“Nathan, I am old and frail; I can hardly walk anymore, I take all kinds of medication, I tire quickly, and yes, sometimes my thinking and memory are a little different, off.”

“Matthew, we have considered this. If you take the mission, you will return to earth a new man.

“You will be God’s sword on earth, fighting for goodness, taking charge, and protecting people who have chosen a path of redemption—protecting them, keeping them safe, and dispatching all evil.”

“What do you mean by dispatch all evil?”

“Matt, please send them to hell!”

“Nathan, has this been approved? Isn’t it murder?”

“No, it is not murder. If you plan to murder and kill innocent people, then yes, it’s murder.

“You have complete authority to complete your mission as you see fit.”

“Okay, so all by myself?

“Nathan, it’s an enormous task for just one person.

"Would you give me help like a large SEAL team?"

"Matthew, you will have help, just not with your old SEAL team. But here, standing next to me, is Benjamin. He will assist you, and you will encounter people on your path to help you.

"Matthew, you will live an exceptionally long, happy life. Stay open and receptive. You will find that times have changed on Earth and have a new life of incredible opportunities."

"So, Nathan, do you know what's going to happen? Can you look into the future and see what will happen?"

"Matthew, I'm not allowed to say. Just know you are not alone. We will all be watching you.

"Now, Matthew, are you ready to go back?"

"Again, it sounds like I have no choice; I love it here!"

"Matthew, you have a choice. This will never be taken from you, and all this will await you."

"Okay, then sign me up!"

"Oh, one other thing: you will not remember our conversation."

*****

Back Home

Matthew woke in his living room, and the sun shone through the window. He tried to get up, but he only passed out again.

Later, he rolled over from his stomach to his back, looking out the window. Now, the sun was bright. He pushed himself up; it was so easy.

He looked at his arms, strikingly young and with muscles of all kinds, a six-pack, and strong legs; he had some extra equipment he didn't have before.

He had no clothes on, so he first had to find something to wear. Matt entered the closet, grabbed jeans, a fishing shirt, and boots, dressed, and headed to the living room.

Matt looked around for Paula and remembered she was on the couch. He walked over to the couch and saw her Green Bay Packers T-shirt, blue jeans, and Nike tennis shoes. Beside her was the needlepoint she was working on.

And Lucy's collar was lying beside Paula's clothes.

They're gone, they're both gone. All he could do was sit on the floor, holding her clothing and sobbing over the love of his life.

Her watch was lying there. He picked it up. It was 7:00 AM, and the lights were not working yet.

Matt wondered if the car would work.

On his way to the garage, he grabbed the key fob.

In the garage, he opened the car door, slid in, put his foot on the brake, and pushed the button.

The engine hesitated to start, but it was rough running when it finally did. He shut it off and crawled out of the car.

Matt went behind the vehicle and manually opened the garage door by pulling on the rope with a red handle hanging from the track.

The garage door was now open. He stood there and looked out at a new neighborhood.

No one was moving around, and there were no signs of life. Chuck's house across the street had burned to the ground, and Matt doubted if anybody had survived the fire.

Several other homes had burned to the ground as well; it must have been the explosions they had heard.

Walking out of the garage, he turned around and looked at the roof. The whole top section of the peak was gone. But no fire of any kind had started.

The other houses in the neighborhood weren't as lucky.

Without the fire damage, it would look like a typical Sunday morning, with everybody sleeping in.

Matt still didn't understand what had happened, whatever the hell that thing was, when it pointed at him and Paula with such disdain and anger and then flew right at them.

Matt didn't know if it was trying to kill them or the reason.

Well, he had to plan; no reason to stay here.

Matt's first plan was to gather all the canned goods from the pantry, grab some clothes, grab his 12-gauge shotgun, and go out and check to see if the rest of the world was the same.

Matt had two totes full of canned goods, two metal frying pans, some silverware and dishes, and cups.

He grabbed his military pack from downstairs, which still had some valuable military equipment, knives, and a few first-aid essentials. He had no weapons.

Matt put everything in the back of the Chevy. *Man, I like this car; I like red, and this Chevy has always been good to us.*

Well, GPS is not going to work. He remembered he had a bunch of maps in his file cabinet: Nebraska, South Dakota, and Wyoming.

Matt was thinking of the Black Hills in South Dakota. There had been plenty of fishing and hunting the last time he was there, and one could hide in the hills and stay safe.

First, though, he was going to the airbase to see if he could find some weapons. The last time Matt was out there, they bragged about all the heavy weapons stored at the Lincoln airbase.

Matt always wanted to be prepared because you never know what could happen. It's better to be prepared than sorry.

Matt loaded everything in the Chevy and took a last look around the house before he left. There was not much else there but memories. Goodbye, Paula, my love.

Matt closed the door from the garage to the house and walked down the steps to look around the garage one last time. He hated leaving all his tools there but didn't know how he would begin taking them with him.

Matt reversed into the garage to load the car. He heard somebody yell as he went around the front to the driver's side.

Matt stopped, turned to his right, and looked across the street. A young, sandy-haired man was waving at him.

Who is that? Matt pondered.

He was running across the street towards Matt.

When he reached the front of the garage, the man stopped.

He looked at Matt strangely.

"Matt, is that you?"

"Yeah, it is me, all right, who are you?"

"Chuck across the street, the one whose house burned down."

"You can't be Chuck; he was an older man in his 70's.

"Who are you really?"

"I could say the same thing about you, Matt; looking at you, what are you 28, 29 years old? And look at all those fucken muscles; you're huge."

Matt was confused. "I don't understand. If you're Chuck, what happened to the old Chuck?"

"I don't know Matt. What happened to the older Matthew?"

"Well, Chuck, what the hell happened? It seems we're both younger versions of ourselves."

"Matthew, I guess I am about 28 to 30 years old. It was tough to find clothes to wear; all my clothing was too small."

"Okay, Chuck, what's your fucken plan?"

"There are no plans at the moment, Matt. My wife is gone, and I am just trying to figure out what to do next.

"Matt, I woke up with all this hair, a muscled body, my old height of 6 feet, and full of energy.

"You are the planner, Matt; what current plans do you have?"

"Right now, I am going to the airbase and try to find some weapons, just in case of any hostile people. Things are bound to be crazy; it will never be normal again."

"Okay, Matt, I was a gunner's mate in the Navy, involved in the operation, maintenance, and training of weapon systems and ordinance equipment. I also had training in small weapons and explosives. I could be an asset if you'd take me along."

"Well, Chuck, I could use the company. Go ahead, climb into the passenger side, and let's get out of here!

"There is nothing more here for us!

"By the way, Chuck, I thought you were dead, burned up inside your house. How did you survive that?"

"When my wife and I heard what was happening outside our house, we went to the back garage.

"My truck was in the garage, so we crawled into the car and locked all the doors.

"Come morning, I was there alone; my wife was gone, with only her clothing left. I don't understand any of it."

"Well, Chuck, I had the same experience. My wife is also gone, and our dog Lucy is as well."

"Okay, Matt, where are we going?"

"Our destination is to go west to Bell Ridge Drive. So, climb in, Chuck, and let's go."

They drove west to 14th Street, south to the US 6 ramp and Cornhusker Highway roadways. Then, they turned left toward NW 24th Street and onto W. Butler Avenue, right out to the National Guard on 2420 W. Butler Avenue, Lincoln.

When they arrived at the airbase, Matt drove to Northwest Hangar, where the Army kept all their equipment for the National Guard and the Air Force.

After they pulled up to the large metal hangar, both got out of the car, walked over to the door, opened it, and Matt walked through with Chuck following him.

Inside, it was dark, but the emergency lights kicked on, and the stupid motion-activated circuit scared them.

Parked inside was a Chevy Silverado 1-ton diesel, colored flat black. Even the chrome was black, and there was nothing shiny on the truck. Attached to the large truck was an extended trailer that resembled an extra-large horse trailer. It was also painted flat black.

Matt and Chuck continued walking forward. They discovered a uniform, boots, and a weapon on the ground, but no body. Walking further in, they found two more uniforms without bodies, which was strange.

"I don't know, Chuck; this is fucken weird!"

"You can say that again, Matt. It's the strangest thing I have ever seen. The same thing happened with Mabel, my wife. There was no body, just clothing."

"Okay, Chuck, let's keep going and look in the back of the horse trailer first.

"Chuck! Grab one of those weapons on the floor, just in case."

Walking to the back of the horse trailer, Matt saw it was open, and another bunch of clothing was on the floor. When whatever happened, it looked like two men were loading a box in the back of the horse trailer.

Matt and Chuck looked inside the trailer at a bunch of boxes.

"Matt, there are plenty of weapons here for you; I count eight attached to each side of the trailer wall, all M4 carbines. More boxes of weapons are on the floor, and food cases are stacked up to the ceiling."

"Chuck, we should look around for anything else we could use."

While Chuck was walking around, he noticed a door open. Walking through the door, holding his carbine in firing position, he found several piles of clothing inside on the floor, once belonging to people who presumably now were all dead.

Several boxes were marked with the words GOLD BULLION. Wow!

Chuck walked out to the main hangar, where Matt was loading other ammo boxes in the back of the horse trailer.

"Hey Chuck, I found some camouflage uniforms, boots, and tactical vests. Let's get out of these clothes that don't fit, okay?"

"Yeah, that sounds great, Matt.

"Matt, you'll never guess what I found in the back room: boxes and boxes of gold bullion. Somebody was planning to be rich in their new life. But it didn't work out so well; they're all dead."

"Gold? Did you see any suits in there with all the dead?"

"Fuck, yeah. Come to think of it, there were 2 or 3 suits, and more people could be in the next room. But I didn't go in there."

"Well, Chuck, I don't need any gold. But if you think you need some, go ahead and help yourself. I'm not sure what you can use it for, but who knows, you might have a use for it someday."

"NO, Matt, I don't need any stinking gold either! Ha, ha."

Matt heard another noise coming from outside. It sounded like a dog. "I'm going to take a look. Chuck, you go ahead and get changed and load your gold! Ha, ha, ha."

Outside the hangar, Matt stopped and listened. He could hear some moaning. To the right of the hangar, about 60 feet in the back, were dog pens. He walked up closer, and there was only one dog, and he was angry, growling, and barking.

Matt was guessing it had nothing to eat or drink for a while. *Let me see if I can find some food.* He found a small wooden structure with one door. Opening it, sure enough, he saw all kinds of dog food.

After filling a bucket with dog chow, he walked back out and found another bucket by the water faucet; he filled another bucket full of water. As he approached the dog pen, a dog with golden brown and black coloring and a black head looked at Matt like he wanted to eat him for lunch.

Matt was thinking the dog was big enough; he could.

The pen was wired, and Matt poured the food down through the wire into the dog's dish, not wanting to get inside to give him food. He did the same thing with the water pouring into a dish; the dog was already chomping down the food and did not notice the water.

Ouch! I better watch my fingers around this dog. He's still eyeballing me like I was dessert. Ha ha.

When Matt finished feeding him, he noticed an old piece of wood hanging on the fence, a sign that said, "Switchblade."

Matt wonders what the term "Switchblade" was all about.

The rest of the sign read: Belgian Malinois. Name: BUCK, aka Switchblade. Please stay clear of this dog; he is very dangerous.

Matt headed back to the hangar, wondering how Chuck was doing. When he got inside, Chuck had changed into military camouflage pants, a black military long-sleeved shirt, leather patches on his shoulders for shooting, and military boots.

"Hay, Matt, what did you find outside?"

"Chuck, I found a dog, starving to death, with no water. Somebody left him locked up to die. All the rest of the dogs, except this one, were gone. I'll check on him before we leave.

"How is everything going here?"

"All's going well, Boss. Everything is secure. I put some food and water in the truck's cab, extra ammo, and a couple of Berettas with ammo."

"Okay, Chuck, don't call me Boss; we are two guys trying to survive."

"Okay, Boss, it's whatever you desire, but you outrank me, so if you don't mind, I will recognize you as Boss because you deserve it.

"Boss, I also loaded some gold bars and hid them in the trailer. After thinking about it, we might want a few for trading."

"Okay, Chuck, that's good thinking.

"I'm going to check on the dog to see how he is doing. I'll be right back."

Matt walked back to the dog pen. Buck was sitting there, smiling at him. It looked exactly like he was smiling, with a mouth full of impressive teeth.

As Matt walked up to Buck, he remained sitting there, so mild-mannered.

Matt guessed after eating and drinking, he was in a good mood.

"Okay, Buck, what am I going to do with you? I can't leave you here; you'll die, for sure. I'll leave plenty of food and water for you. And turn you loose." Matt lifted the latch just a little so Buck had to push open the door, and he would be out.

But Matt didn't plan on being there when it happened.

"Good luck to you, Buck!"

Matt headed back to the hangar. He went around to the driver's side of this huge Chevy. Wow! What a machine, what a beast.

Chuck was sitting there waiting for him, an M4 beside him, drinking a Diet Coke and eating at a Hershey's candy bar.

"Where the hell did you get those, Chuck?"

"Well, I went back into the building, into the second room, and lo and behold, there were all kinds of Coke and candy bars, so I loaded some in a cooler with ice and put the coolers in the back of the truck.

"And Matt, I also found a bunch of meat sandwiches and a couple of loaves of bread and put those in another cooler in the back. I noticed electrical plugs built into the sides of the truck's bed. The coolers run off electricity to keep cool.

"So, I went back and grabbed two more coolers, and after plugging them in, I added more food. The truck bed has a Tonneau cover, which can be pulled over and securely fastened at the back to ensure it is watertight."

"Well, Sergeant Chuck, it looks like you were busy. That's a good deal. You did well; it was good thinking.

"Okay, let's see if this truck will start." Matt reached into his pocket and pulled out the thingamabob because, as everyone knew, the newfangled vehicles start with a gizmo in your pocket.

"Chuck, I found two keys in an officer's uniform on the floor. I'll give you one key.

Matt put his foot on the brake and pushed the button, and the truck started running smoothly without a problem. The steel building must have prevented anything from happening to the truck's engine.

Matt eased into gear, D, or drive. He started pulling out of the building, but a dog blocked his way. Okay, what the fuck now?

Matt started to get out of the truck. Buck stood up, his tail wagging ferociously, and walked towards Matt, who stood still as the dog approached him, sat down, and held his right paw for Matt to shake.

Matt reached down and shook the dog's paw. Before he could stop it, the dog ran around him and jumped in the truck.

Scared the crap out of Chuck when Buck jumped in the back seat of the truck. Buck then turned around and looked at both of them. Matt was shocked. Buck was just sitting there and looking at them with a goofy grin.

"Chuck, this is Buck. I guess he is going to be part of our team." Matt had to laugh at the disbelief on Chuck's face.

"Chuck, we need to make room for dog food. Do we have room in the back there? Chuck?"

After they stopped for dog food, Matt drove over to his Chevy Traverse, grabbed his duffel bag with his clothes and backpack, and tossed them in the back of the truck bed.

He returned to get his 12-gauge shotgun. As he was walking back to the truck, he turned and looked at his Traverse for the last time, reminiscing about some excellent memories with Paula at his side.

Suddenly, Matt heard motorcycles approaching. He stood there, wondering what was happening as five angry-looking men on motorcycles rode towards the air hangar.

They stopped, looking straight at Matt. "What do you guys want?" Matt asked.

The leader, a rough-looking man with a beard, mustache, long hair, and sunburned skin, replied, "We're looking for an asshole named Matt Dylan. Is that you by chance?"

“And what if it is?” Matt responded.

“You’re worth much gold, whether dead or alive. We’d just as soon as you were dead. It’s easier to handle a dead body than a live asshole,” The leader said, at the same time reaching for his pistol. The rest of the bikers did the same.

Matt possessed only his 12-gauge shotgun and a .45 caliber pistol that Chuck had recently given him. He wasn’t even sure if the pistol was loaded. He raised his shotgun and fired three rounds toward the motorcycles, realizing he only had birdshot. He hoped it would keep their heads down long enough for him to draw his sidearm.

Before he knew it, to his right, a vast automatic weapon started firing; 10 rounds burst at a time. Matt drew his .45 and fired toward the leader. An explosion rocked Matt backward; his shotgun must have pierced the biker’s gas tank, causing the explosion when he fired his pistol, killing four of the bikers. One managed to get back on his motorcycle and started to ride off. Just as Matt was about to take a shot, Buck flew through the air and took the guy out by the head and neck, knocking him off the motorcycle.

It was a sight to see. Chuck ran over to check on the dead man. Buck stood there for a second, then trotted back to the truck.

Matt turned to Chuck, “I don’t know what the hell that was all about, but it’s time we get out of here.”

Walking back to the truck, Matt opened the driver’s door, Buck jumped in the back seat, and Chuck got in and looked at Matt. “What the hell did he mean? You’re worth money, dead or alive?”

Matt reached over and pulled the Nebraska map out of the briefcase; he then looked Chuck in the eyes, “I don’t know what the fuck they were talking about; can we just drop it?

“So, Chuck, can you be the navigator? I need a road out of Lincoln. Stick to the off-roads and avoid the interstate, large towns, or heavy-traffic roads.”

"OK, Matt. We'll have to travel a short distance north from the airport on the interstate until we reach the Raymond turnoff."

"All right, here we go!"

Chuck continued that after the Raymond turnoff, they were going north to Highway 92, then turning west on 92, going through Rising City, Shelby, and Osceola on the way west to Clark's, St. Paul, and north on Highway 11.

"Matt, it looks like when we get to St. Paul, we continue west on 92 until we get to Highway 2 West, and then we take it all the way north to Chadron, Nebraska, with half a dozen little towns in between. I estimate 8 to 10 hours."

"Yeah, that sounds about right. Chuck, I've been up to South Dakota a few times; I like it up there—Black Hills, destination: Custer State Park.

"It looks like we're about to hit the Raymond turnoff."

As Matt looked out his window at the rearview mirror, he saw something was happening behind them. So, he pulled over and stopped. Getting out of the truck, he said to Chuck, "Let's go back and look behind the trailer."

They walked to the back of the trailer and looked south at the city behind them. Matt couldn't believe his eyes. "You see it, Chuck? Is the city melting?"

"Yes, Boss, it looks like it is all falling, like sandcastles."

All the buildings were gone, and nothing was left; what the hell was happening now?

"I don't know, Boss. I have binoculars and see that all the roads are gone. It's now all dirt and grass. Everything is disappearing, returning to the original prairie."

"We need to get going. It's headed this way."

They jumped in the truck and took off. They took the North Road, going straight to Highway 92.

"Chuck, I'm maintaining a speed of about 60. I don't know if more cars are ahead on the road; we have already encountered a couple."

"Yes, Boss, I certainly wouldn't go faster. It is best to avoid having an accident. I guess there aren't any tow trucks, mechanics, or bodywork people around anymore."

Matt maintained speed and used the mirrors on the side of the truck to keep an eye on what was happening behind them. All the telephone poles and power lines were gone.

"Everything has just kind of fucking disappeared, Chuck.

"You know, Chuck, Paula was trying to tell me some of the crazy things in the Bible about miracles. She said there would be two miracles after this three-day thing with no lights.

"The first must have been when they took all the good people and left the rest of us behind. The second miracle must have returned the earth to its natural state before mankind. That would explain why everything is disappearing except for grass and trees.

"If it's the case, and it is coming from behind us, we must go as fast as possible to get to our destination before it catches up with us. That's the only thing I know we can do."

"That sounds good to me, boss. Just keep an eye on it and keep moving.

"What is funny is that Buck never got out of the truck. Do you think he somehow knows what is going on?"

"That wouldn't surprise me with all the strange things happening now; nothing would surprise me."

Matt was driving north at a steady pace on Highway 92. After turning left, they spotted a guy standing on the right side of the road, dressed in a bright-colored shirt and pants. He looked like he had escaped from a paint factory.

"He is waving at us to stop, Boss!"

"I don't think so, buddy, not today; things going on are too crazy, and as far as I know, he might be crazy; what do you think, Chuck?"

"I wouldn't stop, Boss; it could be an ambush; things are too new to take any chance."

"Alright, let's keep moving."

"Boss, I have my rifle. I can roll down the window and show him we mean business, and he will leave us alone."

So, as they drove by the painted guy, Chuck pointed his rifle out the window at the stranger, and they drove by, continuing west.

"South of David City, Boss, there is a little jog on the highway, and then it continues west again on 92 to Shelby."

After Matt came around the little jog in the road and over railroad tracks, suddenly, in the distance, something bright was on the right side of the road. What the hell was it now?

Matt hit his brakes as hard as he could. SHIT!! Coming to a screeching halt was complex, with a fully loaded trailer behind, pushing you. When the truck stopped, Matt looked at Chuck, who was looking at him.

Matt said, "I can't fucking believe it!"

"I fucking can't either, Boss!"

Were Matt's eyes deceiving him? Was that a fucking angel? How could it be?

Was Paula right all along about good and evil?

"Chuck, I am getting out and taking my M4 with me; I'll find out what the hell this is."

Matt opened the door and stepped out, leaving it open in case he needed a quick retreat. He stood behind it and looked through the window.

Finally, Matt stepped out from behind the door and approached this figure standing there with wings, enormous white wings, and from above, a white light shining down on this figure, who was holding a mighty big sword.

"Who the fuck are you, and what do you want with us?" Matt demanded.

The figure slowly descended to the ground and folded the wings behind him, placing his sword in a scabbard behind his back. He then started strolling towards Matt. It was in no hurry, whatever it was, and suddenly, the thing's body changed when about 20 feet from Matt.

Oh crap, it's the guy they passed up on the highway, who was dressed as a fairy in those brightly colored clothes.

Matt raised his weapon, "Who are you, and what do you want?"

At that point, Chuck jumped out of the truck with his rifle, standing beside Matt.

Chuck was charged up. "OK, fucker, I'm ready to blast you to hell!"

The figure suddenly pointed a finger at Chuck, who froze, his mouth open.

"My name is Benjamin, and I am here to help you with your mission to the Black Hills."

Matt was now pissed, "What the HELL did you do to Chuck?"

The gaily colored man pointed at Chuck. "I will not stand for cussing or swearing; have I clarified myself?"

"Yes, all right. You made your point. Now turn Chuck loose." With a wave of his right arm, Chuck was freed.

"Matt, do you know anything about a mission this fairy is talking about? And how does he know where we're going? Who told him?"

"I don't know anything, Chuck; I don't know who this is or what he knows."

Benjamin looked at both of them. "I know exactly where you two are going; it's predetermined. I was sent here by request to help you as much as I can, and no, you don't have any choice.

"So, Matthew, who is your friend?"

"His name is Chuck Mazeroski; he was my neighbor in Lincoln."

"Hi, Chuck, how are you doing? I also see you have a dog; I haven't seen one in a long time."

Benjamin looked around. "Matthew, shall we get going? We have a long way to go before nightfall, and I can tell you one thing: it is unsafe to travel at night!"

Still irritated, Matt said, "I don't know who you are. Trusting somebody we don't know is a big deal now. So, who are you?"

"Matthew, you've seen me before; you know who I am, where I am from, and who sent me."

"No, Benjamin, I don't know who you are. And until I have some idea, you're not going anyplace with us."

Matt turned and walked away, yelling, “I need to think about this for a bit. “This was too much.

The whole day was happening too fast for Matt. First, Chuck joined him, then a dog, and now, some kind of multicolored person or thing.

Matt turned back. “Chuck, what do you think?”

“Well, Matt, it seems this guy came from somewhere other than planet Earth, as weird as it sounds. It’s been the norm; crazy stuff going on since day one.”

“Is that an affirmative response, Chuck?”

Chuck just shrugged his shoulders.

Matt decided. “Okay, Benjamin, get in. You’ll ride in the back with the dog and fight him for a place to sit.”

Benjamin opened the back door and climbed in next to Buck.

“Hey, Matt, there is a lot of room back here. Buck and I will be quite comfortable here, don’t you think Buck?”

Buck just looked at him and gave a little growl to tell him, “I got my eye on you.”

On the open highway, Matt decided to open her up to 70-75 mph and make some time. The next time they stopped, they would be in the sandhills, a good place to stop for the night.

Chuck turns around and looks at Benjamin, sitting behind Matt in the back seat.

“Okay, I want some answers, Benjamin. And you look like you might have those answers. So, why are we so young when we both were 70+ years old and on our way out? And while I am at it, what is happening with all the towns melting down and all the roads disappearing? Do you have any explanation?"

"Yes, Chuck, I do. If you want to call it a miracle, there is one miracle: God took all the good people to heaven, sent many people to hell, and had many people left over who needed redemption, which could take 120 years.

"To help these people with redemption, Chuck, each human is given more time to start over and make better choices. Also, it is going to take younger people to rebuild this country.

"Every person is going to need more time, just like Moses. You know, he lived for 120 years. Buildings, roads, telephone lines, power lines, and any human-made structures will be removed, leaving behind a landscape without constructed elements, representing a fresh start.

"Does this answer any of your questions, Chuck?"

"Some. I didn't ask for any of this. Life was challenging the first time, you're telling me I must continue living. Another 120 years?"

"Of course, Chuck, it all depends on your life and what happens along the way. It could be extended or very short. It would not hurt to pray occasionally to help pave your way.

"Do you know what I mean, Chuck?"

Matt had heard enough. "Okay, you two, stop for now. We have other things to think about.

"Chuck, there is a military radio on the floor between us. See if you can get someone on the radio. Don't say anything; just turn it on and listen. Any chatter could help us figure out who else is out there."

"OK, Matt."

Turning on the radio and setting it to keep scanning for open stations. “Are you looking for anyone specific?”

“Yes, Chuck. Military personnel, the CIA, or government bigwigs must have had a plan to go somewhere. You found a briefcase with all the maps and paperwork. When we get time, we need to sit down and review the material. See if we can figure out where they were headed.”

Chuck turned on the radio and scanned but only heard static, indicating no activity on the military channels.

They drove through Osceola and neared Clark’s. Matt was looking ahead. A bridge was coming up, and it looked intact. So, Matt crossed it, and another one was coming up. The second bridge looked like some of the sides were starting to melt.

Matt pushed the accelerator to the floor, and the big diesel kicked in. They took off across the bridge to the other side and down the road. Matt slowed down, thinking they wouldn’t have any more bridges along the way.

“Chuck, I think we are about 20-25 miles from St. Paul, a Bomgaars farm store, and it will have clothing, boots, and other items. I want you to take Ben into the store and get some decent clothes. And get rid of the crap he’s wearing. Find some new clothes for the two of us while you are shopping.

“While you are shopping, Chuck, I’ll give Buck some water and take him for a walk afterward. He needs to stretch after being penned up in the truck for so long.”

It wasn’t too long before Matt pulled into the Bomgaars parking lot. Getting out, Matt opened the door so Ben could get out. Buck came right behind him, jumping down onto the pavement.

Matt walked back behind the truck and opened the tailgate. He grabbed a couple of water bottles and Buck’s water dish, set it down on the ground, poured some water in it, looked around, and Buck was gone.

Matt walked around and found Buck on the grass, doing what he needed to get done.

After Buck finished, he bounced back to the truck and went right to the water, and you could tell he was happy because his tail was wagging.

Matt grabbed a bottle of water and sat on the tailgate, drinking it down. He reached into one of the coolers and grabbed a Baby Ruth candy bar. It had been quite some time since he had last eaten one. Humm, good, it hit the spot.

The boys were coming back; Ben was in Levi's jeans, Roper boots, a red cowboy shirt with pearl snaps, and, of course, a cowboy hat, carrying a couple of bags of clothes.

Chuck also carried several bags stuffed with clothing. He approached Matt and said, "I found some jeans and shirts so we can change out of these fatigues. I also found dog treats, more bags of dog food, orange slices, and peanut clusters. Do you have any requests, Boss?"

"Chuck, see if you can find me a dark red double-buttoned shirt like John Wayne used to wear. And grab me a size 11 tan Roper boots."

"You got it, boss. Do you want a cowboy hat?"

"I would like a Stetson hat in size 7¼, preferably in white if available."

It wasn't too long before Chuck was back with several more bags. He headed to the trailer, opened the side door, and put all the bags and stuff inside. He returned to the truck cab and said he had put everything in their sleeping quarters.

"Sleeping quarters, what are you talking about?"

"Oh, Boss, I forgot to tell you. When I checked the trailer, I found sleeping quarters in the front: one large bed and two bunk beds. It looks like there is air conditioning and heating. It was for officers or the CIA."

"That sounds good, Chuck. We won't have to sleep on the ground. You made my day.

"All right, boys, let's get mounted.

"What's next, Chuck?"

"Boss, take 92 West to Loop City. Then turn at Ansley onto Highway 2 past Broken Bow and Anselmo, then to Dunning, which looks like some kind of forest."

"Yes, it is, Chuck.

"It would be Halsey. It's a man-made forest and would be a good place for us to stop for the night. We can get back up in the hills high enough to watch anything coming up the road."

"Boss, you know a lot about this country."

"Yes, I've been to Halsey a couple of times. I went deer hunting with my brother-in-law and my sister Rita, which was a great time. Yes, it's a beautiful place."

Matt drove through the town of Dunning and up to the Halsey National Forest entrance.

Matt stopped. "I forgot about the bridge crossing here into the forest. We sure don't want to get stuck there if the bridge fails. We'll return to Dunning and find a spot to park for the night."

Matt turned around and, while driving back to Dunning, thought the high school was a good place to park for the night.

"Boys, it has plenty of parking places, bathrooms, and maybe showers if we are lucky. We could all use a hot shower, right Chuck? Ha, ha."

"And like you smell like a bed of roses, Boss!"

Shortly thereafter, Matt arrived at the high school. After shutting off the engine, they got out and walked up to the front doors.

Matt thought they would need to break the glass to get in, but as he pulled on the door handles, the doors opened; they were unlocked. *Stay on your guard*, he thought. *There might be someone else interested in this place.*

They all walked in, and the hallways were spooky. Nobody was around, and no lights were burning. Buck went to the front to lead them down the hallway. Eventually, they found the gymnasium.

Matt was the first to read the sign "Locker Rooms." The showers should be in the locker rooms.

"Let's see if there is water in the showers."

Walking through the gymnasium to the locker rooms, Buck, of course, was in front, and Matt was behind him. They all walked into the locker room. The coach's office was to the left, and it looked like the showers were up ahead to the left also. Once in the shower, Matt turned on what he thought was hot water. It took a while, and suddenly, he felt warm water in his hand. *Holy cow, we've got hot water! Wonderful!*

"Hey, Boss, there's another room over here."

Chuck entered the room and there was a washing machine and dryer, a stack of clean towels, and several bars of soap and shampoo.

"Who would like to go first?" Matt asked.

"Boss, why don't you go first? I'll check around the rest of the building to see what else is available. What about you, Ben? Are you taking a shower?"

"Chuck, I've never taken a shower, so maybe after you folks finish, is that okay?"

"Sure, that's no problem, Ben. Let's go check the rest of the building together."

While Chuck and Ben were checking the rest of the building, Matt grabbed some towels, shampoo, and soap, returned, stripped down, jumped in the shower, and soaked up.

Then Buck came into the shower and joined him. Buck stood there and let the water run over him, so Matt reached down, put some shampoo on Buck, and scrubbed it in. Loads of dirt just washed away from Buck, and then Matt used more shampoo, and finally, Buck looked clean.

Buck then left the shower, went over to the side, and started shaking his body dry.

Matt hadn't been around a dog in a long time. Buck for a vicious dog, sure enjoyed the shower.

Matt was wondering if Buck had ever allowed a person to give him a wash before.

Matt wrapped himself up in towels, and with nobody around, he walked out to the truck for some clean clothes.

As Matt walked through the hallway, Buck followed him out to the sleeping quarters in the trailer, where Matt found jeans, a clean shirt, underwear, clean socks, and a pair of Roper boots. But the cowboy hat stayed, even though he would look good in a Stetson.

Before he left the trailer, Matt grabbed a bag of doggy treats, stepped out, and gave one to Buck, who was so excited.

Matt walked back into the school, down the hall, and found Chuck and Ben.

"Okay, guys, what did you two find?"

Chuck turned and said, "We found the kitchen, lots of food that hadn't spoiled yet, and a working gas stove. After I have my shower, I am going to fix a feast for all of us. I also found some coffee and made a pot. It's in the cafeteria. Help yourselves."

"That sounds good, Chuck. Thanks."

Matt walked down to the cafeteria.

"Did you find any donuts Chuck?"

Matt could hear Chuck laughing as he walked down the hall to the showers, with Ben following him at a minimum distance.

"I guess there are no donuts. Come along, Buck, let's go get some coffee."

Walking into the hall, Matt grabbed a nice, heavy coffee cup, poured it full of coffee, and sat down.

Humm, cafeteria benches had not changed since he had been at school.

"Oh, Buck, I'm sorry. I'll see if I can find any water in the kitchen."

Yeah, the water worked, and Matt found a big pan, filled it with water, carried it back to the bench, and set it on the floor. Buck was happy to get a drink. After drinking his fill, Buck found a place to lie down for a nap.

Matt was happy the coffee's good. Now he had some time to think about things.

Matt realized that all his memories of people in his past were fading. He did not want to lose his memories of Paula, but he could feel them beginning to fade. Was this part of the process, that they had to leave their memories behind and move on to a different future?

Chuck walked into the cafeteria sporting a new outfit: blue jeans, boots, and a white button-down cowboy shirt.

"Hey Chuck, where's Ben?"

"Well, Matt, believe it or not, he is showering.

"I will begin preparing some food, Matt."

"I am getting hungry, Chuck. It's been a long time since we've had anything to eat. Do you need some help?"

"No, I like to cook. Thanks; I am good. How's the coffee?"

"Coffee is good, so if you don't need any help, I'll sit down and drink my coffee without doughnuts, ha-ha."

"Coffee is just one of my many talents. Please wait until you taste these omelets I am fixing, they're award-winning. Bet nobody else in the world can fix them like me. Ha, ha-ha-ha."

Ben entered the cafeteria and walked up to them. With a big smile on his face.

"Hey, Ben, how was your shower?"

"Matt, it was wonderful, my first shower ever, and soap and shampoo—a wonderful experience."

"What do you mean, first shower ever?" Chuck asked.

"I've never been on earth before, so this is my first experience with everything, and it's all new to me. I heard stories from others, and they said it was a great experience."

"Okay, Ben, sit down here and have some coffee; you will either like it or hate it. Chuck is out in the kitchen fixing us a feast and says he is the best cook in the world."

"Okay, boys, here's one omelet for the Boss, another one for you, Ben, and one for me. I also made some toast, and here is some strawberry jam. Enjoy, or bon appétit!

"And I cut up some ham pieces with scrambled eggs for Buck."

Not realizing how hungry they were, nobody said a word for a while until they finished.

"Well, Chuck, it was surprisingly good, but why aren't you eating yours, Ben?"

"Matt, I've never eaten food before, not sure how this body would react to it."

"Well, I guess Ben, you are not going to know until you try it. Chuck went into all the effort of fixing it. You should at least take a bite.

"You drank the coffee; how did it go down?"

"Yes, the coffee was a little bitter, but yes.

"OK, I will take a bite. It does look delicious, and I am sure Chuck is the best cook in the world.

"Here goes. Wow! It does have good flavor—or what is the word, taste good."

Matt laughed, "Congratulations, Chuck. The two of us voted you the best cook in the world.

"Ben, if you have not eaten food before, what happens when you do? I mean, do you have the same physiology as we do?"

"Matt, as I understand, I don't have the same physiology as you. In my other form, we didn't eat or drink, only on special occasions, we might drink some wine."

Matt thanked Chuck again. "I am going to find somewhere to lie down and sleep; I don't want to sleep in the truck."

"Boss, when I looked around, I found a room. It was an elementary or kindergarten room. It had all kinds of floor mats, blankets, and pillows. It could be a good place for tonight."

"Good idea Chuck, Ben, you coming with me?"

"Matt, I don't require sleep; I will be walking around keeping guard all night."

"Ben, if you are going to be up all night, I'll make a list of things you could do to save us some time in the morning; okay, Ben?"

"I would be delighted Chuck."

"It sounds like you two have a plan. I'll be heading out to the kindergarten room to get some sleep so we can get an early start in the morning. Come, Buck!"

*****

Next Morning

After a good night's sleep, they all woke up about the same time. Buck was snuggling up to Matt. But when Matt didn't wake up fast enough, Buck started tapping on Matt's arm with his right paw. "What the heck Buck, no sleeping in?"

Chuck was off fixing breakfast, pancakes, eggs, bacon, sausage, and coffee. He felt they all needed a great breakfast to start the day.

After they all finished eating, everyone picked up their gear.

Matt strapped on his backpack, with two Beretta M9s tucked in the back. He left his .45 in the truck.

They then headed for the front doors, Buck in the lead, followed by Matt and Chuck.

Buck stopped at the glass front doors, which allowed them to see outside. Buck was growling when Chuck came up beside Matt, whispering that something was wrong.

Both Matt and Chuck looked through the glass doors, at three strange people standing in front of their truck, with knives and machetes, banging on the hood of their truck.

Matt was using hand signals and pointing outside.

"Chuck?"

"Yeah! I see them."

Matt pointed at Chuck and then his backpack and told him to grab one of the Berettas and give him one.

"No quick movements, Chuck, and keep your weapon hidden.

"Ben, you stay here with Buck.

"OK, Chuck. Let's go see what's going on with our neighbors."

Matt pushed through the doors; Chuck followed him out.

Matt went to his right and Chuck to his left, spaced five parallel feet apart.

They both started walking towards the truck.

It looked to Matt like three Mexican migrants.

As they approached the front of the truck, Matt and Chuck were 30 feet from the men pounding on their car when the one in the middle, chunky in appearance, who must be the leader, started talking.

"Hey amigo, you have a very nice truck. We would like to buy this truck from you. What do you say?"

Matt casually answered, "Well at this particular time, no, I don't think I want to sell my truck."

"Señor, if this is your truck, do you have any papers stating it is yours? If you do not have any papers saying this, it may be our truck.

"So, Señor, I think we will just take our truck and go. Please give me the keys, Señor."

Matt stared into the leader's eyes. "I don't think it will be possible; I like my truck."

Matt continued, "What are your names, bucko?"

"My name is Diego, I am the leader of this group."

"Well, Diego, the answer is no. This is not your truck. This is my truck, my trailer, and it's best if you leave while you can!"

"Well, Señor, I guess we must just come and take those keys from you the hard way. You are most un-agreeable!"

The migrants came out from the front of the truck, spread out, and started to walk with grim determination towards Matt and Chuck, swinging their machetes. Matt and Chuck stood their ground. The migrants got about 10 feet from them when Matt pulled his weapon and shot the guy on the left twice in the chest, once in the head.

Chuck did the same thing with the guy on the right, twice in the chest, once in the head. Before either could get a shot at the third one in the middle, from somewhere, a big sword came flying through the air between Matt and Chuck, striking the third one right in his gizzard, pushing him back 10 feet. Dead!

Then Matt heard Buck growling behind him, and when he turned around, he saw Buck running towards the back of the trailer at top speed. Buck jumped up in the air—it must have been 6 feet—and Matt heard a scream, so he ran to the back of the trailer.

Buck had jumped up in the air, came down, and tore the throat out of another hostile, who was trying to break into the back of the trailer.

Then Matt heard another round of shots, also coming from around the back of the trailer.

Matt was at the back of the trailer, where he found another migrant lying on the ground dead; Chuck must have shot him.

"The ones in the front had been a diversion, Matt. It's good that Buck heard those two behind the trailer; it could have been a different story if they had gotten into the trailer with all the weapons."

They returned to the front of the truck, where Ben was retrieving his sword. Matt looked at Ben and said, "I thought I told you to wait in the building with Buck."

"You did, Matt, however, I am still a warrior. I just cannot stand by and do nothing, and Buck stopped those hostiles from getting in the back of your trailer and getting automatic weapons as well."

"Matt looked at Ben, "Where did that sword come from?"

"Matt, I have access to weapons. I have my sword, a bow and arrow, and knives. They are at my disposal when I need them."

"Okay, where did your weapons come from? You don't have them now!"

"Matt, I won't tell you everything because you don't need to know everything. But if it helps, I simply raise my hand in the air, and weapons appear when I need one."

"All right," Matt said, "enough for now. We need to get out of here, they might not be the only ones.

"Chuck, help me move the bodies off to the side of the road.

"While I'm cleaning the blood from Buck, you two grab our stuff."

Matt found a hose hooked up to a faucet and cleaned Buck up.

"Well Buck, I now know why the sign at your pen said, you were the jack-knife, because you got up into the air and cut that guy's throat. You deserve a couple of dog treats; glad you are on our side."

Buck and Matt walked back to the truck. Everyone had already loaded, so Buck jumped in the back, Matt in the driver's seat.

Matt stepped on the brake and pushed the button. The big diesel roared to life—it had so much power.

Matt thought he remembered a gas station somewhere along this highway as they headed out of town. He needed to check and see if they had any diesel. It was about time to fill up; the tank looked half empty.

As they drove out of town west on Highway 2, off to the right was Sinclair station, sitting up on a little hill.

As they approached the station, Matt could see that all they had was gas—no diesel. *Okay, well, I know another station coming up, not too far away. We are heading in that direction anyway.*

"Chuck, you are the navigator. How far is it to Thetford and Sandhills gas station? If I remember right, it's not too far."

"Well, Matt, according to the maps, it's about 15 to 20 minutes. It looks like quite the station."

"Do you know if they have diesel, Chuck?"

"Yes, Boss, there is another map here, in the briefcase, which has all the eating places, gas stations, and sightseeing places along the way. This highway has several interesting places to visit if you want to stop and do a tour."

"No, just stop and get diesel, and Chuck, if you want to go and pick up some stuff, it is okay."

BANG!! BANG!!

"What the hell was that? Did we hit something?"

"No, Chuck, somebody is shooting at us; I didn't see them come up behind us, it looks like two trucks, one older truck, one newer, trying to get beside us, shooting with what looks like shotgun blasts. They must be some of the same bunch we ran into this morning."

"Boss, I guess they want to fight; they must have found the other guys."

Matt looked in the mirror outside the truck and said, "I don't think they can stay up with us if I push the pedal to the metal.

"Let's see if we can outrun them, hang on."

Matt knew he had plenty of power in this truck, so he pushed the pedal to the floor and, he was not disappointed. The big diesel kicked in and they were hauling ass.

They continued pulling away from the older pickups, which couldn't keep up with the big diesel. Even pulling the trailer, there was no match.

Matt had a plan. "We're going to pull ahead as far as we can. Then, we'll block the highway with the truck and the trailer, jump out, and take them out as they come down the highway towards us."

"You know, Boss, I have the sniper's rifle in the back of the trailer; I could pick them off easily half a mile away."

"Okay, Chuck, get your gun when we stop."

Matt shouted, "Hold on!" He hit the brake and turned the truck to block the road. They all jumped out.

"Ben, you and Buck, get behind the truck and stay down."

Chuck came running to the front of the truck.

"Boss, I'm ready. I loaded my sniper rifle, CheyTac M200 Intervention, with 408 rounds.

"OK, Boss, if I set the tripod on the truck's hood?"

"Yes, I'll spot it for you Chuck.

"Chuck, sighting a truck a little over 1000 yards away, get ready. Six hundred yards, the first truck is a Ford double cab, 300 yards, fire when ready."

And with a solid, BOOM! The driver in the lead Ford truck lost his head; the truck immediately veered off the road, turned over, rolled 3 or 4 times, and burst into flames, killing all four occupants.

"Chuck, the second truck is a Dodge, also a double cab, right behind the first, 200 yards, fire when you are ready."

BOOM! and the driver of the second truck also lost his head, left the road, rolled end over end a couple of times before ending up in the side of a ditch, all 5 of the bad guys dead.

"That was impressive, Chuck. Where did you learn to shoot? You said you were in the Navy."

"Well, I did a little stint with the Special Forces and had a lot of training in firearms and explosives for a year."

"I knew there was a reason I brought you along, Chuck, besides your cooking. You can shoot."

Chuck went around the back, put the sniper's rifle back in its case, locked up the trailer, and went back to the truck, getting in.

They headed out for the Sandhills gas station only about 15 miles ahead.

As they rolled along, Matt felt Buck's paw on his shoulder. Buck kind of emitted a little growl. "Oh, wow, I forgot Buck. Sorry."

"Chuck, open the console in the middle. There should be a bag of dog treats. Grab a couple for me."

Matt took one, reached over his shoulder, and felt Buck gently taking it from his right hand, settling back, and chewing on his prize. It wasn't long before Buck was back for the second one.

What an intelligent dog.

*****

Apple Pie

Matt was cruising about 65–70 mph so it didn't take them long to cover 15 miles. On the right of the road was the Sandhills gas station; he pulled up to the diesel pumps and stopped.

"Hey boss, there are lights on inside and the pumps have power."

"All right, Chuck, you and I will check it out.

"The two of you stay here, Ben!

"Take your rifle with you, Chuck."

Walking up to the glass front door, Matt could see inside, it looked like there were people inside.

"Chuck, you are right, GO!"

Busting through the door, they found 25 people with their hands up. A tall, thin guy with gray hair said, "Please, we do not want any trouble. Take whatever you want. Please don't hurt us."

Matt looked at all of them, older people. Now what was going on?

"Okay, folks, we are not here to hurt anybody. We are just here to get some diesel so you can all relax. We're the good guys; put your hands down.

"My name is Matt, and this is Chuck." Then the doorbell dinged, and there came Ben and Buck. "And they are Ben and Buck, also harmless."

Both lowered their weapons. Matt asked, "How did you survive the three days?"

The man with gray hair said, "We were all at home. We stayed home. When it was over, we found each other on Main Street. We knew the gas station had a natural gas generator, and the grocery store also had a gas generator, so we gathered everything we could from the grocery store, came up to the hill, and stayed here ever since.

"Later we carried our beds here. We had food, water, bathrooms, and safety. Until the Mexicans found us, they had been coming around taking whatever they wanted, and they killed one of us and cut another one. We saw you pull up and thought you were just as bad."

"Don't you have any weapons in this town?" Chuck asked.

"We did have shotguns; they came and took all our guns, all our ammunition. So, no, we don't have anything to defend ourselves."

Matt looked at the big guy with gray hair and said. "Well, you don't have to worry about the Mexicans anymore, they are all dead. We killed them all!"

All of them started clapping and praising the Lord. "Thank you, God!"

"You are safe now," Matt said, "we will make sure you have some weapons and ammunition to protect yourselves from now on."

And then they all were hugged, handshaking all around. What a happy bunch of people.

The tall, gray-haired man, whose name was Frank, came up and said, "Is there anything we can do for you?"

Matt said, "We just need diesel and then we'll be on our way."

A gray-haired woman, "How about something to drink? We can get you something to drink."

Another gray-haired woman, "How about something to eat? We just made some fried chicken, potato salad, beans, and apple pie for dessert."

Matt said he would take a Diet Coke. Chuck? Also, Diet Coke. When Ben was asked what he would like, he said, "Do you have any coffee?"

"And, of course, if you can, give my dog some water.

"And none of us will never turn down a free meal with apple pie. Thanks."

So, they were taken to another room—a massive room with an 8-foot table and several folding chairs. In the back was a big kitchen, where several ladies were cooking up a storm.

As they sat down, a woman started bringing them plates of food, Diet Cokes, and Ben's coffee. There was great food and good cooking, and Chuck was even more impressed.

As they talked with Frank, some other gentlemen, primarily farmers, sat across the table and visited with them. Some were townspeople who had businesses. One was the barber. Matt looked at the barber and said, "Hey, you have your tools with you. Could you cut my hair?"

"I sure do, I cut hair around here all the time for men and women. You need a haircut, young man."

"Yes, I do. Can you give me a military cut?"

"Sure can; it's where I started: I was in the military cutting hair. When you finish eating, I'll just go to my little shop and take care of you."

Matt finished eating and followed Dudley to another small area that looked like it had once been a supply closet. Dudley had his barber's chair, so Matt sat down. Dudley started by putting a cape around Matt's neck and covering his front. Then, he began cutting, and Matt just relaxed. It had been a long time since he had a haircut, since he had been bald most of his adult life.

Matt was sitting there thinking about what had happened the past few days and wondering what was next when Chuck and Ben walked in and sat on folding chairs.

Dudley looked at the boys, "Hey, you gentlemen want a haircut next?"

Both nodded their heads yes.

Ben had long, curly blonde hair, which would be a substantial change for him. Chuck had taken a pair of scissors to his hair, and he needed it shaped a bit.

Dudley rubbed some smelly stuff on Matt's hair when he finished cutting it. It was nice. Dudley then finished with a shoulder and neck rub. Matt had forgotten about going to the barber shop and being treated so well.

Dudley helped Matt out of the chair. "Next!" Chuck got up and took his place in the chair.

Matt walked out the door, returned to the kitchen area, and sat down to visit with more of the gentleman farmers. This was a nice stop for them, and they appreciated the food and the hospitality.

"As soon as my boys finish getting their hair cut, we'll bring in a couple of M4s, automatic weapons, and pistols. Are there any military people here who can handle weapons?"

A big man with a nice-looking mustache and beard stood up. "Young man, most of us know how to shoot almost any gun. Some have been in the military, but most of us have been hunting most of our lives, using high-powered rifles and shotguns. We are so familiar with weapons, yes."

Matt continued, "My intent was not to embarrass anybody. I just wanted to make sure nobody would be accidentally shot."

The group's mood changed; everybody laughed, and everything was fine.

Wasn't too long before Ben, Chuck, and Buck walked into the cafeteria, and they saw Matt sitting there with the town elders.

Matt turned when he heard them walk in. "You two look slicked up and surprisingly good."

"Yeah, Matt, you know the smelly stuff he put on your head. Your dog walked up and stood there until he put some on his body and rubbed it in his hair. Can you believe he wanted some of the same smelly stuff we had?"

Everybody sitting at the tables had a good laugh over that one.

"Okay, Chuck, let's get some weapons and ammunition for these people and show these fine fellas a little about how to operate the weapons."

Matt and Chuck went back inside and gathered the fellas together. First, the guns were unloaded. Matt then instructed them on how to load the weapons. Second, precautions: proper safety precautions at all times. It wasn't long before they had taken all the guns and gone through the motions.

Matt could see each of them was experienced. "Okay, you are good to go. We're leaving you eight clips for each rifle and four for each Beretta. Are there any other questions? If not, we'll be on our way. If it's all right, we want to fill the truck with diesel."

Frank got up, there was no need. We filled your truck, checked all the tires, and checked the oil, you're good to go.

Matt and his team got up, shook hands, and walked toward the door. They were just about to open it when two older ladies approached them.

"Just a minute, young men, we have fried chicken for each of you."

Each lady handed them brown paper bags and hugged them, "Impressive ladies, thank you." They finally made it through the doors and outside to the truck.

Matt returned to the tailgate, pulled it down, reached inside for his backpack, unzipped it, and reached inside." Yah," he said, "Here it is, my Green Bay Packer hat. Now I'm good to go."

Matt climbed into the driver's seat, put his foot on the brake, and pushed the button to start the truck. Looking at Chuck, he said, "Okay, navigator. What's next?"

Chuck turned around and looked at Ben. "What the hell do you have on your head? Oh, hell no!"

Chuck grabbed Ben's hat off his head, opened the door, ran back into the store, and returned with another hat. After getting in the truck, he turned and handed it to Ben: a Nebraska black hat with crossbones.

Ben looked confused. "What's wrong with the hat I had?"

Chuck turned to face Ben. "It was a pink camouflage hat, a woman's or girl's hat. Pink is for girls."

"Why didn't somebody tell me this stuff before?"

At the same time, Matt and Chuck said, "We just did," and started laughing—a good laugh to start the morning.

"Okay, Chuck, back to navigation."

"Boss, next up are the small towns of Seneca, Mullen, Whitman, Ashby, and Brigham. Do you want to go all the way to Alliance?"

"No, when we get to Highway 250, we're going north to Rushville and back to Highway 20 towards Chadron. Once we get close to Chadron, I know the country roads well enough to get around the town and north to Hot Springs.

"By then, it will start getting dark. South of Chadron, there's a campground that might be a good place to pull over and spend the night. The last time I was there, they had great cabins, cooking facilities, and showers."

"How do you know all this, Boss?"

"Back in the day, after military life, I lived here, taught at the college, and loved this area. It has great fishing and hunting, and I walked all over this part of the country."

"Boss, I have a question: Why didn't you tell those older folks what might be happening to them, you know, with all the cities melting and things returning to nature?"

"Well, they were having too much fun; why spoil it? We don't know if it's going to change for them or not. It might stay the same, and they might live out right there."

"Turn left here, Matt, if you want to take the gravel road to Highway 385, south of Chadron, where the State Park is located."

"Yes, Chuck, it's just a few miles."

"Boss, if you would like another route, I found one to Hot Springs; we could go up to the Pine Ridge Indian Reservation and cut across west to Hot Springs."

"Chuck, I considered going through the Reservation. But, with all the changes, the Sioux Indian tribe could now be hostile, with complete freedom to do whatever they want, which means scalping all-white men and taking all their land back. I'd like to avoid a confrontation, and I don't want any of us to get hurt. And sure, I don't want to kill anyone unless it's necessary. Agreed?"

"Yes, Boss, I agree with you; Ben agrees with you. I don't know about Buck; he's not saying."

*****

Old Home Week

They arrived at Chadron State Park at about 7:00 PM. All the roads were paved, so it was no problem getting up and down the hills. About an hour before dark, they found a nice cabin.

Chuck grabbed the three bags. "I don't know about you two, but I look forward to fried chicken."

It didn't take them long to unload what was needed from the truck and trailer. Going inside, they found 2 queen-size beds and a nice kitchen area. They had supper and hit the hay for the rest of the night. Of course, Buck jumped up on Matt's bed and stretched out; clearly, he had chosen Matt as his sleep buddy.

Ben needed no sleep; he went outside to guard the perimeter. Keeping them safe through the night.

Matt felt secure knowing someone was constantly on watch. He asked Ben one time what he did all night long.

Ben told him, "I check in with my superior and report what has been happening. Then, I spend time praying and reflecting on what I've seen here. And I might make a pot of coffee."

Sunrise was at 5:40 AM. Buck patted Matt on his back, saying he needed to go outside. Matt understood; he needed to pee himself. He got up to let Buck out.

When he was finished in the bathroom, he walked outside to check on Buck and see how Ben was doing.

"Ah, Ben, how was your night?"

"Everything was great, Matthew. I'm just sitting here drinking a cup of coffee. I did make another pot so you can have fresh coffee this morning. It looks like a big storm is headed this way. I've been keeping my eye on the weather; you can feel the change in air, and I believe we are in for a big thunderstorm, heavy rain, and strong winds. It could be rough, Matthew."

"Thanks, Ben. It's good that you spotted the storm. Do you think we should hunker down for the day and just take it easy until the storm passes through?"

"Yes, it might not be a bad idea, Matthew. Getting out and driving in this stuff, and not knowing what's down the road, could be dangerous"

"Yeah, Ben, I can feel the wind picking up, lots of lightning to the northwest, it does look like a big storm, WOW! Big raindrops.

"Okay, Ben, let's go inside and tell Chuck what is happening.

"Ben, did you see Buck? I let him outside."

"Yes, I did see him; he was headed for the trees to the north, he was picking up some scent. He will come back when he's ready."

The rain started picking up pretty well now. They went inside and shut the door. Chuck was still sleeping. There was a big crack of lightning. Thunder sounded like a bomb had been dropped not too far from them. Chuck woke up with a startled scream. "What the hell was that?"

Matt had to laugh. "It's a storm moving in. It looks like it will set in and rain for a few hours. We also need to be aware of lightning. Lightning can start a fire in the forests; we don't want to get trapped in one."

Matt looked out the window. "Once I was up in the hills west, scouting new deer hunting areas up in the high hills, I saw smoke to the east on the other side of the hills. So, I started down the mountain and got to a spot where I saw the eastern ridges were on fire. As quickly as possible, I got down the highway and went north into Chadron. Before they closed the highway, the fire was raging towards Chadron.

"When I finally got home, it was just in time to hear everyone needed to evacuate; the fire was headed for Chadron. Most townspeople evacuated, went to Alliance, and spent the night there.

"The next day, we discovered the fire had stopped at the college football field. If it had jumped, it would have burned the whole town down.

"Chuck, Ben made hot coffee for you if you are ready to get up."

"I also made some pancakes while I was making coffee. There in the oven, keeping warm."

"Well, thanks, Ben. It's mighty nice of you."

Sitting at the table, Ben brought over a stack of pancakes, butter, maple syrup, and coffee.

Chuck finally got up, went to the bathroom, came out, grabbed a cup, poured some coffee, sat down, and grabbed some pancakes.

Matt heard a scratching at the door. He opened the door, and Buck sauntered into the room in no hurry. Buck sat next to his bowl, looking for food. After feeding him, Matt went back to his table and pancakes.

The rest of the day was spent cleaning their weapons and going through some military maps left behind in Lincoln at the Air Base. Chuck was trying to figure out where the military guys were going with all the gold.

"Boss, it looks to me like they were heading to Wyoming. Some mountains are marked on the map. I wonder if this is a military compound built in the mountains."

The storm lasted until about 6 PM, so they just sat around playing cards, checking on provisions, and mapping a route to the Black Hills. They went to bed early, knowing it was going to be an early rise in the morning.

Matt was up at 6 AM, and Buck needed to go out. Matt got up and walked to the door to let Buck out. Ben was sitting in one of the Ozark chairs, drinking his coffee.

"Good morning, Ben. Did anything happen during the night?"

"No, it's been quiet. After the storm ended, I took a walk down the road. Several trees are down, one across the road, and they need to be removed before we can leave.

"Also, Matthew, another storm is coming from the west again. It looks like another heavy storm."

"OK, Ben. I guess we're stuck here for another day. We should look around for equipment to move those trees when the storms are over."

"I made fresh coffee this morning, Matt, but I didn't make breakfast because I was strolling down the road."

"Don't worry about it, Chuck's turn to make breakfast. I'll get him up and let him know the plan for the day. It looks like Buck went back up over the hill again, huh?"

"Yes, he took off in a hurry. I will sit out here for a while and finish my coffee. I'll keep an eye out for him."

"OK, Ben, I'm going inside.

"Chuck, get up. It's your turn to fix breakfast, and another big storm is moving in."

"OK, Boss, I'm up."

When they had finished eating, Matt told them they needed to look around for something to remove the trees off the road so they could leave that place once the storms ended.

"Boss, I found a chainsaw, some axes, and something like logging equipment in one of the drawers underneath the trailer. That should take care of the trees."

"Great, Chuck. That should help." About half an hour later, a big storm moved in with heavy rain, wind, and thunder, which lasted all day.

Matt remembered good times with Paula back in Lincoln when he was old. He would sit in the sunroom with her, drinking coffee, and watching the storm—thunder, lightning, and heavy rain. They both used to enjoy a good storm.

I so loved that woman.

CHAPTER 6

Few Are Chosen

Save the People

Oh, my head, where did all this pain come from?

I've never had pain in my head this bad.

Even on my biggest drunk.

Why is it so foreign to me?

Father sat up and finally opened his eyes, as blurry as they were.

He could see light coming through Mary's stained-glass window.

It must be morning! *I am alive. I can't believe it. I thought I was dead for sure.*

He was sitting there wondering what had happened. He felt so strange; his body was different. With his right hand, he started running it over his left arm, shoulder, and stomach. *Jesus, I've got muscles.* His eyes started to focus.

As he looked around, the people he was seeing were all naked. He looked at himself, also naked. What the heck? He reached over and grabbed some clothes lying on the floor, tight-fitting clothes, but at least it covered him. He was seeing other people doing the same thing, trying to fit clothes on, all too tight, too small.

Walking around, he could not recognize these people. They were all younger, some older, but none of them were old people. They were all different ages—younger, stronger, and healthier. He didn't understand it.

Father Mike found a couple sitting on a pew whom he thought were Lee and Dolores, husband and wife from 3 Horse Ranch. It looked like they were 30 years old, which couldn't be.

Father walked up and asked, "Are you Lee?"

"Yes, it is. And who are you? Oh! You must be the priest in a black shirt and pants. I remember them from before. Do you know what's going on, Father?"

"No, I do not understand it at all. I see your peacemakers sitting beside you on the bench. I know, pretty hard to explain. Dolores, you look young and strong as well.

"I'm going to see how the other people are getting along and try to figure out what's going on."

In another pew were Donald and Monica Stratford, both looking in their mid-30s.

"Donald, your cast is off. You look pretty fit, cowboy. Monica, you look pretty good yourself, ready to take on the world."

"Father, is it you?"

"Yes, and before you ask me—no, I do not have any answers either. But I am glad to see you are okay. I'll talk to you later after I get around to visiting with everybody."

"You must be Bill, the Ace Hardware man, shown on your red shirt. How are you, Bill?"

"I really don't know. I certainly didn't want to be younger; the first time was hard enough."

"Yeah, Bill, I agree with you. The first time was bad enough, so no fun to have to go through it again, but I don't think we have any choice. It looks like everybody was dealt the same hand. I'll get back to you later."

Father Mike recognized Fran and Dakota. They had not changed at all, still in their 20s.

"Hi, Fern and Dakota. I am so glad to see you both made it through."

"Father, what's going on?"

"I don't know what it is, I can't explain it, talk with you later."

A young girl was sitting by Joseph's statue. She was 5′ 9″, couldn't be more than 140 pounds, and had long black hair. She was dressed in black jeans and a black shirt. It must be the girl who walked in before the storm. Looking at her now, she is much prettier. All the marks on her face and the tattoos are gone.

As he walked over to her, she looked up at him.

Father said, "I don't believe we met."

"No, Father, we haven't, you tried to talk to me before, but I was not interested."

"Okay, how about now? Are you interested?

"My name is Father Mike. This is my church. It looks like you made it through with the rest of us. We're all in the same situation for the time being, anyway."

"My name is Elaine. I was backpacking and came from Wyoming.

"When it looked like a storm was coming, I ducked into the church to escape the weather. The rest, you know."

"How old are you, Elaine?"

“I am 19 and ran away from home two months ago. If you think of sending me back, I will be gone before you can even make the call.”

“No worries, Elaine, no one is sending you back, but I hope you will stay with us until we figure out what is happening.

“So, trust me, Elaine, we are on your side.”

“It’s not like I never heard that before!”

“Elaine, I can understand. How about you go along with us and make up your mind later? At least for now, we will feed you.

“Okay, I will see you later and continue talking with you.

“Right now, I need to find out how many people are alive.”

He found Christopher and his wife Joan sitting in front of the altar.

“Reverend, I see you and your wife both made it through the three days of darkness, and you also look in your 30s.”

“Yes, it’s us, Father Mike. We made it through.”

“Christopher, I’ve been talking with several people, but a few are missing. I can tell by the empty pews, with only clothes, that people are missing from the church. Also, I don’t know who is alive in the basement, so we should go downstairs and check for any living people.”

Three young people came running towards Father Mike from the other side of the church and yelled.

“Father, Father, is it you?”

“Yes, it’s me. I am glad you all made it okay, Randy, Kimberly, and Linda. Have you any ill effects?”

"No, Father, we are okay; in fact, we are feeling great and glad we didn't die."

A lady came up from the basement wearing a great big dress. She must be 29 years old. She walked over to them and said, "Father, I'm Helen, from downstairs, the head cook, or at least I was the head cook. I don't know who I am now or what I am."

"Oh my gosh, Helen, it's so good to see you."

"Father Mike. You can only be, what, 30? What has happened to us?"

"Helen, I don't know what to tell you. The rest of us are trying to figure out what happened. We are all younger versions of ourselves, in perfect health and physically fit. What about the basement? Is everyone else alive down there?"

"No, Father. I am the only one; the rest are just a pile of clothes. I believe there must have been around 40 people down there, all gone."

"Reverend Chris, we should gather everyone and discuss our options."

"We'll help Father." The three college kids took off down the middle of the church and started rounding people up and bringing them up to the front of the church.

Father Mike took the opportunity to talk to Helen.

"Helen, how much food do we have?"

"Father, I've been trying to cook up all the food in the refrigerators and freezers after the power went out. Most of it's gone. We have a bunch of canned and boxed food. Not much else. All the bread now is old and moldy; I threw it away. We have flour, sugar, salt, pepper, and some spices, but that's about all. Any food sitting out for three days is not any good anymore."

"Thanks, Helen. If you have any promising ideas, don't be afraid to come to me and tell me. I'm open to any idea to find a way to feed all these people, not just today but in the days to come, so any help you can give me will be appreciated."

Father walked up to the front of the church next to Reverend Chris and his wife.

People were sitting in groups around the front of the church, waiting for any information on what had happened to them and their town.

Father Mike addressed the problem. "Reverend Cris and I will first check outside and ensure it's safe for everyone before you all venture out. So, sit tight.

"OK, Christopher, let's go look outside. Walk with me." They both walked to the back of the church. Father Mike took the wooden plank down from the doors, threw open the double doors, and then stepped outside. It was a beautiful morning. The sun was shining, and there was not a cloud in the sky.

There was no sound, no wind, no cars, no people, no noise of any kind except for a few birds singing. It was deathly quiet. Father Mike had never seen it like this before.

"It looks safe enough, Chris. Let's go back in and talk with our people. I would like you to take the lead on this, Chris. Okay?"

"Sure, I'll be glad to. Let me know how I can help, and I'll be there."

"Okay, Chris, go ahead; I will close the doors now and put the bar back on. Then I will meet you in front." After Father Mike finished locking the doors, he turned and walked up the aisle towards the altar.

Christopher was waiting for him, smiling.

"Reverend Chris, I will put you in charge; I will sit down in the front row. Go ahead; you are the man in charge."

Father Mike was thinking. *I will give Chris the ball and let him carry it for a while. He needs experience, he needs to lead, and I will follow instead.*

"Thank you, Father Mike, for the vote of confidence. Yes, I will be glad to speak to these fine people and reassure them we know nothing more than they do. But we can start to make a plan.

"Ladies and gentlemen, I am Reverend Christopher Merkatz, the minister from the Methodist church here in Hot Springs, and my wife Joan is here with me. Several people from the Methodist Church came here for shelter, and we are so grateful to Father Mike from the Catholic Church for taking us in during such a trying time.

"I know how tough these last few days have been. There has got to be a lot of stress, doubt, and anxiety. I am trained to help you. So, I would like to set up a plan to meet in the back of the church and use Father Mike's confessional to hold meetings with each of you.

"So, if you have problems with emotions, fear, or anger, I would be glad to help you. I will circulate a list; add your name so I can meet and pick a convenient time for you. Mental health is our primary concern; we want to get strong for the days ahead.

"Are there any questions?"

"Hell, yes," came from one of the ranchers. "What the hell's going on? We want to know what we're going to do to survive this. Has this happened here only or in other places? We need answers; we don't need mental health help. Jack Daniels will take care of our mental health."

After the rancher's remarks, snickers could be heard in the crowd, and several others were yelling questions at the Reverend, who was backing up, unsure what to say or do next. He was lost, trying to find answers.

Reverend Chris looked at Mike, who was sitting there stretched out, trying to look supportive but not wanting to get involved.

I suppose I should, or we will all die if the Reverend stays in charge.

Father Mike got up from the pew, stretched a bit, and walked to the front of the church. With his back to the crowd, he leaned over to Chris and said, “Go sit down!”

Father Mike turned around and said, “Okay, people, here is the deal. We have no idea what caused all this, but we are all young, strong, and healthy, so we have that going for us. We don’t know if this has happened anywhere else, and we have no way to contact anyone else.”

Father Mike was on a roll. “So we’re going to do a scavenger hunt. I want you to pair off in twos, yes, we’re going outside. Search for people, food, and vehicles, and you can all go down to Bomgaars or some of the other ranchers’ clothing places and get some decent clothes to wear, maybe a couple of outfits, and good strong boots. Don’t wear flip-flops, don’t wear skimpy little shoes, or tennis shoes. Good boots, rain gear, backpacks, anything else you might think we could use; and bring it back to the church.”

Father looked around and said, “It would be better if you could find a vehicle that runs. None of the new cars and trucks will work; they all have computer chips. Look for old trucks and cars without electronics.”

Father Mike raised his hands. “If there isn’t anything else, it is about 10 AM. Pair up and be back here in two hours. Okay, GO!! And be safe!!”

Everyone was eager to go, so they rushed towards the back of the church, took the bar off the doors, opened them up, and went outside, spreading out, covering the town, looking for anything or anyone they could find.

Father Mike turned around, genuflected, and made the sign of the cross, saying “Thank you, God, for this day.” As he got up and turned around, heading towards the back of the church, Joan was on his left side, walking with him.

"Father, can I visit you a little bit on your way out?"

"Yes, Joan, what can I help you with?"

"Well, Father Mike, Chris feels terrible about not understanding what was required of him when he gave his speech. But, looking at it, you, Father, I am guessing you have a military background. The way you took charge; you are good at leading."

"Well, Joan, why would you be assuming that?"

"Well, first of all, Father, I was a Navy nurse. Before that, I was an Iowa farm girl, so I have been around a bit. I recognize military stature in people by the way they walk, by the way they carry themselves, and by the way they take charge, and that would be you, Father."

"Joan, you were a military nurse. That is impressive; I would never in the world have guessed it. And yes, I have an army background; I was a Green Beret for 10 years in the sandbox.

"And as for your husband, Chris! It's not a problem that he is a spiritual leader. He should take on all the spiritual leadership because people will need some time with someone willing to listen to them as they go along on this journey.

"I'm thinking, Joan, God has another mission for me. I could feel it when I thought I was dying. I'm not sure I really understand yet. Hopefully, it will come to me as we go along.

"Right now, Joan, I would like to go back to the rectory. I have some clothes I can change into that should fit me better. You should take Chris and go find some clothes for yourselves, and we can all meet back here later."

Father Mike was just about ready to leave the church when he heard a loud noise, which sounded like a plane. He looked up towards the south. High above in the clouds was a twin-engine Beechcraft 55. It started approaching the town and looked like it was going to land. Oh no, the pilot was trying to land on the football field, which Father Mike didn't think had enough room.

Father watched as a bunch of townspeople rushed to the football field. *So, I guess I'll let them take care of it. I need to get changed.* A miracle, a plane.

Father Mike walked around the east side of the church towards the church rectory where he lived. He stopped and listened for a plane crash. Instead, he heard the engines dying back, so maybe he was going to make it. It looked like the pilot knew what he was doing.

When Father opened the door to the rectory, he knew exactly where his clothes were: hidden in the back of the closet. He had his old military footlocker, with clothes he used now for deer hunting, a pair of camouflage pants, comfortable military boots, a black camouflage shirt, and a camouflage coat. He grabbed his backpack, his hunting bow, and arrows—all the stuff needed to survive in the wild if he needed to.

He was heading back to the church, seeing people heading in with equipment, all dressed in different clothes, carrying food and backpacks, all loaded down with as much as they could carry.

Father Mike greeted them and helped them take their stuff into the church, putting it all in the pews at the back of the church. Several other people had already returned to the church, and they all looked like they did well.

Donald and Lee walked into the church and started hollering, "Father Mike!"

"Yes, guys. What is it?"

Father could see they were followed by two other people, a man and a woman. He hadn't seen either of them before. Both of them were in their

30s, dressed in jeans and gray button-down shirts with an airplane logo on the left side of their shirts.

Lee introduced Father Mike to Eugene and Kay Dawson, the ones whose plane landed on the football field.

Father Mike shook hands with them. “That was a masterful flight, Eugene, quite a bit of flying. I’m glad to see you both survived.”

“Thank you, Father. My wife and I are from Amarillo, Texas. We were flying up from Texas to meet with Kay’s mother in Hot Springs. My intent was to land at the airport, but I started having engine trouble and had to put her down where I could. I’ve had some experience flying F-15s in the Air Force, including several missions in Afghanistan. Landing on aircraft carriers is much easier than landing on a football field.”

Lee interrupted. “Father, Eugene was telling us he was on the way out from Amarillo. Something happened.”

“Yes, Father, on our way here, all the towns, and I mean all the towns, all the highways, all manmade stuff, everything is gone. Everything melted into the ground, turning into soil, grass, and trees. Flowers are popping up, and no more highways or towns exist. There are no more wires, fences, or anything artificial. And it’s headed this way, so I’m guessing it will be here in a short amount of time.”

Father Mike looked at Eugene. “I’m not sure how to respond. I was hoping we had seen the worst of it. But did you find your mother? You said you were headed this way. Did you find her in Hot Springs?”

Eugene shook his head. “No, we didn’t find her. We stopped at her house, and there was no sign of her. It looked like she had left. I don’t know if she went to work or where she is. We do not know.”

“Okay Eugene, what kind of work does she do? It would help us find her.”

"She's a cook, Father. She said she cooked part-time at the high school and other places here in town."

"You said her name is Helen?"

Yes, Father, Helen Hardy.

"Eugene, I have some excellent news for you. Your mother Helen is downstairs in our kitchen taking stock of our food. She is going to be so happy to see you both."

And they both took off running down the hallway in the back of the church.

"Stop!" Father Mike hollered. "You are going the wrong way; go the other way to the stairs on the right." So, they took off to the right and went down the stairs.

Father and Lee could hear the whooping, hollering, and yelling, which gave both a good feeling. "Something good just happened, Lee."

Father Mike turned around. Okay, back to work. More young people were coming in, including a couple of new people.

"Linda and Kimberly, who do you have with you?"

"Father, this is Patricia Digmann. She is a doctor at the hospital. We also found a nurse, Sally Johnson. Both were hiding in the hospital kitchen."

Father had seen Patricia before when taking people to the hospital. He remembered that she had dark curly hair and a nice figure, and she was about 5′ 9″ tall, dressed in green scrubs. Sally was a little shorter, more round, and had washed-out blonde hair. She was 5′ 5″ tall, also dressed in green scrubs.

"Welcome. We can use a doctor and a nurse. Please make yourselves at home."

Kimberly was trying to get Father Mike's attention.

"Yes, Kimberly, what is it?"

"Father, I saw Reverend Chris and his wife driving two school buses to the church parking lot."

"Kimberly, that's great news. Let's see what they have for us."

They all ran outside, down the steps to the road. Coming up the driveway were two yellow school buses. You could tell both were diesel by the sounds. It made sense; diesels have two batteries each, enough power to start them. Gas engines have one battery, which hadn't survived the initial blast that killed all batteries, flashlights, cell phones, and Father Mike's watch.

The buses came to a stop, and Chris and Joan stepped out.

Father Mike was happy. Chris needed a public win this time, so he gave both a big hug. "Way to go, Chris, smart thinking. Finding buses with diesel engines and loading them with food and clothing is another smart idea, Chris and Joan."

As Father thanked Joan and Chris, several people came up the drive with all their belongings. A couple of people he didn't know, one was a big, tall black guy in scrubs—*Yeah, I don't remember him.*

The new black guy, in a hospital gown, approached Father Mike and said, "I hope I can join your group. It looked like that's where everyone was headed. My name is Ethan Jones. I don't know what's happened to me. The last thing I remember is that I was dying."

Father Mike stared at him and couldn't believe his eyes. "You're Ethan Jones, Sergeant Ethan Jones. You were in the VA hospital the last time I saw you. We all figured you were going to die: no legs, you lost one arm, and several metal fragments were taken out of your body. You, sir, are a miracle, and yes, you are so welcome to join us."

"How do you know me, Father?"

"Doesn't look like it now, but I am the priest of this parish. I walked up the hill to the VA Hospital to visit all the soldiers. Especially you, giving you the last rites. The last time I saw you, nothing more could be done for you. Doctors tried everything and nothing was working. Your body was just tired and couldn't go anymore.

"I am so happy to see you, Ethan. You just don't know how pleased I am.

"Go inside, Ethan. You will find piles of clothes, shoes, and boots. Help yourself, and there will be food later. Make yourself as comfortable as you can."

Father Mike was now excited. He needed to talk with the whole group again, so he grabbed Chris, and they walked into the church and down towards the altar. "Christopher, I would like you to be the spiritual leader of this group. You are so good at helping people with emotional problems; that is your strength.

"Chris, I told your wife Joan that my mission is to effect change. God's mission for me now is to be a warrior priest."

"Father, what makes you think God wants you to give up your priesthood?"

"Chris? It came to me when I died, or thought I was dead. And I'm not entirely giving up my priesthood, just taking on more duties kind of thing."

"Father Mike, I am so sorry for my blunder this morning. I don't know how to take over like you did, taking charge and telling people what to do. I've never been that kind of person."

"Christopher, must have been somebody else's hand at work. It showed what you're calling is, there's no doubt about it. God's given you a major skill of helping people. I will try to do the best I can to help you."

Joan was waiting for them at the front of the church.

Father Mike walked up to the front of the church and turned. He was about to ask for everybody's attention when he noticed they were all talking, moving around, and doing lots of activities. Then Joan put her fingers to her mouth and gave this shrill whistle, followed by, "Everyone! Pay attention!"

"Thank you, Joan. There are some pressing matters we need to talk about, one just came to us this afternoon, but before I do, I want to thank everyone for all your efforts in finding all this food, clothing, and equipment. And welcome all you newcomers who joined us. We are so happy you are here with us and made it through the bad times."

Father Mike continued. "I assume most of you know about the airplane landing on the football field. Eugene and Kay Dawson from Amarillo, Texas flew the airplane. They had some disheartening news. As they were flying north from Texas, they could see that all the small to large towns, all the highways, all electrical wires, phone lines, and fences were gone. All disappeared, and everything was returning to the natural prairie as it was in the beginning."

Father Mike made the sign of the cross. "You all know the only person who could make it happen, is God himself. We also know it's headed our way. We don't want to be caught in any building while they disappear. Or on any highways when they disappear.

"This leaves us with one choice: We must go somewhere safe and away from buildings. Luckily, Chris and Joan found the school buses we could load up with people, some food, and supplies, and see if we can find trailers to hook behind them.

"We all need to leave Hot Springs as quickly as possible. We need to start today!"

Fran had raised her hand and was frantically waving. She stood up. "Father."

"Yes, Fran, what is it?"

"Dakota and I were going through several warehouses when we found two big military trucks. We didn't try to start them, but they are in a steel building, so maybe they were protected."

"That's a good idea, Fern. Would you take a couple of people with you to check it out? If you can start them, it could help us a lot.

"Helen has some food for everybody downstairs. Go ahead and get something to eat. We can finish packing later.

"Oh, I see all of you are looking at me in a strange way. Yes, I am not wearing black. I don't have any priestly clothing that will fit me, so I am wearing my old military clothes, so you must excuse me. Thank you all for understanding.

"Before we go eat, I will bless us in the name of the Father, the Son, and the Holy Spirit. Bless us, oh Lord, for these are gifts which we are about to receive from thy bounty through Christ our Lord. Amen. Let's eat."

Father walked downstairs to get something to eat. Helen had done an excellent job: ham sandwiches with lettuce and cheese, and bowls of potato soup.

He noticed Helen's son and daughter-in-law were helping in the kitchen. It is nice to see a family working together. Everybody was relaxed and eating their food. He couldn't help but contemplate what was going to happen and where they were going to end up. A plan must be made; he needed to round up his trusted fellows.

He needed Chris and his wife Joan; he might include the new guy, Eugene from Texas. He should also see if Sergeant Jones would join them. Helen should also be included, Fern, Dakota, and Lee Peacemaker. There should be nine of us getting together—*a good group*. Okay, the next step was to get ahold of the team and find a place to meet. The best place was the rectory: out of the way, and they wouldn't be disturbed. *We need to meet today.*

Father Mike got a yes from everybody except Sergeant Jones, who looked at him, and said, "I don't know if I want to get involved."

"Sergeant Jones, you have valuable experience we could use to form a plan for all these people. You would be welcome. If you change your mind, we will meet at 3 PM in the rectory."

Father was walking over to the rectory. He was just thinking that the church and rectory were over 100 years old. It could all be gone in a short amount of time, lost to the world. He never locked the rectory door; if anybody wanted to get in badly enough, the door wouldn't stop them anyway.

Walking in, the main floor included a galley kitchen, dining area seated 12, living room, bathroom, and the main bedroom. It had been remodeled several times over the decades; nothing fancy. Comfortable, the only luxury he had was his color TV. His passions were football, baseball, and college basketball, the Final Four. Could anything be more fun to watch than college sports?

It just came to him: There would never be college sports, pro football, or any sports. It was all history now. TV, radio, electric lights, telephone, cell phones—all gone. No police officers, firefighters, rescue personnel, no more 911. The government would be gone—no more Army, Navy, or Marines—nothing, except for the few of us still hanging around and given a new lease on life.

Father was interrupted in his thoughts. Someone was at the door. "Come in, please take a seat at the table." As the committee members filed in, everybody showed up except Jones, of course.

Father took his seat at the table. "Now, shall we get started? I have several maps: North Dakota, South Dakota, Nebraska, Wyoming, and Montana. Our objective should be to find an open area with no buildings or highways, so we don't get involved in the takedown and get caught in a building and go down with it. Does anybody have any suggestions?

"Fern, you have your hand raised, but you don't have to raise it if you want to speak. What is on your mind?"

"Father, Dakota, and I are the youngest here. We have no experience. There are other people with more experience; they should be here at this meeting."

"Yes, Fern, I understand what you are saying. Here's my thought: you and Dakota have traveled all over South Dakota and Wyoming into Nebraska. With you running track and Dakota's rodeo competitions. Both of you have covered more of the countryside than any of us. If we start talking about a location, chances are you two already know something about the area and can give some input on what it looks like. So yes, you're valuable at this meeting and your age has nothing to do with it."

Father Mike got up from his chair. "I would like to open this meeting with silence and prayer. If you are so inclined, please join us.

"Okay, thank you. Now, does anybody have any ideas for a place where we could migrate? We're talking about 30+ people, equipment, food, and clothing. It would be quite an undertaking to move so many people safely to an area where we can hopefully stay alive."

"Father …"

"Yes Eugene?"

"Going south is out of the question. You'll just run into the problems we're trying to escape, so maybe we should go north or northwest and stay away from big cities."

"Yes, Chris, what are your thoughts?"

"Father, going to North Dakota is not a good plan either. I was in a small town and a smaller church for a few years. Pardon my language, it was just too damn cold."

"Good point, Chris; I know it gets cold; I've been up there myself. We wouldn't have any way to keep people safe from the cold, not such a severe cold anyway.

"Okay Lee, do you have any ideas?"

"As you know, Father, I've been on the open prairie most of my life, in fact, all my life, as I was raised on a ranch. It's hard living; you must have water, there is not much game, some antelope, maybe a few deer, it's flat when the wind blows, and it's cold. And it blows a lot, so I would vote no on going to Wyoming unless you can get to the mountains, and then again, you are running into lots of buildings, highways, bridges, and manufactured structures. Also, it's an extraordinarily long trip across Wyoming to get to the mountains. Again, it's not a good option with so many people."

"Thank you, Lee. That is insightful, and I must agree North Dakota and Wyoming are not viable ideas for us. We have too many people to move across Wyoming."

Father was looking at the maps. "What do you think about Montana? Is that …"

He stopped in midsentence as the door opened and Sergeant Jones walked in. *Praise the Lord!*

Sergeant Jones pulled up a chair at the table and sat down.

Father welcomed Sergeant Jones. "I am glad you can make it; at this point, we have eliminated North Dakota, Wyoming, Nebraska, and eastern South Dakota. We are now talking about Montana as an option."

Father again looked around. "Anyone care to comment?"

"Father …"

"Yes, Dakota?"

"I've been to eastern Montana, and it's horrible. There are many sulfur pits, and the ground is poor and flat. You can see forever, but there is nothing to see, little protection, and little game. Unless you go west to the mountains, and then again, you must go through too many cities over bridges. I don't think we can get there."

"Again, good insight, Dakota; we must find another place."

"Father …"

"Yes, Helen, do you have any ideas? You have something on your mind."

"Father, after looking at the maps, I thought we could make it to the Black Hills, Custer State Park. We would be safe from any highways, power lines, or buildings, with plenty of water and abundant game and trees to build a shelter. This is just my thought."

Finally, Sergeant Jones put his two cents' worth in. "While it sounds like an easy decision, it's close. You have enough fuel to get there, so why go anywhere else? You don't have any food or enough fuel to go long-distance anywhere else."

Helen stood up, "It's decided we're going to the Black Hills if nobody objects. Amen."

Father Mike ended the meeting. "Now, we have to go back and tell everyone the plan and mobilize to move as quickly as possible."

As everyone was getting up to leave, Father approached Sergeant Jones and asked him a question.

"Hey, Sergeant Jones, how about you be my second-in-command? You're the most experienced person compared to the students, farmers, or ranchers, none of whom have your expertise or background. What do you say?"

"Father, I don't know how I would feel about taking orders from a priest who cuts the heads off three people right in front of me: it's hard for me to look at you as any kind of leader."

"Fair enough, Sergeant. How about you look at this as shared leadership, maybe with you taking more of a leadership role than me? I will try not to give orders, just suggestions, and you can feel free to correct me if you think I am pushing you. That is not my intention."

"Alright, Father. I will try it. If it doesn't feel right to me, I'll do my own thing."

"Okay then, Sergeant, we're calling it a partnership. First thing, we need to tell people what the situation is and where we plan on going. It's 59 miles from Hot Springs, so it should be an easy transition. I have hunted in the area for a few years and found a valley with plenty of water on one of my hunting trips. It's not out in the open, protected by three sides of hills and trees, should provide plenty of cover, and we will be away from any buildings, wires, roads, anything man-made."

"Okay, another thing. I am not much of a talker, Father. Would you explain the plan to people and all the organization stuff? I would like to take a trip downtown. I heard there could be military vehicles in a building. I would like to check it out. It could be a National Guard holding center. They have guard training down here in the summer. And I am sure the Army would not haul all its equipment back and forth from Sioux Falls.

"So, Father, if you don't mind, I'll look and see what I can find."

"Okay, Sergeant. I'll organize things and put some people in charge of signing up individuals to divide them into groups. We now have two diesel school buses, each carrying 40 passengers. We can start loading backpacks, etc., get everything loaded tonight, and in the morning, we can eat breakfast and go."

Father Mike walked up to the front of the church and went inside.

Sergeant Jones went down the steps to talk with several ranchers standing on the street.

Suddenly, Father heard the noise of an old Chevy pickup, coming down the road approaching the church, and coming to a sliding halt.

Two young men got out, dressed in blue jeans, red button-down shirts with a ranch logo, straw cowboy hats, and boots.

They walked up to Lee, and Father could hear the conversation.

"Señor Lee, Mr. Lee, it's Tom and George from the ranch. Do you remember us? We look different, but we're still Tom and George."

Lee walked up to both and hugged them. "It's so good to see you boys. I'm glad you made it. What about your wives?"

"Sí, yes, Señor, they are safe out at the ranch, having stayed in your house. I hope it's okay; we had nowhere to go."

"Fine boys, I see you got the old Chevy started."

"Yes, and we started the big diesel truck in the Quonset to feed all the cows and the horses.

"Señor Lee, we had a bit of trouble. Some renegade Indians from the reservation came after us, wanting the truck. They had small rifles and bows and arrows and didn't give us any choice, we had to kill them, all four of them. I am so sorry, boss."

"Boys don't worry about it. It sounds like you had no choice. I'm glad you both are okay."

Lee turned around and approached Donald Strafford. "Hey, I will go with these two boys to the ranch, remove the fences, and run all the cattle up north as far as possible.

"Then Donald, I plan to load up all the horses, take them up north close to Custer Park, and turn them loose. They might be our future transportation."

"Okay, Lee, that sounds like a good idea. Also, round up all your tack. We need as many saddles as we can find. There could also be shops around town with saddles and gear. I'll take a look.

"Lee, when you are finished taking your horses to Custer, we can go to my ranch, load 15 of my best horses, and turn them loose in the park."

"Donald, that sounds like a plan. I'll meet you later." Lee turned and headed for the truck. Sergeant Jones ran after him and caught up.

He said, "Hey, you know where the Quonset hut and all the military trucks are?"

"Yeah, I know where it is. Do you need a ride?"

"Yeah, great. I'd like to go down and check things out and see if I can find anything we can use."

After Lee drove out of the church parking lot, Jones, riding in the back of the truck, started looking around town, each side of the street, expecting to see people going in and out of shops. Instead, there was nothing but quiet. A little breeze was blowing up dust and dirt, but no people. It was such an eerie feeling.

As the truck pulled up to the Quonset hut, Jones noticed the hangar doors were open. He jumped out of the back of the car and said, "See you folks around later. Thanks for the ride."

Jones walked up to the Quonset doors. Inside, a few people were working on the trucks.

"Hello, guys. Have you had any luck starting those trucks?"

"We're about to see if this one will start; okay, Dakota, give it a start."

Dakota turned the key and pushed the accelerator down in the truck, which thundered to life. Everybody was excited, jumping up and down. You'd have thought it was a touchdown.

"Well, that is the first one we started, and who are you, sir?"

"My name is Ethan Jones. I'm working with Father Mike to organize transportation to leave tomorrow morning. If I can help, I will be glad to. I have some experience with military vehicles. But it looks like you guys have everything well in hand. I'll look around, see what else's here."

Jones started walking around. He first spotted two Humvees on the left side of the Quonset hut and another on the right side, which looked like it was filled with radio equipment.

He continued his walk. There was a big door—no, it was double doors. He opened them up. Inside were trailers, three of them. It surprised him to see what was inside; he couldn't believe it. Camping equipment, big tents, cots, blankets, cooking equipment—all things they could use. Turning around, he walked back out to the trucks, where it looked like they had gotten the second one started too. It was a good deal.

"Guys, excellent work, has anybody tried to start the Humvees?"

"No, we haven't gotten to those yet. We've just been working on the trucks. We know the plan is to load all our equipment and food in the trucks."

"Well, if you do not mind, I'll work on those Humvees and see if I can start them. Also, in the back are three trailers with various camping equipment. So, if I can get the Humvees started, we can hook those up and take them with us."

"Okay, young man, that sounds like a plan. We'll take the trucks up to the church parking lot so they can be loaded. I'll return and bring some guys with me; we can help you work on the Humvees and get those started.

"Ethan, my name is Angus. I was a rancher down south of here before all this happened. I'm glad to meet you, Ethan, and glad you're with us. We'll be back as soon as we can."

At the first Humvee, Ethan popped the hood; the first things to clean were the battery connections. He found a big tool chest on wheels, rolled it over to the Humvee, grabbed a 9/16–1/2 wrench, undid the cables, found a steel brush in the toolbox, cleaned the posts on the battery on both connectors, and hooked everything back up. He turned the key, and by golly, it took off and started running. He could see by the gauge that the batteries were low, so he drove the Humvee outside to let it run for a while and charge up the batteries.

Good, he thought. It was the first one; back to the second. He repeated the same steps as before, turned the key, and it really kind of didn't want to start, so he tried again. It groaned and moaned and then finally took off and started; he drove it outside, letting it run a while.

While contemplating what to do next, Angus walked through the doors with four others. Walking over to the doors, he looked in. "How are you doing, Ethan Jones?"

"Well, I got two of them started. Right now, they are running and charging the batteries, but this one here, the batteries are completely dead. I imagine that the radio equipment draws most of the juice from the batteries."

"Ethan, I think you need jumper cables, and I have some in the truck. So, let's take the truck and drive it in here, jump the batteries on the Humvee, and see if we can get you started. If not, we'll have to find different batteries, which will be challenging after everything dies."

"Angus, good idea."

"Okay then I will drive the truck in and see what we can do."

Angus drove the truck next to the Humvee, opening the hood. Ethan Jones opened the hood on the Humvee. He got jumper cables, put them on the car, and then put the wires on the Humvee's main battery, letting it charge for a little bit. He jumped it, and it started running even though it didn't want to start. But it was rough, so he drove it outside and let it run to charge the batteries.

Jones came back in; Angus was standing with his four buddies. "What's next, Ethan Jones?"

"Well, if you want to jump in those Humvees and back them up, I'll hook them up to the trailers. Pull them out individually, then take them to the church parking lot."

"Right, Jones. We've got this. If you want to take my truck, you can drive it back to the church. We will follow you as soon as we can."

"Thank you, Angus. Is there any kind of gun shop in this town?"

"Oh yeah, there is an armory gun shop that is pretty good in size. What are you looking for?"

"Well, I think we are going to need some weapons. I will see what I can find; I will meet you later."

Jones climbed into Angus's beat-up old Ford pickup, a faded-out blue. He turned the key, and the V-8 started right up. You can't beat American-made trucks; they will last forever. He started looking for some kind of armory on Ouachita Street, they said, and a place called Mountain Valley Gun Shop. He pulled up. It was quite a big building, with a Western-style front porch.

Pulling up to the front, he exited and walked up to the front doors. He was not surprised to see they were open. Nobody around here had locked their doors when the three days hit.

Walking around the store, he was amazed at all the equipment, clothing, knives, binoculars on glass counters, handguns, and behind the counter along the wall shotguns, 308 rifles, and AR-15s. Yeah, this would do.

It took him a while to load all the guns. He needed boxes to load all the ammo for the shotguns, 308 rifles, NATO rounds for the AR-15s, 9 mm for the handguns, a few binoculars, and, he reminded himself, *mustn't forget knives. Need some good knives*. He found winter clothing, grabbed some, and threw them in the back of the truck. As he looked around to see if he had forgotten anything, he guessed he could always come back; right now, he needed to get back to see what was happening at the church.

Now ready to leave, he started walking to the front door, and out of the corner of his eye, he spotted an old weapon he had used.

He walked over and picked one up, a Ravin crossbow R29X built for stealth and accuracy up to hundred plus yards; 400 FPS crossbow bolts are now made from fiberglass, so he grabbed 1000 of those in all. And all the broad heads he could find. Most of them were 2-3 blades. Then he was ready to go, and he walked out the door, got in the truck, and headed for the church, proud of his finds.

He approached the church parking lot and saw everyone loading the trucks. It looked like everyone was organized; it had to be about time to eat. *Stomach is getting a little gnarly.* Walking up to the church, he saw Father Mike over by the baptismal font. "What's going on, Father?"

"Hi, Sergeant; I had Joan pick up some quart Mason jars with lids. I wanted to take all the holy water with us. The Catholic altar will have to stay, and the tabernacle and chalice will go. I'm also taking some of my robes in case I am needed as a priest.

"What have you been up to, Jones?"

"I went down to a gun shop and loaded up with some rifles, handguns, and ammunition; assuming we are not going to be alone, we could run into some bad guys, so I want to be prepared."

"OK, Sergeant. We'll eat and get everybody to bed early so we can get up and be gone by sunrise. Everything is organized for a 59-mile trip into the Black Hills."

And the day ended.

*****

The sun was about to rise. Father Mike needed to get up, after deciding to sleep on one of the church benches rather than sleeping in the rectory. He hadn't felt like sleeping by himself. This way, he was still around the people, and given what had happened in the past couple of days, he would be available if someone needed his help during the night.

Jones had brought him a watch he found at the military store with a lovely leather band. It looked like it was 5:30 AM, time to wake everyone up. At the altar were the bells used during mass. He walked up and down the aisle, jingling the bells. People were not happy, moaning and groaning. "Sorry, people. You need to get up and move."

Downstairs in the basement, Helen and her family, plus a couple of others, were fixing scrambled eggs, bacon, pancakes, cinnamon rolls, hot coffee, and orange juice—quite a spread.

"Helen, breakfast looks good."

"Yes, Father, we had to use up any food we couldn't take. We've already loaded nonperishable food in the trucks. And I plan to walk out leaving all the dirty dishes.

"Oh yeah, Father, we made ham and chicken sandwiches for an afternoon meal, using the rest of the lettuce and mayonnaise. We were going to be busy for the first day."

"Planning is one of your strong points, Helen. I will take scrambled eggs, bacon, hash browns, a cinnamon roll, and a big old cup of coffee." Sitting down to eat, he noticed the other people were starting to file in.

Not long before Sergeant Jones walked in, grabbed something to eat and a cup of coffee, and came over to sit across from Father Mike at the table.

"Good morning, Sergeant Jones."

"Good morning, Father. I see you were up ringing bells this morning. It was a rude awakening."

"Yeah, I know I was, but we need to get started. Once everyone is seated, it's time to introduce you."

"Okay, Father. I've been working with some of the guys already. I know Angus, Lee, and his wranglers, and Donald. I hope you don't mind. I gathered a few guys and distributed some of the weapons I found. But only to those who I feel are capable and have some knowledge of how to use AR-15s, shotguns, or handguns.

"I was surprised to learn that Donald, Lee, and two of Lee's wranglers already have six shooters that look like 45s. They wear cowboy hats and boots and carry their guns on their hips.

"They look like old-time cowboys.

"Dolores and Monica also have strapping six-shooters. I asked Lee if they could handle those guns. Donald and Lee just looked at me and laughed."

"Did Lee get his horses up north to the Black Hills?"

"Yes, he did. He came back, and they took Donald's horses. About fifteen of them went up to the hills and were turned loose. They just returned, and those young people in their late 20s worked day and night."

"Yeah, sure they do, Jones. They are used to working hard their whole lives and then have to slow down as they get older. And now they are taking advantage of this newfound youth, working hard and loving every minute."

"Another young guy, Father, drove a John Deere tractor into town. He said his name was John Conradt, and he was looking for his mother and father, who had not returned from town.

"Father, do you know Amel and Genevieve Conradt, and has anybody seen either of them?"

"Yes, I know. Amel and Genevieve didn't make it, so my job is to tell him. Wait a minute. It is Chris's job now. Yeah, it's time he started working on some of the hard stuff, beginning with this young man, telling him his parents didn't make it.

"It looks like everybody's down here in the cafeteria, Sergeant Jones; it's time to introduce you to our small community."

Father was standing. "Okay, everyone, can I have your attention?" From behind him, Helen put her fingers to her lips and, with a loud whistle, said, "Everyone listen up. Father's going to speak."

"Thank you, Helen," he chuckled.

"First, I would like to introduce you to Ethan Jones, Sergeant Ethan Jones was a Navy SEAL. We were in Afghanistan simultaneously, and I asked him to be my second-in-command. Second, all of you have your instructions, assignments, and vehicles assigned to you.

"I will start in the lead Humvee with Sergeant Jones; the rest of you will follow us. We have about 25–26 miles. Don't drive any faster than 25–30 miles an hour; it is plenty fast enough. We are not in a huge hurry.

"Finish eating, then meet in the church parking lot. Move to your vehicles and mount up."

"Head them up and move them out!!!"

Father Mike was surprised at everybody shouting and clapping. They were anxious to go.

He and Sergeant Jones got up and went outside to the lead vehicle, taking the Humvee with all the radio equipment. They were going to lead the pack out of town. As he walked outside down the steps to the parking lot, he saw Chris talking to John Conradt, who was shaking his head. Chris looked over his way.

Father gave him a thumbs-up, turned around, and entered the Humvee.

Sergeant Jones turned on the radio to a military channel and listened in for anybody else talking; there was nothing but static. "I'll keep trying, Father, shutting it off for now."

It was not long before everyone emerged from the church's front doors, down the steps, and into the vehicles.

To make sure, he asked Helen to be the last one out with her family and checked to make sure everybody was out of the church. He looked for her and saw Helen at the front door. She looked at him, waving her arms to ask whether she should close the doors. Father waved back NO, because leaving them open would not make any difference. Somebody could use the shelter if it lasted a few days.

Father got out and checked up and down his side, making sure everyone was ready to go.

Jones got out of his side and checked up and down also. "Looks like everybody is loaded, Father."

Father circled his arm above his head to signal the drivers that they start the engines. When all the engines were started, he jumped back into the

Humvee, and they took off out of town, going north to the Black Hills at a steady pace of thirty miles an hour.

Father Mike was taking his time to be safe; a little over 1½ hours later, they arrived at the turnoff, from the highway to the grass. Heading cross-country, about 8 miles over an old game trail, he had to keep an eye on the vehicles behind them and ensure they didn't get stuck in the sand. After a while, they looked down at the hill, and he said to Sergeant Jones, "This is the place, and it seems like it will rain on us.

"Sergeant, we must get the tents up and shelter first."

Shelters were in place, and the storm pounded the new campers.

CHAPTER 7

Death is Coming

Pledge Your Soul

Prison Sioux Falls, South Dakota: Everyone in the prison who was still alive started to wake up, looking around, staring at each other, not recognizing anyone. "You all are so much younger," remarked creepy William.

Preacher was also standing there, looking around and wondering what was happening. "All right, Billy. What do you think is going on here?"

"I think, Preacher, we made a deal, and those of us alive are because of the deal. Looking around, not everybody made it; all the cell doors are open. Let's get out of here and see who else is alive. I hope we don't find any guards alive to stop us from getting out of here."

Billy Stone (Wolf), Preacher, and Creepy were in the first floor cells. They walked out of their cells and down the corridor of the main floor, where they ran into Vern Two Shoes, leader of the Native American group, and some of his allies.

"Okay, Wolf, what the fuck is going on here? All our tattoos are gone. I have all my teeth. I'm 30 years old, we're all younger. How did this happen?"

"Vern, as I was telling Preacher, we made a deal with the guy in black who came into the prison and turned the lights on. Remember him, all dressed in black and creepy-looking? This is the result. We can start over and do anything we want. It looks to me that most of the prison population is dead except for the ones who stood up and accepted his deal."

John Washington, or Snake, came walking up to the group. "I see all of you are standing here trying to figure out what the fuck happened. Does anybody have any answers?"

Snake had also shown up with his group of Black prisoners.

"What about it, Wolf? Do you have any fucken answers?" asked Dustin Toby, or Bulldog, leader of the Latino prisoners.

"As I was saying to Vern Two Shoes, it's the deal we made with the guy in the black suit who came in and turned the lights on. He said we would all survive if we went with him and did his bidding.

"I am guessing this is part of it being younger and stronger, faster, so we can conquer this country. But first, we need to go down and check and see if any guards could stop us, and then we need to find out how to get out of here. It looks like all the gates are open. Find the offices and see if any guards or the Warden are still alive."

As the group of ragtag prisoners walked through the prison, they found clothes lying on the floor—no bodies, frightening all of them. As they kept going, they found more piles of clothes until finally they reached the warden's offices—nobody was there.

Wolf naturally took charge, and everybody followed him downstairs to the armory. There were no guards there, and it looked like they were all dead. Let's get the weapons out of lockers. For now, only the leaders are going into the locker rooms. Vern Two Shoes, Snake, Bulldog, and I will look and get back to you all."

The small group leaders entered the locker rooms and found guard uniforms on the floor. Wolf said, "Look around for keys in some of those clothes. We need to unlock the lockers." It wasn't long before the Snake found a set of keys.

"Snake, go ahead, see if they work, open the locker!"

Searching for the right key, he finally opened the first locker, where he found M-16s, Glock handguns with ammunition clips, bulletproof vests, all kinds of equipment.

"Here is what I think we should do, Wolf. Let's divide this equipment up between the four of us so that everybody has an equal share to give to their people. Afterward, let's get something to eat. The cafeteria refrigerators and freezers run on generators, so food should still be good."

It took several trips to remove the weapons from the lockers and distribute them among the convicts. Once everything had been distributed, Wolf called everyone over to a cafeteria room where they could all sit down so he could address them on the next steps.

"While Badger and Skippy fix us something to eat we can talk about what to expect outside.

"First, though, we can't all travel as one group. For one thing, we don't have good relationships with each other. Several of us would kill each other before we got to our destination, the Black Hills.

"There are three ways to go west: the first is down through Nebraska along the border, the second is Interstate 90, and the third is cross-country Highway 44.

"Do you have any preferences in which one you want?"

John Washington was the first to speak, "I will take my guys, we're going to take the interstate. We are going to leave, and find some fucken vehicles, of some kind."

"All right you have first choice. Who is next?"

"I think we will take Nebraska. We can travel the border, hitting all the Indian reservations along the way to the Black Hills. See if we can find some recruits along the way!"

"All right, then. My group will go cross-country on Highway 44. First, we need to get transportation. We're going to need food and some new clothes. Those should be your three priorities. Spread out in Sioux Falls with your groups, find what you can, and try to avoid each other.

"Go back and tell your people, and as soon as we finish eating and you are ready to take off, remember our priority is to kill every person we meet. It was our agreement. And especially someone named Dylan."

"Bill, what is this Dylan thing all about?"

"I don't know. The only thing I know is they tried killing him before, and it did not work out, we're to look out for him and finish the job."

"Wait a minute, Boss. Are you fucken forgetting something? What about our people?"

"No, Dustin. I have not forgotten about your people. Your small group is welcome to travel with my group. We don't have any problems getting along, but if you choose, you can take your Latino people and try it on your own, no hard feelings."

"I will go back to talk to my people and see what they have to say. It's indeed better to have numbers."

Bill looked around, "All right, let's go eat and then conquer the world."

Everybody got up and went through the chow line for the last time.

After eating, each group got up, grabbed all their equipment, and headed out the front doors. They stepped outside the prison into the sun. A strange feeling came over all of them: They were free. There wasn't anybody watching them, nobody to stop them. Evil had been turned loose on the world.

Billy Stone was standing in the prison parking lot; of course, everybody else was trying to start the cars, but had no luck; the batteries must be dead. So, he took stock of who he had with him: Joseph Kelly (Preacher),

William Haglund (Creepy), Skippy (had trouble walking), Lefty (only had one arm), Smoke (had to keep him from burning everything down), Roy Cowboy, and Bear—who smelled really bad and needed scrubbing with lots of soap.

Dustin Toby and his group of Hispanics, Jeffrey Plugge, José nicknamed Rabbit because he is so fast, Luis Badger's face like one, and the worst, Raul Zero, the deadliest killer. No one lives when he is on a rampage.

"OK Skippy, is there any food remaining?"

"Yes, there are lots of ham and chicken sandwiches. Putting them all in coolers with ice should last three days."

"Skippy, I believe we should keep it our little secret. So, we're going to wait here until everybody leaves. I plan to walk north for about 1½ hours to the Army National Guard buildings, where we should find plenty of vehicles and equipment. And yes, Skippy I understand you have difficulty walking, we'll take our time. There is no hurry."

"Bill, have you experienced any changes recently? In the old days, you would've left everybody behind and taken off by now. But you're going to take time so that Skippy can keep up?"

"Preacher, I have been given a second chance; we all have. Am I still going to hell? Probably. I was just thinking this time I could be a little kinder when I can. Doesn't mean I wouldn't kill you if you crossed me.

"Let's move to the highway and follow it north for half a mile until we get to the turnoff for the National Guard Armory."

Struggling along, they had to carry the coolers, occasionally stopping for Skippy and the others to rest. Even though they were all younger, they hadn't had any kind of work for years.

Finally, they reached the gates to the National Guard compound.

Bill found the gates were not locked, and it didn't look like anybody was around. Several vehicles were sitting around: big one-ton trucks, Humvees, jeeps, pickups, and tankers.

First, Bill headed for the offices to see if he could find the vehicle keys.

They walked across the compound to the office doors, which were, sure enough, open. Nobody had locked up, so Bill walked in.

Someone had asked Bill how he knew where the keys were.

Bill irritated now, answered, "I know because I served, and this is where I was stationed."

"You mean you were in the Army?" Preacher asked.

"Yes, who do you think taught me how to kill? The only thing was, I did it too well. So, they got rid of me and sent me to prison. Here are the keys."

Bill opened the cabinet. All the keys were there, so he grabbed a handful and passed them out. "Now, see if you can start some of these vehicles."

While a few searched for supplies, Bill headed to the armory. Down the hall to the right, he found a big steel door. The handle turned quickly, but inside all the weapons were gone.

Bill returned outside to the yard. "Okay, everybody, spread out, check every room, find anything we can use, and bring it to the yard. I'm especially looking for clothes, food, and camping equipment."

Bill then walked to see how they were doing, starting the vehicles.

Preacher walked to Bill and said, "We started one of the big trucks, two of the Humvees, and one of the pickups. We had no luck with the rest."

"OK, Preacher, I understand. Could you make sure they're full of fuel? I had no luck with weapons. I am wondering if this facility was being phased out. Walking through the office areas, I noticed that there wasn't any paperwork on desks or computers. They looked pretty picked and clean."

Toby and a couple of his Mexican friends came out carrying big boxes.

Bill walked over, and shouted, "Toby, what did you find?"

"Bill, we found uniforms, boxes of boots, some camping equipment, a couple of tents, some pots and pans, and some kind of stove, but no food.

"Oh, there are a lot of blankets and sleeping bags, all in plastic, looking like they are ready to be shipped somewhere."

Bill, in charge, set the orders for the day.

"Preacher, take the truck back to the office area. After everybody has changed into fatigues and new boots, let's load up all the rest of the clothes, boots, camping equipment, sleeping bags, blankets, and anything else you think is useful.

"It is too late in the day to take off; after loading everything up, we will spend the night here and leave in the morning."

Bill looked around at his rag-tag group, "Tomorrow, we'll try to find a grocery store where we can get food and water to last us a while."

"And tequila!" yelled Zero, followed by shouts from the rest of Toby's group members—yeah, yeah, yeah!!!!!

In the back of his mind Bill thought, *This Zero person will be a problem. His reputation isn't good, and he doesn't play well with others. Alcohol will undoubtedly make things worse.*

But, it was going to be Toby's problem. He looked over at Toby and gave him an evil stare, and Toby knew exactly what he meant because Toby looked away from him and down.

The following day, they were up and going by 8 o'clock. Bill and Preacher took the lead Humvee. The rest filed behind in the other Humvees, pick-ups, and the 5-ton 6 x 6 military truck. Behind the truck was a large trailer they had found empty.

Bill drove the Humvee out the front gates and made a right-hand turn south, heading towards the Hy-Vee distribution center. As he went along, he noticed all the stores were empty. There was no one on the streets or driving around, which was spooky, and there were no sounds except their vehicles.

It wasn't long before they pulled into a Hy-Vee distribution center and approached the front doors. Again, Bill found the front doors were open, so he walked in.

Bill said, "This is a warehouse of food." He walked towards the back into the storage area, which was stacked with food, canned goods, and boxes.

Bill addressed the group, "Alright everyone, let's load the 5-tonner and the trailer with as much food as possible. We want canned goods and boxes, especially canned meat. Make sure all food is in boxes. Right, move out."

Amazingly, it didn't take exceptionally long before they were loaded with weeks' worth of food—and water, lots and lots of water bottles by the case.

Everybody was standing around waiting for Bill's directions.

Bill said, "I think we should stop at a hardware store. Ace Hardware would be a good place along the way. We will need shovels, axes, and stuff to build fires with; we won't have any electricity."

Diving out of the Hy-Vee parking lot, Bill turned south for a few miles and found a big Ace Hardware store. Pulling over, he stopped, got out, directed people on what to look for in the store, and turned them loose.

Bill then walked over and grabbed Toby. "I see Zero, and his buddies got hold of alcohol, especially tequila."

"Yes, Bill, they did, and so did your guys. They grabbed all kinds of whiskey and cigarettes, and they also loaded up with candy bars, nothing like having prisoners high on sugar and alcohol."

"Toby, we will have to keep an eye on them now they are armed with weapons, they could kill all of us.

No sooner had Bill said it, than the rest of them came out of Ace Hardware with shovels, axes, and chainsaws, and Zero came out with a machete. *Why would that sight scare the crap out of him, he wondered?*

Bill looked at his watch. "Good, we made a suitable time today. It's 10:30. Get into your vehicles. We're going to head down Highway 44. It's not too far from here. We will take a right turn. Stay a couple of vehicles or so away from each other. Don't crowd on the highway. All right, let us go!"

"Preacher, you have all the maps, and I have a couple of books on towns and cities in South Dakota, so you are the navigator. What is our first destination?"

"First, Bill, we must turn off at Lennix to Highway 44. Then, we're going to go west to Parker. Our first stop for the day should be down the highway to Platte Bovee. According to the book, Bovee is a ghost town, so we shouldn't have anybody give us a problem."

"Okay, Preacher, what is the first sizeable town?"

"Parker's population is approximately 1200. There might be a gas station. If we need fuel, we can go right through town on 4th Street. There is a food center, grocery store, and two gas stations. The first one is a Sinclair gas station. The second one is a Phillips 66. They are all close to 4th Street."

"Preacher, what we don't need is a grocery store. Let's stop at the first one, Sinclair, and see if they have diesel for these vehicles. We should top off the tanks when we can."

The drive west was quiet; Bill was not much of a talker. When they were getting closer to Parker City, a pickup truck was on the side of the road, and people were standing around.

"Hey Bill, some people are near that pickup truck on the right side of the road. Looks like two women and two men, waving at us and wanting us to stop."

"Okay, Preacher, I'll stop. I didn't expect to find victims so soon on the trip."

"What do you mean, Bill?"

"You know what happens when we meet people and what we should do, have you forgotten already?"

"I just think, Bill, we should find out first what's going on and talk to them. They want to join us and can help us in some way. Don't be too quick; that's all I am saying."

Bill was out first, followed by Preacher. "OK, let's talk to them."

As Bill walked up, the two couples looked all excited.

"You are from the Army, thank God. Our truck broke down, and we have been stuck here for hours." This came from a pretty girl about 26 years old, with blonde hair and a nice figure.

"No, lady, sorry. We are not from the Army. We're out here, just trying to survive."

"I do not understand why you all have Army uniforms and trucks, and you are not Army. What are you?"

Before Bill could answer, Zero, several of his friends, and some of his people rushed towards her, drunker than skunks. Zero was the first one to reach the young blonde gal, grabbed her, ripped off her clothes, and threw her to the ground. Before she knew what was going on, he was raping her. The others were standing around looking, waiting for their turn. One grabbed the other woman and did the same thing to her. At the same time, others tied up the two men.

Bill stood there, uncertain about what to do next.

Zero had his pants down to his ankles and was on top of her, and she was fighting, scratching, and biting him in his face, drawing blood; Zero swore, "You fucking bitch." He got up, grabbed his machete, and slashed her right between the eyes, killing her instantly. Blood everywhere.

Smoke and Cowboy, along with one of the Mexicans, had the other girl on the ground and tore her clothes off before anybody could do anything. Zero ran over and cut her head off. He was in a rage and killed both the men, who were tied up, before anybody could stop him. He was drunk and crazy, a crazy man, and everybody was afraid to get involved, fearing he would cut their heads off too. With a machete in his hand, raging around, blood covering him from head to toe, he looked like the devil himself.

All the others were pissed, yelling, yelling, and in a rage.

"What a waste."

"What did you do that for, asshole?"

"What a waste now we can't get our turn."

None of them had seen a naked woman for years; they had all been charged up, and now it was gone.

Bill stood there with his hand on a .45 handgun, not sure if he was going to kill Zero now or later. *It would give him a lot of pleasure when he did decide to kill that son of a bitch.*

"Preacher, let's go into Parker, get some fuel, and keep moving west until we get to Bovee, where we can stop for the night."

"Bill, what about the others?"

"Preacher, I don't care; they can catch up. They know where we are going, and they know where on Highway 44 all the way. Right now, I am too pissed to be around any of them."

"What is in your head, Bill?"

"Preacher, I haven't seen my share of dead bodies or even caused my share of dead bodies, but to see somebody hacked to death for no reason doesn't sit right with me. When he cut them up with a machete like that—I am going to kill him.

"Wait a second, Preacher. I see Toby. I'm going to have a word with him."

Bill got out of the Humvee. Toby saw Bill coming towards him. He turned to walk away, but Bill grabbed his arm.

"Toby, what was all that about? I told you, dammit, Zero is a problem. You need to do something about him. If you don't, I will, and you will not like my results."

"Bill, I don't know what I can do, I can't stop him."

"What you are saying, Toby, are you afraid of him?"

"Bill, you saw what he is like; he is crazy; he will kill all of us if we oppose him."

"I'll take care of the problem, Toby. Did you understand we needed intel from those people? Are there more people in the area? Are they armed? Now, we have nothing!"

"Okay, Bill, yes, I understand."

We are going to Bovee. Find a campsite where we can spend the night. You follow up behind us. Make sure you stop and fill up your vehicles if you can.

Skippy and Lefty came up to Bill. "Are you leaving?"

"Yes, we're leaving. Where were you two?"

"We were hiding, afraid we were going to be next. Can we go with you?"

"Yes, climb in the back," Bill got into the passenger seat.

"Okay, Preacher, you drive, let's go."

Preacher was driving, and they were heading down the highway when Preacher started a conversation about Bill's past again.

"Bill, you are upset about what happened, but didn't you get prosecuted for being a serial killer?"

"Yes, Preacher. You've been after me for years to find out how many people I killed to get prosecuted as a serial killer?

"I will tell you that it all started when I was a sniper in the Army Rangers. I was in Iraq and Afghanistan and enjoyed my work—so much that I would go out alone. Sometimes, the military doesn't appreciate personal initiative without orders, so they discharged me dishonorably.

"I moved to Pierre, South Dakota, and enjoyed fishing in Lake Oahe. I had a good job working in a boathouse fixing boats and motors, and nobody gave me any crap. Perfect for me.

"One day a terrible thing happened to a 70-year-old woman who was raped, beaten, and robbed by this gang member. He was apprehended, taken to court, and released on bail. It didn't sit well with me; I was in the courthouse on another matter. When he came out the front doors of the courtroom with his buddies smiling and laughing, he was turned loose to continue his reign of terror.

"I had the skill; I took matters into my own hands and found out where they were hiding out and by nighttime, I was outside their house. There was little light in those cheaper parts of town, so it was easy to lie in wait. Wasn't long before this character came outside to get something out of his car. He opened his car door and reached to the driver's side. He never knew what hit him; he backed out, and I stabbed him in the neck with a 12-inch blade and ripped it down his back to his spine. And I was gone.

"But of course, it was in the news, and people just thought it was another gang member who killed him. So, I was in the clear if I had only stopped.

"A couple of weeks later, two punks robbed a local bank and in the process killed the female teller and also the bank guard, and they got away.

"They were caught going south out of town by the state patrol and taken to jail. They went before the same judge, who set bail and then turned them loose. Of course, the town was outraged because two people who were well-liked had been killed.

"I just couldn't shake it out of my head—it was so wrong—so I waited a week, actually 10 days. I had already scouted where they were: in a trailer near the Outpost Lodge north of town. After scouting the area several times, I was sure I was set with a plan. They would go to the Outpost Lodge for supper and return to their trailer.

"Only that night when they returned to the trailer, I was waiting for them. They drove in their car, climbed out, and the driver shut the door. The passenger walked around to the front of the vehicle and up to the driver. I was in the dark behind them; I took the first one, thrust my knife to his neck, pulled downward to his back, spun around, and kicked the other one in the stomach. As he bent over, I stabbed him in the neck and cut his throat. Easy for a Ranger.

"The problem was somebody next door with one of those video cameras caught me on camera, so the police had my picture on TV, and it was not long before they arrested me. The rest, you know, I went to trial and was convicted as a serial killer because I killed three people the same way, and the police looked at my military record and figured I was a threat to society. Life in prison, no parole."

Skippy was in the backseat taking all this in. He commented, "So you're military, just like Captain Kirk."

Bill said, "Captain, who?"

Skippy was excited. "You know Bill. Kirk, from Star Trek."

"Oh, Skippy, you and your Star Trek and Star Wars."

"That's right, Captain Bill."

"What Captain Bill? What's he talking about, Preacher?"

Lefty said, "You are our leader, so you need a title. What about Captain Bill? It's perfect."

Skippy looked at the others, and they said yeah, great idea Skippy, Captain Bill. Perfect.

Skippy, "So, make it so."

A short time later, they arrived at Bovee Campground, grabbed wood to build a bonfire, and found chairs to put around the fire. Captain Bill brought out 1/5 of Jack Daniels. He handed out a cup to each of them and poured them all a healthy shot.

"It's been a long time since I've had Jack Daniels," Captain Bill took a long sip, and said, "yes, this is good."

"Captain Bill?"

"Yes, Lefty," You have a question?"

"You and the Preacher are younger, larger, and faster, while Skippy and I are the same. We may be a little younger, but we still have deformities. How do you explain that?"

"All I can tell you is I'm about the age I was when I first started in the Rangers in Iraq before I went off the rails. I'm also guessing I'm getting a second chance to avoid repeating the same mistakes.

"You were younger, relatively younger, when you lost your arm, and Skippy was also younger. So, whatever affected us didn't go back as far for you two. What about you, Preacher?"

"I am about the age when I started preaching way before I did anything wrong. And you two were imprisoned for life, assuming you must've killed somebody. Think about it: are you at the age when you did anything wrong?"

"We both talked about it and yes! We are younger, and it was before we did anything to warrant arrest. Which means what?"

Preacher looked at Bill asking for help with his eyes.

"Don't look at me, Preacher. You started this, go ahead and finish."

"I'm also guessing you both have second chances in life. It's the only logical explanation I can come up with."

"So, Preacher, does it mean we are virgins, never killed anybody, never robbed anybody, never stabbed anybody, and we're starting over brand-new?"

The silence was broken by the sound of trucks approaching the campground. Bill decided he was going to go ahead and have a few more drinks, eat some of the leftover sandwiches, and call it a night, and deal with the crap tomorrow when the sun comes up.

Bill picked up a sleeping bag and blankets, went over to a big pine tree, spread out his blankets, put his sleeping bag on top, and crawled in, reflecting on a long day.

It wasn't easy to sleep; everybody was still drinking, yelling, hollering, and playing music loudly, and he couldn't get any sleep with all the noise.

Somehow, he finally fell asleep. Then the sun shone in his eyes, waking him up.

Skippy walked over to him and handed him a cup of coffee. "Good morning Captain, did you sleep well, sir?"

"Please don't refer to me as Captain, thank you for the coffee. Is anyone else awake and active?"

"A few, mostly our guys, are fixing something to eat, and they made the coffee."

"What about the Mexicans? Are they up yet?"

"I think they were sleeping by the trucks. I did hear some of the gang members getting up; they were up longer than anybody else, drinking, screaming, hollering, and fighting with each other."

"Wow, Skippy, this is good coffee. I could use another cup, and then check what is happening in camp.

"I also have a chore I need to take care of first thing this morning, so Skippy go tell everybody to stay by the bonfire, eat their breakfast, and drink coffee."

"Is there anything I can do to help you, Captain?"

"No, thanks. I have to take care of this myself, and it shouldn't take long. I'll be back for breakfast."

Bill got up and stretched. *Yeah, sleeping on the ground is not good for my back.* He strapped on his .45, leaving his 9 mm behind.

Bill started walking toward the trucks, about 70 feet away. As he approached, Bill saw others getting up, stretching, and walking toward the bonfire. He stood there looking at them as they passed by him. Of course, the one he was looking for would be the last one to get up. Zero lazily walked toward Bill and smiled from ear to ear.

"Bill, you son of the bitch! Do you want something, pendejo motherfucker?"

He was about 10 feet from Bill. *Zero looked at me, and he could see it in my eyes!!*

Zero reached for his machete, which was strapped to his back. He raised it, smiled at Bill, and charged. Bill put one round in his head and one in his chest. And that was the end of Zero.

Bill walked back to the bonfire. Skippy came over with another cup of coffee and some kind of egg sandwich.

Bill stood there looking around, waiting for some kind of response from the other Mexicans. They all looked at him; they could see it in his eyes. If anyone tried anything, he would kill them just as easily. Besides, all his men had their weapons out, holding them in front of their bodies. If there were going to be a fight, it would end right here; the tension was high.

Toby stood up and said, "Everyone, when you are finished eating, let's get mounted on the trucks. We've got a long way to go."

Toby's way of defusing the situation.

Preacher and Bill were looking at the maps. "Bill, we need to cross the River Lake Francis Case. After we cross into the Badlands, we'll turn north and go through the Pine Ridge Indian Reservation."

"It might be nothing, but we might have a fight getting through, Preacher."

Preacher was loud, "Listen everyone. We are going through the Indian Reservation. Make sure your weapons are loaded and ready for action. Once through the Indian reservations, we will turn west to the Buffalo grasslands.

"Is that right, Bill?"

"Captain Bill," piped up Lefty, "he is now Captain Bill."

"Yes, Preacher, that's the plan. When we reach Buffalo, the grasslands will run out of roads, and some vehicles will be useless.

"I've been talking with Cowboy, who tells me there will be several ranches along the way with horses, and yes, they will be our transportation from now on. Let's head out if everybody's finished eating and loading their gear."

Preacher was driving. Lefty and Skippy were in the back seat. And Preacher always had to be talking about something.

"Bill, you are pretty damn handy with a .45."

"Well, there are some things you never forget. Now drop it. Concentrate on your driving. I plan to stop in Winner, a large town where we can find fuel for the trucks and may pick up some more food. Look for more transportation. Cowboy says we're going to need a lot of saddles, bridles, and stuff for horses. He said it should be a good place to look, the last large town."

"Yes, Señor Captain Bill, you are our fearless leader."

"Preacher, you smartass, don't think I won't get even, ha, ha, ha."

The rest of the trip to Winner was without incident; everybody was getting along fine. Once they got to the town, it was time for Cowboy to do his thing. First, they needed to find him an oversized truck to load all the horse stuff in.

"Preacher, let's stop here by this GMC truck lot, and see if we can find a diesel truck for Cowboy to load his saddles and stuff in."

As Bill climbed out of the Humvee, he waved Cowboy over. "Cowboy, pick yourself a nice big diesel truck and see if you can start it.

"We'll just wait here while you go get your saddles, bridles, and whatever else you need. Take Smoke with you and Jeffrey Bear."

"But Captain, Jeffrey smells; I don't want him in the same truck."

"That's a good point. Right, here is what we are going to do. This is a big dealership, and in most big car dealerships, they have showers, bathrooms, lunchrooms, and suchlike. Take Bear in there and wash him down with soap and water. It should solve your problem."

"Captain, who will tell him he will be taking a shower? He's a big man; I don't want to tangle with him."

"Okay, Cowboy, I'll take care of it."

"Jeffrey, come over here. I want to talk to you."

Bear sauntered over to where Bill was standing, and Bill didn't want to stand too close to Bear; one could tell he needed a shower.

"Okay, Jeffrey, here's the deal: you either go in there and shower and soap down to clean off and change clothes, or I will leave you here when we go! You understand?"

"I don't need a shower Captain..."

"Jeffrey, you stink, we can't stand it anymore; now do as you're told."

"I smell?"

"Jeffrey, it's more than a smell. It's a rank specter. Now go!"

Cowboy, Jeffrey, and Smoke went to the building to take care of Jeffrey's shower.

Bill walked over to the Humvee and looked to see if there was any more coffee.

"Here, Captain, you want a doughnut with your coffee?"

"Lefty, have you been hiding donuts?"

"Just my private stash and I share it with Skippy."

"I'll take one, don't let the others find out you're hiding food."

It didn't take as long as Bill had thought. Cowboy and his crew found the keys to a big GMC 1-ton diesel. They got it started, backed it up and hooked it to a four-wheel enclosed white trailer. As they drove out of the lot, Cowboy waved, and then they went down the street, with the radio blaring country-and-western music. They had to have found a CD because there were no radio stations anymore.

Cowboy returned about three hours later, loaded with equipment.

Bill gave everybody the signal to load up, and the Preacher turned the Humvee around.

As they headed out of town, Bill's thoughts turned to their next stop, the White River Bridge, where they could cross the river.

It wasn't too long before they were at the bridge. Bill got out, walked up to the bridge, and checked it out, making sure it was still solid and in one piece.

The others got out and stood behind him. From their conversations, he gathered that they had never seen this river before.

"Yes, it's white," Bill said, "it's the dirt, the clay, that turns the water white, not suitable for drinking or anything else. We're starting in the Badlands and going through the Pine Ridge Indian Reservation, so be on your guard. The bridge is safe; we'll go first.

"Alright, Preacher, let's GO.

"Do you want to wait, Lefty and Skippy? To make sure we make it before you go cross?"

"Oh no, Captain. We are with you all the way." And they climbed in. They drove across the bridge without any problem and started to head west at about 60 miles an hour, beginning to get into the Badlands. Preacher asked, "How does anybody live out here? How did the Indians end up out here anyway?"

"It was the good old USA. The Army pushed them into this part of the country. There are Indian reservations all along the borders of Nebraska and South Dakota. Some are better than others, but it's pretty barren around here. Just keep driving, keep your eyes on the road. The rest of us will watch to ensure we don't get surprises."

They had to drive through the Indian Reservation to Cedar Bluff and then Wanblee. Nobody was in sight except a couple of stray dogs. It looked like nobody had survived in this part of the country.

"Okay, Preacher, head north on Highway 44 towards Cedar Pass and the interior, about 30 miles to the Buffalo Gap Grassland."

The next hour was pretty quiet until they got to the town of Scenic.

"Okay, Preacher, I'll take over."

Preacher and Bill got out and traded places. Bill got behind the wheel and immediately turned off the road into the grass. They slowly headed southwest for about 45 minutes until the perfect spot.

Bill climbed out and walked up to the front of the Humvee. Preacher and the others joined him, looking at the rolling hills and grasslands. *Yeah, this is what I had in my visions: this exact place.*

Bill turned to face the others. "The first task is to set up some sort of camp. Toby, if you take your guys and unload the trucks, my guys will start figuring out how to set up the tents. Cowboy, you and Creepy go ahead of us and find a good way down the valley for our trucks.

"We are looking for a flat area near a stream of water. OK, Cowboy?

"Sure thing, Captain. But where's Creepy? I haven't seen him for a while."

"When was the last time you saw him?"

"At our last camp, he was helping the new Mexicans load the truck."

"What new Mexicans, Toby?"

"Two came into camp during the night; I told them they could stay."

"Without talking to me?"

"I was not interested in talking to you after Zero, and you never told me your plans for Zero. Isn't that right?"

"Preacher, Cowboy?"

"We have you covered, captain!"

"Well, Toby, I am guessing we would find Creepy hacked to pieces at our last camp?"

Bill stared at Toby. Now is a good time for us to cut ties. "Toby, you are going to unload half of everything. Then you will take your men and leave with the other half. If I have more problems with you, I will deal with them like Zero."

Then two young Mexicans stepped forward. "Toby, why do we listen to this white trash? Let's just take everything. How is this pendejo going to stop us? They look weak."

Toby held up his hand. "Slow down, you two; I will handle this!"

"Now get to it, Toby, unless you want to make a stand right here, right now. I will oblige you either way. Make your play!"

"We will leave, but I don't think this is the end of it, Bill!"

"Oh, I think it is!"

After Toby's men unloaded all supplies and equipment, they drove off in a Humvee, a 5-ton truck, and a pickup and headed south.

"Captain, I feel a lot better with those men gone. Creepy did not deserve to die like he did."

"Preacher, I feel the same, now let's get busy and start building a new camp.

"Let's load everything up; there's a spot that looks pretty good and has a flat area on a hill. We'll have to cross a stream and climb a hill, but it will be fairly easy."

Bill realized it took more time than he figured to get to the top, but once they did, it was a great spot from which one could see forever.

Bill felt good for the first time in a while. After unloading everything, he turned to Smoke. "I can't believe I am going to say this, but I will put you in charge of building and keeping the campfire going. We can cook some food when we've finished setting up the tent. Lefty and Speedy, you're going to be our cooks. The rest of us will do hard labor.

"We only have a few hours of daylight left, and I am hungry."

Everybody laughed, they needed a good laugh.

After a dinner of fried potatoes and spam, they went to bed pretty early; it had been a long day.

*****

Next Morning

Speedy and Lefty were up early, fixing breakfast.

Bill got up and walked out of the tent. Lefty handed him a cup of coffee. He grabbed a seat and sat down. Bill gazed towards the east, admiring the sunrise. *What a beautiful day.*

"I see we have plenty of wood, where's Smoke? We don't need any more firewood."

"I haven't seen him this morning, Captain. We've been up cooking pretty early."

Getting off his chair, Bill started looking for Smoke and then spotted a column of smoke to the south.

Bill, concerned, wondered what it could be, he hoped it was not Smoke out there starting fires; he could burn this whole forest down around them.

"Preacher, Cowboy, wake up and get out here. We need to go look for Smoke."

*****

About 35 Minutes Later

After walking through trees and brush, they stopped at the forest's edge. About 30 yards away, they could see what was burning. Someone had tied Smoke up to a tree and set him on fire.

Bill grabbed Cowboy by the arm, "Stop. You can't do anything for Smoke. He's been dead for a long time, and not much remains. He's almost burned up completely; you could just see some of his face."

"Captain, we need to do something for him!"

"I understand how you feel, Cowboy, but this is a trap. If you step out in the open, somebody will cut you down. Let's return to our camp, pack everything, and leave before they come for us."

Packing up took about two hours. They headed west through some pretty rough country.

The plan was to get to Highway 40 and go northwest to Keystone Dakota. They should be able to find an area to get lost in and hide away from the Mexicans.

Bill thought it had started to be such a beautiful day, and now he was down two men. Both were killed and died horribly.

They now had to run for their lives!

CHAPTER 8

Chadron Hills

Days of Rain

After two days of heavy rain, fierce winds, thunder, and lightning, the weather finally let up on the third day, giving Matt's team a window to leave.

Benjamin walked into the cabin. "I've been out scouting, and all the trees crossing the road are down due to the wind. I've cut a path through them to get down to the highway. So, right now, I would like to have a cup of coffee."

"What time is it? Does anybody know?"

"Yes, Boss, it's almost 7 o'clock."

"Okay, let's get things moving. We should plan to leave within 60 minutes. We've already loaded our gear, so all we have to do is eat something and go.

"Thanks, Ben, for doing all the work cutting drowned trees and moving them out of our way.

"Was Buck outside with you, Ben?"

"Yes, he took off over the hill as usual but returned a few minutes ago. He is sitting outside now, eating the food and water I put out for him."

"Ben, you want some scrambled eggs and hash browns, Chuck fixed up?"

"No thanks. I am good with coffee."

"Okay, Chuck, who's first in the bathroom this morning?"

"Your turn, Boss; I was up earlier, getting antsy about moving on."

"Okay, I won't take too long." *All I needed to do was pee in the morning, brush my teeth, and wash my face. I gave up shaving.*

Matt exited the bathroom and crossed to the front door, taking one last look around. This was a wonderful place.

Matt decided to ride and let Chuck drive for a while. He had a thermos of hot coffee along with his coffee cup. He poured some for himself and handed the thermos back to Ben. "Chuck, do you want some coffee?"

"No, thanks. I had plenty this morning."

Chuck was driving along when Ben suddenly told him to pull up on that hillside.

"Boss, I want to show you something." They all got out and walked over to the side of a prominent hilltop, from which they could see the town of Chadron.

Ben handed Matt a pair of field glasses.

"Matt, see how it's catching up with us. If you look at the town, you can see buildings disappearing."

"Yes, I can see, over to the east, they're starting to disintegrate.

"See the big, tall building to the left?" Matt pointed, "That's where I did much of my teaching on campus. I taught there for six years; it was one of the finest periods of my life.

"Right, we need to get out here before it catches us; Chuck, you're still driving."

They slowly drove down the hill, dodging trash and tree limbs on the road. Eventually, they reached Highway 385 North Road.

It was a pretty clear road now. As they turned the corner to go west, Walmart was on the top of a hill to the left. Next to the airport, there was a car dealer. They turned at the airport, going north up 385 to Hot Springs, South Dakota. In a few hours, they hoped to be in the Black Hills.

"Are we going straight through to the Black Hills, boss, or are we making any stops on the way?"

"I want to stop at the Stateline Casino to pick up some additional food."

On the drive to the Nebraska–South Dakota border, the landscape was hilly, with grassy sandhills and a few antelope and cattle.

They were gradually climbing on the way north to South Dakota. It wasn't long before they reached the Nebraska–South Dakota border. A large building was visible on the horizon to the left side of the Highway. As they got closer, a sign announced the Stateline Restaurant and Casino.

"Pull in here, Chuck. Let's check this place out. Usually, places in the middle of nowhere have big diesel generators, and electricity lines are not always dependable in these far-out places. Pull in here and park."

"Look, Boss. A couple of pickups, two older cars, and one big self-contained camper are by the building. That's a sweet-looking ride."

Matt wasted no time exiting the truck and heading for the front doors.

He pulled out his .45 and kicked through the doors. Buck was first in, and Matt walked in, ready for action. But nobody was there. It was quiet, and nothing other than people's clothes lay on the floor and around the bar.

Chuck followed him in with his M-16 at the ready. "I'm here just in case you need backup, Matthew."

Ben followed Chuck in; they all stood there looking around at all the alcohol, the usual casino games, and signage around the walls. Gambling never really appealed to Matt; several people he had known in the past had serious problems with gambling, which then ruined their families.

But Matt didn't mind taking a drink, he should grab a good bottle of whiskey on the way out.

"Chuck, let's check the freezers and see if we can find anything frozen.

"Ben, see if you can find some ice and coolers."

Chuck found several packages of hamburgers, frozen bread, T-bone steaks, rib-eye steaks, sirloin steaks, and a couple of frozen hams.

Ben returned with the two big coolers. "I didn't find much ice, but I did find a lot of dry ice. There are a couple more coolers in the back if you need more, Matt."

"Perfect, Ben. Let's pack up, using the dry ice around the steaks and hamburgers.

"Ben, I'll need a couple more coolers to finish packing the stakes."

"OK, Chuck is coming right up."

Matt was helping load the coolers. "Chuck, I noticed an ice chest outside. All the ice could be out there. Let's get a cooler filled with as much ice as possible."

A couple of hours later they had everything loaded up in the trailer.

As Matt and Ben finished loading, Chuck started the RV quickly.

"What do you think, Boss? This would make a suitable place to sleep instead of on the ground. It has two pullout extensions on each side, so it's huge inside."

"I think it's great, can you drive it?"

"Boss, you know I can drive anything."

"Okay, Chuck, I'm just checking. If you can drive the RV, I will drive the Chevy.

"Let's go back in and check around to see if we've missed anything."

They walked back into the casino. Matt walked up behind the bar and grabbed two bottles of Kentucky whiskey. "Guys, go ahead and grab whatever you want. This is the last opportunity."

They didn't need another invitation, each grabbed what they liked to drink. Chuck had a box filled with Wild Turkey bourbon and was surprised to see Ben grab two big bottles of Scotch, black label. Good for him.

All three went back into the casino and hauled out cases of their favorite drink. After a short confab, they realized that it could be the last time they saw bottled alcohol again.

*****

On The Road Again

Matt drove the Chevy straight out of the parking lot onto Highway 385 N. to Hot Springs, South Dakota.

Ben and Chuck were in the RV. Ben had never seen an RV, so he pushed all the buttons, walked around, checked the bathroom, and so forth. He discovered the RV had a kitchen and two queen-size beds. A TV had several CDs he thought were pretty cool and, of course, country-and-western music CDs. He was in his element, and Chuck was also, so they got along pretty well. And they tapped one of those bottles.

Buck was in the Chevy with Matt, who was taking the lead. They were driving down the highway at 65–70 mph, which, as Matt remembered, was a good way to Hot Springs.

A few hours later, they pulled into the edge of Hot Springs and pulled into a campground, It was time to stop for the day; Matt needed something to eat, a little Jack and Diet Coke. He wondered if it tasted the same as it did years ago.

Ben and Chuck were busy setting up the camper. It looked like they found some briquettes to put on the barbecue pit. Buck jumped down behind Matt as he got out of the Chevy, and they walked back to the RV to see how they were doing.

"Hi guys, you made it okay. It looks like you are setting up a barbecue. What are you cooking?"

"Chuck is going to barbecue some of those steaks we found at the casino. He thawed about four out on his way here."

"Chuck, sounds delicious!"

"I thought, Matt, we would have rib-eye steak, potatoes, and baked beans. Ben found some French bread in the casino. And for dessert, Rocky Road ice cream."

"What? I can't wait. Chuck, that's another reason I brought you along. Ha, ha."

With a little chuckle and a smile, Chuck just waved.

After eating such a fine meal, Matt went and took a shower, said his good nights, and crawled into bed in the back bedroom. *Humm, it even has a fabulous bathroom. It's time for sleep. Wait a minute.* "Yes, Buck, you're welcome. Jump up here."

Ben went outside to make his rounds and report to the relevant person.

What's pushing on my back? Matt rolled over. "Okay, Buck, do you want to go out? I'll get up and let you out. I slept so soundly last night, which makes it harder to get up and go." He got his jeans, shirt, socks, and boots and headed for the door. No sooner did the door open than Buck was out like a flash.

Come to think of it, I also need to relieve myself. Matt exited the door and walked over to a tree, relieving himself.

"Shit Ben don't sneak up on a guy like that, you could get shot. Make some noise when you walk up behind somebody, it could keep you alive."

"Sorry, Boss, I didn't mean to frighten you."

"You didn't frighten me exactly; you just startled me slightly.

"How was your night? Are there any new developments?"

"None; it's the same quiet with many stars out last night."

"No information from your friends?"

"Evil has been turned loose, and it's headed our way from three different directions. It is looking for someone important to them, but the person's identity is kept from me.

"Boss, I see you found some fishing gear."

"Yes, it's out of the RV; the owner has many fishing and hunting equipment!

"I'm taking the spin rod and a couple of lures down to the stream to see if I can catch us some breakfast. It's been a long time since I've been able to fish."

Matt put on a trout lure and cast it out in the stream, slowly reeling it in. WOW! He got one. What a thrill! He made another cast, but nothing this time. He moved up the stream, cast again, and caught another one. It was a nice rainbow trout. *Let's see if I can get one more.*

He made another cast out, slowly reeling it in, and BAM!! A third one. Christ almighty, what a great feeling. It will take me a few minutes to clean and wash them off in the water. He should go back to the camper and find a frying pan. He liked fried fish, fried potatoes, and hot coffee—a perfect breakfast.

By the time Matt returned to the RV, Chuck was sitting at the picnic table drinking coffee; Ben had already fixed coffee for them all that morning.

Grabbing a few pieces of wood and throwing them in the fire pit started a small fire. Matt looked inside for a frying pan, potatoes, oil, flour, salt, and pepper. He also needed a mixing bowl.

Matt asked Chuck if there were any mixing bowls in the RV.

Ben said he would get one. "What else do you need?"

"Grab some plates, forks, knives, another frying pan."

Matt grabbed a knife and started peeling potatoes. Looking over at Chuck, he thought he looked slightly frayed that morning.

"Chuck, did you have a rough night ?"

"Just leave me alone and let me drink my coffee peacefully."

Ben came out with the needed items, so Matt put the grill over the fire pit and cut up the potatoes, which went first in the frying pan. He splashed oil in the second pan, and set it beside the other one in which the potatoes were cooking, then rolled the trout in flour, put on salt and pepper, and within 40 minutes they had a great breakfast,

Chuck was a little queasy and lost his cookies when he saw the trout on his plate.

"Ben, it looks like there's more for us. Chuckie, you must have the Turkey Bourbon flu; I hear it's going around.

"Chuck, did you see the flock of turkeys this morning?" Matt had to laugh at that one, ha, ha.

"Did you want any of this, Ben?"

"I will try a little taste of the trout because I'm curious. I ate steak last night, so I must be careful how much I eat. Remember, I've never eaten before I came down here. So, it's all new to me, but another cup of coffee with this little fish is undoubtedly allowed."

After breakfast, they cleaned up the area and loaded everything. Matt checked with Chuck again to make sure he could drive. After another puking session behind a tree, he returned and said he was good to go.

Buck and Matt started down the highway to Hot Springs. The first thing Matt thought about was finding somewhere to get diesel fuel; it might be the last stop for fuel.

Matt drove into Hot Springs and pulled up to the first gas station. He could tell somebody had already wired the pumps, so he had to hook up their generator and start pumping fuel into the vehicles.

Matt looked at Chuck and Ben. "Do you know what this means? Someone else is around besides us. So, keep your eyes peeled and keep your weapons close."

"Boss, do you plan to stop anyplace else here in Hot Springs?"

"No, we will keep going and move through town as fast as we can; we don't want to get ambushed."

They finished filling the vehicles and the extra fuel tanks.

They climbed in the vehicles and took off through the middle of Hot Springs on 385, north, turning towards Evan's Plunge. Then, they jogged eastward and back to the north, closing in on the Black Hills.

Heading down the road at a good clip, Matt saw detour signs. It wasn't long before they saw that the road ahead was all torn up on both sides of the interstate. It looked like significant construction. His only option was a detour on a gravel road to the west, road 333.

Matt stopped the Chevy truck, got out, and returned to Chuck's window. "It looks like we have to take gravel roads the rest of the way. Do you have the radio phones hooked up and charged?"

"Yeah, they're all charged up. I'll get your pair. Here, take this set."

"Chuck, going down gravel roads is a little different than going down a paved highway, so we must stay in touch. Start at about 40 and see how it goes. Let me know if you have any problems. The RV may experience some difficulties navigating gravel roads. Okay?"

Matt turned the Chevy left onto the gravel road and picked up speed to about 40. He had driven gravel roads before, so it wasn't a big deal for him, even pulling a loaded trailer. He kept checking the rearview mirror to see how the RV was doing. It wasn't long before Chuck was on the headset.

"Matt, there's too much dust. I can't see anything. You need to slow down."

"Okay, Chuck, I see it is pretty dry around here; I'll slow down; there's no real hurry."

After driving about 15 miles, Buck became restless beside Matt, whining and fidgeting.

With a diesel, you have a lot of noise. Matt opened the window, and then he could hear what upset Buck—gunshots, more than one, several.

Matt shouted into the headphones, "Stop!" He could see Chuck was 100 feet behind him. Chuck slowly came up behind Matt and stopped.

Matt told him over the headphones, "I can hear some gunfire ahead, and it seems like we are driving right into it."

Chuck and Ben got out to stand beside Matt. "Can you hear it?"

Both Chuck and Ben stood there for a second and nodded. "Yes, we can hear it. It sounds like it's just over this hill before us."

"What do you think it is, Boss?"

"I don't know. We'll need full gear, headphones, extra ammo, and water. We're going to creep up this hill, look over the top, see what we can see. Get your binoculars out."

They walked up to the base of the hill, got down, and started creeping through the grass. They could smell the grass and the dust from the road. It was a good thing none of them had allergies; otherwise, they would be sneezing their heads off.

Matt was ahead, flattened out, scoping down the hill with his binoculars. Beside him, Chuck started doing the same thing; Ben was sitting behind them, holding Buck so he wouldn't take off down the hill after the bad guys if there were any bad guys.

"What do you see, Boss, anything?"

"Well, I see a truck pulling a trailer loaded with hay bales, one Humvee with several men pinned down behind the bales, looks like 6–7 guys. The firepower is limited: one M-16, and the others are handguns."

Matt scanned left. "The other group is behind the trees with five long rifles, 30-30s, and a 3.6 rifle, old military rifles, single-shot with a six-shot clip. I can't tell what the other one is. At first, I thought it was a shotgun, which sounded like a 12-gauge. But it would be stupid because you don't have any distance to the road to do any damage. So, it also tells me they're not very bright."

Matt continued. "Further down the road, I see somebody set up a barricade so the guys on the road couldn't go forward or backward. The guys on the road look like diligent men who don't have the firepower to defend themselves. They probably didn't expect any trouble, and I'm guessing the guys among the trees set the barricade up to trap them. If I were to pick sides, I would go with my gut and pick the guys on the road.

"So, this hill goes to the west quite a long way; we can follow it on this side, staying hidden. Go about a half mile west, cross north into the trees, and come up behind the bad guys, who will never see what is coming."

"I like it, Boss. We have about six hours before dark, so we should get moving if we're going to go."

"All right. I'll start with Buck taking the lead, and you two can follow. Keep a reasonable distance between us. We can move at a good pace hidden under this grassy hill, move out, move out."

Buck took the lead, and Matt followed him. Buck was looking and sniffing the air, trying to pick up any scent. He could hear the shooting, and Buck was headed in the same direction.

Buck came to a halt; Matt cautiously crept up in the grass to the top of the hill beside Buck and lay down in the grass, very still. Buck then turned back and looked at Matt with extremely cautious eyes.

Matt quickly looked over the hill, spying two men coming their way. They were armed. Matt turned, signaled Chuck and Ben to join him, and whispered "Two guys coming this way. I'm sure they're trying to do rear action on the people on the road. We're going to cut them off here. I prefer to do it quietly and use my knife; I don't want to warn the others among the trees.

"Chuck, you and Ben cover us. Buck and I can handle these two.

"Get ready, Buck. Go." Buck was up and running and took the first one in the front by the neck. Matt was behind Buck, taking the second one and stabbing him right in the neck. No sounds were made.

Buck was so efficient he went back hunting, but Matt had to stop him. He looked at Matt and understood, so he backed up, sat down, and waited for his following command.

"It should leave three more. Let's go; we need to hustle down to the trees. Go, Buck!"

Taking the lead, Matt quietly headed down to the trees, through a path in the trees to the other side. The tall buffalo grass was waving in the wind; and he could smell the scent. Using hand motions only, Matt moved Chuck and Ben to the back where the bad guys hid among the trees.

They were so intent on watching the people on the road that they had no idea Matt's team was crawling behind them. Buck was in front of Matt, waiting for a command.

Matt raised a hand, and everybody stood up, locked, and loaded.

Matt decided to warn them, "All of you raise your hands, you are covered, don't make any sudden moves." Any rational person would have seen they were covered and had no exit. These guys weren't sensible. They turned in unison and started firing; and Matt's group cut loose. Chuck was on the left of the line, so he took the little guy on Matt's left with two shots in the chest and one in the head with his M-16. Matt took the middle one and did the same.

Ben was on the other side, and to Matt's astonishment, he had a bow and arrow. His guy was sitting there with an arrow right through his head. It was over in seconds.

Matt looked at Buck, and could tell he was disappointed. Buck had wanted to get into the fight.

Satisfied with the firefight, Matt said, "Chuck, Ben, let's greet the guys on the road and give them the good news."

Matt called out, "Hello! You all on the road! We are friendly; don't shoot us!!"

CHAPTER 9

Lee's Ranch

The Hunt

Fern Singletree was on her hands and knees crawling up a small sandhill to peer over the edge at a small grove of trees below. She had spotted a big, fat, four-point, white-tailed buck sniffing around the ground. Over her shoulder, she could see Dakota nocking an arrow in his compound bow

Fern, on the other hand, liked her Browning Cobra two-cam bow. It might be an older bow, but she still had a good 60-pound pull, plenty to bring down even a buffalo.

Fern nocked a 3–3 blade arrow into her bow, each blade razor-sharp. She got up on one knee, drew her bow, and, with a slow breath, let go. It whistled through the air towards the four-point buck, who had no idea he was now dead.

Dakota and Fern waited about 15 minutes to ensure the deer was dead. Then they walked up the hill and back down the other side toward the trees. It was a nice, fat, four-point buck. They pulled out their knives, and in no time, they had gutted it and were ready to take it back to camp.

Dakota ran back to fetch the horses they had tied about 100 yards away—two riding horses and one packhorse to carry the deer. After loading the deer on the packhorse and securing it, they returned to camp, about five miles away.

Fern figured they'd arrive around sundown to hang the deer in a tree to cool off, clean up, and get something to eat.

The camp was taking shape with four big army tents in four areas, like a four-star resort; people had been divided by age and sex, which determined who lived where. The cooking area was covered with an overhead tarp, and some of the ladies, with Helen in charge, took care of all the cooking duties.

At a makeshift corral some distance from the camp, Fern and Dakota tied up their horses, unsaddled them, and let them loose into the corral. As they returned to camp, the two hungry hunters found several tables where people were already eating.

Fern could see Father Mike, Master Sergeant Jones, Lee, and Donald at another table with a couple of maps spread before them. They were having an intense discussion. Father Mike noticed Fern and Dakota enter and waved them over.

"Did you two have any luck?"

"Yes, Father, a nice, fat, white-tailed buck. We have it hanging in a tree outside camp, high enough that no predators can reach it."

"Wonderful. It will feed us for at least a few days. Why don't you two get some food and come back to sit with us at the table? You might be interested in what we're discussing."

Fern and Dakota returned to the table just as Lee talked about hay. "I have several big round bales on my ranch, each weighing ninety pounds or more, and we're going to need more feed for the horses and animals. We'll have to go somewhere to pick up some feed. I have forty bales at my ranch.

"We still have our big diesel trucks, all four passenger vehicles, and if we take one of the Humvees, we should have enough room for people to help load the trailers. I have trailers down there, so we can hook up the truck to the trailers, load the bales on, and haul them back, stacking them by our corral; what do you think, Father Mike?" "

"That sounds like a plan, Lee."

"I'm going to go," Father Mike, responded.

"Are there any volunteers?" Lee looked around.

Master Sergeant Jones was the second to volunteer.

"What about you, Donald?"

"Father, I still need to do more work on the corral fence and prepare a good spot for you to unload those bales."

"Fern and Dakota?"

"I'm sorry, Father. We need to finish the deer in the morning. It must be skinned, butchered, and put on ice as soon as possible."

"Okay, then I'll talk to Angus and Jarvis Sanchez to see if they'll be willing to go along."

"We could use one more Father."

Fern suggested, "You could take Bradley. He's young and strong, and you could use him."

"Okay, see everyone at 7:00 AM." Father ended the meeting. "Get something to eat; it's going to be an early morning, so get as much rest as possible."

Morning came too soon. Father Mike had slept deeply, and it was tough to get up and move. He noticed it was becoming harder after working so much. Being a priest, he never had to work this hard.

Father left his tent and headed to the cook's shack. Ellen, of course, had breakfast and coffee ready. It looked like he was the last to get up and get to the table.

Father waved a good morning to everybody.

They all slightly nodded or waved, concentrating on coffee, eggs, bacon, and toast.

"Ellen, good morning. I see you have eggs and bacon. Where did you rustle those up from?"

"On one of our trips back to town, I knew where some chickens were, we gathered them all up, all egg layers, and brought them back here with plenty of feed. The bacon was the last from Jim's grocery store, where the generators were still running and everything was frozen, so enjoy it, it's the last of it, at least until we get some hogs and make our bacon."

After Father had finished eating, he got up and dug in his pocket. "Here, Ellen, a tip," he said, and gave her a crisp $20 bill.

"Thank you, Father, and where exactly will I spend this money?"

"You can go buy a hog, Ellen," and they both had to laugh at how absurd a comment it was.

When everyone had finished eating, they started heading for the trucks. Father climbed into the driver's seat of the Humvee, Jones claimed shotgun, and the Sanchez brothers climbed in the back. Lee was driving his truck with Bradley. Ace Hardware Bill hopped into Lee's truck at the last second.

"I want to go along; I need some exercise."

They angled south and took country gravel roads to the west and south again to Lee's ranch, a 60-minute trip.

As they came over a hill and down into the valley, they could see Lee's ranch. Driving up to the house, they saw the hay bales laid out in the field, ready to be picked up.

Father Mike looked at the hay bales. "Our work is cut out for us. This is my first time picking up bales, and what a beautiful place this is!"

Lee walked over to a big John Deere tractor that had a big fork hook at the front of it. Lee waved at Bill to bring the truck over. Lee opened the back door, reached behind the back seat, pulled out some jumper cables. Lifting the truck's hood, he hooked them up to the positive and negative and hooked the other ends to the tractor's batteries. Lee waited a little and jumped in the tractor. It took a little urging, but it started, making life so much easier for them rather than trying to load hay bales by hand

With hard work, it took them around three hours to load 20 bales on the flatbed. Lee was the only one experienced, so the rest of them followed his lead, and it went pretty smoothly.

With Father Mike taking the lead again in the Humvee, they headed back to camp.

They were about 7 miles down the gravel road when Father started slowing down the first hill. Approaching the bottom, it looked like something was blocking the road ahead, near the tree line.

It didn't make sense. They had just come through there that morning on their way to the ranch. Father Mike slowed down to about 100 feet from the obstruction. He could see trees and brush lying across the road, blocking it and stopping him from going further.

Yeah, this is a trap. Father stopped, and everyone got out. He pushed the boys outside the passenger side and told them to stay low.

The truck hauling bales was just coming over the hill towards them. Now back behind the Humvee, Father waved his crossed arms for them to stop. Of course, it takes a while for the truck with a loaded trailer to stop. They ended up about 10 feet behind the Humvee. Father was standing there talking to Lee when shots rang out from the trees on the west side of the road towards them, pinging off the Humvee and truck.

Even though he was a priest, he still carried a 9 mm Beretta with two extra clips. He was still a Green Beret at heart. "Everybody stay down. Master Sergeant, you have your M-16. Bradley, do you have the other M-16?"

“Yes, and two extra clips”. Shots were pinging close around them, getting ever closer.

“Lee, you and your boys all carry .45s. How many rounds do you have?”

“Six and 12, six in the gun 12 in the belt, each of us.”

“Okay, Bill or Ace, stand behind Bradley and help him when possible.

“What do you think, Master Sergeant? Do you have any ideas about how to get out of this?”

“It appears they have us in a nice trap. We can’t go forward or backward; we’re pinned down as near as I can tell, at least four or five possibly in among the trees. I can’t get a good shot; we must wait it out and see if somebody makes a mistake.

“The worst scenario is darkness. They could creep in on us at night and wipe us all out. It’s my biggest fear right now. I’ll keep firing a few rounds now and again to keep their heads down, not sure I’m even close to where they are hiding.”

“Did you hear more shooting? Sergeant?”

“Yeah, Father. Sounds like they are shooting at each other, except the gunfire sounds like all M-16s.”

“They’re yelling something. Can you hear what they are saying, Sergeant?”

“Father, I think I’m hearing that they are friendlies and not to shoot them.”

“Fat chance. What kind of trick is this? Do they think we are going to fall for any more traps?”

“I don’t know, Father. Something sounds familiar: ‘ Don’t shoot. We are friendlies.’ I’ve heard it before, but I can’t place it.

"Father, ask him his name and see if he will tell us."

"Hey, you in the trees, what's your name?"

"Matt Dylan!"

"Come on, Sergeant, he thinks he's Matt Dylan of Dodge City.

"He has delusions of some kind! He is nuts; it is another trap."

"Ask him if he's ever been in Afghanistan."

"What for? They just tried to kill us!"

"Humor me and ASK HIM!"

"OK. Were you in Afghanistan?" Father Mike yelled as loud as he could.

Answer back, "Yes!"

"OK, now ask him what unit he was in."

"Tell me why we're doing this again."

"Because I think I know him, Father."

"OK, what unit did you belong to?"

Another long pause....

"I was in the Navy special forces."

"Navy special forces is pretty vague, Sergeant."

"It means, Father, that he was a Navy SEAL. Their identity will always be kept secret from civilians, which I guess is why he's so cagey."

"What are you talking about, secret identity? I call it bullshit."

"Yes, a secret much like my own.

"Matt! This is Master Sergeant Jones. From Team 3.

"We'll hold our fire, walk to the road, and wait for us to meet you. All guns down!"

"Jones, is it really you? You son of a bitch, I heard you were dead!"

"Still alive, Lieutenant, meet us on the road."

"Jones, you know this guy?"

"Yes, Father, he was my team leader in Afghanistan; he saved my life and the lives of others many times over."

"Lee, I want you and Father along with me and Ace.

"Ace, grab Bradley's M-16.

How is Bradley doing, Ace?"

"He was shot in the shoulder, fortunately the bullet went clean through, we bandaged him up the best we could, but we need to get him back to the Doc as soon as we can."

"The four of us will go. I'll take the lead, and Father, you will fall behind and cover the rear.

"Do you have any questions? Let's go slowly and keep your weapons down. Please don't make any moves unless they do. If it is my old lieutenant, he could kill all four of us in the blink of an eye."

As they walked down the dusty road, Sergeant Jones saw the other group coming out of the trees and walking towards them, 40 yards apart. The men on both sides were moving slowly and cautiously, and soon, 30 feet from each other, Sergeant Jones immediately recognized a younger Lieutenant Dylan.

"Master Sergeant Ethan Jones, I can't believe my eyes. You look good for a dead man."

"Lieutenant Matthew Dylan, I thought you had retired, living in the suburbs of Lincoln, Nebraska."

"Yes, I was until all this happened and now, I'm here killing bad guys again."

"Matt, who's with you?"

"This tall sandy head is Chuck, my neighbor from across the street in Lincoln. We both survived, so we got together and came north. We ran into this other guy, Benjamin, along the way.

"Oh, both are extremely capable and deadly regarding a fight."

Buck was sitting beside Matt and gave a little growl!

"Oh, and Buck is an incredibly valuable team member!".

"Is he one of those Belgian dogs?"

"Yes, Sergeant, he is, and it's true what they say: He is deadly. But he is also a sweetheart and poses no threat to anybody unless you're a bad guy.

"And who is with you, Sergeant?"

"The tall, skinny cowboy is Lee. We were down at his ranch getting hay bales when we were hijacked.

"The big guy is Ace, I call him Ace. He owned the hardware store in Hot Springs. And you should remember Father Mike. He was in Afghanistan, and we were sent to rescue him on our last mission."

In an instant, Matt shed all his gear, ran over, and punched Father Mike in the face, driven by some unknown grudge. Matt threw the first punch, catching the priest off guard. The priest quickly regained his composure, his training kicking in; what followed was a true donnybrook—a chaotic and fierce brawl. Matt's SEAL training, which was initially an advantage, was short lived as the priest countered with a series of powerful strikes, his movements a blend of martial prowess and disciplined control.

Dust swirled around them as they exchanged blows, each drawing on his extensive combat training, the SEAL's agility and speed were matched by the priest's strength and resilience. The fight was intense, with neither willing to back down.

Onlookers could only watch in awe as the two warriors clashed, their battle a testament to their skills and determination. Despite the fight's brutal nature, an underlying respect grew with each passing moment. It was a battle not of physical strength but of willpower.

As the sun dipped below the horizon, casting long shadows on the road, both men were battered and bruised. The fight ended not with a clear victor, but with mutual acknowledgment of each other's strength and resolve, both on their knees leaning against each other for support.

Sergeant Jones walked over to both. "What the hell is wrong with you, Matt?"

Neither could speak as they were both breathing heavily.

"Sergeant, because of this guy, two of my men died on that mission."

"Matt, because of this guy you're alive!"

"What— the— fuck— are— you— talking— about?" he huffed and puffed, trying to speak.

"When you were in the hut and stabbed twice before anybody could react, the priest was up and on the guy, disarmed him, stabbed him in the neck, and pulled the knife down through his chest. He then could see how badly you had been hurt, were hurting, he picked you up, carried you outside, and immediately started working on you—, put a tourniquet on your arm, stopped the bleeding at your wrist, and stopped the bleeding at your stomach. While the rest of us just stood there and watched."

"I thought it was you who killed Alhaji. I thought it was Doc who patched me up."

"No, it was Father Mike, you were completely out the whole time. He's the one who got you ready for transfer to Kandahar.

"Nathan and Doc both demanded to go with you, so I let them, and I went with the others. So, if you want to blame anybody, Matt, it should be me for letting them go with you instead of myself"

Matt sat there momentarily and reached his hand up to Sergeant Jones. After Sergeant Jones helped him up, Matt reached down, offered a hand to Father Mike, and pulled him up to stand beside him. Both of them leaned against each other, dusty, sweaty, and bleeding; nothing more was said.

After both men had cleaned up, been bandaged, and had some water to drink, it was time to move on to new things.

Chuck, who was talking to Sergeant Jones, asked him where they were headed.

"Well, we have a camp in the Black Hills with around 30 people. We came to Lee's ranch to get hay to feed our horses and cattle."

"Okay, that's also where we were headed: the Black Hills. Matt had the idea of taking us there. Would it be possible for us to tag along?"

"Yeah, I don't see why not, as soon as Matt's ready to go."

"It might be a little bit before he's ready to go. Can one of your guys drive our truck and trailer? I'm driving a big self-contained RV."

"Ace, would you go up and drive the hay truck back?"

"Yes, Sergeant. Be glad to."

About 45 minutes later, they were ready to go. Sergeant Jones drove Matt's Chevy pickup. Matt sat on the passenger's side with a wet compress held to his face. On the way, he told Sergeant Jones about their encounter with the bad guys they had ambushed and reminisced about old times.

When they arrived at the camp, some men came out to help unload the hay, while the rest of the hay crew went to get something to eat.

Meanwhile, Sergeant Jones explained to everybody who the newcomers were.

Chuck went up to the RV and came back with a bottle of Turkey bourbon and Kentucky whiskey. After he handed glasses out to everyone involved in the day's activities, he passed around the bottles of Turkey and Kentucky.

He noticed Matt had taken some of the ice from the compress on his face and put it in his glass, along with a big shot of Kentucky. Matt, Father Mike, and Sergeant Jones were all sitting together at the end of the table together, sipping on their whiskey. Three warriors, nothing more had to be said.

And that was how the day ended.

*****

The next morning, although not too early, Matt struggled to get up. The priest packed a fairly good wallop, and Matt was still feeling all the bruises on his face, and his body ached.

Matt's objective that morning was to get a cup of coffee—four or five or six—and a tub of ice for his whole body. As he walked out of the tent, he saw Chuck and Ben sitting at the tables by the cook's shack having breakfast. Matt sat down, and Helen brought him a cup of coffee. And no, he didn't want anything to eat right now, thank you.

Chuck was giving him the eye. "What are your plans, Boss? Are we staying here, or are we going?"

"I'm not sure yet what's your suggestion?"

"Matt, during our last two days, something unique happened, we met other people, and in my opinion, we are exactly where we need to be. Remember our mission is to help others and keep them safe."

"Okay. Ben, and what are your thoughts, what do you think?"

"I agree; I like it here; they are charming people, they have food and doctors, but certainly can't take care of themselves. If there is a fight, except for the priest who knocked the crap out of you, Boss, the rest would be slaughtered."

"Humm, I can't deny it; he packs a surprisingly good punch for a priest.

"Okay, it's settled. We're going to stay here, do what we can to help out where we can, and kill anybody who threatens these people. I'll talk to the priest and Sergeant Jones, find out what we can do to help out."

It took Matt four cups of coffee to feel good enough to get up and go look for the priest, who seemed to be the leader of this group. They offered him their services.

He found Father Mike with Sergeant Jones sitting at a little table with their coffee pot, having an enjoyable conversation.

"Good morning, Matt. I see you are up and around. Would you like a cup of coffee?"

"Yes, Father, thanks; I would never turn down a good cup of coffee. Did I interrupt something?"

“The first thing, Matt, I wouldn’t call this a good cup of coffee. Father made it. He always had a housemaid to make all his coffee for him, so he had a learning curve, and what we were discussing.

“Father has an idea; I will let him tell you.”

“I have just an idea. When we were at the church in Hot Springs and the demons were attacking us, I took holy water and anointed all the doors and windows to keep them out. I wonder if we anoint all our tents and equipment, one or two vehicles, with holy water if it would keep them from dissolving into the ground. If it works, I wonder if it would work on buildings, specifically those at the Sylvan Lake Hotel.

“You all know we can’t stay here in tents through the winter; we must find permanent shelter. So, if I anointed the hotel all around and inside, would that keep it standing?”

“Matt, what do you think?”

“Sergeant, I am uncertain. All I can tell is that my wife did the same thing to our house with holy water, doors, and windows. It seemed to keep the demons out. Would it work now on a building? I don’t know, but it is worth a try. Keep in mind we don’t have a lot of time. It was behind us moving up north from Chardon.”

“Well then, Sergeant, we need to go today.”

“Matt, would you and two of your men go with us and help with protection? We’ve never ventured out in a northern or western direction before.”

“Father, we would be glad to. Let you help me get everybody up. Give us about an hour, and we should be ready.”

“Fine, that would be great, Matt. We will take one Humvee. I’ll meet you at the Humvee in about an hour.”

“OK, Father.”

Walking into the tent, Matt rousted everybody up again and told Chuck and Ben they were going on a mission, and to get dressed, while they put on their gear.

Matt asked Ben about the priest's idea of taking holy water and going west of here to bless a hotel and some buildings to keep them from crumbling. "What do you think?"

"It's true, Matt; holy water has some astounding properties. Does it work on buildings to keep them standing? I'd say it's 50–50. I wasn't given any instructions or told when anything was going to happen or how to stop some of it from happening, other than to kill the demons. So, it is a possibility, yes."

"Okay, we have about 45 minutes to pack some water, food, and ammo. Clean your weapons if you need to. Be ready to go in 45 minutes. We're going to meet at one of the Humvees."

*****

Later That Morning

After piling into a Humvee, Sergeant Jones took the driver's seat. Father Mike was on the passenger side. The three of them, Ben, Matt, and Chuck, sat crowded in the back seat.

Ben asked, "Are you not taking Buck on this trip?"

"No, I left him home. I knew it was going to be crowded in the Humvee."

"Okay, Father Mike said we were going up to 385 and west to Pringle, then north on 385 to a town of Pringle south of Custer, and up north on 89 to Sylvan Lake."

It wasn't long before they got to Pringle, South Dakota. Father was telling them about the town, which was home to about 100 people. The only significance was that they had a bar called the Hitch Rail Bar, famous in the area.

"And I also heard they have a Mormon compound of some kind, surrounded by barbed wire and towers."

"Where are you getting your information, Father?"

"Oh, Chuck, I have several maps and books on South Dakota, with lots of information on small towns and attractions."

"What do you think, Father? Should we check on the Mormons and see if they survived? It might be interesting to see if God accepted their practice of multiple wives."

Ben, hearing the conversation, butted in, "Chuck, I don't think it's a clever idea; we all know what happened to all the organized religions in the world; they are now extinct."

"I guess you would know Ben."

Sergeant Jones, who was driving, turned his head and said, "What do you mean, Chuck? He would know."

Matt jumped in right away. Ben has a unique ability to sense things nobody else can. He is a savant. He certainly didn't want to offend anyone. He's simply different from the rest of us and has sometimes sensed trouble ahead of us."

Ben looked at me, Matt, and winked.

Sitting between Chuck and Ben, Matt was extremely uncomfortable as they started pulling into Senator, South Dakota. It was a small unincorporated town with no people, so they kept driving through. Next was Custer, Dakota, a much bigger town. "How big is Custer's Father?"

Looking at his guide, he said, “It’s about 2000 people. They used to hold the Buffalo Roundup around here, a couple thousand buffalo herded around the hills to where they could be vaccinated and sorted out. Another reason for coming to this area is all of the wildlife.”

Sergeant Jones looked at Father Mike. “Are we going to drive through or around town on the back roads?”

“Yes, Sergeant, take the back roads. There is less of a possibility of running into people. We’re not sure who our friends or foes are yet, so I would rather not provoke confrontation on the first trip. We’ll have time later on to scout some of these towns and see if we can find more people needing our help.”

Still sitting in the middle, Matt looked out the front window of the Humvee. All he had seen so far were abandoned cars, some in the ditches, some on the roads. They had to drive around cars occasionally, but there was still no life other than animals. Sitting in the middle reminded him of when he was a little boy and had to sit between his older brothers because he was the youngest. He hated it then and didn’t care for it now.

They were about to turn off the road and head to Sylvan Lake when Matt heard a BANG! “Stop!”

Sergeant Jones hit the brakes hard. “I also heard it, Matt!”

Matt was struggling; he needed to get out of the backseat. “Let me out!!”

Chuck opened his door and bailed out. Matt was right behind him, with his weapon ready.

Sergeant Jones got out of the driver’s side, his weapon ready, and looked around. “Did anyone hear where the shot came from?”

By then, everybody was out, crouching close to the Humvee, weapons ready.

Matt finally stood up and walked over to Sergeant Jones. “We should just keep going, I haven’t heard anything else or seen anyone.”

"Yeah, Matt, I haven't either. Could it have been an echo?"

"Well, Sergeant, I suppose with all the hills and rock, it could have been."

Matt was going to change the seating arrangement. He walked around to the left side of the Humvee, where Ben was standing.

Matt motioned to Ben, "You're in the middle this time."

They were on the move again down the road, following a sign on the side that read: Sylvan Lake, straight ahead.

Father Mike held the map of the Sylvan Lake Lodge area. As they pulled up to the front of the lodge, he realized he hadn't expected it to be such a massive building.

Father Mike got out, put on his priestly robes, and, with his holy water, started walking around blessing the outsides of the buildings. Then he went inside the building and did the same thing. Later, he went to each one of the cabins in the area and did the same thing, also with the general store and any outbuildings he could find.

When Father Mike had finished, he came back to change clothes. Looking around, he thought *Well, that's that. I don't know if it's going to help or not, but it's done. I hope God will take pity on.*

Matt walked up to Father Mike. "When I first saw your box with all the quart jars in the back, Father, I thought it was moonshine. I figured you guys were making your own moonshine. I almost took a drink."

Father Mike started laughing. "There was no moonshine, just holy water. Before leaving, I took all the holy water from the church and filled up the quart jars.

"Matt, you mentioned that you saw some of Chadron disappear and melt into the ground. Is that true? "

"Yes, Father, it was a sight to see. The town just melted into the dirt and was gone. Nothing remained but grass and trees."

"Matt, how long do you think it will be before there's trouble in the Black Hills, where we happen to be camping right now?"

"Father Mike, I am shocked and surprised it's not here already. I'm guessing no later than tomorrow."

"Our next step then should be what? Matt, what is your suggestion?"

"Father, I'd say first, we need to get back and move all the vehicles up on the road so they aren't close to people. When everything starts disappearing, no one should be anywhere around them.

"Second, we have everyone sleep outside the tents tonight—all are man-made. I recommend sleeping on the ground away from the tents. It will be rough on some people, but I think it's safer."

"Matt, that's good advice. When we get back, I'll initiate your plan."

Some time later the Humvee returned to the campground and Father Mike started initiating Matt's plan.

Ben watched people moving personal items out of their tents, but he couldn't tell Matt it would happen first thing in the morning, and it would be something to behold. What he had learned from his celestial friends had to remain hidden until he was told differently.

Matt and his team offloaded the contents of their trailer and piled everything on the ground. The next step was to park their trucks on the road, knowing they were about to witness something monumental.

As the last hum of the engines faded from the road, Matt's thoughts were of creation and destruction, interwoven with the last remnants of human civilization vanishing.

He held on to the promise of a new, fresh start. His thoughts returned to Paula. As difficult as it was, her memory still drove him to be a better person and effective in this new world. *Ah, my love, I miss you.*

Sergeant Jones took over and got everybody something to eat, and then got them organized to pack out their belongings and take them up a hill about 100 yards away. He pointed it out to them on the southwest.

As the sun slowly sank in the west, the last glimmer of sunlight cast shadows over the hillside. Father Mike looked at his flock, all bedded in for the night with their sleeping bags, blankets, and pillows, unsure of what the next morning would bring. Sleep came to all.

*****

Morning Sun

The warmth of the morning sun woke up Matt and Buck. It wasn't long before Matt noticed others were starting to get up, stretching to begin a new day. The air was warm and comforting, with the smells of pine trees, flowers, and dewy grass. It looked like it would be a gorgeous, sunny day.

Father Mike and Sergeant Jones observed the scene, their faces etched with awe and solemnity. The night had been long and arduous, yet the morning's transformative power offered a glimpse of hope amidst the chaos. Sergeant Jones, a stalwart figure of determination, turned to Matt with a firm nod.

"Matt, we've been through thick and thin together. This place, this moment, is a testament to our resilience. We need to ensure everyone remains calm and focused."

Matt met his gaze with a sense of unyielding resolve. "Agreed, Sergeant. We'll guide them through this, just as we have always done."

CHAPTER 10

Magnificent World

New Beginnings

Matt, Buck, Chuck, and Ben sat together, taking in the morning, when suddenly, it felt as if the air were charged with divine energy. Everything shimmered with pure, unblemished light; the scene before them took on an almost otherworldly quality. Every man-made structure dissolved into the ground, and a sense of sacredness surrounded the process of nature reclaiming its throne. Their pasts were now just memories.

The earth itself heaved and transformed, swallowing every trace of human ingenuity. Concrete jungles crumbled into the ground, towering skyscrapers dissolved as if they were never there, and a pristine new world emerged from the ashes of the old.

Ben was the first one to speak. "Such magnificent power and glory—it's how it was before man took it over."

Father Mike and Sergeant Jones came over and sat with Matt, Chuck, and Ben. "It looks like the holy water worked on our tents. They're in decent shape. We have one Humvee and your truck, Matt. The rest of the vehicles are all gone."

"My truck, Father?"

"Well, I decided to use the last of my holy water on your truck, something we can all benefit from. If you don't mind sharing, Matt?"

"Okay, Father, it works for me, and we have plenty of diesel for the trucks. Also, outside our tent, is another solar-powered generator you can have, keeping the one you're using to run the ice machine."

"Yes, Matt, our doctor required an ice machine to treat small injuries, bumps, bruises, etc. Yours can also power the lights in the medical tent, which the doctor will be happy with."

"Father, I could use some coffee. What say we all go down, get some breakfast, and start making plans for the rest of the day?"

"Excellent idea, Matt!"

Everyone got up and moved down the hill toward the tents. Chuck looked at Matt. "What are your thoughts for today? I can't see you just sitting around here all day."

"Chuck, I'm thinking about discovering where the shot we heard came from. It's kind of been nagging at me; it just doesn't feel right. We should check out parts of this country before we send any civilians out on their own."

"Boss, I'll fill up the truck with diesel, and then we can leave after we eat."

"Chuck, sounds like a plan."

Matt and Ben sat at the table, had breakfast and hot coffee, and then Matt informed Father Mike of his plan for the day.

"Sounds like a promising idea, Matt. We need to get out and make sure it is safe around this part of the country. We haven't taken the time to check if others might need our help. Do you need any more men?"

"No, Father, you have your hands full here. Take whatever you want from our tent. We have a lot of food and some other equipment. Help yourself. We should be back by sundown. If we are not, don't come looking for us; that means we ran into trouble."

"Do you have any idea which way you arc going? Could you possibly go to Sylvan Lake and check it out?"

"Yeah, Father, that's where we're going to head, where we heard the shot. We will also check on your buildings to see if they survived after the purge."

Chuck had the keys in his hand. "You want to drive, Boss?"

"Nah, you go ahead, Chuck. I'll sit on the passenger side, and Ben and Buck can sit in the back; it's like old times back in the saddle again."

They drove to the old roadbed.

"This is a different-looking Boss. There are no roads anymore, just prairie grass. It will be slower going."

"Yes, I can see how bad it is. I'm unsure how long the truck will last in this new world. If we have any breakdowns, we'll leave it sit.

"Chuck, do you know where the turnoff is to Sylvan Lake?

"Considering the roads are all gone, it's going to be harder to figure out where to turn."

"I think it's just right up here, a tree break. It looks like it might have been a road at one time; I'll take the turn and see where we end up."

Chuck was driving steadily as the pathway they were following became increasingly rough.

"Boss, going up and down the hills and dodging all these big potholes is getting rougher, keeping the truck on the grass path."

"Slow down, Chuck, take your time we're in no hurry."

Matt looked around the countryside, and it didn't look familiar. On each side of the path were so many big rocks and boulders, some big canyons, and even bigger trees.

"Chuck, stop when you get up on this next big hill."

"Okay, Boss." The truck struggled to climb the next big hill. Chuck pulled the truck to the top and stopped it.

"How's this, Boss?"

"Good. I will review some of this area before we proceed further. You should all get out and take a break. I'm sure Buck needs a break."

"I'll give him some water, Boss, what do you see?"

"I'm good Chuck, thanks"

"Looks to me, Chuck, the countryside up ahead is rough and hilly, with lots of rocks and trees. I don't think we'll be driving too much further in the truck, and I don't see any buildings. So, we're either in the wrong area or those buildings didn't survive."

Bang, bang, bang, bang!

Matt shouted, "Get down!" Even though the shots sounded far off, they all ducked behind the truck. "Does anyone have any idea where the shots came from?"

"Boss, I think," as Chuck reached into the truck and shut it off, "the shots came from up ahead, half a mile ahead."

"All right, let's gear up. We're going to take a look. Chuck, you take the lead; I will take the rear; Ben, you in the middle; Buck, you're in the lead with Chuck."

When they started, the spacing between them was 5–6 feet apart. Walking easterly, climbing hills and over rocks; coming closer, they could hear the sounds of different weapons firing.

Buck was up in the lead, getting low. He uttered a little growl and stopped, the hair on his back standing up, a clear sign of trouble.

"Everyone stay sharp," Matt ordered, feeling the familiar adrenaline rush. The forest's quiet seemed to close around them, and every rustle of leaves was a potential threat.

Peering through the trees, Matt spotted a hillside where three black men and two other unidentifiable men had four people pinned down in a clearing below them.

Matt took his binoculars and looked at both sides, realizing the guys on the hill were shooting down at the guys hiding behind an old truck in the clearing. He still didn't know if the guys on the mountain or the people in the clearing were the bad guys.

And then he recognized O'Reilly who lay dead, fallen beside the truck, a grim reminder of the stakes they face. Matt's breath caught in his throat, anger and sorrow intertwining. He clenched his fist, pushing past the grief and focusing on the fight.

Matt signaled for them to spread out, taking flanking positions. Chuck moved swiftly, his eyes scanning for threats. Buck stayed close to Matt, ready to spring into action. The five bad guys, focusing on the trapped people below them, had not noticed the team's approach. Matt's heart pounded as they drew closer, the tension familiar.

Matt's team quickly assessed the situation, working with precision that only years of training could produce.

With a nod from Matt, they launched their ambush, determined to save the remaining captives among their fallen brother.

Without hesitation, Matt and Chuck annihilated three gangsters. They tried to shoot the other two, but the bullets just bounced off of them, Ben stepped forward and with his bow, shot an arrow into one of the other two, and suddenly his body just disappeared, and the other one was gone in a flash.

Matt sighed with relief; the fighting was over, and none of his men had gotten hurt. Amidst the chaos, they had managed to rescue the three remaining pinned-down individuals: two women and one remaining man, who Matt recognized as Chris King, a former Marine Special Forces operative. He stood tall at 6′ 4″, with long blonde hair and now sporting a full beard, standing in a composed demeanor with a sharp focus.

"Chris King," Matt shouted, "we are friendly, don't shoot us."

Chris shouted back, "Do I know you?"

"Yes, Matt Dylan, U.S. Navy."

"Matt, yes, welcome to the fight."

Matt and his team walked down the hillside and greeted Chris with handshakes.

Matt took Chris by the shoulders, "Sorry about your loss."

Chris nodded, a silent understanding passing between them. The hostiles had momentarily retreated, giving them a brief window to regroup.

Matt took a deep breath, looking at the newly saved individuals. They had just witnessed a miracle earlier in the day, and he realized their journey had only begun.

Matt knew with people like Chris by their side, they stood a chance in this reborn world and whatever it might throw at them next.

Matt's team quickly regrouped and reloaded, taking defensive positions.

Chris had two young women with him, standing tall, radiating strength and readiness.

Chris introduced them. "This is Cynthia Naylor and Pauline, Star," he said. Both are trained US Army Rangers. They're tough as nails and two of the best soldiers I've served with."

Matt nodded, recognizing the determined fire in their eyes. "I'm glad to meet you both," he said, clearly showing respect in his voice. Cynthia's long blonde hair glinted in the sunlight, cascading past her shoulders. Her tall frame made her one not to be underestimated. Her eyes were sharp and vigilant, constantly scanning their surroundings.

Next to her, Pauline's long brunette hair flowed down her back like a dark river. She stood tall and confident, her presence commanding respect. Both women exuded a blend of strength and grace, their military training evident in every movement.

Cynthia and Pauline exchanged glances before Pauline spoke up." We're ready to fight," she said, her voice steady and unwavering.

Chris King leaned against a 1970 Ford Club Cab, the truck's vintage lines contrasting starkly with the transformed world around them. The vehicle was rugged and dependable, a relic of the past that survived retribution.

Matt admired Chris's nice truck.

"I've always had a thing for red and white classics," Chris remarked, patting the truck's hood. They just don't make them like this anymore. "

"Where did you find it? Most every vehicle is gone?"

"We were living in a military retirement home near a Catholic Church, and a nunnery called Sisters of Mercy had this truck. If you look on the side of the door, you can faintly see Sisters of Mercy. So, I'm guessing it's blessed. We just borrowed it."

Matt could not help but feel a sense of camaraderie as they loaded up their gear. The addition of an old Ford, carrying the scars of countless adventures, seemed almost poetic. They were all relics of a bygone era fighting for their place in the new world.

"There is a tarp in the back of the Ford, I would like to wrap O'Reilly in it and put him in the back of the truck and take him someplace better for burial."

"Chris, we have a great place back at our camp for O'Reilly to rest."

Matt approached Chris, "I would officially like to welcome you to our camp and hope you will become part of our group. We have many people willing to fight to the end against the evil we have been facing lately."

"Matt, that sounds good to me, I can't speak for the girls."

Cynthia jumped in, "It sounds good to both of us."

"Okay, Matt, I need to turn around here. This is a dead end. When we came down this way, we thought it was a road to the west. It looks like the road to nowhere now. We had another choice: to go right. We'll backtrack, take the right road west, and hopefully meet you on the road."

"Okay, Chris, that sounds good. We'll wait out west of here on what looks like the road going north and south until you find us."

With everything said and planned, Matt took his team back to the truck. Once they were inside the truck, Matt looked at Chuck and said, "Give me a sit rep on what you found."

"Matt, the three black guys were gangsters or prisoners at one time. The other one shot with Ben's arrow was a pile of ashes. We couldn't find their vehicle, I'm guessing the one who got away must have taken it. They all looked menacing, their weapons were not great, so we destroyed them. They did have some papers but no identification."

“Papers? What kind of papers?”

“Papers identifying someone they were looking for; someone who’s wanted, dead or alive, stressing mostly dead, in the worst way. The name on the papers is Matt Dillon. It’s your name, Boss.”

“I don’t know how it could be me; why would somebody go to such lengths to kill me? I am not special in any way. And besides, my name is not spelled that way.”

“Boss, I think you should know. The note looked like it was written in blood, and it gave me the creeps to handle it.”

“What happened to the note, did you bring it with you?”

“No, Boss, I handed it to Ben to look at, and it burst into flames when he touched it.”

“Ben, what do you make of it?”

“Matthew, the reason you couldn’t kill the fourth man with your bullets was because he was pure evil, masquerading as a man. The only way to kill him was with my golden arrow, and the note must have been written by evil because when I touched it, it just burst into flames.”

“Here come Chris and the girls. Let’s keep this letter stuff, the golden arrow killing evil, and the wanted poster on whoever it is between us.”

Chuck had turned around the Chevy truck and was heading back towards camp.

Matt was reflecting on the day. “I am ready for a drink.”

Some time later, they arrived back at camp. As Chuck pulled up, people came out to greet them, and noticed the other truck following them.

Father Mike was in the lead. He approached Matt and asked him, "Who are your new friends?"

"Father, this is a good friend of mine from the old days. Chris King and two of his friends, Cynthia Naylor and Paula Starr, all agreed to join us."

Matt continued, "We also have a casualty; we would like to bury him on the hill where we spent our first night. With all the flowers, the trees, and grass, it would be a perfect resting place for our friend O'Reilly. Father, would you mind doing the burial service?"

"Of course, Matt. I would be happy to. And let me be the first to welcome your friends to our camp. Please make yourselves at home. We have food at the mess tent and will find you quarters to sleep and hang your hat.

"Chris, I will find some guys to dig a grave for your friend O'Reilly."

"Thank you, Father, but I would rather dig the grave myself. He was a warrior and deserves special honors."

"Okay, Chris, I certainly understand; we have enough military people to give him a military burial. Let's plan it for today before sundown."

"Chris, would it be okay if I helped dig the grave? I also knew O'Reilly from the past; we were in a couple of skirmishes together."

"Yes, Matt, it's fine; I want some company."

"Chris King, is it you? I thought you retired, old man. What are you doing here?"

"Sergeant Jones, hell, man, I thought you were dead!"

"Exaggerated rumors, Chris. I am well and good. I am happy to see you alive, old friend. How did you end up here?"

"I got into a little skirmish, and Matt and his friends came in and saved our bacon. He invited us to join your organization, and also, we're here to bury our old friend. Sergeant Bill O'Reilly was killed in the skirmish."

"Oh, sorry to hear that, Chris. I also knew O'Reilly from my time in Afghanistan."

Matt and his team were standing on the hillside along with several others, the burial was complete with a United States flag draped over O'Reilly and a 21-gun salute, and somebody back at the camp was blowing taps on the trumpet to finish the services.

Matt and the others returned from the funeral to camp, sitting around tables by the mess tent. Chuck brought out a couple of bottles of whiskey and handed out glasses to everyone at the tables. He then passed around a bottle; everyone took a shot. Chris gave a short eulogy in Sergeant Bill O'Reilly's honor; everyone raised their glasses and drank a salute to O'Reilly. Most everyone departed after about 20 minutes.

Matt, Chris, Chuck, Sergeant Jones, Ben, and Father Mike stayed behind. After more drinks, the conversation turned to the ambush earlier in the day.

Chris described how they had been ambushed, and he remembered something. "Matt, you asked me about buildings before. When we returned and took the other road to the right, we drove by several cabins and a lodge. They looked pretty intact, near some kind of a lake. Sorry, I just remembered. I hope it wasn't too important."

Father Mike jumped up. "Hallelujah, we are saved! Get up and start packing; we are moving to our new home. It worked. Thank you, God!!"

Matt was the first to speak. "Whoa, Father, hold your horses. It will take some planning to move all these people and supplies to the Lodge. Father, you will have to wait until morning to start."

Matt continued, "We should send a team over first to check everything out and ensure it is safe."

"Yes, Matt, you are right. I just got excited. I'll let everybody know tonight that they can start packing tomorrow. We'll move as soon as you say it's safe for everyone."

"Okay, I'll take Ben and Buck with me. We will go over it and check it out and then get back to you as soon as we can. Chuck, I want you to stay behind and help organize the move. It will take several people working together, and you are a good organizer."

"Matt, I would like to go with you if you don't mind."

"Chris, sure, I'll get you outfitted with new equipment; we'll leave at sunrise."

Matt returned to his tent and crawled into his sleeping bag. He made himself comfortable, Buck lying right next to him, as always, keeping him company and safe. He was thinking of the day and how it went. And what was this with angels now? And demons? *How are we supposed to fight things from hell?*

CHAPTER 11

The Lodge

Sniper

Matt, Chris, Ben, and Buck drove steadily through the winding paths of the Black Hills to their destination: Sylvan Lake. The serene spot was now their hope as a potential haven for their group. The tension in the air was high as they neared the Lodge.

Buck sniffed the air, alert as always. "Stay sharp," Matt reminded everyone, his voice cutting through the silence. "We don't know what's waiting for us."

The lake's surface shimmered in the distance, reflecting the surrounding pines. As they approached, they were in awe of all the natural beauty. Chris scanned the area with military precision while Ben kept a conventional compound bow at the ready if needed.

Chris's eyes never left the horizon, "I hope it's secure before moving anyone here."

Matt nodded, gripping the steering wheel tighter. The lake would be their sanctuary or a trap; they had to ensure it was the former.

Matt parked the Silverado about 100 yards from the Lodge. They approached cautiously on foot. Matt and Chris scanned the area with binoculars, intent on seeing if anybody had made changes since they had last been there. All they saw were two deer feeding on the grass around the cabins. Matt felt it was a good indication that nobody had been around.

Matt had them spaced about 5 yards apart as they moved up the hill towards the Lodge.

Matt reached the front door first; it was still locked. Luckily, Father Mike had given Matt a key. As they checked the inside, everything was as they had left it, which was all good news.

With everything clear, the drive back to camp was exciting, and they were filled with optimism. Sylvan Lake was secure; they could finally offer some hope to their people. Matt drove the Silverado with a newfound urgency, eager to relate good news.

As they pulled into the camp, Matt opened his door to climb out when a shot rang out, clipping his tactical helmet, knocking it off, and knocking him to the ground. Matt was lying on the ground as the sharp crack echoed.

Chris jumped out of the truck, taking cover while trying to locate the shooter, and at the same time, concerned about how badly Matt had been hurt.

Ben got out of the truck and pulled Buck to safety, and they all took defensive positions around the truck.

Matt's heart pounded as he lay on the ground, not moving; the good news was that he didn't seem to be injured, but he still didn't know where the shot came from.

Chuck was in the camp when he heard the shots and ran out to see what was happening, realizing his buddies were under fire. He turned, ran into the tent, and grabbed his sniper rifle. Then he ran up a hill, climbing it at top speed.

Chuck glassed the area in front of him, not finding the sniper. Then another shot rang out. That was it, he saw the muzzle flash in the trees and brush a hundred yards away. Chuck lay down, took aim, slowed his breathing, and squeezed the trigger. The bullet whizzed away, finding its mark with a perfect headshot.

Hearing the shot from Chuck's gun, they all looked up and saw Chuck waving an all-clear.

Chris and Ben rushed over to the other side of the truck, apprehensive about what they might find. Buck reached Matt first, licking him in the face. Matt got up from the ground and was hugged by Chris and Ben.

Matt was safe. They all climbed the hill to find Chuck, who had found the sniper. He found a Mexican gangster type, chains, rings, and gang tattoos. Chuck checked his pockets and found a wanted poster similar to the one seen before, but this time, there was a crude picture, unmistakably recognizable as Matt.

Matt and the others reached Chuck, who handed Matt the wanted poster.

Matt's heart sank as he looked at the poster. "It seems like someone's put a bounty on my head," he said, his voice tight with anger.

Chris examined the poster more closely. "We need to be extra careful if they're targeting you. Specifically, they will not stop, especially with a bounty of 50 pounds of gold. I wonder how this asshole got here."

Matt and Buck walked north through the forest. About 60 yards in, Buck growled softly. Tied up to a tree was a buckskin-colored horse. Matt untied it and led it back to his friends.

"Good looking horse, Matt, are you going to keep him?"

"You know Chuck, I think I might, he made friends with Buck already."

The weight of the realization hung over them as they made their way back to camp. The world had become even more dangerous, but Matt knew they could not let fear hold them back. They had to press on and protect their people, no matter the cost.

Matt and his team reported their findings to Father Mike, giving him the information he had been looking forward to. The Lodge was safe, and they could move as soon as possible. However, now that the Lodge's population had grown to 33 souls, it was going to be difficult.

Father Mike said that it was a blessing. Despite the looming challenges, the Lodge offered a glimmer of hope. "We must be careful, and it will not be easy, but it is our best shot."

The camp buzzed with a mix of anxiety and anticipation as they prepared for the move. Each person carried their fears and hopes, contributing to the collective effort. The path to Sylvan Lake required both safety and caution.

The move's planning demanded careful coordination with their vehicles. They estimated they could transport all the supplies and equipment in several trips. As for people, they could move 12 to 14 individuals each time.

Matt and his team began organizing the first group, prioritizing the most vulnerable. Father Mike helped him instill a sense of purpose and hope in everyone. "We will do this in stages," Matt explained to the group. It will take a few trips, but we will get everyone there safely."

Chris, Cynthia, Pauline, and Ben organized the convoy, ensuring every journey was as safe as possible. The first vehicles were loaded, and as they set off toward Sylvan Lodge, everybody felt apprehensive.

The journey had begun and with every mile, they moved closer to a new beginning.

Matt took the lead in the Silverado, pulling the trailer loaded with weapons, ammunition, and food. The others followed, each vehicle a few lengths apart. As they were coming up on the turn to Sylvan Lake, a sudden BOOM!! tore through the back end of his pickup; luckily, the pickup was bulletproof. No one inside was hurt, although some of the merchandise in the back had been damaged.

Matt got out and took a look, quickly assessing the situation. Smoke billowed from the damaged truck bed, and the air was thick with the smell of burning rubber from the tires burning, a sickening odor.

Chris and Ben immediately took defensive positions, scanning the surroundings for further threats.

"Stay alert!" Matt called out steadily despite the adrenaline coursing through him. Buck growled, sensing the danger.

Cynthia and Polly, the new Rangers, moved up to help secure the perimeter.

"This is a trap," Chris murmured, examining the blast site. "We need to determine who is responsible for this."

The convoy stopped, worry evident on every face. Moving forward, they knew each had to be even more vigilant when traveling to Sylvan Lake, which had just become much more perilous.

The Silverado was beyond repair, so they left it behind; they had no choice. They unhooked the trailer and hitched it to the 1970 Ford. Despite the setback, they pressed on, determined to reach Sylvan Lake.

The convoy moved forward cautiously, every sense on high alert. The explosion rattled them, but their resolve was unshaken. The tension eased slightly as they neared their destination, though they remained vigilant.

It took the rest of the day to finish moving all the people and their belongings. Upon reaching Sylvan Lake safely, they quickly moved everyone into the lodge.

Matt gathered everyone together. "We have made it this far," he said, his voice filled with resolve. "We won't let anyone stop us now. This place is our chance for a fresh start." The group nodded, drawing strength from each other. They knew challenges lay ahead, but together, they were ready to face whatever came their way.

Matt grabbed his gear and left the Lodge with Buck at his side. They headed to the Senator's Cabin, a beautiful log cabin set off by itself.

Matt was surprised at how nice it was as he walked in the door. According to the pamphlet, it had three bedrooms, and he picked the nicest one with the biggest bed. There was a fireplace, and he planned to start a fire as soon as he got his gear set down and had a shower.

A knock at the door brought him out of the bedroom to the front door where he found Chuck.

"Hi Boss, you want to be alone?"

"Not at all, Chuck, there are two other bedrooms, take your choice."

"Thanks, Boss. Oh, here is a housewarming gift."

"What do you have? Ah, a fifth of Jack. After I shower, I'll start a fire in the living room fireplace. We can sit back and open this bottle."

Matt had just settled on the large, overstuffed couch with a glass of whiskey when there was another knock at the door. Buck walked over to the door, his tail wagging.

"Come in, Ben!"

"How did you know it was me?"

"Buck gave you away, he went to the door and started wagging his tail."

Matt sat back again, sipping his whiskey, watching the fire crackle and pop. Relaxing, Buck found a place by the fire. They were on the verge of closing their eyes—another knock at the door.

Chuck and Matt, in unison, "Who the hell can that be?"

Ben got up and walked to the door. Of course, Buck was at the door first, wagging his tail. Ben opened the door and found Chris King and Sergeant Jones.

"Ben, we come bearing gifts," they chorused, each holding a bottle of whiskey.

Ben turned and looked at Matt for confirmation.

Matt hollered, "Come on in, gentlemen, make yourself at home, *mi casa, su casa*."

After all the howdys were done, each sat in the remaining two overstuffed chairs.

Jones was the first one to speak. "Now we have everyone moved and safe, what do you think we should do next, Matt?"

"Humm, domesticated is not really in my vocabulary. Plenty of others can take care of what needs to be done here. I was thinking about scouting."

"Scouting? Where and how are you going to accomplish it? Now that your truck has crashed and burned, what will you use for transportation? Are you going to walk?"

"Sergeant Jones, no, I am not going to walk. I have a horse and plan to go out on horseback with enough supplies for three days. I have an overpowering urge to find out who thinks I am worth 50 pounds of gold."

Jones was surprised. "Do you plan on doing this all by yourself?"

"Well, sure, Sergeant, I am more than capable of doing things independently."

Ben was a little agitated with Matt. "Boss, you're not going by yourself. I am at least going along. We're tied together. Where you go, I go."

Looking at Matt, Chuck said "Don't think you're leaving me here either."

"Okay, Chuck and Ben, you'll have to round up a couple of horses. Do either of you know how to ride?"

"I do; although it has been quite a while, I am unsure about Ben."

"No, Matthew, I have never been on a beast."

Matt looked at Chris, "Do you have any plans?"

"Cynthia, Pauline, and I are going back to the campground with Lee and Donald to load what is left of the hay and round up all the horses to bring them here. Lee and Donald have taken some time to build a corral down below the Lodge in an open area."

"Sounds good," said Matt. "Chuck and Ben, if you're going along with Buck and me, Lee could help you pick a couple of horses.

"I've asked for a horse, and I plan to use my talent to hunt for fresh meat. I know Fern and Dakota have been providing most of the meat. With everything going on, I hate to send those two out not knowing what's out there."

"Matt, what's your plan, do you still plan on leaving tomorrow?"

"My plan has changed until the boys learn how to ride while you take care of the hay and horses. I will unload the trailer, take all the weapons and ammo, find a room in the Lodge to store everything, and then start loading more magazines so we don't run short.

"Next, I plan to leave at sunup in a couple of days, which should give Chuck and Ben enough time to get situated with some horses.

"Right now, I am going to bed. I will see all of you when you get back."

*****

Morning at the Lodge

Morning came early, and the sun rose in the east before 6 AM. Lee and Donald located a pickup with a large horse trailer at French Creek horse camp south of the lodge. Chris drove his 1970 Ford with the idea that it could pull the flatbed trailer loaded with hay.

With both trucks being club cabs, there was plenty of room to bring all the newfound help. Lee told Don about how much military training their helpers had, and how much safer he felt knowing how deadly they could be in a fight.

Sometime later, they reached the camp, and all looked safe. They quickly loaded all the hay on the flatbed, and Lee loaded the horses in the horse trailer.

About to start on their way back to the Lodge, Cynthia raised a closed fist in the air, meaning freeze, don't move.

Cynthia strained to hear the sound again.

Pauline came up beside her, "What is it?"

"I think the sound I heard was a motorcycle; there it is again. Did you hear it?

"Yes, I did, it sounds like it's heading this way."

"Pauline, get everyone under cover, defensive positions!"

A Harley Davidson motorcycle with a sidecar and two-wheeled trailer came over a grassy hill. The rider was dressed in black leather, a helmet, and goggles. In the sidecar was a cute Pekingese poodle also wearing goggles. The rider pulled up and stopped. Getting off the motorcycle, he raised his arms over his head, recognizing they were armed, and the weapons were pointed at him.

"I am not armed; my weapons are in the sidecar with Dolly. I'm not looking for any trouble. Instead, I'm looking for people who won't shoot at me," he said, removing his goggles and helmet to reveal his curly black hair.

Humm! thought Pauline.

Cynthia was a little more cautious, "Who are you?"

"My name is Jake Savage, and I'm from Kansas City."

"What do you want, Jake Savage from Kansas?"

"Shelter, something to eat for me and my dog, a place to lay my head for the night."

Cynthia asked Lee and Donald, "What do you two think?"

Lee and Donald exchanged looks.

Lee was in charge of the operation, so he spoke first. "Well, Cynthia, we always seek people who need our help. Take his weapons and have him follow us back to the Lodge."

"Chris, what are your thoughts on this guy?"

"I agree with Lee; give him a chance until he breaks our trust."

Cynthia nodded OK.

"All right, Jake. Here is the plan: We are taking your weapons, and you can follow us back to our current shelter. If you try anything funny, you're dead!"

"I understand, and I'm OK with you taking my weapons for now. You won't have any trouble with me."

Lee's hay team arrived at the Lodge late in the afternoon. Matt and Father Mike met them at the corrals.

Jake Savage reported to camp on his Harley-Davidson. The engine rumbled, turning heads. In the sidecar sat his loyal dog, Dolly, her ears perked up, and alert. He stopped and dust settled around the bike. Jake dismounted, his eyes scanning the camp. "Jake," he called out, his voice carrying over the camp. "Looking for a place to lay low, me and Dolly. We've been on the road a long time."

Matt stepped forward, gauging the newcomer. Something about Jake's hard-edged resilience spoke of his survival. Sensing the tension, Dolly wagged her tail and stayed close to Jake.

Father Mike welcomed Jake by extending a hand, saying they always had room for those willing to contribute.

Jake grinned, shaking Father's hand firmly. "Thank you, I'm pretty handy with tools."

The camp was buzzing with curiosity as Jake and Dolly entered their small community, and new faces brought new stories.

Cynthia and Pauline filled Matt in on the day's happenings.

"Jake, if you follow us up the hill, we'll get you something to eat."

"Father, what about my dog?"

"We can find something to eat for your dog."

After the horses were in the corrals, the hay crew was hungry. Walking up the hill to the Lodge and into the cafeteria, they were not disappointed. Helen had put out a pretty good spread. Most people in the Lodge had already finished eating, so they were the last ones, and she still had plenty for them.

*****

Horse Sense

The next day, Lee and Don spent most of the day working with Chris and Ben, finding a couple of horses they could ride.

Chuck got up early in the morning, picked out a horse for himself, saddled up, and took off riding out to the prairie.

Chris picked up riding pretty fast, but Ben was a different matter. He had never been on anything like a horse before. Most of it was just getting him on a horse and getting him comfortable. It took a while to lead him around the corral on a horse until he felt like he could do it himself. Late in the day, he was riding outside the corral, finally confident.

Matt postponed his scouting mission for a couple more days, giving Ben some much-needed time to get comfortable on his horse. The delay was frustrating but necessary.

Matt decided to take the downtime and do a little fishing. He grabbed his fly rod and started for Sylvan Lake. Arriving at the lake, he took a deep breath, savoring its peacefulness. His fly rod in hand, he cast his line into the ripples of the water, soothing his mind. It was one of those perfect days when the world's troubles seemed far away.

*****

New Adventure

A couple of days later, Matt finally set out. Chuck, Ben, and Buck were prepared for what lay beyond their territory.

The sun dipped low as they traveled the rugged landscape, casting long shadows. Matt first saw her on the second day as they navigated a dense forest path. Maggie emerged from the trees, riding bareback on a mighty steed, her long honey-colored hair flowing behind her. She wielded a bow and arrow with precision and grace, taking down a deer in a single shot.

Matt signaled for his team to stop, watching as Maggie dismounted fluidly.

She approached them, her eyes sharp and curious.

"Who are you?" she called out, her voice steady and commanding.

Matt stepped down from his horse and walked forward, keeping his hands visible. "We're scouts from Sylvan Lake. Just trying to learn more about what's out here."

Maggie nodded, a small smile playing on her lips. "Welcome to the Wild, then. I'm Maggie. It looks like we have a lot to discuss."

After loading her deer on the horse, Maggie led them through the forest to her camp, where four other women were waiting. The camp was small but well organized, with shelters made from natural materials and a central fire pit that provided warmth and light.

"Welcome to our camp," Maggie said, pointing them to sit by the fire. These are Annie, Lisa, Sarah, and Tricia." She introduced her companions, each nodding in acknowledgment.

Matt looked at each of them. "Maggie, how did you five get out in the middle of nowhere?"

"Matt, we were all in a rest home, just waiting to die. Then we woke up, young, in our late 20s. Given a chance to start over with a new life, I can't explain it.

"We walked out of a rest home, which was more of a hospice than a home. Wearing hospital gowns and dragging IV lines out the door, not knowing what the hell had just happened."

Matt was nodding, "It is not just you; it happened to all of us, and NO, none of us can explain it. One day, we were old, then after the three days of darkness, we were young again, and all of the people we had known were gone."

The five of us found no one in North Dakota and didn't see anybody alive, so we started heading south. We picked up supplies, found a few horses, and started south into South Dakota. We ended up in the Black Hills, which looked like a good place to call home. There was plenty of game, and it was beautiful.

"You've heard our story, Matt. What is yours?"

"I was living in Lincoln, Nebraska, with my wife, when everything went to hell. I woke up with this new body. My wife, dog, and neighbors were gone, except for Chuck. Chuck was my neighbor across the street; he lost his wife also. So, we got together and decided to head north to the Black Hills. On the way, we ran into Ben, and he joined us, and we all ended up here in the Hills."

Buck walked over, sat beside Matt, and looked up. "Don't let me forget Buck; he also joined us in Lincoln."

"What did all of you do in your previous lives?"

Matt was careful about how much information he shared. "I am ex-military, went to college, became a teacher, and finished my career in education."

"Chuck?"

"I was also an ex-military, retired farmer with my wife. We had a great life living in Lincoln, Nebraska, with four children and eight grandchildren."

Maggie looked at Benjamin. "What's your story, Ben?"

"I am a servant of the Lord, spending my existence praising his magnificent glory."

Matt looked at Maggie, who was sitting on a stump of wood. "Your story has to be more than just a rest home."

"In my previous life, I was Maggie Andrews, a wildlife biologist dedicated to studying and protecting endangered species. My knowledge of these species has helped me with survival skills."

"My name is Anne Thompson. I was a paramedic who saved lives in urban areas. Now, I do what I can to treat injuries and illnesses in camp with whatever resources I can find."

"My name is Sarah Mitchell. I worked as a mechanical engineer, solving complex problems and building innovative solutions. While here, I built a solar-powered system to power the batteries for our walkie-talkies."

Maggie introduced Tasha Reynold. "She's shy, and after an unusually violent life, it takes a great deal for her to trust anyone. Please understand it's not personal. Tasha was a chef with great culinary talent. In camp, she made sure everyone was well-fed with limited supplies."

Matt could see the strength and resilience of these women, who were forced by circumstances to survive in this wilderness. They exchanged stories of their past experiences, finding common ground for survival.

Maggie's group had carved out a life in the wild, relying on their skills and each other. They had learned to be self-sufficient, but there was safety in numbers, she said, her eyes meeting Matt's, perhaps we could help each other.

Matt nodded, appreciating the offer. "We're all in this together," he replied. "Strengthening our alliances is the key to surviving and thriving in this world."

As the evening wore on, the two groups began to form a bond united by their shared experiences and common goals. They planned to ride together to Sylvan Lake, knowing cooperation would be their most significant asset in the days to come.

Matt found it hard to tear his gaze away from Maggie. There was something magnetic about her presence and undeniable attraction. Knowing they'd be riding together meant she would always be near, a thought that stirred something deep within him.

As they prepared for the journey back to Sylvan Lake, Matt felt the connection between them. Every shared glance and brief conversation hinted at a growing bond adding complex feelings among the many challenges he faced.

Matt still felt the ache of Paula's absence, and her memory was constantly in his heart. Even as he found himself drawn to Maggie, the pain of losing his wife lingered. It was a bittersweet past love, and now, there is the potential for a new one. Each day, he honored Paula by pushing forward, knowing she would have wanted him to survive and thrive.

The journey to Sylvan Lake was not just physical but also a road toward healing and finding a new purpose amongst all the chaos and his path to salvation.

The journey back to the Lodge took one and a half days by horseback. Matt took the lead, sending Buck up ahead to scout for danger. The women riding bareback followed, and Chuck and Ben brought up the rear.

Matt took a different route back to the Lodge, going over the hills and coming in from northeast Sylvan Lake. It was the most unprotected way to the Lodge, allowing him to check if anybody had been making tracks or leaving any signs.

Late in the afternoon, they arrived in front of the Lodge. Matt climbed off his buckskin, walked over to Chuck, and asked him if he would take the ladies into the Lodge, introduce them around, and find suitable quarters.

"What are you going to do, Boss?"

"I plan to take these horses to the corral, ensure they are fed and watered, and rub them down. Then, I will return to the cabin, take a long, hot shower, and wear clean clothes.

"There should still be some food in the refrigerator. After eating something, a big drink of whiskey, then bed, sleeping on something other than the ground."

Chuck and Ben took the ladies into the Lodge and introduced them. Father Mike came up and started talking to Maggie as she was the group's leader and spent some time talking to her and invited all into the cafeteria for something to eat.

"While you are eating, I will arrange rooms in the Lodge. I am sure you would like some hot showers, and we have lots of clothing stored in one of the rooms. Help yourselves. And if you can't find something you want, just ask, and we will try our best to help you. And if I have not said it enough, you are so welcome. Welcome."

Maggie and the girls sat at the cafeteria tables, enjoying hot food, and meeting new people, like Helen, the chief cook, and her friends helping her with the meals. Then Ben and Chuck came over and joined them.

"Chuck, where did Matt disappear to?"

"Auh, he took all the horses down to the corral to feed and water them, and then he was going to rub them all down. After he was finished with the horses, he planned to take a hot shower, get something to eat, and sit down with a big glass of whiskey. I know he was looking forward to jumping into his soft bed after sleeping on the ground for so many nights. It sounds good to me, too. So, I will say my good nights and see you later."

Chuck walked down the hill to the cabin. When he walked in, he saw Matt sitting, watching the fireplace, drinking a nice glass of whiskey with a couple of ice cubes, and relaxing.

"Oh, so nice to be off that horse for a while Chuck."

Then, of course, there was a knock at the door.

Buck got up from the fireplace and ran to the door, his tail wagging.

Matt was too tired to get up and answer the door, so he just hollered. Come on in.

Chris King walked in with a big wave and a howdy. "Would you mind if I joined you briefly, Matt?"

"No, not at all. Come in, Chris, grab a glass and help yourself."

"I reckon you are the man in charge around here, Matt. I wanted to let you know my plans for the next 2 or 3 days."

"I am not in charge of anything. You should talk to Father Mike, even Sergeant Jones. I think they are more in charge."

"I did talk to them, and they said to go see you and let you know because you are the man in charge now."

"Crap, I don't need that. I just want to be left alone; I don't want to be in charge of anybody."

"Well, sorry about that, but it is what it is, and right now, it is you. So, I plan on hunting for three days to the west of here and maybe circling up north. It depends on how much luck I have when I return. Thanks for the drink. I'll be leaving early in the morning. See you in a couple of days. Boss!"

"I figured you were a wise ass, Chris, good luck!"

*****

Elk Hunt

Even before sunrise, Chris King was up, saddling his roan-colored horse. Next was the packhorse outfitted with a double pack and everything he would need for three days.

Chris mounted up and rode out with the warm sun on his back. He smiled, patting the cloth bag tied to his saddle horn. Helen had packed him breakfast—some ham sandwiches with a big thermos of coffee. What a sweetheart she was.

After riding for about four hours, he was due for a break. He spotted a lovely big tree. Getting off his horse, he loosened the cinch on his roan and the packhorse and gave them a breather. It was time to have breakfast and a hot cup of coffee. While he was sitting against the tree, he pulled out his binoculars and started looking around. This looked like a nice spot. On the way here, he had seen lots of signs of elk.

It was a good place to make his camp, sheltered and with plenty of water. Later, he could scout the area and set up his tree stand. He still might have a couple of hours to hunt before sundown.

Walking down a trail, he found a sturdy tree to set up his tree stand. After setting up the tree, he surveyed the landscape untouched by man. The wilderness was impressive. Waiting for elk to appear, the quiet attuned his senses to every sound moving through the forest. It was a good time for reflection while connecting with nature.

As he waited, he could hear a bull elk bugling in the nearby forest. A sudden surge of adrenaline and excitement surged through his body.

Distant voices and the crunching sound of footsteps on the forest floor shattered the silence. Chris peered through the foliage in the tree. He could see a group of armed men moving cautiously through the woods. They looked rough, and their body language indicated they were trouble, possibly outlaws.

Chris tightened his grip on the bow; his senses were heightened as he assessed the situation and noted their weapons and numbers. They were heavily armed, but their movements were undisciplined, suggesting they were not trained soldiers.

Trying not to make any sound, Chris reached for his Glock strapped to his hip, ready for confrontation. He had a Glock in his front pack too but couldn't get it or the automatic weapon on his back without making too much noise. Considering his vulnerable position in the tree, avoiding a fight would be ideal, but he was prepared if a fight was the only option. The men drew closer but were unaware of his presence, high above them in the tree stand.

Chris watched them intently, hidden above the armed men who continued to approach. Their intent was uncertain, but they seemed potentially harmful.

Chris decided to remain silent and hidden, trying to gather as much intelligence as possible and determine their potential. As he carefully watched, noting their movements and listening to their conversation, he heard them speak in hushed tones, discussing plans and revealing their motives.

From his vantage point, he could see their tattoos, rugged appearance, and different ethnicities suggested they were working together as a gang or criminal group. He heard them mention a camp nearby and caught a little about their planned raid.

Chris knew this information could be vital for the people at Sylvan Lake. As the men moved on, he quietly descended from the tree stand and returned to the horses. Although it was too dangerous to make the trip tonight, he would leave at sunrise to return this intel to Matt and the others before it was too late.

*****

Matt was brushing his buckskin horse at the stables, and Buck found a place to lie in the morning sunshine. Lee and Don were headed that way; they looked determined and obviously had something on their minds.

"Morning, Matt!"

"Lee, what can I do for you two? I can see you have something on your mind."

"We located a great big barn not too far from here, one we could keep the horses in when winter rolls around. The problem is Matt, we can't pick it up and move it; it's too big. We need some idea of how to get it from there to here."

"Okay, so why did you come to me?"

"The word is Matt, you are the boss. Now, everything has to go through you first."

"I need to straighten this out. In the meantime, you should talk to Sarah Mitchell. She has an engineering degree and experience solving difficult problems."

Both nodded in agreement and started for the Lodge.

Matt was back brushing his horse, when Buck started barking agitatedly and jumping around, looking to the west.

Chris came galloping in, pulled his horse up short, jumped off, and ran up to Matt.

"Matt."

Matt's eyes widened as he heard Chris's urgent news, and his mind raced. "First, we need to fortify our defenses here, warn everyone, and prepare them to defend if needed."

Chris nodded, still catching his breath. "And what about the intel? They mentioned a raid on a camp nearby."

Matt paused, considering his options. "We need to scout out their camp and disrupt their plans before they can strike, but we'll need a precise, co-ordinated effort. Let's gather the team and map out our strategy."

Matt felt apprehensive about running into Maggie, but there was no time for hesitation. He had to get his team together and plan their next move.

He called a meeting at the Lodge, bringing Chris, Ben, Cynthia, Pauline, and the rest of their group together.

Maggie and her team also expressed a mix of curiosity and concern.

"We have a situation," Matt began, his voice steady but urgent. "Chris has intel on a dangerous group of men planning a raid. We need to fortify our defenses here at the Lodge; some of us will find them and disrupt their plans before they can strike."

Maggie stepped up, her eyes meeting Matt's. "We're with you," she said firmly, "whatever needs to be done, we'll do it."

He nodded, grateful for her support. "All right, let's divide into two teams. One group will scout their camp, and another will strengthen our defenses here. We need to be ready for anything."

As Chris showed Matt the map position, where he spotted the group of men. The team gathered around, intensely focused, as they planned their next move.

Matt said they would form a team of 8 on horseback, and pointed to key routes on the map. "We'll track them down and neutralize the threat before they can move."

The members nodded in agreement, leaving to prepare their gear and check weapons.

Sergeant Jones, Chris, Ben, Cynthia, Pauline, Maggie, and Chuck were chosen for the mission. Each ready to face whatever dangers lay ahead.

Matt's apprehension faded, replaced by pride and determination to protect his people and unite against any threat.

As they mounted their horses, Matt felt a surge of resolve. They had come this far together and would protect their camp and people at all costs. With a final nod to Father Mike, who stayed behind to oversee the defenses, the team rode into the unknown.

They moved through the dense forest, their horses' hooves barely making a sound as they moved in single file on the thick ground cover.

A few hours later, they found their quarry. Smoke from a fire curled up into the sky, marking the location of the enemy camp.

The tension was strong as Matt and his team prepared for the confrontation.

Matt signed for everyone to dismount and take cover. They moved silently, positioning themselves around the camp.

The men were unaware of Matt's team's presence and engaged in their activities, arguing and drinking.

Chris whispered, "We need to hit them hard and fast, with no room for mistakes."

Matt looked at Chris, "Warning first."

Chris hesitated, not understanding Matt's sudden urgency for fair play.

"OK, Matt." Chris yelled at the men before them, "Drop your weapons; you're surrounded!"

The hostile group turned and opened fire on Matt's team.

With Matt's final nod, they launched their attack. The forest erupted into chaos as gunfire and arrows flew. The enemy scrambled, caught off guard by the sudden assault. Matt's team moved precisely, and their training and coordination were evident.

The fight was fierce. Matt's heart pounded as he fought alongside his team, each driven to protect their people. The enemy was completely overwhelmed and utterly destroyed; the air, once filled with the chaos of battle, grew silent.

Matt looked around, making sure everyone was accounted for. A sense of relief and accomplishment was at hand. "Good job, everyone," he said, his voice steady. "Let's secure the area, take anything we can use, and destroy the rest."

Matt, "What about the bodies?" Ben asked.

"Leave them where they fell!

"Ben, if you want to say something, feel free."

The journey back to camp was filled with stories of triumph, a renewed sense of purpose, and confidence in the team's abilities to protect themselves.

CHAPTER 12

Blackness on the Horizon

Traveling the Interstate

John Washington and his small group of prisoners finally found the transportation they needed to leave Sioux Falls. They found two diesel GMC Club cab trucks and one diesel Ford Club, just enough for his eight members. One stop at a grocery store filled all three trucks with food and water.

John drove one of the GMCs, keeping his buddies close to him. He, Darrell, Brent, and Kevin had known each other for several years. He was unsure of the other four men, just from checking files. They were all guilty of petty crimes where they killed somebody more from stupidity than anything else.

Darrell was riding shotgun. "John, do you have a plan?"

"Yes, driving north out of town up to Interstate 90 West. On the way to the Black Hills, I plan to stop at every small town, checking police stations and sheriff stations for weapons and continually looking for people to kill."

The next town was Mitchell, South Dakota, with a population of 16,000. "We should be able to find weapons or food and maybe some women. Is anyone interested in finding women?"

A rousing yes from everybody in his truck.

"Well then, it's my plan. Any objections, you should now say so, and if you are gay, you better stay here in Mitchell if you want to stay alive.

"Another thing, do any of you know who the four guys behind us in the pickups are?"

"I do not know any of them, John; I don't think Darrell or Brent know them either."

"All right, Kevin, let us watch them for now.

"There are many abandoned cars and trucks on this interstate highway. You three should keep your eyes out for any police cars. If you find any, I'll stop and see if any weapons are left."

John Washington and seven others had made a pact with the demons in prison. When they reached Mitchell, South Dakota, they turned off the main road, their destination shrouded in secrecy and danger.

Driving through Mitchell, South Dakota, John and his group noticed the side streets blocked with abandoned vehicles, forcing them to continue into the business district, where suddenly several people confronted them, standing in the street armed with automatic weapons; the tension was tremendous as the armed individuals signaled for them to stop.

John slowed the truck, his mind racing, knowing a confrontation would not end well; he glanced at his companions, who were armed and ready. The other two pickups pulled up on either side of him, and the occupants bailed out of their trucks with automatic weapons, standing behind the doors of their trucks facing the main street.

John got out to talk with the new guys on the street before anybody got killed.

John's heart pounded as he stepped out of the truck, raising his hands in a gesture of peace. "Easy fellas," John called out, his voice steady despite the tension. "We were just passing through looking for a place to rest. There is no need for bloodshed here."

One man was clearly in charge. He stepped forward and said, "Now you need to leave. This is our town."

John kept his hands visible, trying to de-escalate trouble while gauging the situation. "We're not looking for trouble; we're just trying to get somewhere safe. Can we negotiate?"

The leader's eyes narrowed, assessing the group. "You have one chance to explain why we should let you stay; otherwise, you turn around and leave."

John glanced back at his team and returned his gaze to the leader. "We can offer supplies, skilled and experienced fighters."

The leader momentarily considered this and nodded slightly, "All right, I will hear you out. But make no mistake: any sign of trouble, and you are gone."

John explained that their destination was the Black Hills, where they planned to search for survivors and a haven. "We've been traveling for a long time and are seeking a place to settle."

The leader considered John's words carefully, "And you think the Black Hills will offer that?"

John nodded. "It's a place of hope, a chance for a fresh start. We could use more hands, and you and your people are welcome to join us."

The leader exchanged glances with his men, weighing the offer. After a tense moment, he turned back to John. "I agree to accompany you, but please understand that we stand as equals, not followers."

The men in town were a mix of Blacks, Mexicans, and Native Americans who had already noticed the southern part of their town disappearing, and knew it was only a matter of time before they had to leave. The realization united them in their determination to survive and find a new place to call home.

John smiled and extended his hand, "Deal, we'll work together."

John and his group prepared to merge with the town's residents, and the urgency of their mission became even more apparent. They shared the goal of reaching the Black Hills and securing a haven for everyone. The combined strength and diversity of the new allies would make them an even more formidable force.

They were about to begin their journey when John took the group leader aside and said, "We have another mission. We're hunting for a man named Matt Dylan. He's responsible for a lot of the suffering among our people.

"We think the devil has recruited him and his evil people to fight against all the good in this world. Our task is to stop them and especially find and eliminate Matt Dylan, the leader chosen to destroy all good in this world."

The leader's eyes narrowed, and he understood the gravity of the situation. "If Matt Dylan is our enemy, we'll do whatever it takes to eliminate him."

"By the way, my name is Stoney Black; who are you?"

"My name is John Washington, the chosen leader of this group, and Stoney, I couldn't help but notice you have several women with you."

"That's right, John. They decided early on that they would make the choice. If anybody violated their choices, harmed them in any way, or forced themselves on them in any way, the individual would be taken care of quickly. We respect their choices, and I expect your people to do the same."

"That's not a problem, Stony. I will tell everybody to keep their hands off unless they are chosen.

"Well, Stony, if you don't have any problems with me leading, everybody else can follow. We're going to head down the interstate to Rapid City."

"It's not a problem with me; I'll let everybody know we're ready to leave."

John gave his men a round-the-head signal to head out. It wasn't long before they were on the interstate heading west, followed by several trucks, pickups, and a couple of Humvees—an impressive moving train of vehicles.

Everything was fine until they reached Pierce, South Dakota's corner, where several men stood out on the road, waving at them to stop.

John was cautious and said to his men, "Keep your weapons close. Let's see what these guys want." As he pulled up and stopped, one of them approached his window.

"I'm looking for John Washington. Is he with you guys?"

John looked at him, "What are you looking for him for?"

"We were told to wait for him here and to join his group."

John asked again, "Who told you that?"

"A big, ugly-looking guy in black told us we were to join your group to hunt down this guy on these posters here. I was to give it to you."

"What else did he tell you?"

"To hunt down all the white people with him and leave no survivors."

"Okay, did you bring any transportation?"

"No, we were told you would provide transportation and all our needs. From here on out."

John, not sure, "All right, find yourselves a place to ride."

Stony approached John's window, "What was all that about?"

"We have more riders, so we're a bigger group now. When we get to Rapid City, we'll have to divide into smaller groups and spread around the country. Each group will have to manage itself."

It was sundown before they finally got to Rapid City and made camp at one of the outlying campgrounds. Everyone had something to eat after. John noticed several men had bottles of alcohol. Where had they found alcohol?

Stony said, "John, what do you think of the guys we picked up at the Pierre corner?"

"What do you mean, Stony?"

"Well, they are strange and weird looking, like evil looking weird, and they provided alcohol for everyone, which is making them all crazy, and talking about killing anybody they find, especially this guy they have on posters that offer 50 pounds of gold for the person who kills him."

"Stony, I've seen a person like him before in prison, and he had come to us with a plan. He told us that for our freedom, we were to go out and kill all evil we found to gain retribution for our crimes.

"I'm guessing the ones we picked up are part of his organization. They're pumping everybody up to go out and face evil, which will be a chore for some of these people. Anyway, let's deal with this in the morning."

*****

Second Day

The following day, John and Stony gathered everybody up and explained the plan of dividing them into groups of 6 to 8 and letting them roam the countryside independent .of each other

John continued, "We don't have the resources to care for everyone, so go around town, get as much as you can, and good luck hunting down evil.

You're on your own from this point on." John noticed the newcomers from Pierre had divided themselves into their groups, with one in each group; evil would lead each with the real agenda.

As the groups moved around town, collecting as much food and water as they could carry, they started their search, some heading east, others south, and west.

Oh, and they were gaining ground. All looking for that 50-pound gold prize at the end of the trail. And, they would kill anyone to collect the gold for themselves.

John joined his specialized group—25 members of the worst of the worst—and went east to establish a camp to work from. He was not foolish enough to go out and take on the enemy until they've been whittled down as far as possible. Until then. he planned to enjoy life, have meaningful experiences, and seek a compatible partner.

CHAPTER 13

Back at the Lodge

Ambushed

Matt was down at the corral taking care of his buckskin, ensuring it had plenty of food and hay. Buck, his faithful companion, had found a place on the hay to nap.

Lee, Donald, and Sarah were headed down the hill toward the corral. They were looking for Matt because they had a proposition to run by him about moving the barn to the Lodge area.

"Good morning Matt, how are you this fine morning?"

"Lee, that's just fine, thank you. What is on your mind? I can tell you have something cooking."

"Well, Matt, we plan to move the barn to this area, to the corrals."

"Lee, will you let Sarah tell Matt, because it is her plan?"

"OK, Don!"

Sarah winked at Donald. "I think we should divide into four groups. Each group will take one side of the building. We have a numbering scheme; they will follow it to number every piece of siding, take it down, stack it, and do the same with the inside timbers. Move the timbers to this area first, set up the barn, return with the siding, and do the same. Easy-peasy.

"What do you think of my plan, Matt?"

"It seems you have a structured plan, Sarah; Please go ahead and implement it."

Matt suggested that Sarah should take charge, as it's her plan, and that she should begin by gathering volunteers.

As the barn committee was walking away, chattering amongst themselves, Matt was pleased, thinking, *It's nice to see people excited about something again.*

Chuck located Matt. "I have been looking for you, Matt; what is on your agenda for today, Boss?"

"I'm going to take a ride down to where this barn is they're talking about moving, and check it out, while also giving my horse some exercise.

"What is your plan today, Chuck?"

"I volunteered to help Jake Savage, with a team of horses, get to your pickup and drag it back here so he can fix it. He seems pretty certain he can find the parts he needs."

Matt saddled his horse, thinking of this new barn they were discussing. *Buck, let's go.* As he was riding out, he thought it was such a wonderful day again, a great day to take a ride.

Sometime later, he arrived at the barn, and WOW! That was a huge barn, and there was another one behind it. *It's pretty ambitious, but I think their plan will work.*

Buck was in front of his horse. Then he stopped and let out a little growl, looking from side to side.

Matt had learned to trust Buck's senses. His automatic weapon was strapped to his back and he pulled it around to the front and started to dismount his horse, when something whizzed past his head into the barn, an arrow. *What the hell,* Matt thought, getting off his horse and slapping him on the rump to move him out of harm's way.

Matt needed a hiding place; he was too much in the open. He lay flat on the ground, motioning Buck to take cover as two more arrows flew over his head into the barn, so close.

It's only a matter of time before they home in on me; looking around behind him was a barn door; he had no idea where the arrows were coming from or where they were hidden.

And then he heard terrible screams, his chance to run for the door. Inside, he looked for a place to hide. The door was still ajar when Buck came running in and found him.

Looking at Buck's bloody mouth, he understood what all the screaming was.

After a while, Matt went through the back of the barn and circled to the front, looking for the people who ambushed him. Buck led him into the trees, where he found a significant amount of blood but no bodies. *Good job, Buck*, giving him some hugs.

It was late afternoon by the time Matt returned to the corral. After putting up his horse, he walked to his cabin.

Once Matt was inside the cabin, Chuck appeared. He had brought some food down from the Lodge. After eating, Matt planned to return to Sylvan Lake, take his fly rod, and do a little fishing. But first, he filled Chuck in on his day and showed him the arrows.

*****

Lake Side

Okay, Matt took a deep breath, savoring the peacefulness of Sylvan Lake with his fly rod in hand; he cast his line. The general ripple of the water soothing his mind was one of those perfect moments away from the morning's troubles that seemed far away.

Matt was focusing on his fishing when he heard a soft crunch of footsteps behind him. Turning around he saw a figure approaching, a woman with an air of confidence and familiar form.

"Maggie," Matt said, a smile tugging at his lips.

"Mind if I join you?" she asked, holding up her fishing rod.

"Not all," Matt replied, feeling the warmth spread through him. They fished side-by-side, the tranquility of the lake providing a perfect place for their growing attraction. Words weren't always necessary; sometimes, being in each other's presence was enough. And of course, she caught the first fish.

*****

Tracking the Enemy

The next day, Matt decided to take some of his closest friends to look again at the area around the barn to see if they could track down who was shooting at him.

First, Matt wanted to discuss the barn incident with Father Mike to emphasize the need for security. He also needed a few people to join him in finding the archer.

"Father Mike, do you understand that security will be needed when we take that barn apart?"

"Yes, Matt. We must ensure plenty of people are armed on the perimeter to keep everybody safe.

"So, what is your plan, Matt?"

"I am taking Chuck, Ben, maybe Sergeant Jones, one other, and a packhorse on a two to three-day trip. We will see if we can track down who was shooting arrows at me and where they went. This might be a threat we have to intervene with before it happens again."

"Right, Matt. Safe travels, see you when you get back."

Matt was walking out of the Lodge when he spotted Maggie to his right, walking towards him. He hurried out the front door, down the steps, and down to the corral, trying to avoid any kind of confrontation with her right now.

Chuck and Ben were already at the corral, saddling up their horses. Sergeant Jones came down the hill carrying his pack and his weapons; behind him was Dakota.

Dakota walked up to Matt; "I would like to go along."

"You understand, Dakota, we're going out to hunt down people, dangerous people. Are you sure you are up to this?"

"I understand what you are saying, Matt. I am ready to carry my share of the load to be more useful. So, if you accept me, I'd like to go along. I don't have any weapons; you'd have to give me something to protect myself."

"Okay, Dakota, saddle up your horse, and I will get you a weapon. Are you familiar with any kind of weapon?"

"Familiar with handguns, maybe 30-30 rifles or 30.6, but no automatic weapons."

Matt returned. "Okay, this is a handgun—a 9 mm with 15 rounds in the clip, four other clips, and a holster; this is a 308 sniper rifle with a scope and several clips. Please put it in your scabbard on your horse's saddle. This is a tactical vest—you wear it constantly in the field. It could save your life. We're going out for two or three days. Pack a backpack with essentials and be here in 30 minutes."

Later, Matt was sitting on his buckskin, looking around at his group, all saddled and ready to go. "Okay, let's move out."

Matt moved his group south from Sylvan Lake to the French Creek horse camp, where the barn was. They traveled in a single file. Buck was always in the lead, followed by Matt, who would keep an eye on Dakota for his first time out. Sergeant Jones brought up the rear.

They were just about to the barn when Buck stopped, turned around, and looked behind them. Then Matt and his team could also hear vehicles moving their way.

"I think it's probably the barn crew, Matt said, getting an early start on their day. Let's check out the area and ensure it's safe for them. Chuck and Ben go east around the barn and check around. We'll check around the west side and meet you at the south end of the barn."

The two trucks and several people on horseback pulled up, preparing to dismantle the barn and move it back to the Lodge area.

Matt concluded it was safe and not anything to be worried about.

Matt took the team south from the barn, Buck in the lead. He then returned to where he had found the individuals shooting the arrows.

After they arrived, Matt's team could see quite a bit of blood on the ground but no bodies. The blood left a clear trail south. When a rider approached, they were getting on their horses and about to leave. Matt recognized it as Maggie.

Maggie rode through the trees and stopped beside Matt.

She said, with a mix of curiosity and challenge, "Have you been trying to avoid me?" She said it just loud enough so only Matt could hear.

Matt glanced at her, feeling the weight of her gaze. "It's not that simple, Maggie. There's a lot on my mind right now!"

She nodded, understanding, but not entirely satisfied with his answer. "Okay, Matt, we're in this together, so whatever it is, we'll face it together. I'm very patient when I see something I want. Be safe," she said, returning to the barn.

Chuck looked at Matt. "That's a very beautiful woman, and she has the hots for you, Boss. What's the problem?"

Matt's responded, "We've wasted too much time already. Let's go move out." Matt retook the lead, riding steadily, trying to keep his mind on the mission.

Dakota rode up beside him. "Matt, I looked at the arrows you left with Father Mike. It's my opinion that some are Comanche arrows. By looking at the markings, they are really a nasty bunch of Indians; the others are Apache, who are even worse."

"Thank you, Dakota. That's excellent information; good thing I brought you along."

They had been following a trail for several hours now. Matt pulled up, got off his horse, and looked at the ground, trying to figure out what kind of tracks he was seeing. He turned and waved Dakota over.

"Dakota, what do you make of these tracks? Looks like horses, but no horseshoes."

"Matt, they look like two unshod ponies, and there's also a blood trail. Someone's been bleeding quite a bit."

"Thanks, Dakota, I heard you were a good tracker."

"Yes, I learned from my grandfather. He would take me out whenever he could, starting when I was young, teaching me how to track and all about nature, the trees. He was a wonderful man."

"Let me introduce you to Buck. This young man is Dakota, Buck. He's with us now. Dakota, please take the lead with Buck and do the tracking for us."

"Thank you, sir, for trusting me."

"Please avoid calling me sir; take the lead and stay alert for hidden dangers."

Sometime later in the afternoon, Dakota and Buck stopped, signaling to the rest of them to dismount and take cover. Dakota signaled Matt to join him. He was kneeling, looking ahead.

"Not sure, Matt, what's lying down ahead on the side of the trail?"

"Okay, let me get my binoculars and see what I can see."

Matt returned, focusing on the thing on the trail. He could tell it was a body, and it was not moving. There didn't appear to be anyone else around. "Good catch, Dakota.

"Sergeant, come with me. We'll go check it out. You're on the right side; I'll take the left. Move cautiously." They moved up from tree to tree until they got to the body.

"What do you think, Sergeant?"

"It looks to me like he has been dead for a while; something almost tore the side of his face off and part of his neck, so he bled to death."

"Yeah, Sergeant, I'm sure that Buck likely caused the damage to his face and neck."

Matt waved at the rest to join them.

"Dakota, what do you think about the body?"

"Well, it's an Apache. You can tell by the painted face, clothing, and the tattoos on his arms and face.

"And, sir, tracks of two horses leading to the south, one heavy track, the other light, led by the first."

Matt turned to the others. "We have about two more hours of daylight; let's start looking for a place to shelter for the night."

Matt waved to Dakota to go ahead and find them a safe place to stop and camp.

A half-hour later, Buck took a sharp left turn into the trees; Dakota followed him, unsure if he had found another body or sensed an ambush. Dakota saw him sitting beside a structure of some kind. "What did you find, boy?"

As Dakota approached, he saw an old hunting cabin in the woods, still in pretty decent shape. "Good job, Buck."

The others had followed Dakota in.

Matt looked at the structure. "Okay, guys, we've got a nice place to spend the night. Go ahead and unpack everything and take it inside. When you are done, stake out your horses for the night."

They could tell the inside had not been used for several years, but it was still clean and had a fireplace. Being this close to their enemies, Matt didn't want to start a fire that would let them know where they were. It would be a cold camp that night.

"Boss, should we set up a guard shift for the night?"

"Sergeant, Ben is going to be our guard for the night. He doesn't need much sleep, so he usually guards all night, and we don't have to worry."

"I am not sure I am comfortable, Matt; somebody watching all night by themselves."

"I understand, Sergeant. If you like, you can go out and walk and sit with him for a couple of hours or so, whatever makes you feel comfortable. I'm sure he would like the company."

Morning Camp

The following day, Matt woke to the smell of coffee, which was strange because they were in a cold camp. Yet Ben was by the fireplace with the coffee pot and skillets, cooking bacon and pancakes for breakfast.

"Ben, I thought I told everyone we should have a cold camp and hide our position, not give it away."

"Good morning, Matthew. Dakota showed me how to make a fire without any smoke, so that's why we're having breakfast. He is a very resourceful young man."

"In that case, Ben, I'll have a cup of coffee, pancakes, and bacon when you've got it ready."

An hour later, when the sun was just peeking over the eastern horizon, they were on their way south again, tracking two ponies—Dakota and Buck in the lead.

About 50 minutes later, Dakota stopped, dismounted, and led his horse into the trees. He motioned for the others to do the same—get off the trail and get in the trees. He motioned for Matt to come up and join him.

Dakota pointed up ahead, talking low. "Somebody's camped up ahead. They even have a little fire, and the two ponies are staked off to the side. This is our man."

"Sergeant, you, Chuck, and Dakota cover us. Ben and I will see if we can surprise the guy."

Matt and Ben walked through the trees as quietly as possible, sneaking up on the guy, sitting there with his back to them, getting warm by his fire, and eating something.

Matt was about 20 feet away and must have stepped on something because the man turned quickly, grabbed his bow, and started to shoot. All of a sudden, a hatchet came from behind Matt right into the guy's head; he fell dead. Matt looked at Ben, and he shrugged his shoulders. "It wasn't me." Matt turned around, and there was Dakota.

Matt walked back to Dakota. "I thought I told you to stay back and cover us."

"Sir, I was until I realized neither one of you had anything but firearms. Since that would let everybody in the country know we are here, I took the initiative to take him out quietly. Sorry."

Matt had to agree and said, "You are pretty handy with a hatchet!"

"That is again from my grandfather's days: learning how to use a hatchet, a knife, a bow, a spear, and whatever else you can get your hands on if you are in danger."

"Dakota, grab those two ponies; we can always use horses at the Lodge."

Matt was back in charge. "Let's keep moving forward. The trail ended with another dead body; they came from someplace."

It was getting kind of late in the afternoon. They stopped to eat something, pulled off in the trees, and were hidden from the open areas.

The team relaxed a little, eating cold meat sandwiches, which were like eating lard, and sat in their stomachs with only water to wash the glop down. Then Buck started growling, looking out towards the open area.

Matt jumped to his feet, walked up to the edge of the trees, and crouched down. He had his field glasses with him and scanned the area.

Chuck and Dakota were right behind him.

Dakota held Buck so he would not take off and run after whatever was in the open.

Matt whispered, "There is a man and three women on foot carrying backpacks with stuff. They seem hurried, constantly looking behind them, coming this way. They are not armed as far as I can tell. Let's intercept them when they get to these trees. Chuck and Ben were behind them, and Sergeant and Dakota were with me. Wait for my signal."

It wasn't long before the small group closed in on Matt's team. He signaled Chuck and Ben to move behind them.

Matt, Sergeant Jones, and Dakota stepped out before the small group and stopped them. They looked around for an escape, but there was none. They finally raised their arms, and the women started crying. "Please don't kill us; we won't tell anyone."

"Who are you? And what are you doing out here?" Matt demanded.

"I am Ravi. This is my wife Anika, and her two sisters, Lila and Maya, are from the Sioux Indian tribe of the Pine Bluff Indian Reservation. People from the reservation are hunting us because we will not go along with their agenda of killing everybody that's white.

"Are you going to kill us?"

Matt stood there looking at his team for an indication of their thoughts. They were all looking down and shaking their heads. *Okay, I guess I know what that means.*

Matt was concerned. "Who exactly is hunting, do you know?"

Ravi looked at Matt, "Bad people from the prison in Sioux Falls, South Dakota, Comanches, Apache, and Sioux, killing anyone who didn't go along with them or opposed them; they were behind us on horseback. We escaped by jumping into a river and hiding."

Chuck looked around. "How many are there behind you?"

Ravi's wife, Anika, was now beginning to feel safe and answered, "At least ten. They have killed so many of us already and raped all the women and young girls. We ran away; they were coming for me and my sisters.

"Tell them the rest, Ravi!"

Ravi continued with his wife's story. "Two leaders came after my 12-year-old sister; I walked in while the two of them were raping her; I grabbed a machete and killed them both."

Ravi told the group, "We had to run. I had killed two of their leaders, and they then killed friends of ours trying to find us."

Matt wanted more information. "How many are in the main camp, and how are they armed?"

Ravi thought for a second. "Around 60, with more coming in each day, armed with small arms and automatic weapons brought in by several evil-looking men working with the leader of the Sioux, Vern Two Shoes, and his pals, Timothy Blackbird and James Red Cloud."

Ravi and his wife kept staring at Matt. Your face looks like the one posted around the area. Are you the one they're offering gold for your head?"

Matt looked at them both and shrugged off the information.

Matt gathered his team together. "Okay, this is what I think. If 10 riders are coming with automatic weapons, we will probably be outgunned. Let's return to the Lodge and not leave any trail for them to follow."

"It looks like we killed the two scouts gathering intel on us, Matt."

"Yes, Dakota, I think you're right. Take Ravi and his family and put them on the ponies." Matt decided to take them along when they returned to the Lodge.

"Dakota, talk to the father and his family and tell them what the plan is. Let them know we will keep them safe and take them to our camp. They have nothing to fear from us; we will provide them protection and shelter."

"Okay, sir, I'm on it."

Matt looked at his team. "The rest of us need branches to rub out tracks so they can't follow us back to the Lodge.

*****

Long Ride Home

It was a long ride, stopping occasionally to rub out tracks. Late in the afternoon, they finally arrived at the barn area.

Matt noticed all the siding was off the barn and stacked on the sides of the barn, and several people were in the rafters taking those apart, making pretty good progress.

Matt led his team past the workers, not looking around. He kept his eyes straight ahead, not wanting to make eye contact with Maggie.

Soon after arriving at the Lodge, Matt took the new people to meet Father Mike and gave him a report on what they had found in the field and possibly a new threat from the South.

When Matt had finished, he headed back down to the corral to take care of his horse. When he arrived, the rest of his team had rubbed down, fed, and watered his horse, turning him loose in the corral.

He thanked them and then headed for the cabin to take a long hot shower, eat some leftovers, sit in front of the fireplace, and drink a little whiskey, contemplating the new threat and how they would deal with it.

*****

Next Day

The following day, the birds' chirping woke Matt. The sun was coming through the window. It was such a nice feeling, just lying there stretched out, thinking a cup of coffee would be nice. He might have to go to the Lodge for a hot breakfast that morning.

Someone was pounding on his door. Buck got up and ran to the door. Matt put on some pants to see who was there that early in the morning.

Opening the door, he found Father Mike and Sergeant Jones standing there. "What the hell are you guys doing here this early morning?"

"Matt, we need to discuss something with you. Can we come in?"

"Depends. Did you bring any coffee with you?"

Father answered first, "No, we did not. But we still need to talk to you."

"All right, then. Come in, sit down, and let me put on my shirt." Matt walked back into his room, grabbed his shirt, and returned.

Chuck exited his room, yelling, "What the hell's going on with all that noise?"

"Chuck, make some coffee, would you?"

"Yes, Boss!"

Matt sat in the living room and looked at Father Mike and Sergeant Jones. "Okay, what is going on here?"

Father Mike started. "Chris King came in this morning with a couple of refugees. According to them, some of their group was murdered along the way by five hostile men. They not only killed their friends, but they also chopped them up and set them on fire."

Now it was Sergeant Jones's turn.

"Matt, we were hoping you could take a group and find these people and take care of them before they kill any more innocent people."

Chuck came over with a cup of coffee, handed it to Matt, and then sat down.

"Father, we have just returned from five days of intensive riding. It's hard for me to ask my team to go back out again so soon."

"I understand, Matt, but I don't know how far away these guys are from us, and maybe finding our camp.

"Matt, I have a map here that Chris drew. He said they are northeast of us, but we are not sure exactly where they are now."

"Boss, you know I am in!"

"Thanks, Chuck, I appreciate that."

Sergeant Jones was next, "I am also going along, Matt!"

"Well, Sergeant Jones makes three of us." Matt looked at the stove where Ben poured himself a cup of coffee. He raised his cup to Matt and nodded. He was also going.

There was another knock at the door. Ben walked over and opened the door. Chris King and Dakota were there. They walked in and waved, so they were in.

"Okay, then. We should saddle up and load a couple of packhorses; it will take a while before we can go, Father."

Father Mike interrupted Matt.

"It's all taken care of, Matt. I had your horses saddled and loaded two packhorses."

"You are pretty sure of yourself, Father, huh?"

Matt got up. "First, I need some breakfast before I go anywhere."

Father waved, "It's done, Matt. Helen, and her crew are bringing down breakfast now."

Father stood up. "If nothing is further, I must return to the Lodge and speak with the refugees who arrived this morning. It sounds like one was a carpenter and another a dental hygienist in their previous lives. We can use both. I wish you well and hope you come back in one piece. God bless you!"

As Father approached the door, Helen and her breakfast team entered, placed the food on the table, and stood aside, waiting for Matt's team to eat.

Chuck looked at Helen, "What an excellent breakfast! This will stick with me most of the day."

Everyone gathered up their gear and headed for the corral. Matt stood there, hands on his saddle, ensuring it was nice and tight. He heard a soft voice behind him. "Matt?"

He knew who it was, without even turning around, "Maggie. How are you?"

"How am I? Is that all you have to say?"

Matt looked confused. "Not sure what to say, I guess."

"Okay, Matt. I guess I am expecting too much from you at this point. I have a little present for you."

"Present? What is it, Maggie?"

"Matt, it's a present, so you have to open it and find out!"

Matt opened the present and found a badge, a US marshal's badge made of metal. You could tell it was quite the handiwork.

Matt was confused, "What is this for?"

"Some of the people you rescued are pretty handy, and they are so appreciative that they felt you needed a badge to go along with your name, Matt Dylan. Now you are a US Marshal, so take it and keep your mouth shut."

She turned around, flipped her hair, and walked off. He guessed he might have pissed her off a little bit, pinning it on his shirt, *Humm, US Marshal!*

Chuck rode beside him and saw the marshal's badge pinned to his shirt, "So now we have to call you Marshal Dylan?"

"Being a smart ass again, are you, Chuck?" Both laughed as they rode out towards the northeast, looking for the next bunch of banditos.

CHAPTER 14

War Party

Chief?

After leaving the prison, Vern Two Shoes and eight other followers walked into Sioux Falls to find transportation. It took them a while, but they finally found sufficient transportation to leave and go south along the Nebraska border to the reservations.

The first stop was the Santee Indian Reservation south of Gavin's Point Dam. As they drove into the reservation, they saw no soul nor heard any sound of dogs or people.

It was eerily spooky. All the doors of the stores were open. They found a gas station that had diesel. Their three trucks were new, diesel-powered, and could hold 40 gallons. Leaving the station, they picked up as much food as possible and moved on to the next reservation.

Vern's second-in-command was Timothy Blackbird; he had the map in his hand.

Blackbird was riding shotgun and giving directions on how to make the next reservation. Vern hoped they would find somebody alive.

"It looks like the next reservation is that of the Ponca tribe around Lynch, Nebraska. Just stay on Highway 12. It is not far, but it doesn't look huge. I don't think we will find any people until we get to the bigger reservations."

Sure enough, when they drove through Ponca, they found absolutely nobody, hardly any stores, and nothing they needed, so they kept moving.

"All right, Tim, what's our next stop?"

"We could go north from Valentine to Mission, South Dakota. The Sioux nation has a reservation there, but looking at the map, it looks like a thousand people, so I don't think we'll have much luck going north. It is even more sparse than the other reservations we came through."

Vern had enough. "We'll head for Pine Ridge and won't stop at the small ones anymore."

Sometime later, they pulled into Pine Ridge and found people standing around everywhere. The town was completely gone—nothing but trees and grass, no stores or highway.

Vern pulled over and stopped.

A couple of young men approached Vern's window and asked if they were there to save them from everything that had happened. They were told to expect a great chief who would arrive in a red chariot. "It looks like your truck is a red chariot, so maybe you are the chief?"

Vern left his pickup and waved at his other followers to get out of the trucks, stand down, and keep their weapons down.

"Do you have any kind of leader?" Vern asked.

One young man stepped up. "No, we don't have anybody leading us, we are all alone. All our leaders are dead; most of our people are dead."

Vern was intrigued. "What's your name, young man?"

"My name is Clayton. I am an Apache and am damn proud of it."

"Clayton, how many people are you?"

"We are 25 men, and we have been able to care for ourselves, so it hasn't been a problem. But we don't know for sure what to do from this point on because our lives are so disrupted."

"Just you 25?" Vern asked.

"There are others at the camp, probably 30, some men and women, and children."

"Camp? Clayton, what kind of camp are you talking about?"

Clayton described the camp. "We found all the teepees from all the powwows we've had over the years. We set those up for people to live in and found enough wood to make shelters for others. There is enough room for you and your men."

Vern was quick, "Right? Clayton, I want to make you part of my inner circle; let me introduce you to Wakiza Warrior, Chaska First Son, Mato Bear, Hotah Strong Voice, and Tatanka Buffalo. All are my inner circle, and you will be helping to give me advice on taking care of our people, our number one concern." There was rousing applause from the energetic young men.

"All of you listen to what I have to say; we have another mission; we're going to take over this whole country, we're going to kill every white person we meet or anybody who disagrees with us and our philosophy. I am looking for people who are willing to join me.

"What say you?"

All 25 gave a rousing yes, whooped, hollered, got excited, and said, "Let us take our country back. It was ours to begin with. We want it back. We're with you, Chief."

"Chief, huh? And what about us, Vern? What part of your inner circle do we belong to?"

"Timothy Blackbird, you and James Red Cloud are going to be my enforcers, it's going to be your job to keep everybody in line by using any methods you deem necessary.

"With that idea, pick ten ambitious young men and make them part of your team. Train them to be vicious and relentless in carrying out our mission.

"Now, let's examine this camp and the rest of the people and start taking control of everything."

Vern followed Clayton to the campground, a short distance away.

As Vern walked into the camp, he noticed several teepees and shelters and went to the last one. There was a nice, big stream of water south of the campground and a great, big bonfire in the middle of the campground.

"Chief, this is your tepee, which is reserved for you alone. Please make yourself at home. I'll find a place for the rest of your men to stay."

Vern went into the teepee, started taking his clothes off, and got comfortable. It was nice how they fixed it up like this. Then he heard a noise outside. "Who's there?"

Someone pulled the flap apart from the teepee and stepped in, a beautiful black-haired woman. "My name is Marisa Little Hawk, and I am yours, Chief Tashu."

*****

Chief Tashu?

Several days passed, and new people were constantly coming into camp. One group of four stood out as they went into the camp with all kinds of arms and ammunition.

They approached the Chief, saying, "We are here to help you."

Vern was skeptical of the newcomers. "How do you think you will help me?"

"Chief, we have been sent here by a tall man in black. You met him. He sent us here to help you, and you have no choice."

Vern could not help but notice they were strange-looking. Ugly is not the word he would use because it doesn't begin to describe how they looked, and they smelled like sulfur. Could it be the demons he had heard about? From Hell? Couldn't be. Those were just old stories to scare children.

A couple of days later, he was enjoying Marisa's company when he heard some guys outside shouting his name, "Tashu!" He got up, put on some pants and a shirt, and walked out to see what all the ruckus was about.

"What's going on here, guys? Red Cloud, why are you shouting?"

"Tashu someone has killed both Matos and Hotah, they were hacked to death with a machete."

"What the hell are you telling me? Somebody killed two of my inner circle?

"Who were they, Red Cloud?"

"Chief, we think it was a man named Ravi."

"How would you know it was him, Red Cloud?"

"I would rather not say Chief."

"Blackbird, do you know what he means? He would rather not say. "I want to know now who it was." As Vern moved closer to them, Clayton handed him a knife. "Now tell me!"

"OK, OK, Hotah and Mato were raping Ravi's 12-year-old sister, and he walked in on them."

Vern Tashu, the Chief now, had just suffered a personal blow when Ravi, in a desperate bid to protect his family, had killed two members of his inner circle.

This act incited the wrath of Tashu's loyal warriors, who now had blood in their eyes.

Vern called Clayton over by his side. "Take your band of warriors and hunt down this guy who just killed two of my friends, bring the man back alive."

"What about the women, Chief?"

Chief Tashu raised his hands for quiet. "Whoever catches this murderer gets the women as his reward, to do as he wishes."

Clayton moved across the camp, shouting for his seven warriors to join him for the hunt. They were fiercely loyal and highly skilled, making them formidable adversaries.

Mounting their ponies, each rider, having been painted with battle markings, had also painted his face for war. The warriors moved with a singular purpose, driven by duty and vengeance. As they attempted to close the gap on the quarry, tensions mounted within each warrior, inflaming their desire to kill and collect the reward.

Chief Tashu grabbed Timothy Blackbird and James Red Cloud, his two cellmates. "I want to see what those two were up to. Let's walk over to the hut and see what happened."

Arriving at the hut, the Chief walked in first; he was not expecting such a gruesome scene with both his men lying on the floor, all hacked to pieces, their heads nearly cut off, and on the bed a 12-year-old girl with no clothes on, also dead.

"One of you grab a sheet and cover that poor girl; I swear if he hadn't killed them, I would have done so myself.

"We don't make war on children. All right, let's get help to bury them someplace outside of the compound, or you can throw their bodies in a canyon, I don't care. And take that poor girl and give her a respectful burial with a marker; she deserves that at least."

As they left the hut and crossed the compound, the Chief asked what they had been doing lately.

Blackbird was the first to speak. "Well, we took several of the warriors, divided them into pairs, and sent them out in different directions to see if they could contact anyone and then report back to us. So far, none of them have returned, so we don't know what's outside of our area yet."

"Tell me about the four Ghostriders and what they are up to."

"Chief, they spend time jacking everybody up, getting them excited, binging on more weapons, training different people to use the weapons, and urging everybody to accept a war."

"Look, you two, you can't have a war until you have somebody to war against; until our scouts return, we don't have any enemies.

"I want both of you to keep an eye on what is happening in our little community, no surprises."

CHAPTER 15

Running Man

Black Hills Canyons

“Captain, you think we can outrun them?”

“I don’t know, Preacher. The hills will make it difficult for anybody to follow us, especially when it rains occasionally, hopefully washing out our tracks. We’re going to have to stop here pretty soon. Big canyons are coming up, which means our trucks won’t benefit us.”

“We also need more food, Captain, which means we must rustle up some game.”

“Yes, I know, and we also need horses, Preacher.

“Preacher, I remember something you said: Cowboy is the expert, so get him. It’s time we started looking for both game and horses.

“Cowboy, we have been running for three days and are mostly out of food. It looks like the canyons are coming up, so we are limited in using these trucks. We need to go out and find some horses and some game.

“So, tell us what you need. We need to get going.”

“Captain, we need to take the small truck. We can get through some of those canyons with it, load it up with saddles and bridles, all the equipment we might need, and enough supplies for two to three days.

“We will have to hunt down the horses. I know there are horses out here, but they are running wild, and it will take time to catch them.”

"Okay, Lefty, you and Skippy stay here and establish a camp; the rest of us are going to go out and see if we can get some horses. It will take some time; we'll be back as soon as possible.

In the meantime, empty out the big trailer; the truck and trailer aren't doing us any good anymore, so we will leave them here.

"Cowboy, you drive the truck, and I'll ride shotgun—the rest of you in the backseat.

"Let's go; we need to get moving."

*****

Later in the Day

"Cowboy, you did a wonderful job driving up and down the hills, shifting into four-wheel-drive, and climbing up and down."

"Preacher and Bear in the backseat didn't care for it, Captain, because it jostled them around, but we made good time."

Every once in a while, Cowboy would get out and check for signs of any horses. So far, nothing. It was almost sundown when Cowboy pulled up and stopped the truck.

He had his window down, listening. They were on the crest of a hill.

"Captain, all of you stay put. I'm going to check out the other side of this hill."

In a short while, Cowboy came back all excited. He had just found seven horses down in a small draw by a stream. "If we walk in from the end, we can block them in, and it will be easy to catch them; everybody grab a bridal, let us go."

Cowboy, Captain, Preacher, and Bear made their way down a narrow canyon. In front of them were seven horses grazing peacefully.

Cowboy and the rest, each with a bridle, were intent on capturing the horses. The trucks were failing them now, and capturing these horses was the only chance to continue the journey with speed and stealth, continuing to run from death.

The canyon walls provided cover as they moved cautiously, avoiding sudden movements that might spook the horses. Cowboy signaled the others to spread out, moving slowly, and closing the distance between themselves and the targets. Captain whispered, "Be quick and quiet." Bear and Preacher nodded in agreement, their eyes never leaving the horses. The team was ready for anything, but capturing these horses without incident would be crucial for their mission.

Cowboy, Captain, Preacher, and Bear held a bridle, moving slowly and steadily toward the horses; they spread out, each choosing a specific horse and closing the gap carefully. The horses, sensing the calm and deliberate approach, mainly remained still, their ears flicking in alertness.

With a gentle whisper, Cowboy reached out to stroke the neck of a dark bay, his movements slowly reassuring. The horse snorted softly but didn't bolt.

A few feet away, Captain extended his hand to a chestnut mare speaking in soothing tones. Preacher and Bear did the same with their chosen horses, using their experience and calm demeanor to gain the animal's trust.

The moment was tense, but each man knew the journey ahead would be easier if he secured his horse. With steady hands and patient movements, they began to close the distance and slip the bridles on the horses.

Captain Bill was happy each had bridled their horse. "Let's leave the canyon and climb up the hill to where the pickup is parked. It's too late in the day to go back to the campsite so we will spend the night here.

"What do you suggest, Cowboy, we do with these horses until morning?"

"Captain, I suggest we tie some rope between some of these trees and picket the horses to the rope for the night. Also, it's starting to rain. I have a tarp under the saddles; if we string another rope, we can make a tent to sleep under tonight and keep the saddles dry; it will get wet."

"It sounds like a plan. As Captain Picard would say, make It SO!" That got a laugh out of everybody.

*****

Wet Morning

Next morning Captain Bill woke up and looked around. At least they were dry but stiff.

As Bill stood up, "All right, the rest of you. It is time to get up. We have to get moving; the sun's coming up."

After everyone was awake and moving around, Cowboy took them to the horses and showed them how to saddle up. None of them had ever done that before.

Cowboy said, "If we don't do it right, we'll know as soon as we fall out of the saddle."

It took them a few tries, but they finally got the hang of it.

The next part was getting on the horse, and it was hilarious watching them all try it for the first time. They were about to leave when Cowboy handed out beef jerky. He called it breakfast, and told them it was all they had.

Cowboy looked at his new students, "It's a few hours' ride back to camp. I'll go slow at the beginning, and then when you get used to it, we'll pick up speed."

Five hours later, they were riding up the hill towards camp. As they crested the hill, the scene in front of them was a horrific, gruesome sight. Lefty was lying on the ground; his other arm, his good arm, had been hacked off and lay beside him, and his head was also cut off. Skippy had both his legs cut off and his head. Somebody had intentionally left a message, and they were angered beyond description that two of their best friends were lost in such a horrible way.

“Captain, we need to do something for them; we need to bury our friends.”

“I understand what you are saying, Bear, but we cannot get any closer. Somebody’s probably watching this site and waiting for us to return. We need to leave now. Let’s get out of here right now. Cowboy, take us out of here. There is nothing left. They took the truck and all our food. There is nothing here for us anymore.”

They turned and rode out, not looking back at their friends lying there, hacked to death most horribly. All of them wanted revenge, but they didn’t have enough firepower to take on whoever was in charge of doing this; all they could do was run.

Captain told them, “There’s going to be a reckoning.”

Cowboy was in the lead. They rode as hard as they could with new people on horseback. And then it was dark. They needed to stop.

Cowboy found a small cove of trees, and said, “It’s a good place to hide for now. Unsaddle your horses. We still have the ropes to picket them to the trees.”

“Cowboy, this is a cold camp, no fires.”

Captain and the rest were under the trees, lying against their saddles, listening to the sounds of the night, hoping they were not being followed. They were too tired to care.

“Preacher, I have a question for you.”

"Yes, Bear, what is it? What kind of questions do you have for me?"

"Just wondering, Lefty and Skippy had fresh starts, does that mean they were without sin, and when they died, did they go to heaven, and if that is true, does that mean the same thing for the rest of us?"

"It's a good question, Bear. The only answer I have for you is that I hope so; we all are without sin and can make it to heaven."

Cowboy was listening, "What if we have to kill somebody or worse, many somebodies? What happens then, Preacher?"

"You don't understand, Cowboy; if you have to kill somebody in self-defense, that is different than if you go out and just kill somebody innocent for no reason. You are allowed to kill to save your life or the lives of others."

"Thank you for that explanation, Preacher," said Captain Bill. "So, it means that when I killed Zero, it was in self-defense?"

"Bill, that is probably on the line; it might have been self-defense. It was justified, but I'll leave it to somebody higher than me to call whether it was self-defense."

"Okay, Preacher, I'll take that explanation. Now, everybody, get to sleep. We need to rise and shine before the crack of dawn."

By early morning, they rode out, heading southeast with a piece of jerky for breakfast again.

Cowboy was getting a little frustrated. He had to stop every couple of hours because the new horsemen had sore butts. They had to stretch their legs and walk around a little. And then they went again.

Several hours later, Cowboy came over a hill and saw Mount Rushmore. It still existed; what a fantastic sight!

The others rode up beside him and marveled at one of the most iconic sites in the world.

"Captain, captain!"

"Yes, Bear, what is it?"

"Captain, I used to work here long ago, and I know of a good place to hide behind the faces. Nobody else hardly knows about it. A good place, I think, to hide away, maybe."

"Bear, take the lead, and we will follow you."

Bear started in the lead, riding down the hill with conviction; he knew where he was going. Sometime later, they found themselves on the side of the mountain surrounded by big granite boulders in a grassy clearing. Behind the boulders, another grassy area enclosed by huge rocks, ideal for the horses.

Captain rode up to Bear. "I must hand it to you, Bear; this spot is nice. Now, all we need to do is find something to eat. I'm getting tired of hardtack."

"Captain, please go ahead and unsaddle the horses, put them down below, and prepare the makings for a small fire. I'll see if I can find something to eat."

"Okay, Cowboy, it sounds like a plan—anything but what we've eaten the past few days. We'll get the horses down below and unsaddle them."

Cowboy returned an hour later with two rabbits. What a festive time they had—fresh meat.

CHAPTER 16

Death is a Nightingale.

Death Riders

Exhausted from their three-day run, Captain, Preacher, Cowboy, and Bear found temporary refuge among the granite boulders behind the faces of Mount Rushmore.

The mix of the pursuing enemies—Mexicans, Indians, Blacks, and now a sinister ghost rider—had driven them relentlessly. Finally, feeling a brief sense of security, they gathered around a small fire, savoring the rabbits Cowboy had managed to catch.

Their meager meal was the first decent food they had in days, and for a moment, they allowed themselves to relax, listening to the night birds singing.

The full moon cast shadows on the monumental presidential faces looming above, a silent testament to their struggle. As they ate, the crackle of the fire and the whispers of the wind provided a rare moment of peace.

Suddenly, without warning, the tranquility shattered. An attack came from all directions, the enemy had tracked them to their hidden spot. Bullets whizzed past in the air, the quiet was now filled with the sound of gunfire and shouts.

Under the full moon, Captain, Cowboy, Preacher, and Bear could see their attackers closing in. As they breached the circle of boulders, a fierce battle erupted.

Captain fired his handguns precisely, while Cowboy shot as fast as possible. Preacher attempted to flank their attackers but suddenly found himself face-to-face with an Apache warrior. With quick reflexes, Preacher fired three shots into the man's chest, watching as he slid down the granite rock, leaving a trail of crimson.

Bear, in a display of raw strength, grabbed two assailants by the neck as they fired into his chest. Despite the bullets, he shrugged off the pain and snapped their necks, dropping them lifeless to the ground. Turning to look at Captain, Bear smiled before a bullet found its mark. Locking eyes with Captain one last time, Bear fell, a warrior to the end.

*****

After two days of hard riding, Chuck, Sergeant Jones, Chris, Dakota, Ben, and Matt set up camp. They had been on the lookout for the banditos but instead found themselves caught up in various little skirmishes with outlaws.

The sound of gunfire shattered the night, pulling them from their brief sleep.

Reacting swiftly, they saddled their horses and rode towards the commotion. Upon arrival, they saw Captain, Cowboy, and Preacher desperately needing help, surrounded and outnumbered by their attackers. Without hesitation, they dismounted and joined the fray, their weapons blazing.

Their sudden arrival turned the tide of battle. Matt, Chuck, Sergeant Jones, Chris, and Dakota fired with precision, taking down as many assailants as possible while trying to save the three trapped individuals. The chaos of the fight was intense, and the combined efforts began to break the enemy's assault.

Except for one, who kept coming, Chris kept firing. *I know I hit this guy several times, but he keeps coming.*

Ben stepped up, pulled out his golden bow, and fired a golden arrow, hitting the assailant—the ghost rider—squarely in the chest. He immediately dropped and turned into ashes.

Chris and Sergeant Jones simultaneously asked, "What the hell was that?"

Matt walked over to Chris and Jones. "I will fill you in when we return to the Lodge. For now, don't worry; we need to go."

Captain, Preacher, and Cowboy were exhausted from the intense fight. They were unsure who came to their rescue until they heard a voice shout, "Hold your fire! We're friendly. We're here to help you. We're coming in. Don't shoot."

Relief washed over them as they lowered their weapons, recognizing that reinforcements had arrived in time. Matt and his team emerged from the shadows, their faces lit by the moonlight, confirming their friendly intentions.

"Thanks," Captain said, his voice filled with gratitude. "We were starting to think we wouldn't leave here."

Matt nodded, "We heard the gunfire and knew someone was in trouble. I'm glad we could help."

Preacher and Cowboy exchanged wary but relieved glances. The unexpected help turned the tide, and now they had time to regroup and strategize for what lay ahead.

After the introductions, Matt asked Bill Stone, "What are your plans now?"

Bill replied, "We have been just running for our lives for days; they've killed several of my people already."

Matt glanced at his team, looking for some kind of acknowledgment, and they all nodded their heads.

"Well, you're welcome to join us. We have a safe place about two days' ride from here. The sun is about to rise, so we need to get moving now."

Bill Stone nodded, looking around at the weary faces of his companions. "We could use a safe place. We'd be glad to ride with you.

"First we need to bury our friend Bear, a courageous man."

Matt looked at the body of a large man with dead hostiles lying around him. "We would like to help, it would be an honor."

As the first light of dawn began to break, they mounted their horses and set off toward the Lodge. The combined group moved with renewed purpose and strength, ready to face whatever challenges awaited them. United, they knew they had a better chance of surviving the pearls of the day that lay ahead.

After hours of hard riding, the group finally stopped to give the horses a breather. Matt's team shared their food with their new companions, and everyone appreciated the short break.

In the saddle again, they continued to ride until it was nearing the end of the day. They found a campsite as dusk fell, deciding on a cold camp without fires to avoid detection.

They sat in the growing darkness, quietly eating and reflecting on the journey. Suddenly, the rest stop was shattered as four Apache warriors rushed them. One of them threw an axe, hitting Preacher square in the chest, killing him instantly. The rest of the crew reacted swiftly, their guns blazing as they took down all the attackers, scanning the surroundings for more threats.

Bill Stone (Captain) knelt by the Preacher's side, disbelief and grief etched on his face. "Oh my God, Preacher," he whispered, the loss of a friend weighing heavily on his heart.

Ben looked at Matt. "I think we're okay for the rest of the night, but I'll keep guard throughout the night just in case.

"Go ahead and sleep. I'll keep my usual watch, and maybe my companions from the celestial heavens will give me some information or answers."

Matt nodded, grateful for Ben's unwavering dedication. The group settled down, trusting Ben to keep them safe through the night.

Bill and Cowboy's loss of Preacher still weighed heavily on them, but they knew they had to rest and renew their strength for the challenges ahead.

As Ben stood watch, he felt a quiet sense of resolve. He whispered a silent prayer to the celestial beings and asked for guidance; hopefully, they would provide some insight and protection they desperately needed. The night was still under the watchful eyes of the heavens as the group found a brief rest in their ongoing journey.

Matt had the group up early the following day. They shared a quiet meal of cold elk sandwiches for breakfast. After eating, the mood was somber as Cowboy and Bill took a moment to give Preacher a proper farewell, burying him with solemn respect.

Matt knew the loss of one of them weighed heavily on everyone, but he knew they couldn't linger. They mounted their horses and rode hard at his hand signal, driven by the urgent need to reach the Lodge before nightfall.

They needed to inform everyone about the potential danger that might be approaching. The ride was grueling, but their determination and sense of duty pushed them forward.

As the sun began to set, casting long shadows across the landscape, they could see the Lodge in the distance. Exhausted but resolute, they knew their next challenge would be to prepare the Lodge and its inhabitants for whatever might come their way.

Matt and his team arrived at the Sylvan Lake corral and dismounted. Their exhaustion was evident, but their determination was unshaken. Matt signaled to Bill, and the two of them made their way up to the Lodge to meet Father Mike.

Father Mike greeted Matt with relief and concern, sensing the urgency of their arrival. "What's the situation, Matt?" he asked.

Matt took a deep breath, recounting the events and the imminent threat they faced. He spoke of their encounters and losses in the relentless pursuit of their enemies as Matt detailed their escape and journey.

Father Mike listened intently, his expression growing more serious.

Matt continued, “We need to fortify the Lodge. We can't let them catch us off guard. We have to prepare for a potential attack.”

Father Mike nodded. We have some supplies and weapons stored. We can start preparing immediately. Everyone in the Lodge needs to be ready.”

Matt and Bill exchange determined glances, “Bill and Cowboy are ready to contribute to the defensive efforts.”

Bill decided to confide in Matt and Father Mike about his past. He revealed that he had been in prison and that two other groups were heading in their direction, one to the north and one to the south. Their primary aim is to wipe out all white people and take over the world.

Matt and Father Mike listened intently, understanding the gravity of the situation. They knew they had to act quickly to fortify the Lodge and prepare for the potential onslaught.

Bill continued, the ones chasing us were a mix of Mexicans, Indians, and Blacks. We broke away from that group, seeking redemption for our past mistakes. Now that we've been given a second chance, we're ready to fight against evil, even if it means dying for it.

Matt and Father Mike exchanged glances, understanding the gravity of Bill's words. This newfound alliance, forged in the fires of battle, provided two new members to their cause.

Father Mike looked at Matt and said, “How are we fortifying such a large area? It's massive.”

Matt looked at Father Mike and said, “Well, first, I would cut down some of the big trees around here, bring them up to the Lodge, and form a barrier around the Lodge—two or three trees deep at least.”

Matt continued, "Second, I would take a group of warriors and take the fight to the enemy instead of waiting for them to come to us."

Father Mike pondered Matt's strategy, recognizing the urgency of their situation. The Lodge's expansive area made it challenging to fortify, but Matt's plan to create a barrier using large trees is practical and a strong barrier.

Father Mike agreed. "Let's get to work then. We'll need everyone we can muster. While we build the barrier, I agree you should organize an army of men and women for an offensive move; taking the fight to them could give us the upper hand."

Matt nodded, "I'll rally the team. We must act quickly; every second counts."

Matt noticed on the way in that morning that significant progress had been made on the new barn; the framing was nearly complete. It was unfortunate to pull everyone off that project, but the priority was fortifying the Lodge for the survival of all.

Matt and Father Mike quickly organized groups to cut down the most substantial trees they could find. They harnessed horses to haul the logs back to the Lodge. Others worked tirelessly to set them up in a sturdy barrier. It was backbreaking work, but over two days, with everyone pitching in, the barrier was finally in place.

Optimism began to take root as all the workers stood back to admire their handiwork. The Lodge was now better defended, and everyone felt a new sense of purpose. They knew the barrier wouldn't be enough, but it was a crucial step in their defensive preparations.

Father Mike informed Matt that while he had been away, everyone in the camp was trained to shoot. "We're well-armed and prepared to take shifts guarding the front and the larger areas."

Matt nodded in approval. "That's good news, Father Mike. With everyone trained and ready, we stand a better chance of holding off attacks. We will establish a schedule to ensure that personnel are always on duty. We need to be vigilant and proactive in our defense."

After two days of hard work on the barriers, Matt's team was well-rested and ready for the next phase of their plan. It was time to take a well-armed group that would go on the offensive, hunting down the people who were hunting them.

Matt knew he needed about 10 to 15 capable individuals, armed and good on horseback, to form a small army for this mission. He gathered everyone together at the Lodge and explained the plan, emphasizing the importance of their mission and the need to act swiftly and decisively. "We can't just wait for them to come to us," Matt said firmly. We need to take the fight to them and ensure our safety."

Volunteers quickly stepped forward, ready to join Matt in this crucial mission. The group was diverse and determined, each bringing unique skills and strengths. They prepared their horses and checked their weapons, knowing the mission's success depended on their readiness and coordination.

Matt's team of fifteen set out early in the morning, accompanied by four packhorses loaded with ammunition and food. They rode under clear skies, shadows following them. Buck was scouting ahead as usual, his keen eyes and ears always looking for signs of danger.

As they rounded a bend in the trail, Matt noticed someone riding up beside him. He turned and saw Maggie, her presence a comforting and familiar sight. They rode side-by-side, and they had a mutual understanding between them.

"It's a beautiful day for a ride," Maggie remarked, her tone light but her eyes serious.

"Sure is," Matt replied, appreciating the brief moment of calm amidst the tensions of their mission. They knew the stakes were high, but having each other's company made the journey easier.

They had ridden hard most of the day, spreading out to avoid bunching up on the trail. Each member of the group maintained a watchful eye. Dakota was positioned at the rear, looking for any signs of pursuit or ambush from behind.

As they rode, the terrain changed, becoming rougher and more challenging. Matt signaled the group to slow down as they approached a narrow pass that required careful navigation. Buck, scouting ahead, raised his head and stopped.

Matt got off his horse and walked up beside Buck, who had spotted something in the distance: a small group of riders moving in their direction.

Matt motioned for everyone to take cover behind the rocks and trees that lined the pass. They waited, silent and tense, as the riders grew closer. It was time to put their plan into action and confront the enemy hunting them.

The pass was wide and long, offering plenty of hiding places. Matt's team waited, their eyes scanning the terrain. Suddenly, they saw their pursuers, a mixture of Indians, Mexicans, and Blacks all on horseback. Then, the riders stopped abruptly, dismounted, and took cover behind the trees and rocks.

The silence was shattered as the fight erupted. Gunfire echoed in the pass, bullets whizzing past as both sides engaged in a fierce and vicious battle. Matt's team responded determinedly; each member focused on destroying the enemy.

The chaos of the fight was intense, with the sound of gunshots and shouts filling the air. The rocky terrain provided cover and obstacles, making the battle even more challenging. Despite the odds, Matt's team fought with everything they had, determined to overcome their relentless pursuers.

Matt's brow showed concern. He looked at Sergeant Jones. "How do you suppose they knew we were here? We were pretty well hidden."

Sergeant Jones scanned the area with his binoculars. "It looks like there were more hostiles behind us," he said grimly. "They must've been in radio contact; we are surrounded."

Matt, realizing the gravity of their situation, quickly formulated a plan. "We need to break through their lines and regroup," he said firmly. "Everyone, stay low and move fast. We'll fight our way out of here if we have to."

The team nodded with determination. They knew the odds were against them, but they were ready to fight their way to safety. They coordinated their movements, using the terrain to their advantage and firing strategically to create openings in the enemy's lines.

Despite the cover of trees and rocks, Matt's team felt the pressure of being surrounded and trapped.

As Matt took cover, he tried to strategize their next move, when the sound of rotor blades reached his ears.

"Chuck, is that a chopper?"

"Yeah, Boss, I hear it." Chuck's face lit up with a glimmer of hope. "I've got my radio here. Let's see if I can contact them."

"Good. Chuck, use the callsign SEAL Team Three."

Chuck quickly set up the radio and began transmitting. "SEAL Team Three, calling Chopper. Come in, Chopper. We are trapped and surrounded. Can you assist us?"

After a tense moment of static heard only on the radio, a voice crackled through: "This is Chopper Thunder, who is this?"

Matt took over the radio. "This is Matt Dylan, U.S. Navy SEAL team. We're trapped and surrounded. Can you help us?" Matt pleaded.

"I'm not authorized." The voice responded, indicating a need to contact the base.

After what felt like an eternity to Matt, a voice returned. "Chopper One, callsign Thunder, I have been authorized to intervene. I have an Apache. Do you have smoke?"

Chuck quickly grabbed a smoke canister, "Yes, we've got smoke; it's purple."

Matt shouted, "Pop it!"

Matt, back on the radio, "We're popping purple smoke, and we're surrounded."

"Roger, SEAL team, this is going to be close," the pilot warned as the chopper approached.

With Gatling guns blazing from both sides of the Apache, the copper swooped in and unleashed a barrage of bullets and rockets. The enemy was surprised, and many fell under the intense firepower. One by one, the hostile forces were wiped out, providing a window of opportunity for Matt's team.

"Now's our chance!" Matt shouted. "Let's get to the horses and get out of here."

The team quickly mounted their horses, adrenaline fueling their escape. With the cover of the Apache, they rode hard, putting as much distance as possible between themselves and the remaining enemies.

As they rode to safety, Matt quickly checked on Maggie, who was injured and riding at the back with several others who were also wounded. Matt knew they had to return to the Lodge as quickly as possible. They rode hard through the night, doing their best to avoid further encounters with hostiles—or banditos, as Chuck would say.

When they arrived at the lodge, they immediately called for the doctors and nurses. The wounded were swiftly taken inside, where they were attended to with care and urgency. Knowing they had returned in one piece despite the challenges, the sense of relief grew.

*****

Day After

The following day, at the Lodge, Matt checked on everyone to see how they were holding up. He found Maggie lying in a cot, her arm bandaged. She looked up at him and tried to smile. "Don't worry about it, Matt. It's just a flesh wound on my arm. I'm fine."

Matt shook his head, a mixture of relief and concern in his eyes. "You're one tough cookie, Maggie. But don't push yourself too hard. We need everyone at their best."

Maggie nodded, appreciating his concern. "I'll be ready when you need me. Just give me a little bit of time to rest."

"Maggie, I'll be back tomorrow. To pass the time, I could find a book to read to you."

"Can you read, Matt?" she asked with a smile.

*****

Next Day Surprise

The following day, the team gathered for breakfast and discussed the events of the past few days. Once again, the familiar sound of rotor blades reached their ears. They all rushed outside to see what it was and what was happening. This time, it wasn't an Apache but a Chinook helicopter descending and landing nearby.

Once the blades stopped, a military officer stepped out and approached them. "I'm looking for Lieutenant Matthew Dylan," he announced.

Matt raised his hand, "I'm here, sir."

"Would you come with me, sir? Our general would like to talk to you."

Matt hesitated briefly, "Sergeant Jones, you come with me."

They both climbed into the Chinook; it took off and flew for about 55 minutes, retracing some of the terrain they had traveled the previous day. Flying in the middle of nowhere, a large mountain appeared ahead. After landing near the hill, the officer led them towards an opening in the mountain, revealing a hidden base within. As they walked in, the sheer scale of the operation became clear. This was a command center equipped for significant military operations.

Matt and Sergeant Jones followed the officer into the compound. The place was massive and well-established, indicating it had been there for a long time. Walking deeper into the facility, they approached a large steel door. The officer entered a code, and the doors opened, revealing a well-equipped command center.

To Matt's astonishment, Captain Engel stood before him. "I don't believe it," Matt exclaimed as he approached, extending his hand. "Captain Engel!"

The officer corrected him, "It's not Captain Engel anymore, it's now General Engel.

"How are you, Matt?" asked the general, shaking Matt's hand.

They spent the next several hours discussing the situation in the area. General Engel revealed they had been monitoring the Lodge with surveillance and scouts. "We know a sizeable hostile group threatens you and your people. Fortunately, several troops and their families who had moved here before the outbreak are on base."

Matt had to ask how all this was possible with everything in the world destroyed?

"Matt, we're not all ignorant in the military. We realized what was happening and what could be done to save things. Following some of the examples that we've seen, we had this whole area consecrated by a bishop. That's what saved us.

"Matt, we will supply you with ammunition and food. If you need anything else, we can get it for you."

Matt nodded, understanding the gravity of the potential situation they were facing. Matt and the general began to strategize on how to deal with the hostile groups by combining resources and coordinating an effort to ensure the safety of everyone in the Lodge.

Matt recounted to General Engel about the Apache helicopter, the Savior that had saved their asses; he had been a real lifesaver.

General Engel nodded. "It wasn't just any pilot; it was Captain Sarah McNally. She's a fierce warrior, one of the best we have. We're fortunate to have her on our side."

"We owe her a lot. Would you give her my deepest appreciation?"

"Matt, our next move should be to set up a barrier of troops around your Lodge and take a defensive stance with troops and armored vehicles. We also have a couple of cannons that should help hold the line."

Matt nodded, appreciating the completeness of the plan. "We need all the help you can give us, sir, and coordinating our efforts will ensure everyone knows their roles."

The Chinook helicopter took Matt and Sergeant Jones back to the Lodge. Upon their return, they met with Father Mike and others to explain the plan.

Matt outlined their strategy: They would form a group to go out and make contact with the enemy. "We'll have reinforcements on standby if needed, as well as air support. The goal is to engage and neutralize them before they get too close to us here at the Lodge."

Father Mike and the others listened intently, understanding the importance of this preemptive strike.

"Will you be taking our best fighters, Matt?"

"Yes, Father."

Father Mike stressed that they also had to ensure the Lodge remained secure while they were out there.

Matt nodded, agreeing. "We'll leave a strong defense here; we can't afford to take any chances."

As the Lodge's community gathered to listen to the plan, members eagerly volunteered, raising their hands, "I'll go, I'll go," they said, ready to step up and defend their home. Matt was impressed with their courage.

Matt noticed Maggie raising her hand, too. "I'll go!" she declared. But Matt shook his head firmly. "No, Maggie, you're staying here." Her eyes blazed with defiance, silently questioning his decision. *What the hell's wrong with you?* her gaze seemed to ask.

Matt couldn't take the chance of losing her, and he felt the weight of his responsibility was to keep her safe.

"Maggie, I need you here," Matt said gently but firmly. "Your strength is required to help defend the Lodge and care for the wounded, and I can't risk losing you out there."

Reluctantly, Maggie lowered her hand, understanding, but still feeling the sting of being left behind.

Matt hand-picked a team of 12 for the mission, focusing on mobility and readiness. He instructed them to rest and prepare, ensuring they had plenty of ammunition, their weapons were checked, and their horses well cared for. They would set out the following day, ready to confront the enemy.

When Matt returned to his cabin, he noticed a Chinook returning, bringing more supplies, weapons, and much-needed radio communication equipment. He also saw his pickup was parked nearby; Jake must've fixed it while he was gone.

Matt decided to take a moment for himself, feeling relief and gratitude. He poured a little whiskey into a travel mug and walked to Sylvan Lake, planning to sit and relax.

Later, as Matt sat by the lake reflecting on the events and challenges ahead, he heard footsteps behind him. He turned to see Maggie approaching.

"Hey," she said softly, her eyes searching his. "I thought you might need some company."

Matt smiled, appreciating her presence. "Yeah I could use some. It's been a rough few days."

They stood together in comfortable silence, finding peace in each other's company amidst the turmoil.

Matt felt a mixture of emotions as Maggie spoke her words, cutting through the lingering silence of the lake. "Matt, I know you've been trying to avoid me. I know you still have attachments to your wife. I'm not trying to take her place, but I go after what I want, and you are what I want. I have strong feelings for you, Matt."

Taking a deep breath, Matt turned towards her, his eyes softening. "Maggie, I appreciate your thoughtfulness. I also have feelings for you." His arms wrapped around her, offering a comfortable embrace.

They stood there, enveloped in the beauty of the lake, finding solace in each other's presence. The challenges ahead loomed large, but they drew strength from their connection in that moment.

In that moment, everything else seemed to fade away for Matt. Holding Maggie close, he could feel her heartbeat against his chest, quieting him amidst the chaos surrounding him. He focused solely on her for a brief and precious while, finding strength in their shared feelings.

Matt watched Maggie walk away, her words echoing in his mind: "You damn well better come back to me." The strength and determination in her voice gave him a renewed sense of purpose. She was beautiful in appearance and spirit, and he knew he had to return to her.

This emotional moment strengthened Matt's focus on what was ahead. He gathered his team, ensuring everyone was prepared for the journey. The next day, they set out with resolve, knowing what was at stake, determined to protect their home and loved ones, and knowing full well that some of them would not return.

Matt returned to his cabin, feeling the weight of the upcoming mission. Once inside, he found Sergeant Jones, Chris, Ben, and Chuck deep in conversation.

Matt knew this moment was inevitable.

Chris broke the silence first. "Okay, what's the deal with this guy, Ben?"

Matt took a deep breath, realizing it was time to reveal the truth. "Ben is no ordinary man. He's a celestial angel sent to protect us and help us on our mission to destroy the forces of evil."

Chris and Sergeant Jones stared in disbelief, processing this new information. Ben nodded, confirming Matt's words. "I'm here to guide and support you in this battle. We face dark forces, but with faith and strength, we will prevail."

Chris and Sergeant Jones started laughing, "You've got to be fucking joking!"

Matt looked at Ben. "Go ahead, Ben."

To everyone's astonishment, Ben stood up and unfolded his gleaming wings—magnificent and spanning wide. At that moment, it was clear: Ben, indeed, was a celestial being, an angel sent to protect and guide them; they were now convinced.

Ben waved his hand, and Jones and Chris were frozen.

Matt was laughing, "Oh yeah. Ben doesn't like swear words."

Ben turned them loose, and with another wave of his hand, they returned to normal. Pissed but normal.

Matt ensured they understood, "And you can't tell anyone about this either."

*****

Morning March

Matt and his 12-person team were ready to go the following day. They all mounted up, headed out to the east, and eventually turned north. They aimed to locate hostiles.

Two days later, they encountered a formidable force of mixed races. Matt spaced his team amongst the rocks and trees, preparing for the enemy's onslaught. Without hesitation, the enemy attacked. The fighting was ferocious, and Matt's team held their own, but they were becoming overwhelmed by the number of hostiles pitted against them.

"Chuck, get on the radio. Call for support!" Matt shouted over the gunfire.

Minutes later, an Apache helicopter swooped in, firing Gatling guns from both sides of the Apache and shooting rockets, decimating the enemy.

Matt yelled, "Mount up! We're going to charge and finish them off."

They all mounted and took off after the retreating enemy, shooting from their running horses. The team split up, going in different directions. Matt and Bill pursued four hostile Mexicans on horseback, trying to retreat. As they got further away from the primary fight, the Mexicans dismounted, ready to make a stand.

Matt and Bill got off their horses. Matt had his .45 automatic pistol, his automatic rifle was out of bullets, and his 9 mm was close to empty. Bill had a .45 revolver and a 9 mm handgun, ready for the showdown.

One of the Mexicans sneered, "Bill, long time, amigo."

Bill stopped. "Toby, you asshole."

Toby laughed menacingly, "Bill, I'm going to kill you today, amigo."

As Toby walked towards Bill, Bill was faster. He drew his .45 and shot Toby twice in the chest; Toby looked at him with surprise and then fell dead. As Toby fell, Bill shot the man behind Toby too. Matt had engaged with the other two, killing both. Bill had taken a round in his side and another in his leg. As they both walked up to make sure the hostiles were dead, Matt noticed Bill was bleeding.

Matt climbed back on his horse. Bill, injured, managed to get on his horse.

Matt told him to go back for some doctoring to his side and leg.

"What are you going to do, Matt?" Bill asked.

"I'm going to circle around and see if there are any more hostiles. I'll meet you later," Matt replied.

Bill rode off to find a medic. Matt turned and rode east to find out where the others were headed. About 20 minutes later, a shot rang out and he was hit in the chest by a sniper who had been hiding in the trees. Matt fell off his horse, which bolted.

Matt was wounded in his chest, and he discovered he had taken another hit in his left leg above his knee. It had gone through, but the one bullet in his chest was still in his body. Matt crawled into the trees. He still had his backpack and a 9 mm, but he had lost his .45.

Matt waited, hiding behind a tree. Soon, the sniper approached with his scoped 308. As the sniper got closer, Matt stepped from behind the tree and shot the sniper twice, killing him instantly.

Brutally wounded, Matt crawled back into the trees and found some rocks to hide among. He took off his backpack and started to apply bandages to his wounds. He tied a tourniquet to slow down the bleeding on his leg, then used a bandage on his left leg. There wasn't much he could do with a bullet wound in his chest; he put some bandages on the wound to slow down the bleeding, then wrapped a bandage around his chest and tightened it down with as much force as he could. Next, morphine. He jabbed the needle into his left leg, knowing he wasn't going anywhere, and he guessed it was his end, like in his nightmares.

CHAPTER 17

Rescue

A Very Upset Lady

The rest of Matt's team was two miles away, still engaged in skirmishes with the remaining hostiles. Suddenly, Army personnel carriers arrived behind the team, carrying 10 rangers. The rangers quickly dismounted and joined the fight, helping to finish off the remaining enemies. Several of the Lodge members were injured, and there were two casualties. The military personnel loaded the wounded into the APCs and returned to the Lodge.

One of the injured was Buck, the dog, who had taken a wound to his upper torso. Dakota stayed by Buck's side as they headed back to the Lodge. The rest of the team gathered the horses and began their journey home, miles away.

The APCs reached the Lodge quickly, where the doctors and nurses were ready to tend to the injured. The military had also sent over a surgeon and another doctor to assist with the injuries as the wounded were brought into the Lodge.

Maggie anxiously searched for Matt, questioning everyone she saw. No one had any answers; he wasn't among the wounded or the returning men and horses.

Desperation set in for Maggie. It was already sundown, and she could do nothing that night. She determined that she would set out to find him at first light.

Maggie returned to the Lodge, helping the wounded and anxiously asking about Matt's whereabouts. As she moved through the Lodge, her concern grew. She found Chuck, who was also aiding the injured.

"Chuck, have you seen Matt? What happened to him?" Maggie asked urgently.

"I don't know," Chuck replied. "Last time I saw him he was with Bill, chasing some hostiles on horseback."

"Bill?" Maggie called out, continuing her search around the Lodge. She was overwhelmed by the sight of so many injured. She found Buck, who was being sewn up and bandaged. They had given him a shot to help him sleep, keeping him off his legs. Then she saw Bill also wounded.

"Bill," she asked anxiously, "where's Matt?"

"I don't know," Bill replied, "the last time I saw him, he was going to look for more hostiles. That's the last I saw of him, Maggie!"

"Where's Ben?" she asked, worry still etched on her face.

"Ben was wounded, Maggie. He should be around here someplace."

Maggie continued her search and found Ben; he had taken a wound to his right side. "Are you going to be okay, Ben?"

"Yes, Maggie, I just took a wound to my right abdomen; I'll be okay after some rest."

"Ben, do you know where Matt is?" Maggie asked her voice tinged with desperation.

"No, I can't say that I do. I lost track of him during the fighting. He took off with others on horseback, running down some hostiles."

Maggie turned away, with no answers yet. Chuck approached her,

"Maggie, as soon as we get things settled here, I'll take off and try to find him," Chuck offered.

"I'm not going to wait that long, Chuck," Maggie said determinedly. "I'm going tomorrow morning, I'll find him."

The following day, Maggie was up early before sunrise, down at the stable saddling her horse. The sky was soft gray, the first light casting a glowing light; a slight chill hung in the air with dew on the grass.

Maggie had a packhorse loaded with food, water, and medical supplies. She had strapped on a 9 mm pistol and an HK416 automatic weapon.

When somebody hollered at her, Maggie was ready to mount and leave. She stopped to look and saw Chuck coming down the hill with Dakota and Buck.

"Maggie, you're not going anywhere by yourself. We're going with you. He's our friend too, you know," Chuck said as they saddled their horses.

They rode out, heading east and north, back to the battlefield area. The surrounding countryside was rugged and beautiful. Rolling hills covered a dense forest and wide-open meadows, which were starting to come to life with the sounds of birds chirping and the leaves rustling.

They rode through the night, cool but exhausting, and the sight of the battlefield where Matt was last seen washed over Maggie, creating a somber stillness.

The area around the battlefield was eerie. The ground was covered with the dead, now seen in the early morning light.

Buck was ahead, trying to pick up Matt's trail while the rest followed closely, their breath visible in the cool air.

An hour later they continued looking, Buck still leading the way. About two miles from the battlefield, Buck started to pick up the scent.

They followed him and soon found Matt's horse grazing on prairie grass. Chuck grabbed the reins and saw the horse's side and the saddle covered in blood.

"Maggie don't look," Chuck warned.

"What do you mean, don't look? You don't think I can handle it? Let me see," Maggie insisted. She saw the blood on the saddle and the horse.

Buck was moving towards a large stand of pine trees. As they approached the dense trees, sunlight filtered through the branches, creating a pattern on the forest floor. They had to dismount and continue on foot.

About 15 minutes later, they heard Buck barking and howling. They rushed up and found a dead man shot two times in the chest. While they were checking the dead man, they heard Buck barking again, the sound echoing through the trees; running now, they found Matt unconscious between some rocks. Maggie checked his pulse; it was faint and slow, but he was still alive.

"We've got to get him back as soon as we can," Maggie said. She replaced Matt's bandages on his chest and leg, as Matt moaned in pain, Maggie administered a shot of morphine. Dakota looked at Maggie; "We needed to build a travois to haul Matt back to the Lodge; putting him on a horse would kill him."

Maggie agreed. She and Dakota used knives and hatchets to cut two long saplings, and they took a rope from one of the horses, along with a couple of horse blankets.

Matt was placed on the travois, and they began their slow journey back, dragging him behind the horse. The first day was slow, so they rode through the night without sleep, knowing time was crucial.

They had to stop for a couple of hours to rest. Maggie told the unconscious Matt, "Matt, I love you with all my heart. You better damn well not die on me."

Two hours later, they resumed their ride. By late afternoon they were close to the Lodge. They saw smoke in the distance.

"What the hell?" Chuck exclaimed.

As they got closer, they were looking at a skirmish, soldiers with arrows lay on the ground. They rode further into the Lodge grounds and found their worst fears confirmed. Someone had attacked the Lodge and tried to burn it down but hadn't succeeded. Dead bodies of hostiles were scattered around the grounds.

They rode up to the Lodge, and people came out to meet them—people also with stretchers. Father Mike's relief was evident on his face. "I'm so glad you guys are safe," he said.

Maggie answered, "What happened?"

"An overwhelming force of Indians attacked us," Father Mike replied.

Father Mike continued, "They came early in the morning, snuck up, and killed most of the military men guarding the outside of the perimeter.

"Then they started attacking us," Father continued, "and then they left, but they took all the horses with them when they rode off. We have several people injured, some of them very seriously."

Father Mike and Maggie walked back into the Lodge, with Buck behind her, following her every move. They reached the area where Matt had gone into surgery. Soon, Chuck and Dakota joined them. After a couple of hours, the doctor came out.

"I don't know who's related or responsible for this man," the doctor said.

Maggie stood up, "I am."

"Well, young lady, I'm not sure how it will go; if we had him yesterday, maybe he'd have had a chance to survive.

"But he's lost a lot of blood; it's just not looking good; I will keep an eye on him; right now, we are going to move him to a recovery bed and wait through the night. I'm just letting you know that it will be a rough night for him."

Maggie started tearing up a little, not wanting to show the others how much she cared for Matt. Several minutes later, she walked into the recovery room where Matt was lying on a bed, tubes coming out of him, on oxygen, he was pale and didn't look good at all. She pulled up a chair, sat beside him, and grabbed his hand; she could only whisper prayers.

Next Morning

The weather had warmed slightly, and the sun shone brightly through stained-glass windows as Maggie sat by Matt's side.

The sound of the birds and the rustling of the leaves outside calmed Maggie while she waited for the doctor's return.

Later, Chuck and Dakota came to the recovery room with a recliner. "Maggie, you need to get a little rest. Let's get rid of that chair and get you into this recliner. We will push it up next to the bed. Here's a pillow and a blanket. You need to get some rest. We will be back later."

As they left, she took Matt's hand and fell asleep.

Ben came over and looked at Matt and saw Maggie was sleeping. He walked over to Matt's left side, put his right hand on Matt's head, his left hand on Matt's heart, and whispered prayers, asking for help. There was a small light glimmering down.

Ben got up and was about to leave when he saw Buck. He walked over, put his hands on Buck's injuries, and whispered a few prayers. "It should help, buddy. It should take care of those injuries. You're a good dog."

*****

Sunshine Smiles

The following day, sunrise came through the windows, and Maggie was still asleep when she felt a tug on her hand. Immediately, she woke and saw Matt turn towards her and smile.

"Oh, Matt!" she exclaimed, reaching over and giving him a slight hug. She was so excited, tears of happiness streaming down Maggie's face.

Later that day, a small military group arrived at the Lodge, with two APCs and several men climbing out. Two large military trucks pulled up; the men started to retrieve the bodies of their fallen soldiers.

All the weapons were gone, but they picked up their bodies and loaded them into trucks. Then, regrettably, they did the same with the dead hostiles, loading them into the other truck.

A sergeant approached Father Mike and Chuck. "We'll take our men back. We have a burial spot for them, and they'll receive full military funerals."

"The others?" Father Mike asked.

"For the hostiles," the sergeant said, "we'll find a ditch or canyon away from everybody and dump them. They don't deserve anymore, Father."

Later that day, Father Mike gathered Matt's team in the cafeteria: Chuck, Chris, Sergeant Jones, Cynthia, Pauline, Dakota, and Ben, who walked in with a slight limp. Maggie also came in and grabbed a cup of coffee and sat down at the table, a dead seriousness in her eyes. Nobody questioned why she was there; they all knew she wanted retribution.

Father Mike stood up. "First of all, two of our people were killed on the battlefield: young Bradley Newcombe, such a sweet young boy, and Heath Sanchez, one of the Lee's cowboys. We need a plan, and our planner is lying wounded in the other room. Any suggestions or ideas from anyone?"

Sergeant Jones was the first to speak. He stood up. "We need to regroup. We must fortify our defenses, stay here, and prepare for another attack. We need to get all our wounded healed up, contact the military, see if they can bring us some more help, and get set. The next battle is going to be horrendous. They finally found out where we are, so we must be prepared."

They all agreed they could do nothing now but regroup and prepare. Everyone got up and left except for Chuck, Chris, and Sergeant Jones. They walked over and sat next to Ben.

Chris was the first to ask, "Okay, Ben, how did you get wounded? I thought you were an angel and invincible."

Ben replied, "I made a mistake. I fired one of my golden narrows at one of the minions. The evil person dropped and turned to ashes, but another evil person picked up the arrow. I didn't notice it at the time. He shot it back at me and hit me in the side. If he had hit me in the chest, it would have killed me. This reminds me that I need to wear my armor next time."

*****

The Third Day

The next few days were spent burying their dead, including Bradley and Heath, and three others from the Lodge, new refugees brought in by Matt Dylan. The three had joined the fight and paid with their lives.

Matt started feeling better; he sat up, ate, and healed fast. When they took the bandages off his leg, it was healed. His chest felt great, but the doctor insisted he stay in bed for at least another day or two. He was okay with it as long as Maggie was with him, especially when she read to him from *Huckleberry Finn.*

The military agreed to send more soldiers, stationing them at the Lodge, this time all armed with automatic weapons. They would keep an Apache helicopter on standby and another Apache circling the area in a 5-mile radius to keep an eye out for the hostiles.

Matt and Maggie weren't the only ones in the throes of a budding romance. Chuck spent much time with Pauline, and they got along well. Matt asked Chuck about it during one of his visits, and of course, he teased him.

"You know, Matt, she's a beautiful woman and damn good with a weapon. She could probably kick my ass in a fight if it came down to it, but I like her, she's fun," Chuck said.

"And Matt, I'm not the only one. Dakota has been hanging around one of Ravi's wife's sisters. I think her name is Lila."

"I thought Dakota and Fern were going to get together, they've known each other their whole lives," Matt said.

Chuck explained, "I thought so too, but they found out they were related somewhere in the past. So, they're just friends with no benefits, just good friends."

When asked how things were going around the Lodge, Chuck responded. "Well, after losing five people, everybody is pretty sad and still trying to cope."

Matt looked puzzled. "What do you mean we lost five people? Who's dead? This is the first I've heard of it!"

"Matt, we figured it was better to keep it from you until you healed up."

"Chuck, you should have told me, damn it!"

"We lost Bradley, a young man; Heath Sanchez, one of Lee's cowboys; and three of the refugees you brought in a while back, a man and two women. They were also killed defending this place. So that's five, and that's too damn many."

Matt agreed, "What's the plan now?"

"We're going to fortify our position. The military is coming in to help fortify the Lodge. We are on standby for whatever happens next."

*****

Young Military

When the military arrived the following day, the rumble of two APCs and one heavy truck ended the peaceful morning. But it also brought the lodge community a sense of relief and security. Overhead, the rotors of an Apache helicopter flying overwatch prompted a cheer from all.

Lieutenant Williams was in charge of the military personnel. He walked up to the Lodge and introduced himself to Father Mike, letting the priest know who was now in charge.

Father Mike responded, "Perhaps we should all go inside and meet with the other militia members. We are anxious to work with you in formulating a plan."

Father Mike turned and led the group into the cafeteria, where he introduced the members of Matt's team. He continued, "Lieutenant Williams is in charge of the military personnel stationed around the Lodge to help reinforce our defenses."

Lieutenant Williams stood up and cleared his throat. "I think you might be confused, Father. I oversee everyone in this complex, and you will be taking your orders from me."

Chris, standing at 6′ 4″, had heard enough and looked down at Lieutenant Williams. "I am a lieutenant. Chris King, Special Forces Unit. I'm sure I outrank you by a hell of a lot. But neither of us is the top-ranking officer here; we have a captain, Matt Dylan. And he is friends with your General Engel because they fought in Afghanistan together. So, if you want to challenge our captain for leadership, I would like to stand back and watch what happens. Until then, little man who probably hasn't shaved yet, have I clarified who's in charge here?

"I said, have I made myself clear?" Chris took two steps to get in Williams's face.

"Yes, sir, crystal."

Father Mike stepped in. "All right, if we are finished with the pissing contest, let's talk about planning the defense of the Lodge and area.

"First, in the wake of the attack, we are left with fewer horses after the Indians took most of them from the corrals. The impact of the loss is crucial, not only because it creates transportation issues but also because the horses were part of our defenses," Father Mike continued.

"Father, we can use our armored APCs to scout outside the Lodge area if you like."

"Well, thank you, Lieutenant Williams. That's a grand idea. For now, let's place our people around the barricades and set up a rotation of guards. We will all reconvene at a later date; you all know what has to be done."

It would be a couple more days before Matt could start planning another hunt for the hostile forces that attacked the Lodge. For now, he decided to check on the wounded.

Matt walked into the room where the wounded were being treated, looking for Bill. The room was filled with the scent of antiseptics and the quiet, painful sounds of the injured. He spotted Bill, who had been seriously injured during the last gunfight.

"Bill, how are you feeling today? I heard you made it back safely," Matt said, his concern evident, given his friend's severe wounds.

"Matt, I'm going to be OKAY," Bill replied. "Ben stopped by to see me, and after he prayed over me, damn if I didn't feel better."

"Yeah, Ben has that effect on people," Matt agreed with a knowing smile.

"Matt, ever since I met you, I've had this nagging feeling we've met somewhere in the past. Where did you serve last?" Bill asked.

"Well, Bill, I spent most of my time in Afghanistan, around Kandahar, then I was injured during a mission and almost killed when the evacuation helicopter was hit by a rocket."

"Now I have it," Bill said, a look of realization on his face. "You're the Navy SEAL we rescued when the Taliban fighters surrounded you. I remember one of them was about to shoot you, and I took a shot, nailing him in the head."

"Bill, you were the Ranger that saved my life," Matt said, a sense of recognition and gratitude in his voice. "I can never thank you enough."

"Matt, you've more than made up for it when you helped me take down that damn Mexican asshole, Toby."

"We need to go back out," Matt said, looking at Bill. "This time we need to go south and find the people who attacked the Lodge and killed some of our people.

"So, Bill, get well soon. I need you at my side. I will check on you again in a couple of days," Matt said, his voice filled with determination.

Matt walked out of the Lodge, heading towards his cabin. After seeing all the injuries, he was experiencing guilt over what had happened to his friends and the fact several had died. He couldn't shake the feeling that maybe someone else should be taking over the leadership role. Somehow, he felt he had failed.

When Matt reached the cabin, he found Chuck, Chris, Ben, and Dakota sitting around the table drinking coffee and discussing the following steps to take to hunt down the ones who attacked their friends.

They all hailed Matt when he walked in. "Come join us,' they invited.

As Matt sat down, he looked at all his friends, thinking, *I don't want to be responsible for any more deaths.*

Matt said, "I think the Army leaders should take responsibility for the rest of the missions and leadership roles."

Matt took a deep breath, his gaze steady. "We have done enough," he said firmly. "I would like us to be a supporting group from now on, not take the lead anymore."

Chuck, Chris, Ben, and Dakota exchanged glances. They could feel the weight of Matt's responsibility.

"Matt, we understand," Chuck said, nodding. "We've been through a lot, and it's time we let the military handle the lead."

Chris added, "We'll still be here to support and assist, but you're right, it's time to step back from the front lines."

Dakota nodded in agreement. But not liking it at all.

Ben looked at Matt, his expression serious. "Is that what you wanted to hear? Because it's crap."

Ben's words seemed to hang in the air, challenging the group's decision.

"Ben's right," Chuck said. "We can't just step back now. We've come this far together and need your leadership, Matt."

Chris nodded, "We've faced everything side-by-side. We're stronger together, and we need you leading us."

Dakota added, "We trust you, Matt. We're in this together."

Matt looked around at his friends, and their unwavering support was very clear. He realized they believed in him despite his doubts, and his feelings of being inadequate faded away.

Matt stood up, wavering a little. He could tell he was still weak. He thanked everyone for their support, said good night, and headed into his bedroom. Buck followed close behind.

Matt shed his clothes and climbed into bed. Buck jumped up and lay at the end of the bed, looking at Matt with his head between his paws, his eyes full of concern for his master. The loyal dog's presence was comforting, a silent guardian watching over Matt as he fell asleep.

Meanwhile, Ben was out guarding the perimeter.

Father Mike finally took a chance to have some time for himself. He had a good cigar he'd been saving for the right moment. He filled a glass full of ice, poured some good bourbon, and walked outside to a spot under some trees where there was a bench. He sat there, enjoying his cigar and sipping on his bourbon, when he heard a slow whistle.

"Father, Father, I'm here. I'm here for you."

Startled, Father Mike looked around. "Who the hell is that? Who are you?"

"You know who I am. You've been a bad man chopping off tree heads. I'm here to collect your soul."

Father Mike stood up, dropping his glass and throwing away the cigar. "What do you mean?

A dark figure stepped into the light, an 8-foot tall black demon angel holding a sword. "I'm here for your soul. You've killed people. You're mine."

Father Mike screamed, "I've repented! You can't come for me!"

Meanwhile, Ben, guarding the perimeter, sensed something was wrong. He started running towards the Lodge, faster and harder. As he ran, he transformed into an 8-foot-tall Warrior Angel, flying with one flap of his wings. He landed between Father Mike and the demon.

"Barabbas, what are you doing here?" Ben demanded.

"Bashaol. Are you the one they sent to defend these people?

"Don't get in my way Bashaol; I'm here for Father Mike's soul. He killed people. He's mine," the demon replied.

Ben drew his sword, "No, he has repented. God saved his soul. He's not yours anymore." With that said, the two angels clashed, their swords ringing out in the night. Benjamin reached up and called to the sky. Lightning struck his sword, setting it on fire. He swung at the demon, hitting him a couple times.

The demon snarled, "I'll be back!"

Ben shouted, "You come back here, and you die!"

Father Mike stood there, unable to understand what had just happened. The angel with pure white wings and gold armor turned and looked at Father Mike.

Then, right before Father Mike's eyes, the angel transformed into Ben.

"Benjamin? What… what…" Father Mike stammered, his mind struggling to process what he had witnessed.

"Father, this has got to be kept a secret. You cannot reveal who I am," Ben said firmly.

"What are you doing here?" Father Mike asked, still in shock.

Ben explained, "I'm here to keep Matthew alive; he is the answer."

"Answer to what?" Father Mike asked, confusion evident in his voice.

"The answer to destroying all evil. He has been given that charge, and I'm here to protect him and ensure he succeeds," Ben replied, his voice steady and resolute. "This must be kept our secret, Father. You can't reveal to anyone who I am."

Father Mike nodded slowly, the weight of the revelation setting in. He knew he had to trust Ben and keep his secret, no matter what.

"Ben, I have some questions."

"I'm sorry, Father. I'm not allowed to divulge any heavenly secrets. But if you think about it, tonight, you witnessed evil, and me defeating evil, which should answer your most significant question.

"Good night, Father."

CHAPTER 18

Change of Heart

Will He Kill Me

Clayton and the rest of his raiding party returned to the Pine Ridge campground with the 20 horses they'd stolen from the Lodge. The mood was tense as they led the horses into camp.

Clayton knew he would have to report the substantial loss of his men; they had lost a third of their attacking force. The weight of this failure hung heavily over him as he prepared to face the consequences, knowing how the Chief dealt with failure.

Tashu, the chief of all the hostiles, came out of his tent when he heard the commotion of the horses riding into the camp. He stood there with his hands on his hips, the near sundown light casting long shadows as the temperature began to drop. Clayton rode up, dismounted his horse, and walked up to his chief to report what had happened.

Clayton stood before Tashu, who sternly surveyed the remainder of the raiding party. "Clayton, it looks like you're missing some of your men. Tell me what happened," he demanded.

"Chief, after two of our men didn't return from the north as we discussed, I took a group of 40 men to go north and find out what happened to them. It led us into the Black Hills and the compound where all the whites had relocated. To our surprise, the military had formed a perimeter around the Lodge. We moved in silently, eliminated the perimeter guards with knives, and attacked the Lodge.

"They had built huge barriers around the Lodge and were unassailable. Armed with automatic weapons, we tried to burn down the Lodge, but they had water hoses ready to extinguish the flames. The fight went on for a couple of hours. We were losing men, so we retreated.

"We took all their horses, about 20, and returned. We lost men, but we now know where they are and their strengths."

"All right, Clayton. Take care of your men and your wounded. We'll speak more tomorrow," Tashu said, dismissing him.

Blackbird and Red Cloud joined the Chief as Clayton left.

They started discussing the next steps. "I think we'll need a few days to round up more men," Blackbird said thoughtfully.

"Clayton has distinguished himself in battle and brought us 20 horses, which we can use to reinforce our fighters," Red Cloud added. "I think it's time we found a more fitting name for Clayton, which will reflect our heritage."

Tashu nodded in agreement, contemplating the honor of bestowing a new name upon Clayton. "How about giving Clayton the Apache name Black Hawk, a solid name for a leader? It signifies his bravery and leadership in battle."

They all agreed, and then each went their separate ways. It was time to find a warm spot for the night. Tashu headed to his teepee, where Little Hawk waited to keep him warm.

*****

Early in the morning, just as the sun was rising, the Chief stepped out of his teepee and stretched, feeling the cool spring air. He walked over the campfire in the middle of the compound, where some of the Sioux Indian women were cooking buffalo stew. He sat at a table, and soon Blackbird and Red Cloud joined him. He sent someone to fetch Clayton.

When Clayton arrived, he figured he was going to get an ass-chewing, if not worse. The Chief stood up and said, "Clayton, sit down here and join us." The Chief ordered some stew to be brought over to Clayton. Clayton sat down, feeling nervous.

"Clayton, we've been discussing changing your name. You need more of an Apache name, so we'll give you the name Black Hawk. It will signify your bravery and leadership in battle, making it a fitting name to honor your achievements."

As they talked, a young Indian girl brought a plate of buffalo stew for Black Hawk. She handed it to him and gave him a big smile before walking off. The Chief asked, "So, do you like her? She is pretty. Her name is Aiyana, which means 'internal blossom.'"

Black Hawk nodded, "Yeah, she is pretty. I had noticed her before."

The Chief stood up and called Aiyana over to the table. "Black Hawk here needs a wife, so you are now his," the Chief declared.

Black Hawk stood up quickly, "I can't accept this. It has to be mutual. I don't know her; she doesn't know me."

The Chief said firmly, "Exactly, Black Hawk. You will get to know each other, and we will set up a place for both of you. It's settled. I made the decision, and I'm the Chief, and you both will do as I say."

The Chief then called over two Sioux Indian women. "Take Aiyana over to that teepee on the edge of the camp and make it nice for her and Black Hawk. I expect your best effort."

Turning back to the group, the Chief continued, "Now, let's discuss what we will do next. Black Hawk, please take five warriors to Hot Springs to see what's left there.

"I want you to leave right away, this morning. You'll be gone at least two days, if not three. That will give us time here to try and get more recruits to form a bigger raiding party for our next trip to the Black Hills. And I'm sending Red Cloud with you."

"What are we looking for?" Black Hawk asked?

The chief replied, "You'll be looking for a way around the Black Hills from another direction to get behind our enemies, so we attack them from two points.

"And Blackbird, I want you to take a group of five or six, go north towards Rapid City, and see if you can find John Washington.

"We are supposed to join up with him, and we need their support to finish off the people at the Lodge compound. Ghost riders have told me that Matt Dylan is still alive and leading all these ambushes and attacks against us. He needs to be destroyed; that's going to be a priority. All right, you'll have your marching orders, take off."

As Black Hawk started to leave, the Chief added, "Black Hawk, just a second. While away, consider what awaits you upon your return. She's beautiful, and she'll be waiting for you."

Black Hawk left and went to round up five of his closest friends to brief them on where they were going and what they would be doing.

"Prepare to be gone for three days," Black Hawk instructed them to ensure they had enough food and water. "It sounds like we will have an overseer; Red Cloud is going with us.

"I don't know why," Black Hawk said, "and I don't want him watching us. But it sounds like we don't have a choice, so get your horses, and let's get mounted up and go."

About half an hour later, Black Hawk and his men rode west towards Hot Springs. Red Cloud was in the lead, setting the pace. It was 50 miles to Hot Springs, and his job was to get there as quickly as possible.

Red Cloud wasn't going to disappoint his chief. He knew the consequences of failure all too well.

Black Hawk thought to himself, *so this is how it will be. I wonder if he could have an accident along the way? No, I shouldn't feel that way. Oh, the price we'd have to pay if something happened to him.*

With Red Cloud setting the pace, they reached the outskirts of Hot Spring, South Dakota, in the middle of the night. They took time to rest their horses and to get something to eat and drink, waiting for sunrise to investigate what was left of Hot Springs.

It was rough trying to sleep for a few hours, but they needed to catch some rest before they had to get up and go again.

Soon, the sun started rising, and they could feel its warmth. Steam was rolling off the creek they were sleeping by. They grabbed some jerky, jumped on their horses, and rode into what was once Hot Springs, now just a field with tall grass and trees.

They spotted a church still standing, so they rode up to it and dismounted. Red Cloud walked up to the church doors, kicked them open, and they stepped inside. It was dusty and dark, with nobody and nothing worthwhile to take. They turned around and left.

Riding a little further, they found a pharmacy still standing, but when Black Hawk looked through the windows, he could see it was stripped bare. There was no reason to stop there either.

They continued riding through Hot Springs, turning north towards the Black Hills. As they rode along, the sun had risen, the dew on the grass was drying up, and the warmth was welcome to their thinly dressed bodies. They continued riding for about an hour until they came across fresh horse tracks leading east; they tied the horses in some trees to keep them hidden and continued on foot.

As the small group walked through the tall grass and pine trees to the east, they saw buildings in the distance, which had to be the compound. The small war party spread out, staying low, hidden in the tall grass. Red Cloud was in the lead, his feathers visible above the grass.

Suddenly, they heard a noise. Someone was coming.

Black Hawk quickly moved up beside Red Cloud. "Who do you think they are?" he whispered.

Red Cloud answered. "I see a tall man with sandy hair and a woman with dark brown hair walking hand in hand; I think it's the one we are looking for."

Black Hawk was now becoming concerned; they were hiding about 35 feet away from the couple.

Red Cloud hollered, "It's him, it's him, Dylan!" He jumped up, grabbed his hatchet in his right hand, and charged the couple, screaming in Apache, "I'm going to kill you."

The sandy-haired man and the dark-haired woman turned, and both were so fast with their pistols that they shot Red Cloud, bam, bam, and he was dead.

Black Hawk and his men retreated to their horses and rode off, dragging Red Cloud's horse with them.

Black Hawk was in shock. "What the hell happened?"

Eagle Eye rode beside him. "I think he must've gone crazy. Now, what are we going to do?"

Black Hawk replied, "I don't know what we're going to tell the Chief," his voice filled with uncertainty, "we're dead for sure."

As Black Hawk debated what to do, his second-in-command and friend, Eagle Eye, asked if Red Cloud was worth dying for.

Black Hawk turned and stared at his friend. "What do you mean?"

"We've been talking amongst ourselves," his friend continued, "and we don't like the fact we're being used and killed off by our Chief, who has yet to fight in any battles. We're tired of fighting and seeing our friends dying."

"I understand," Black Hawk replied, "what do you expect to do?"

Eagle Eye added, "What's to stop us from gathering our wives and families and leaving?

"Going someplace else, getting away from all this death and killing. What would you say to that?" Eagle Eye asked.

Black Hawk sighed, "I understand how you feel. I thought about it myself. I've lost a lot of men, and I am not sure of the reason anymore. Let me think about it. I'm not saying yes; I'm not saying no; I'll just think about it."

Black Hawk rode along, formulating a plan in his mind. Could they pull it off? There weren't too many warriors in camp anymore because the Chief had spread them out to look for more reinforcements. Would it be possible to slip in and gather their families?

Yes, there were 20 new horses at the camp that would help. And now he had someone waiting for him; he couldn't leave her behind.

As Hawk rode along, he decided to propose a plan. He pulled his horse up and turned to face his men. "This is what I think we need to do," he told his men. "We must slip into the camp quietly at night and gather your families. Bring as few possessions as possible. We've got several horses; get your families to the corral and help them saddle up and leave.

"Next, a couple of you will help guard and kill anybody that comes towards us who is not friendly. Once you are out of camp, head west. I'm not sure exactly where we will go, but we don't want anyone following us. So that's my plan."

It was getting close to dark, and there was a slight chill in the air for this time of year. The smell of the campfires marked the village. The group rode in and dismounted, about a mile away from camp, deciding to go on foot. They spread out, walking through the tall grass and around the trees, hidden from sight. There were no guards guarding the camp as they approached, which was a surprise to Hawk.

Black Hawk turned his men and said, "Be swift. Get your people and get mounted. As soon as they're mounted and you're with them, leave. Please don't wait for the rest of us. Go!"

They started leading their horses to the corral, tying them up, then heading off to collect their families.

Black Hawk had only one person he was interested in. He walked over to the tipi, threw the flap open, and walked in. There was a small fire in the middle, casting shadows around the inside of the tepee. Aiyana sat there, huddling in a blanket, staring at him with fear.

"I'm here, and I'm not going to hurt you. You have nothing to fear from me," Black Hawk said softly.

"But we're leaving. We've decided to go. Do you want to come with us?"

She looked at him, confusion and fear evident in her eyes. "I don't understand."

"There's too much dying, too much killing," Black Hawk explained gently. "We're sick of it. We want to go someplace else and start over. Do you want to come with us or not?"

She thought for a second. "But what if they catch us?"

"There's enough of us; if they catch us, we will kill them," "Black Hawk said to reassure her. "Yes or no?"

"Yes," she finally agreed.

"Then bring your blankets and your things. Let's go quickly," Black Hawk instructed.

They left the tepee and headed for the corral. His friends had saddled a horse for her, and he was tied at the corral. The rest had already left with their families and headed out. Black Hawk looked around to see if anyone was following them. All was quiet.

He helped her onto her horse, then mounted his own. Together, they rode out to start a new life, leaving the death killing behind.

*****

Blackhawk and his new girlfriend rode swiftly to catch up with the group that was escaping from Pine Ridge. He finally caught up with his friend Eagle Eye and the rest of the group, which consisted of old women, wives, and children.

Breathing heavily, Blackhawk spoke to Eagle Eye, "I have a place we can go. It's a secret valley that my friend Haskia and I discovered when we were children. It's well-hidden, easily defensible, with plenty of water and wild game. We'll make our way there and spend at least the summer."

With that, Blackhawk took the lead, guiding the group towards the hidden sanctuary.

*****

The Second Group

Blackbird had six of their best fighters, going northeast, towards Rapid City, looking for John Washington. He figured it would take them at least two days, if not three, to get there by horseback.

Blackbird rode his horse hard, and the others tried to keep up.

Blackbird was concerned. The distance to Rapid City was 73 miles, and it would take them days to get there. Even riding day and night would be close to meeting the Chief's timeline; failure was not an option. He had seen first-hand what happened.

Haskia Spirit and his four friends rode hard to keep up with Blackbird. Haskia kept asking Blackbird to rest their horses, and though Blackbird would stop for a short time, they soon were back in the saddle, pushing on as hard as they could. After two days, they arrived at the outskirts of what used to be Rapid City, which now consisted of grasslands and trees.

Blackbird was in the lead as they rode up to the front gates of a large camp. Two big guards stepped out with their weapons pointed at them, ordering Blackbird to stop.

"Who are you?" they asked.

"I'm Blackbird, here to see John Washington; he expects me."

The two guards looked him over. "Leave your weapons here. You come with me," ordered the tall guard with long hair and a full beard. "The rest of you stay here."

Blackbird handed over his weapons and followed the guard further into the camp to find John Washington. Meanwhile, Haskia looked at his friends. "These horses are winded. They are no good to us anymore. Take off their saddles and turn them loose. We'll have to find some other form of transportation."

Blackbird followed the guard into the camp, up to a big tent, where he found John Washington. As he walked in, they both recognized each other from prison.

"Well, Blackbird, what are you doing here?" John Washington asked.

"John, when we left prison, the plan was to meet and form an army to take out our enemies. Vern Two Shoes, now our Chief, sent me here to get you to meet him in the area east of Sylvan Lake Lodge.

"The Chief has a vast area where we can set up a base camp. Then march to the Sylvan Lake area and take on the assholes and wipe out all the holdouts of white people," Blackbird explained.

"All right," John Washington said. "I understand. We'll get our people together and meet you southeast of here in two days. Tell your Chief to meet us there. We'll form up together, and we'll wipe them out."

John Washington was about to return to his desk when he stopped and turned around. "Hey, Billy Stone and Toby with the Mexicans, will they join us?"

Blackbird looked at him and replied, "My scouts told me that some Mexicans and some other Black guys they didn't recognize were wiped out by Matt Dylan and his group of mercenaries—the worst kind of all people, those who kill for money."

Blackbird left John Washington's command tent, jumped on his horse, and started to the front gate at a gallop. Suddenly, his horse stumbled and went down, throwing Blackbird into the dirt. He rolled several times before coming to a stop. He dusted himself off and grabbed the reins, but the horse wouldn't get up. After trying to pull the horse up, he realized the horse was done. Blackbird was pissed; he pulled out his pistol and shot the horse in the head, killing it. Some of the camp people standing around weren't happy with him killing the horse in the middle of their compound.

Blackbird walked up to the front gate, where the two guards stood. "I need a horse," he said.

The bearded guard replied that they only had one, and that his other guys would have to wait to get new horses.

"What do you mean, new horses? Where are their horses?" Blackbird asked.

The shorter guard answered, "They turned them loose. They were finished, almost dead; you could tell they were not taken care of."

"All right," Blackbird said. Finding his five companions, he said, "I'll take this horse and ride back to meet our Chief. I plan to see the rest of you in a couple of days."

He walked up to Haskia. "You know where the meeting place is. As soon as you get some horses, meet us there as fast as possible. We will assemble an army and take on those people at the Lodge. It's time we ended this and killed them all."

The shorter guard, with long hair colored red, white, and green, brought a horse to Blackbird, who climbed on and took off at a gallop. Haskia looked at Tall Bear, his long-time friend. "I don't know what the hell's going on here; Blackbird worries me.

"What you think, Tall Bear?"

"I think a lot of us are getting killed to further somebody else's agenda; we could all be killed if our Chief or Blackbird gets pissed at any one of us. I also know those demons are pulling the strings, forcing our people to fight and die, killing people who haven't done anything to us, but they retaliate when we strike against them first," Tall Bear replied.

"What are you saying, Tall Bear?" Haskia asked.

"Let's get some horses, and get out of here. Nobody is going to miss us when the shit starts," Tall Bear said. Haskia looked at his friends, who were standing behind him. They nodded in agreement.

Red Hand said, "We were good people before all this happened, Eagle. Before, those evil people came to our camp and demanded we kill people because they were white."

Haskia understood how they felt. "Here is what I think we should do: get some horses, gear, equipment, food, and water. We'll go as slowly as possible when we leave here heading south. We're not in any hurry to get in the fight." All nodded in agreement.

"OK then, I know a place we can go that is pretty much a hidden valley. Black Hawk and I found it when we were children."

Haskia, Tall Bear, and their friends quickly gathered the necessary supplies, determined to leave before they became further entangled in a battle they did not want.

Haskia and his men dreaded returning to the site of the pounding drums of war and the craziness. By going on a much longer route back to the war party, he hoped to preserve their lives and return to the ways of proud Sioux Indians.

Haskia took one final look around. They mounted their horses and rode south, avoiding a Crazy Chief and Blackbird, hopefully towards a future free from the violence and control they had known for so long.

*****

John's Crazy Camp

As the camp came alive the following day, excitement and anticipation rose with the morning sun. The air was energized, and everyone looked forward to the impending battle. Some warriors ate their breakfast silently, while others drank theirs from a bottle, strengthening their nerves for the bloodshed ahead. The sounds of screaming, shouting, and gunfire filled the air as if they teetered on the edge of madness.

Amid all the chaos, a lone figure stood apart: a young Indian warrior, Sam Thunder. He had a faraway look in his eyes as he contemplated the path that had brought him here. Unlike his comrades, his heart was not filled with bloodthirstiness but deep unease. He had joined the camp hoping for glory, but now, standing on the brink of battle, he couldn't shake the feeling that they were all marching toward their doom. He missed his chance to go with Haskia and Tall Bear and leave this craziness behind.

Thunder's fingers tightened around the locket he wore around his neck. It was a gift from his sister, a small reminder of home. As he glanced around the camp, he noticed others seemed as conflicted as he was. Were they all pretending to be ready for the fight?

The break of dawn marked the beginning of the day. As the sun rose higher, so did the tension. Thunder knew that the landscape around them would be alive with color in a few short hours. He only hoped that he would live to see another sunrise and maybe, just maybe, find the courage to protect the little remains of his humanity.

John Washington stood outside his tent, taking it all in, relishing the others' excitement; in the pit of his stomach, his excitement started to rise. He was so looking forward to killing Matt Dylan. For decades, others had missed their chance and ended up dead; he had no plans of dying but of killing and maybe even collecting 50 pounds of gold.

John Washington gave the signal to mount up. They had two days to join their brothers and start a campaign of war against the Lodge, the last holdout standing in their way before they could take over the whole country. John took the lead, and the rest of his warriors followed quickly, covering as much ground as they could in one day.

As John rode along, his thoughts returned to finally facing Matt Dylan. And how he was going to kill Matt Dylan by shooting him. Or kill him with a bow and arrow? No, that didn't sound like him. Maybe with a spear, no, not with a spear either. But, killing someone with a knife is a personal thing—looking into the victim's eyes, seeing the fear. And then he would cut Dylan's head off, take it back, show everyone, and claim his prize. *Yeah, a knife. Personal, up close, looking into his eyes as I kill him. Yes, I can see it now*!

CHAPTER 19

Heart Felt

New Bodies

Matt, his crew, and their girlfriends ate breakfast in the cafeteria. Matt was next to Maggie, and everyone was laughing and joking. He was so happy that everyone had healed well after the many injuries his warriors had suffered.

Suddenly, he felt a hand squeeze his under the table. He looked at Maggie and whispered, "You know there's a honeymoon cabin on these premises?"

"What are you saying?" she asked with a playful smile.

"Just throwing it out there," he replied, grinning.

A small communication system connected to the military base had been set up in the other room. They had given the Lodge radio equipment to stay in touch; a young man came into the cafeteria looking for Matt.

"Excuse me, sir. The military just radioed. They found some people about 10 miles from here, mostly on foot, looking for a safe place. They wanted to know if they could bring them here."

Matt thought briefly, "Sure, go ahead, radio back, tell them to bring them in, and we will look and see who they are and what they're all about."

Later in the afternoon, military trucks pulled up into the compound and unloaded about 12 people. Matt, Father Mike, Chuck, and Maggie went down to see who they had brought into the compound.

Matt walked up to Sergeant Brown.

"Who do we have here?" Matt asked.

"Well, sir, the leader of this group is Stony Black. They are from Mitchell South. Dakota.

"John Washington recruited them by giving them the impression they would fight evil. Finally, they realized that they were being lied to. Several of their people had died fighting for the wrong side, so they left," the sergeant explained.

Matt approached Stony Black. "So, you're the leader?"

"Yes, sir, I am. We are no threat to you, sir," Stony replied.

"Tell me, what's going on, and how did you end up here?" Matt asked.

"The sergeant asked me to repeat what I had told him. I can tell you this: I know the plans of the group gathering east of here; all the people from the north, the east, and the south are making one big push to come here and wipe everybody out. That's the plan, and we want no part of it. You can lock us up if you need to, just so we don't have to kill any more people who don't deserve it," Stony said solemnly.

Matt looked at the others in the group, then turned back to Stony.

"So, Stony."

"Yes, sir."

"And who do you have with you?"

"This is my wife, Emma," Stony replied, gesturing to a woman staying close to him, "and this is my best friend, Tom, and his wife, Ella."

Stony pointed to a couple standing nearby. "I have known the rest of these people most of my life—we went to school, graduated, hunted, and fished together. They are all good people who will not harm you or anybody else."

"Okay, sergeant, take these people to the cafeteria, get them something to eat, and find a place for them at the Lodge."

Then, turning to Chuck, Matt said, "Get everybody together. It looks like we're going to have at least one more battle. We need to get ready for another fight. I won't let them get to us again, surround us, and do what they want. We will find and try to finish them before they arrive."

"Okay, Boss, I'm on; when do you want us to meet?" Chuck asked.

"Let's plan to meet in about two hours. Give these people some time to eat, and then we'll meet in the cafeteria."

Matt hoped to put together a group of fighters and warriors, at least 45 of them, and with maybe another 50 from the military, that would make around a hundred. With the military's helicopters, they would have a chance to win this war against evil for the last time, the last battle.

Matt went back to the Lodge and walked into the radio room. He told the young man to get the general on the line so he could talk to him. The young man nodded and began calling, trying to reach the general's office, giving Matt time to gather his thoughts and find the right words.

The connection was established, and Matt spoke. "General, we have been notified that to the east of us is a massive round-up of all our enemies in one place. The plan is a big push to come here, surround the Lodge, and try to finish us off. I have approximately 45 warriors ready to go.

"I want to fight them on their ground rather than ours. Could you come over here and meet with us? We can start planning. We need to act quickly because I'm not sure how much time we have."

"Roger, Matt, I'll be over within an hour," the general replied over the radio.

Matt went to the cafeteria, grabbed coffee, and contemplated the plan. He knew time was of the essence; they needed to be ready for the impending battle.

Father Mike was busy with the newcomers, helping Stony Black and his people get settled and assigning them rooms where they could shower, clean up, and change into fresh clothes.

Stony approached Matt, "Sir, I know you don't trust us yet because we're new here, but I'm willing to throw my hat in the ring if you need us to join you in the fight. We've been lied to and lost so many of our friends, I want to get some payback. These are just my thoughts. If we disagree, that's okay."

Matt looked at Stony and said, "Let me think about it for now; take some time to clean up and get fresh clothes. We plan to meet in about two hours."

Maggie came rushing into the cafeteria, looking for Matt.

"Matt, Fern, and two girls went out hunting; they are long overdue."

Matt again felt the weight of responsibility on his shoulders as he gathered the search parties and split them into two groups.

The two groups moved quickly, their faces showing determination.

Chuck and his team headed north, scanning the dense forest and listening for any sign of missing girls. As they advanced, they felt tense, their hearts pounding with urgency.

Meanwhile, Matt led another group west through the rocky terrain and called out, hoping for a response. Shadows lengthened as time wore on, but they refused to give up.

The journey west took the search team through rugged terrain. Urging their horses onward, they felt their anxiety growing with each passing hour. The only sound was the gentle thud of hooves on the ground, mixed with occasional calls that went unanswered.

Finally, a thin plume of smoke rose against the distant horizon, a hopeful sign in the vast wilderness. Urgently, they spurred their horses into a gallop, and the anticipation built with every stride.

As they crested the rise, they saw a small makeshift camp sprawled below them, the smoke from a modest fire. Matt signaled the team to approach slowly and cautiously. They could see several crude shelters alongside a few tattered teepees.

Two horsemen riding bareback approached Matt's group with wary eyes.

Matt raised his hand, signaling for calm. "We're looking for three girls who disappeared. Have you seen anyone pass through here?" he asked, meeting the young Native American man's gaze.

With an unwavering stare, the man replied, "No, we haven't seen anyone.

"Who are you? And where are you from?" asked the young man.

Matt looked him straight in the eye. "The young man to my right here is Dakota. Next to him is Sergeant Jones. And we're from a lodge east of here."

Matt, in turn, asked, "And who are you?"

"I'm Clayton, and this is my friend Timothy. You didn't say who you are, tall man."

"My name is Matt."

Clayton now sat up straight. "Your name's Matt? It's not Matt Dylan by chance?"

"Why yes, it is. What difference does that make?"

"Absolutely none. Just curiosity." Clayton exchanged a glance with Timothy. Both realized who they had in front of them.

Clayton looked over his shoulder. As the three riders joined him, he added that those approaching were his mother and wife, and Timothy's woman, visibly pregnant, rode with a gentle sway.

Matt looked at Clayton and told him they were welcome at their lodge. "We have a doctor and shelter when winter comes."

Clayton then turned to Dakota, conversing quietly in Sioux, their words blending with the wind. After a short while, Clayton nodded, "We appreciate your offer. We must stay here for now, but we may seek shelter when the time comes."

Matt and his team began to ride back, thanking Clayton and his family for their time. Then, the camp receded into the distance.

Matt couldn't shake the feeling of unfinished business, but they had to return and regroup. The girls were still missing, and their search had to continue.

*****

Chris King had been trailing through the trees, keeping hidden and scouting to the north and east, careful not to be seen by the enemy. He listened intently for sounds that might give away their position, knowing that such a large group couldn't hide well. As he came over a rise, he spotted a group of people below. He dismounted, tied off his horse, crept up the hill, then scanned the scene below with his binoculars.

Shocked, he saw Fern, Kimberly Morgan, and Linda King tied to trees. It was late afternoon, and two rough-looking characters were prodding and yelling at them. Chris knew he had to devise a plan to free the girls. He only had one horse, so he had to go on foot.

Slowly, he walked down the hill, hiding among the trees until he reached the bottom.

As darkness began to fall, he pulled out his knife and crept up behind the two men guarding the girls. With swift precision, he sliced one man's neck and stabbed the other in the throat, killing them both.

Chris quickly untied the girls and whispered, "Follow me quickly." Fran stopped and grabbed an automatic weapon and some clips from one of the dead guards. "All right, I'm ready to go," she said.

They reached his horse. Chris instructed the two girls to take his horse and ride back double. "Fern and I will make it on foot. When you get back, send help." He slapped the horse on the rear, and it took off with the girls.

Chris and Fern began running, hiding, and running again, trying to distance themselves from the camp as much as possible. "I hope you can keep up," Chris said.

"Don't worry about me, old man," Fern laughed.

They continued their escape, knowing that once the bodies were found, an alarm would be raised, and they would be hunted down.

Traveling primarily through treacherous terrain in the dark was a dangerous endeavor. Matt and Fern had managed to cover only a few miles, and the going was getting more challenging. Matt had decided it was time to make a call. He turned to Fern. "We need to hole up someplace. Someone will get hurt out here in the dark, and we can't afford an injury."

They both slowed down as they reached the crest of a hill, where they found several trees. Some had fallen over, providing decent cover.

They settled in to rest, making as little noise as possible, knowing that sound carried better at night. The silence also worked in their favor, allowing them to hear any approaching threats. The distant shouts and yells confirmed that their pursuers were on their trail, but tracking them in the dark would be challenging.

"Fern, try to get some sleep if you can. I'll stay awake and guard," Chris suggested.

Fern shook her head. "I'm not tired."

"Yeah, but we've got a long way to go. See if you can't rest a bit," Chris insisted.

Fern pulled her coat close, tied it around her shoulders, snuggled up with her automatic weapon, and closed her eyes.

Chris moved out, a little distance away, and positioned himself to take on the blunt force of any attack. Standing vigil in the dark, he heard someone approaching from behind. He turned quickly, just in time to see a large man lunging at him. The impact knocked the wind out of Chris as he hit the ground hard. The man got up, ready to attack again, but Chris rolled to his right and got to his feet. The man stumbled, and Chris seized the opportunity to jump on him. Chris pulled out his knife and stabbed the man in the neck three times to ensure he was dead, because he was the big one.

Breathing heavily, Chris rushed over to check on Fern. She stood there, axe in hand, bleeding but alive.

Fern looked at him and said, "One came at me, and I finished him off."

"Man, I'm proud of you, Fern," Chris said, admiringly. "Are you hurt?"

"A small cut on my hand."

Let me put a bandage on it, then we need to move. Let's go."

They quickly gathered their things and set off again, determined to put as much distance as possible between themselves and their pursuers.

It was now after midnight. Chris and Fern had been traveling for hours, and they finally reached flat ground, which allowed them to move faster. The tall grass whispered against their legs as they pressed on, Chris in the lead and Fern following behind. Chris held up his hand to signal a stop. But Fern couldn't see him in the darkness.

She crashed into him, knocking him down in the tall grass and falling on top of Chris.

"This is nice, Fern, but we don't have time right now."

She smiled at him and punched Chris in the gut.

Chris heard a whistle, familiar from his time in the military. He whistled back and listened to another whistle follow, and a voice called out.

"Chris, it's us, Matt and Chuck."

Relief washed over Chris and Fern. They hurried to meet their rescuers. Matt and Chuck had arrived with horses, water, and supplies. They mounted and rode out without wasting time, knowing their pursuers weren't far behind.

Chris turned to Matt. "They're right behind us. We need to keep moving."

They pressed on, riding through the night until they finally reached the lodge at around 3:00 AM, exhausted but safe, and filled with relief and gratitude. The search for Fern and the girls had come to a successful end, but the night's events were a stark reminder of the dangers still ahead.

Matt and Chuck were exhausted from riding all day and night. They turned their horses over to Cowboy, who had become the chief wrangler. He would feed, water, and rub them down while Matt and Chuck crawled into their beds to get some sleep before morning broke. As Matt walked through the door of his cabin with Chuck in tow, he noticed a small light was on.

Maggie was on the couch, curled up in a blanket, sound asleep, with Buck lying on the floor beside her. Buck stirred, and Matt put his finger to his lips to be quiet. But it didn't matter. Maggie heard him, and she woke up. "Matt, you're home. Is everybody OK?"

"Yes, Maggie, everybody's safe. We're all back safe. Now, go back to sleep. We're going to bed. It's going to be an early morning."

"Not just yet," she said. "Come over here and kiss me."

Of course, he was ordered, and he obeyed. He gave her a loving kiss. "Goodnight."

Matt's night was a fitful one. Knowing he only had a few hours of sleep before setting up everything, plans swirled through his head. He felt lucky they found Fern and Chris alive, but now they had to prepare for the next battle.

Matt and Chuck rose early the following day, whether they wanted to or not. Maggie was still sleeping on the couch, so Matt quietly walked out, motioning for Buck to join him. They went up to the cafeteria at the lodge to get some coffee and breakfast and start their day. Slowly, the rest of his crew began walking in, sleepy-eyed, everyone waving to each other, and saying their hellos. They all grabbed coffee and breakfast and sat with Matt and Chuck at the tables. Chris came in, Fern followed, and they sat down.

Chris looked at Matt. "What's the plan, big guy?"

"Well, we're waiting to hear back from the general. We're going to try to plan a group attack. We need to work out the logistics before we do anything." Just then, the radio operator came in looking for Matt.

"Sir, I have an urgent message from General Engel. Please follow me."

Matt exited the table and followed the radio operator to the radio shack, where he was handed the microphone.

"This is Matt."

On the other side, the general was talking. "We're under attack. It seems like they have surrounded us out front. They can't reach us because of the mountain, but we're blocked in. We can't get out to help you either. They're keeping us pinned down. I don't know their plan, but we can't help you now. You're on your own."

"Roger that, General. Good luck," Matt replied.

He handed the microphone back to the radio operator, turned, and walked off, thinking, *Ooh, crap, they're coming after us sooner than we all thought.* He rushed into the cafeteria and shouted, "Everybody get ready, the general is under attack. That means they're probably coming after us next; get everybody up. Get your weapons—prepare for an assault on the lodge."

With that, somebody rang a bell in the hallway, waking everybody up. People screamed and shouted, "Get ready; they're coming."

Matt had called a meeting for all the members to gather in the cafeteria. Once everybody was seated, he addressed them and ensured everyone had the same information.

"First, the general and his troops are trapped in the mountain. Some enemies hunting us have trapped them, so they cannot help us. This leaves it up to us; we know they're coming for us. It sounds like they've split their forces, and I'm guessing they will hit us from two different directions. We need to be ready.

"We have 20 military soldiers—and all of our fighters. Ensure your weapons are clean, and you have plenty of ammo, water, and food. You might be at your station for quite a while.

"And here's my other plan: I will take 12 fighters. We'll ride the horses south and hide. Once the enemy starts attacking the lodge, we'll come up behind them and hit them from behind, and you will hit them from the front.

"We have snipers at the top windows of the lodge and the Gatling gun in the middle. It should give them a tremendous fight. We also have grenade launchers provided by the military. Some of you have been trained to use those, so be ready. I know it's going to be a struggle and a big fight. And yes, some of us are going to win, some of us are going to lose. But keep this in mind: we're making it safe for people in the future to have a place to call home. Now everybody to your stations. Good luck."

After Matt finished talking to the group, everyone started to splinter off. They grabbed something to eat and drink to take with them and walked out. Everyone left, except for the usual 12 or 15 members standing by awaiting their orders.

"OK," Matt said, "those of you who want to volunteer for this should know it's not going to be easy. We're going to have to be pretty stealthy. But we need to hit them from behind. If we hide and use arrows, we can eliminate several of them. Then, with automatic weapons, we should be able to finish them off. We will use a hit-and-hide technique and try to draw them away from the lodge to chase us. Alright, go ahead and get your equipment, and gather your horses. We need to be going as soon as we can."

Everyone got up and walked off except Maggie. She came up to Matt, "I want to go with you," Maggie said.

"Maggie, you know I greatly respect you and admire your abilities. I know you can take care of yourself, but for my peace of mind, so that I can do my job, I need you to stay here where you're well protected. This might be a suicide mission for some of us. I don't want you involved. You have to take my word on that," Matt replied.

"Very well, Matt. I'll do what you say as long as you promise to return to me. Oh, and by the way, I'm fixing up the honeymoon cabin. I'm just throwing it out there," she said with a smile as she walked off.

Well, that is certainly something to live for, Matt thought.

Matt was down at the corral, getting his horse and saddling up. They rode off to the south and embarked on the most significant battle in their history. Matt hoped it would be the last fight. If they could wipe out most of their enemies, it would bring peace to the survivors.

CHAPTER 20

Suicide Mission

Rendezvous Point

Washington and his small army arrived at the rendezvous point, where they met up with the Sioux Indian chief and his second-in-command, Blackbird. Despite their mutual disdain for each other, they agreed to work together to kill everyone in the compound and take over the area for themselves. They decided to deal with each other later. They also agreed to send a joint force to the military mountain compound to hold the military inside, preventing them from joining the fight with their helicopters and firepower...

As they finalized their plans, tensions were running high between the groups. The atmosphere was charged with the weight of the uneasy alliance. They knew this was a rare collusion born of necessity and ambition, each party driven by the urgent need to eliminate their common enemy. John Washington was a man of few words but calculated actions. He had meticulously mapped out the compound's defenses. His mind raced through the potential scenarios and countermeasures. Meanwhile, the Sioux chief was wrapped in quiet intensity, only his eyes betraying the storm of strategies forming his mind. Blackbird, ever a shadow, silently communicated with his chief. Their understanding was built on years of shared battles.

The plan was set. Washington's group would approach from the northwest corner, while the chief and his small army would strike from the east. They aimed to hit the compound from two different directions, catching it by surprise early in the morning before they could wake up and fully organize their defenses.

As they marched, the night cloaked their movements, and the chill in the air mirrored that still unresolved in their hearts. They moved purposefully, and each step was calculated and measured toward their violent objective. The quiet rustling trees and the muted sound of the horses on the forest floor were the only witnesses of their deathly procession.

Hours later, they were in position. The first wave—John Washington's group—rode in precisely, initiating the attack with automatic weapons, setting off the alarm that pierced the stillness of dawn and awakened the compound to the assault.

The Chief and his warriors emerged from the shadows from the east with a fierce battle cry. Their presence was a sudden and terrifying sight to the defenders. The compound erupted into chaos as the defenders scrambled to respond to the dual front attack.

Inside the compound, Father Mike and his teams heard the commotion. The time had come. They readied their weapons and prepared to engage. They knew the odds were stacked against them, but their resolve was unshakeable. This was their home, their sanctuary. They would defend it with every ounce of strength they had.

The defenders fought with a tenacity born of desperation as the battle raged. The initial shock of the attack began to wear off, replaced by a fierce determination to repel the invaders. The enemy's gunfire was answered with gunfire, and hand-to-hand combat broke out in the compound quarters and courtyards with a few Indians who had managed to get over the barricades. They were dispatched immediately by highly trained military personnel.

Washington and the Sioux Chief watched from their respective vantage points. Aware of the delicate balance of their alliance, they knew the outcome of this battle would shape their futures in terms of territory, power, and influence. The tension between the two simmered beneath the surface and provided a menacing undercurrent during the chaotic clash.

Matt and his team, who had been hiding, grabbed their horses and started riding toward the chaos and noise of the raging battle.

As they got closer, they dismounted, and the people with bows and arrows took the front line. They released several rounds of arrows into the fighting enemy, killing many. The enemy soon realized they were being attacked from the rear.

Several enemy fighters mounted their horses and charged towards Matt and his team. But Matt's team had already disengaged, riding down the trail and setting up an ambush in a pre-screened clearing. They prepared as the horsemen approached; Matt's team was ready. There were only eight enemies, and it didn't take long to dispatch them all.

Matt's team returned to the front lines, finding many of their enemies dead. They had been surprised by the ferocity of the firepower of the people in the lodge. The Gatling gun in one of the windows devastated the attackers.

Matt's group jumped off their horses and joined the fight, spreading out with automatic weapons and charging what was left of the enemy fighting force. Several hostiles retreated and ran for cover in the trees to the west.

Hiding with a few of his men, John Washington spotted Matt Dylan. He grabbed his knife and charged at Matt, yelling. Matt turned and saw him coming.

John Washington stopped and said, "How about we settle this the old-fashioned way?" He waved his knife.

Matthew laid down his automatic weapon and grabbed his knife. They both lunged at each other, swinging their knives. Minor nicks and cuts marked their fierce battle, but nothing serious. Matt Dylan, a skilled knife fighter, took John Washington aback.

"Who are you? Where did you learn to fight like that?" John Washington panted.

"U.S. Navy SEALs," Matt replied.

John Washington backed up, realizing he was fighting a highly trained Navy SEAL. He threw down his knife, reached behind, and grabbed his pistol. As he brought it up to shoot, Matt backed up, and then Buck leaped out of nowhere, knocking John down, sinking his teeth into John's throat, and ripping it out, leaving John Washington to bleed to death. Buck looked at the assailant to ensure he was done, then returned to his master.

Matthew looked at Buck and said, "You've saved my life again, Buck!"

Suddenly, out of the darkness, four demons emerged from the trees, followed by a substantial 8-foot tall black figure with black wings, burning eyes, and smoldering flesh. The demons charged towards Matt and his team. Several arrows fired from the lodge struck and killed the demons.

Ben, positioned by the Lodge, had anticipated the demons and armed his people with arrows capable of killing them.

As the black angel advanced, Ben leaped onto the barriers in front of the lodge, raised his arms, and instantly transformed. He stood 8 feet tall, clad in golden armor, with enormous white wings and a massive golden sword.

When Ben waved the sword over his head, lightning struck it, charging it with energy. He then flew down towards Barabbas, the Black Angel, and they crashed together in the compound yard. The battle was on. Ben swung his sword with all his might, clashing with the Black Angel. Fire and darkness in the sky marked their epic encounter.

The ground became cracked and scorched, and the air was thick with a sulfur smell as they both rose into the sky above. The fight turned into a swirl of dark clouds occasionally pierced by flashes of lightning. In the center of this barren landscape, the White Angel with wings of pure white stood tall, radiant, emanating a soft golden light that contrasted sharply with the darkness around the demon who was a menacing, cloaked, shadowy figure with eyes that burned like embers and horns that curled evilly from his head.

The ground beneath them trembled as they prepared to clash again, the forces of good and evil poised for an epic confrontation. There were crackles of energy as the world's fate hung in the balance, and these two powerful beings faced off in a battle that would determine the future of Ben's friends.

The fight continued, and neither side was willing to back down. The White Angel's resolve was fueled by a desire to protect and bring hope to his friends, while the demon was driven by his pursuit of chaos, destruction, and killing.

The White Angel triumphed over the devil with an enormous swing of his sword that cut through the demon's black hide. The White Angel's unwavering determination and the purity of their cause gave him the strength to deliver the final, decisive blow. The devil, weakened and unable to withstand the White Angel's light, was forced to retreat into the shadows.

The sky cleared and radiant light shone from above. Ben stood in the middle of the compound. He turned around and looked at his friends, raising his sword over his head. And in an instant, he was gone.

Matt and his team were still kneeling on the battlefield, trying to comprehend what they had just witnessed. Ben had overcome such a formidable force before he disappeared. Matt got up to return to his group.

As they headed to hide behind some hay bales stacked in the corral, Chuck, who was covering Matt's flank, was hit twice in the chest, and fell.

Matt continued fighting and moving towards cover. When he looked back and saw Chuck lying bleeding on the ground, he ran back into the firefight without hesitation to rescue his friend. As he reached Chuck, Matt checked his friend's tactical vest, and found that two bullets had penetrated his vest enough to cause some bleeding. But not seriously.

Despite the enemy fire, Matt grabbed Chuck into a firefighter's lift and rushed to cover. Paula immediately took over and administered first aid to Chuck who was still unconscious.

Suddenly, Chris heard a voice on his radio. "Hey, Boss, it sounds like the Apache helicopters are coming to join our little skirmish." He handed the radio receiver to Matt, and they could hear the call coming in from Thunder, who was calling SEAL Team Three.

Matt answered, "SEAL Team Three. We have hostiles on the east and the west hiding in the trees. Some are retreating. We're going to pop green smoke to mark our position."

"Roger that. SEAL Team Three popping green smoke, neutralize anything else moving on the ground," Thunder replied.

With that, the first Apache helicopter appeared, followed by a second one. They spread out and stretched the tree line where the enemy hid, targeting all hostiles. They then moved to the east, circling and firing until they were satisfied they had neutralized everyone. Rockets exploded as they circled, providing cover for Matt's team.

Army trucks began rolling into the compound, loaded with soldiers who jumped out in groups at predetermined intervals. They circled through the trees to finish off any remaining stragglers. The soldiers moved with practiced efficiency, ensuring no enemy escaped their sweep. The once chaotic battlefield was now systematically being cleared of any threat.

Matt felt immense gratitude. The fight was over, and they had won—the end of a long, arduous battle.

However, the battlefield was still tense, and the air was thick with smoke and fire. Matt and his team, though weary, stood ready. They knew the value of vengeance and vigilance even in the face of apparent victory. Matt allowed himself a moment to breathe.

"Chris, we must ensure we account for every team member."

Matt's voice was steady but firm. "Chris, check on the military soldiers and ensure they are all safe."

Matt quickly relayed the orders to the rest of his team. They moved methodically, sweeping the area and ensuring all the civilians were accounted for and safe. Relief was evident on the faces of those they encountered.

Meanwhile, the Apaches continued their air patrol, their presence a reassuring sight in thc sky. Ground forces supported them, ensuring a comprehensive sweep of the area. Every corner was checked, every potential hiding spot scrutinized. As the soldiers moved through the trees, they found pockets of resistance, small groups of enemies who had managed to evade their initial onslaught.

These skirmishes were quickly dealt with, and the soldiers' training and determination ensured no enemy was left standing. Matt's thoughts turned to the future. This battle had been hard, but it was just one chapter in their ongoing struggle. He knew that as long as they had each other and remained vigilant, they could face whatever challenge came their way. The bonds forged in the heat of battle were unbreakable and would carry their strength forward.

As the dust settled and the last echoes of the battle faded away, the survivors sighed with relief. They had made it through another day, and their resolve was stronger than ever. They would rebuild, heal, and be ready to face whatever came next.

Matt looked at his team, pride swelling in his chest. They had fought bravely and prevailed. The future was uncertain, but together they were unstoppable.

Matt's team climbed the hill to the lodge, their bodies aching from the intensity of the battle. As they walked through the front doors, they began checking on everyone.

Matt's eyes looked for one familiar face.

He saw Father Mike and approached him.

"Father, do you know where Maggie is? Is she OK?" Matt asked anxiously.

"Yes, Matt." Father Mike replied that she was caring for some of the wounded in the hospital.

With that, Matt took off, navigating the crowd and the halls of the lodge. He walked through the doors of the hospital room, his heart pounding. She was there, knelt over a young man who was bleeding, helping to secure his bandages alongside the doctor.

Matt stood there watching her work. She got up, turned, and spotted him. Unable to contain herself, she ran towards him. Matt stepped forward, and they met in the middle. Maggie jumped into his arms and smothered his face with kisses.

"Oh, Matthew, I love you so much," Maggie said, her voice filled with relief and joy.

"I'm rather fond of you myself," Matt replied, smiling and laughing.

"How's it going here, Maggie?" he asked.

"We've contained all the injuries; they've done surgery on the people who needed it. Right now, we're just making everyone comfortable. We have about eight who have died, so we'll need to bury them," she explained, her voice tinged with sadness.

Matt's concern deepened. "Who has died?" he asked softly.

Her eyes welling up with tears, Maggie told him that some of the newcomers who recently joined them stepped up, took their part, and died for it.

"Chuck is coming in, wounded in his chest, but he should be OK."

Matt kissed her again. "OK, I'll check with you later."

With that, he turned and walked away to find his team members. Some needed attention for scrapes, cuts, and other minor injuries. He got hold of them and sent them to the hospital area to be looked after. Buck followed him closely, his loyal presence being a constant comfort.

Matt went back into the cafeteria and sat down. Helen brought him a cup of coffee and a dish of water for Buck. She sat down across Matt and looked at him with relief.

"Matthew, you did it. You conquered the hostiles. The evil is gone. We're free. We can now establish a home for everyone.

"Be safe," Helen said, her voice filled with gratitude and hope as she walked away.

Matt sipped his coffee, the warmth spreading through him. He looked around at the faces of the people who had fought so hard for their survival. They had faced incredible odds and came out victorious. Now, they could begin to build a new future, one filled with hope and safety.

There was only one sad duty to perform.

It took a couple of days to bury the dead. They returned to their original camp on the hillside and buried them all together, believing it was right to keep everyone in one place. People brought flowers and flags. Every burial was solemn with a trumpet in the background, a fitting tribute to each great warrior.

Matt and Maggie returned to the camp, hand in hand.

Chuck and his girlfriend, Pauline Starr, were walking around together while Chuck was recovering. They also noticed that Chris and Fern were growing closer.

Chuck thought to himself, *That's a good thing. They're the same kind of people—a perfect match.*

Holding Maggie's hand, Matt returned to the truck they had used to transport the bodies to the cemetery.

They returned to the compound and parked in front of Matt's cabin.

Both got out; Maggie wanted him to follow her. "I want to show you what I did with this other cabin."

They proceeded up the hill to the recently designated honeymoon cabin. She opened the door, and Matt walked in, his eyes widening with amazement. "Wow, this is pretty awesome. You fixed this thing up.

"It's meant to be ours?"

"Yes, Matt, all ours."

Matt turned around and grabbed her in his arms. "OK, then I can move in today."

She looked at him and said, "No, if you want all this and me, then we're getting married.

"We have a priest here who can do it. So that's the next step. If you want to move in here with me, marriage."

Buck was lying nearby, watching them with his head between his front feet.

"Marriage." Matt tasted the magnitude of the word. "I didn't know that was in my future."

"You can't have this unless you marry me. And believe me, it's worth it," she replied with a playful smile.

"Let's find Father Mike and set it up as soon as possible." Matt agreed.

They left and went back to the lodge. Father Mike was busy helping others, but he saw Maggie and Matt approaching. He thought, "I saw the handwriting on the wall, and I was right!" As they approached, he said, "Yes, what can I do for you two?"

"Father, Maggie, and I would like to get married. Can you do that for us?" Matt asked.

"Well, yes, I can. When would you like this done?" Father Mike asked.

"As soon as possible," Matt said.

"All right, how about tomorrow at 13:00?" Father Mike suggested.

"Tomorrow. Do you mean we have to wait another day?" Matt asked, impatience in his voice.

"Yes, Matthew, things have to be arranged. You need to return to your cabin, and she needs to return to her room here in the Lodge until you two are married. That is my final word," Father, Mike insisted.

With that, they walked off. Matt walked down the hill to his cabin. Opening the door, he saw the room where Ben usually sat drinking his coffee.

Ben was missed profoundly, and all felt his absence.

Matt walked over to Chuck and Chris, who were sitting with their girlfriends. Chris got up, poured a shot of bourbon with ice, and handed it to Matt.

They all sat down. Not much was said, as they were exhausted from the past few days.

Matt looked at Chuck.

"Chuck, Maggie, and I are getting married tomorrow at 13:00. I'd like you to be my best man and Chris, I'd like you to be there too."

They clapped their hands and said, "It's about time." They all hooted and hollered in celebration. That night, as Matt fell asleep, he thought about how much his life had changed and how happy he was to have found someone to love again.

Matt slept in the following day. Until Buck decided to get him up. Still stiff and sore, Matt groaned as he got out of bed. He put on his clothes and walked to the front room, where Chuck had already fixed coffee and set aside breakfast.

"Well, Matthew, this is the big day," Chuck said with a grin.

"Yes, Chuck," Matt replied, quietly drinking his coffee and eating breakfast. Chuck, however, didn't stop talking.

"So, what are you going to wear? You can't wear army fatigues," Chuck continued.

"What do you mean I can't wear army fatigues?" Matt asked.

Chuck pointed out that it was a wedding, not a military action.

"Chuck, I'm thinking. I do have those new Levis you got me from Bloomberg. I also have a red shirt and boots. I guess I have a cowboy hat, too. Would that work?"

"Well, it has to, since you don't have a tuxedo. I'll dress up too. I have some appropriate clothes to wear," Chuck continued.

They sat around drinking coffee and talking. Matt wanted to know all about Chuck's girlfriend.

Chuck looked at Pauline, she nodded, he told the story about how they first met.

"And you remember I told you about that Indian we came across. We were walking out west of here. She claimed she outshot me. I'm sure I outdrew her and shot first, but she wouldn't give it up. She says no, she outdrew me because she's faster. You know, she's so much fun. We have such a great time.

"Yeah, I'm falling in love with her. I guess it's a matter of time before it's my turn." Looking at Pauline who had a lovely smile.

*****

Wedding Day

The time had come to get married. Matt got up and walked out, dressed in his outfit and ready to go, with Buck following him closely. They walked up the hill to the lodge and went inside. The community had set up a makeshift chapel. As Matt walked in, Chuck and Chris met him, and the three of them went to the front, where Father Mike was waiting.

Someone was singing, and the music began. Maggie walked in. She was gorgeous, dressed in a white gown, with a big smile on her face. As she walked towards Matt, two of her closest friends followed. Matt clasped her hands in his, and they turned to face Father Mike, who began the marriage vows. "I do," they both said. And just like that, they were married.

They walked out with everyone shouting and celebrating. The whole community sat watching. They were directed to the cafeteria, where Helen had prepared a feast in their honor. The party lasted all afternoon, until close to sundown.

Matt and Maggie finally walked through the hall doors and down the hill to the honeymoon cabin. Buck, of course, close on their heels.

When they reached the front door, Matt picked Maggie up and carried her through, setting her down and kissing her. "I love you so much," he told her.

It was late afternoon, near sunset. After all the celebrations and food at the lodge, they went outside. Matt poured a glass of Jack Daniels on ice—for both of them. They walked outside and sat on the swing on the deck, facing the western sun as they swung and talked and loved each other. Buck was on the ground, content to be part of their group.

Matt was looking to the west when he noticed something. "Who's that coming towards us?"

"It seems like another straggler," Maggie said.

Matt was still strapped with his .45.

Straining to see into the sunset....

"Maggie, I think it's Ben," Matt said, filled with disbelief.

"It can't be," she replied.

"Yeah, I think it's Ben. Look, he's walking towards us," Matt insisted.

They both sat there amazed, watching this man walk up the hill towards them.

Matt got up and approached him. "Where have you been?" Matt exclaimed.

"Matthew. Good to see you both!

"Matthew, I asked to come back. You're all my friends. I didn't realize how much I would miss you when I left. I was granted permission to finish my life here as a man, as your friend," Ben explained.

With that, Maggie jumped up, hugged him, and kissed him.

"Matthew, I'm so glad you two are married. Of course, I knew that would happen," Ben said with an annoying smile.

"Sure, you did, Ben. Sure, you did," Matt replied with a laugh. "But you never told anybody."

Ben shrugged. "I couldn't tell anyone anything."

The three of them sat down on the swing. Matt poured Ben a glass of bourbon and ice. They all clinked their glasses in a toast and said, "To the future. With love."

The End

www.ingramcontent.com/pod-product-compliance
Lightning Source LLC
Chambersburg PA
CBHW070641310726
48982CB00001B/368

* 9 7 9 8 9 9 8 6 6 2 5 1 5 *